I0565261

TRADEMARK ACKNOWLEDGEMENTS

The authors acknowledge the trademarked status and trademark owners of the following wordmarks mentioned in this work of fiction:

Star Wars: LucasArts

Rocky and Bullwinkle and Friends: TM &© Ward Prods.

SCOOBY-DOO, THE FLINTSTONES and all related characters and elements: Hanna-Barbera

Get Smart: HBO

Guinness: Diageo Ireland Private Unlimited Company

Marvel Super Hero character names & likenesses: Marvel

Lara Croft: Square Enix Holdings Co., Ltd

Praise for CHRIS ALMEIDA AND CECILIA AUBREY:

"A riveting, clever spy story full of intrigue, modern-day espionage and a scorching hot romance."

—Misty Evans, award-winning author of romantic suspense

"Almeida and Aubrey had me from the first paragraph and I couldn't put it down. Electrifying thriller!"

—Becky Condit, Mrs Condit and Friends Read Books

"It is beautifully written with the perfect mixture of action and suspense and in the midst of all that there is a beautiful emotional love story entwined."

—Rhayne Risque, Guilty Pleasures Book Reviews

"I highly recommend Countermeasure for any fan of a fast paced erotic romance. I know I'm looking forward to checking out the duo's next collaboration!"

—Silla Beaumont, Just Erotic Romance Reviews

CHRIS ALMEIDA & CECILIA AUBREY

TO RUSSIA WITH LOVE

To Russia with Love

ISBN 978-0-9879217-7-2

ALL RIGHTS RESERVED

To Russia with Love © 2012 Chris Almeida & Cecilia Aubrey

Edited by Emmanuelle Hertel

Typesetting by Győrgyi Balogh

Cover art by Chris Almeida

To Russia with Love is a work of fiction. Names, characters, places and incidents either are the product of the authors' imagination or are used fictitiously. Any resemblance to actual persons, living or dead, events or locales is entirely coincidental.

ACKNOWLEDGEMENTS

Someone once told us that being a beta reader was an honor, and that if someone was offered that position, they should be thankful for the opportunity.

We see it differently. To have the amazing people we have as our beta readers and critique partners is not only an honor but crucial to *us*.

We thank the following crucial people for the guidance in the development of our craft, for the encouragement to continue spinning our tales, and for the great friendship and laughter we share:

Candy Chapman, Harriet Vallero, Micquleta Williams, Sarah Davis, Heather Von Ohlen, Hope Sloper, Karen Lorio Piper, Sandra Zapp, Lori Freeman, Jennifer Murray Thompson, Maria Mercedes Prieto, Shannon Adamson, Cathy McCarron, Dianne Steverson Vickers, Victoria Iankova, Alan Langford, Anders and Nina Karlsson, Melissa Berlese and the members of the OMB Role Play group.

Thank you for believing we could make it happen a second time.

Contents

"The single biggest problem with communication is the illusion that it has taken place."

—George Bernard Shaw

Prologue

Chicken-scratch

"So, HOW IS THE NEW guy doing?" Roy Denner, Chief Financial Officer of Mark Devlin Software, asked Mark Devlin, owner of MDS. They often held their casual meetings over the phone, and that day was no different.

"New guy? Oh…you mean Antonín Mucha? Amazing. He had an impressive resume. Worked with some big names, including Conor Brennan." Over the line, Roy heard Mark take a sip of his coffee.

"Brennan? Why is the name familiar?"

"Big name in biometrics. He led some major projects in the field."

"Ah."

"Mucha helped him with an algorithm for voice recognition some years back."

"I see."

"Apparently they were close for a while. Mucha mentioned he had some of Brennan's notes. I bought them from him. They will be worth a fortune down the road—even though they look like chicken-scratch to me."

"Why?"

"Don't you remember? Brennan died in a boating accident some five years back—"

A knock on Mark's door sounded over the line.

"Hi, Paul. Everything okay?" Roy overheard Mark's question followed by a pause, then Paul's muffled reply in the background.

"The decrypter, Mr. Devlin...I don't know how...the files are gone." Paul Faber, the lead developer at MDS, was in charge of their main piece of software—which was also one of his projects from inception.

"Mark, what's going on?" Roy asked over the line.

"Roy. Grab Harold and get over here. My office. We have a situation." His voice was thick with tension.

Mark hung up and Roy immediately called Harold Preston, MDS's head of security, and instructed him to meet them at Mark's office on the double. It was going to be a hell of a day.

★ ★ ★ ★ ★

George scanned the latest assignments and prioritized their order of attack for the day. It would be handled as soon as he could get a hold of Trevor.

With that in check, he scanned the latest report generated on their little keyword list—something he had been keeping an eye on for his buddy. He had to take a second pass at it to make sure he had gotten it right. When he did, a small smile played on his features.

"Trev's going to want to hear this one..."

Chapter One

Heaven and Hell

T HE SOUND OF FLESH POUNDING flesh followed by grunts, curses, and thumps was audible from the front door. Downstairs, in the renovated house that belonged to Trevor and Cassandra Brennan, the air was thick with the pungent smell of sweat and the sounds of struggle. The origin of the noisy fracas was the gym, the largest room in the basement.

Two bodies were involved in a brutal confrontation. Trevor sported several bruises from it while Cassandra fared better. In a blur of movement, the heel of her hand connected with Trevor's chin and his mouth snapped shut, the resonance of teeth grinding against each other filled the room.

"Fuck!" He tackled her to the ground and slammed his fist into her cheek, snapping her head to the side.

"Oh no, you didn't!" Cassandra growled savagely as she shoved him off her, rolled to her feet, and landed a direct kick square in the middle of his chest.

Trevor grunted as he fell hard on his back. Cassandra flew at him but, at the last minute, he rolled across the mat, avoiding her tackle only to feel the side of her foot slam into his ribs.

"Holy hell!" he screamed as pain flashed hot through him.

She relentlessly followed with another kick to his stomach. Trevor rolled, cupping his balls to protect the boys from a third, more damaging strike.

"Come on! Is that all you got?" Cassandra taunted as he curled tightly into a fetal position to protect his stomach and assets from further harm, heaving in pain. She straddled his side and pushed him to his back. His painful grimace was proof she'd gotten more than a few good blows in.

"At least you didn't give up after only a few minutes this time," she sneered.

"What are you talking about? We've been at it for over two hours!" Exhausted and drenched in sweat, Trevor lay on the floor with his arms spread wide.

"Crying 'Uncle'?" The undercurrent of laughter in her voice was evident.

Trevor pushed up to rest on his elbow. "Can I? I should be on chat with George right now." He collapsed against the mat again when Cassandra knocked his elbow and shoved him.

Before meeting Trevor, Cassandra had let her own training slide after leaving the CIA, thinking she no longer needed it; but the encounter with Niklas Möeller—a deadly mercenary—in France the previous summer had proven otherwise. A week after moving into the new house, Cassandra had enforced a heavy training schedule to keep them in shape and physically prepared for the unexpected.

During the six months Trevor and George had been working under the Operation Countermeasure cover, they had handled a couple of tough cases for the NSA. One of them had required physical intrusion into a facility—an adventure that had almost cost Trevor dearly. Cassandra had then intensified their workout, putting him through a modified version of Navy Seal training, similar to what her father had imposed when she was younger.

During the renovations, they had converted the basement into a fully equipped gym. Mats covered the floors wall to wall. All types of martial arts equipment filled one corner of the room, while another housed a set of punching bags and free weights. The treadmill, elliptical, and rowing machines lined the back wall.

Their training was not for the faint of heart. Cassandra didn't hold back. She had been kicking his ass for almost six months now, and although his body was fitter than before and he was larger than she, he still hadn't come to terms with the idea of hitting her, which always meant he ended up with a larger share of bruises by the end of each session.

"No, sir." She pinned him and captured his mouth with hers in a deep wet kiss.

"Hmm…I like this part of the training. Can we just tackle this part first next time?" Trevor mumbled in her mouth.

"Shut up and kiss me."

"Yes ma'am," he grinned against her lips before threading his fingers through her hair and thrusting his tongue into her mouth.

★ ★ ★ ★ ★

Trevor and Cassandra had moved into their new home in Dublin, Ireland, after getting married the previous fall. Trevor, who had lived in Ft. Meade, Maryland, and worked for the NSA before the move, had accepted a consultant position after his resignation had been summarily denied by his superiors. The government organization considered him a huge asset and retained him as a part of their arsenal to intercept and decrypt sensitive data. As a consultant for the NSA, Trevor was given limited access to Echelon computers via a highly secure remote connection.

Trevor's best friend, George Miller, was his liaison within the NSA walls. In addition, George handled all data intercepts and watched their back like an extra set of eyes and ears.

Cassandra had left her security position with her father's firm, James Security Agency, and never looked back. Since their move to Ireland, she had applied her skills and expertise honed in the CIA and security work on Trevor and George's projects, but most of her efforts centered on tracking any leads tied to Trevor's investigation into his parents' disappearance. She was the strategist while he was the go-with-it expert. Their union was one made in heaven.

They had decided to maintain Trevor's mother's maiden name, the one he took when he moved to the United States, as a cloak for their façade as a data recovery and investigations business, Bauer Enterprises. They planned to use it to handle any information related to their search for answers whenever they were on the hunt. It gave them a much-needed disassociation from their true identities, since they had no idea what or who they would come across while working on NSA cases or his parents' investigation.

Trevor sat at his office desk, freshly showered and invigorated by the exercise. When he signed into the secure online chat application used to communicate with George, he found several messages waiting for him.

Where the fuck are you?

We need to talk.

Seriously. You should be here by now. No need to explain what you've been up to. I can imagine it involves Cassie.

Trevor chuckled as he typed a quick note letting his good friend know he was online. George immediately responded with a request for voice chat.

"Finally!" George's excitement was almost palpable.

"What's up?"

"Caught some intercepts through your father's filter on Echelon."

Trevor's stomach clenched tight and a wave of apprehension swept through him. It was like that every time they discovered a new clue or tip tied to his father. They hadn't come across any of late, and the little they had uncovered had led to dead ends. He was afraid to believe this time it could turn out differently.

"It sounds solid," George added.

"Send me the deets." The file transfers immediately popped on the screen. Trevor saved and promptly opened them.

The furrow on his brow grew deeper as he scanned the transcript. Once finished, he leaned back in his chair and processed the information. There wasn't much to be considered. "We need to get our hands on those notes."

"I thought you'd feel that way. I already have taps in place."

"Thanks, George."

"No problem. I'll let you know if anything more pops up. Later."

Trevor disconnected the call and thought about how to best to make contact with the man in possession of his father's notes. He wasn't about to openly disclose his interest in them or the possible link between them and his parents' disappearance. It would only elicit bogus information based on a perception of what people thought he wanted to hear. Trevor wanted it straight and unadulterated. The use of the Bauer name as a cover would come in handy masking his connection to the Brennan family. If he collected any useful intel, he would toss it Cassandra's way to get her take on it.

★ ★ ★ ★ ★

Cassandra had grown to love the odd set-up of their new four-story home, and still chuckled over the forced exercise it provided.

The façade of the Georgian rarity had been preserved during the renovation of the four above-ground floors and excavation of the basement. In addition to the gym, the basement also housed their cellar; the main floor consisted of the foyer and a spacious comfortable sitting area. The open-concept kitchen and media room—a feast for the senses, decked out with both high-tech appliances and entertainment equipment—were located on the second floor. Their geek's dream office shared the third floor with a spacious master suite that offered amazing views of St. Stephen's Green from its tall Georgian windows. Last but not least, the top floor of the house was split between a guest suite and their computer equipment room, where they stored the tech gadgets they used on the rare occasions physical infiltration was needed in order to retrieve data.

The equipment storage room was another never-ending source of amusement for Cassandra. To the naked eye, it looked like a regular storage room, but a tap of fingertips on a hidden panel embedded in the back wall revealed the room where they stored their prized high-tech equipment, firearms, and munitions. Each time they unlocked the room, she felt like she was channeling Lara Croft.

Cassandra shook her head at the whimsical thought as she carried a steaming cup of tea up the stairs and into the office. She handed Trevor the cup and noticed his contemplative expression. Without missing a beat, she leaned down and tipped his face for a quick kiss on the lips. "Penny for your thoughts."

Trevor brushed his thumb gently along the blackish-blue bruise discoloring the left side of her jaw and grimaced at the knowledge he'd put it there. His eyes shifted to the monitor. "George was just on."

Cassandra straightened and casually moved over to her desk to begin her routine. "And?"

"He snared some intercepts from the filter we set up on my father."

Cassandra swung her head to look at Trevor. His brows were drawn together, lining his forehead. Her heart-rate revved. "Whatever it is, we should follow up on it. No stone unturned, right? At some point it'll pan out."

"Well, we have a name and George just sent me the deets. I'm going to dig into it first."

In the months that they'd been together, Cassandra had quickly caught on to Trevor's mode of operation: read the file, check out the players, plan next steps. She respected that and knew once he wrapped his head around it, he would pull her in and they would work through it together. Until that happened, she gave him space and left him to it.

She settled at her desk and sent a quick email to Jessica Forrester, her best and oldest friend. *Hey, hit me up as soon as you get this.*

They had been like sisters since high school and missed each other terribly since Cassandra's move to Ireland. They compensated for the distance by spending countless hours on chat. It was because of the many hours on text and video calls that Cassandra had known for some time that something was niggling at her friend. Cassandra hoped Jessica would break and finally spill the beans about what was bothering her before she had to resort to brute force.

While she waited for Jessica to show up, her thoughts returned to Trevor. So far, his commitments with the NSA hadn't interfered with their true quest. But the lack of activity on his parents' case was getting to him. The couple of times they had come across leads she had seen his hopes dashed, each dead end a bitter pill to swallow. Her heart ached every time she saw the disappointment cloud his face. They had discussed the possibility of adding resources to their search, and Cassandra was thrilled at the opportunity to offer the job to Jessica for good. More like an ultimatum.

Almost on cue with her thoughts, a flashing light in the task bar caught her eye and words appeared on the screen.

Cassie, you there?

Here. Thanks for getting back so quickly!

Think you read my mind. I was about to call you. What's up?

Remember when I mentioned that if you ever wanted a change in scenery to let me know?

Yeah?

I'm changing that to a direct job offer. We are. Trevor and I would love if you would consider helping us out with a few aspects of our business and other things. It would require that you also move here.

OMG! Did you say job? YES! Of course I'll take it! Wait…what about Bob?

I've talked to him. He isn't happy to let you go, but he understands we need you here. Business is booming!

So I don't have to fight to leave? Yay! LOL!

Nope. Your passport is up to date, right? We'll need to get you set up with a work permit and registered with the Garda National Immigration Bureau once you're here.

Yes. Everything is still good. No worries. Work permit? Registration? Damn, sound ominous!

Nah, just a pain. We're glad you're coming! It will help with our load for sure.

Get ready Ireland, here I come! Let me know what I need to take with me for the work permit and I'll let you know when I've squared everything here.

As Trevor would say, "Brilliant!" I can't wait. You'll stay with us until you find a place of your own. We have the space and you'll have a floor all to yourself. We can spend more time together that way. Send your flight info when you're booked. We'll meet you at the airport.

Jinkies! Already bossy. Did you learn to be pushy from Trev? It's working.

Velma? LOL! I'm looking forward to kicking your ass.

Just so you know…the office is not the same without you. It's quiet now, no snoring to be heard.

Watch it, buster, or I'll take back the offer.

NO!!! Okay. Looking forward to seeing more of you and the hunk. I gotta run! Give Trevor my love! Later!

★ ★ ★ ★ ★

Trevor had listened to the call and read the transcripts several times. He'd used the initial information provided by George to trace the call to Mark Devlin Software, a budding computer development company out of Austin, Texas. Assuming that Mark Devlin was the man captured on the recorded conversation, Trevor sifted through the digital maze for details on him.

A quick search on Devlin revealed a sharp businessman who had picked the right time to invest in software development in a city that promised to be the next technology hub in the United States. Although Devlin himself was not a developer, he had the knowledge and instincts on how to harvest the best brains in the field. That explained why he was aware of Conor Brennan's work. Trevor would have to tread softly with that one—or not.

Trevor hoped George's taps would yield additional information on Mucha and the notes. He wanted to find out more about the man who apparently had been in close contact with his father. It was still too early to know if the taps would bear any fruit. For now, he had no time to waste.

With only a glimpse to check the clock, he picked up the phone and made the call.

"MDS Enterprises. How may I direct your call?"

"Mark Devlin, please."

"May I have your name?

"Trevor Bauer."

"One moment please while I connect you."

After a brief pause, a curt prompt sounded on the line, "Devlin."

"Mr. Devlin, I'm calling in regard to some scientific material you have in your possession that's of interest to me."

"Who is this again?"

"Bauer. Trevor Bauer."

"I don't think I know a Bauer. Have we met before?"

"Not yet. But I think after our talk you'll want to."

"Exactly what material are you referring to? Everything regarding our current product line can be found on our website—"

Trevor cut in before Devlin could continue to spew the standard company sales pitch. "Dr. Brennan's notes. Word on the street is you're in possession of them." Trevor held a tight rein on his eagerness to get a hold of the notes. While talking, he cradled the phone against his shoulder and composed a succinct email to Devlin.

"How did you—"

Trevor interrupted him again. "I'm curious. How much do you want for the notes? I'm sure you must have a figure in mind."

"I don't know how you found out about them, but they're not for sale. Now if you don't mind, I've things to do." Devlin's response was terse and clipped, forbidding further discussion.

But Trevor wasn't about to give up that easily. The email would be another pitch for the notes he wanted so badly. "Nevertheless, I've sent you an email. I recommend you read it."

"I'll think about it."

Trevor had thought hard about what he could offer Devlin in exchange for the notes. As he had run through the options in his mind, he recalled the dark undertone in Devlin's voice when his conference call had been interrupted. Based on the little Trevor had been able to hear, the stolen files were of high value to his company.

"Hey! Hold on a second. How do you know my email?" Devlin asked in a rush.

"All that matters, Mr. Devlin, is that I can be of assistance with a more pressing situation—more like the big pickle—your company is facing at the moment."

"What? How do you—?" Devlin sounded decisively flabbergasted.

"I've explained it in the email. But let me make it simple for you. I can track those missing files. My price, the notes. Think hard before you make your decision. Ask yourself, what's more valuable to you: your company files, or some old man's chicken-scratch?"

Trevor hung up and met Cassandra's eyes trained on him.

"What do we have on our hands?"

"Nothing yet. Let's hope he bites."

"Give me names. Let me do my part."

Trevor raised his eyebrow humorously. "Antsy, are you?"

"Just trying to help," Cassandra shrugged. "Besides, if he bites we'll be way ahead of the game."

Laughing, Trevor sent the information to her computer and Cassandra began her background checks. The only sound that filled the office was the clack of the keys as their fingers danced across their keyboards. Trevor stretched back in his chair and was about to call it quits when he heard the familiar beep of an email hitting his inbox. He opened the application to find Devlin's name on the screen. He cleared his throat and called out to Cassandra, "Heads up. I think we've got a bite."

Cassandra swiveled her chair to face him as he opened the email. After a few minutes of deep silence she asked expectantly, "So?"

"Yep. A big bite. He's agreed to the exchange. But I still need to stipulate a condition."

"Condition? What condition?"

"That Mucha has to handle the exchange in person. I need to meet the man."

"To pick his brain about your father?"

Trevor nodded. "If he spent time with my father right before he disappeared, he might have pertinent information and not even realize it." He composed a second email to Devlin to which he received an immediate response.

Agreed.

"We're on. I gotta let George know."

A rush of adrenaline hit Cassandra. They were a go. The hunt was on. She loved working these cases with Trevor because it gave them time together. Granted it was busy time, mostly spent buried in work, but it was an enjoyable partnership. The ring of the landline startled her, and she quickly grabbed the phone.

"Hello?"

"Hello, Cassandra."

"Stephan! What's up?"

"I'm calling to see if you two are free for dinner tonight. It'll be a four-some, as Terese will be joining us."

"Not tonight. We're up to our ears in work. Maybe another time?"

"Maybe another time then. Has Robert mentioned when he'll be visit-ing? I still have that Bushmills bottle I mentioned waiting for him."

"No word yet, but I am sure it'll be soon. Oh, by the way, remember my friend Jessica? You met her at the wedding."

"Yes," he said hesitantly. "I remember her. Sweet lass."

Cassandra's excitement at her friend's visit inundated her voice, "We ex-tended a job offer to her to help alleviate some of our load, and she's accepted! I'm hoping to have a nice dinner to celebrate when she gets here. You'll join us, of course." Silence filled the line. "Stephan, are you still there?"

"Yes. Yes, I'm here. That's great Cassandra," he said in a low, composed voice.

"Well…make sure you block some free time in your busy schedule when she gets here."

"I need to go. Just tell me when and I'll put it on my calendar."

"Do you want to talk to Trevor?"

"Something's come up. I'll call him later. Goodbye Cassandra."

"Goodbye." Cassandra stared at the receiver in her hand and wondered at Stephan's reaction. During the rehearsal dinner and the quick fare-well after the wedding ceremony, she had caught Jessica's eyes hovering on Stephan Connellan, Trevor's honorary uncle. Between both Stephan's skittish behavior and Jessica's strange reference earlier, one would think they were interested in each other.

Trevor glanced up at Cassandra and noticed her raised eyebrows. "Who was that?"

Cassandra turned to him with a bewildered look. "Stephan."

"And?"

"Let's just say for the record, I expect Jessie's move here to be an interesting one."

"That's brilliant. She accepted! Why will it be interesting?"

"Don't ask me; just a hunch."

★ ★ ★ ★ ★

Stephan dropped the phone in the cradle, fell back in his chair, and laid his head against the headrest. His heart raced in his chest and anticipation rippled in his gut, tightening his stomach muscles in knots. Jessica. When he had traveled to California for Trevor's wedding, he hadn't thought he'd get a surprise in the form of Jessica Forrester. He had been seated next to her at dinner the night before the wedding and was immediately intrigued and attracted to the pixie. Thoughts of her had plagued him ever since.

During the wedding, Stephan hadn't been able to keep his eyes off Jessica and had been thrilled that hers had seemed to seek him out, too. He'd been blown away as he watched her come into the church. Her petite slender frame had been perfectly adorned with the delicate maid-of-honor dress, her skin lightly tanned as if kissed by the sun. Her large eyes were as blue as a bright summer sky and radiated happiness for her friend. His heart had been captured and, for an instant, he'd tuned out the niggling voice babbling about their age difference.

After the wedding, an impulse, one he could only describe as a streak of masochism, had him offering Jessica a ride home so he could spend more time in her company. It was an offer he had come to regret.

Many a night he'd tossed and turned. His thoughts kept finding their way to her. The idea of having her within reach again filled him with excitement and his blood stirred at the memory of her mouth under his— until guilt punched him square in the face: she was almost seventeen years younger than him, a man in his forties. Doubts began to consume him. Had she been playing him that day? He could have sworn he had seen a real spark of interest in her eyes, but then again, it could have been wishful thinking on his part.

Stephan had returned to Ireland and buried himself in his work, but this time it didn't make up for his loneliness or block images of the captivating American girl who had stolen his heart in only two days.

It was then he had decided it was time to move on, and he had made the effort to come out of his self-imposed shell. He had called on Terese, the woman Maeve had planned to set him up with, in an attempt to wash away his memories of Jessica. In the weeks and months that followed, they had come to an understanding, but Terese didn't tempt or whet his appetite the way Jessica had.

Distance and time apart from Jessica had been instrumental in numbing his feelings; he thought he had finally put her behind him until Cassandra had mentioned the latest developments. Jessica. Would he be able to withstand temptation a second time?

Chapter Two

Meet & Greet

THE BULLET TRAIN SPED DOWN the tracks, blurring the landscape along its path. The cruel glint in the blonde man's eyes gave full indication he was not joking around when he pulled the trigger. Cassandra's scent wafted in the air as she appeared out of nowhere. The pain. Her pain. His rage. Then everything blurred to that last moment.

"I wouldn't do that."

"You don't have the guts." The man's sneer grated his nerves.

"Try me, asshole…"

The shot rang out.

Trevor sprang up in bed shivering, his body covered in a thin film of sweat.

Cassandra stirred in bed beside him and once her eyes focused on him, alarm flooded them. She sat up and wrapped an arm around his back. "What's wrong?"

"Nothing new."

"Niklas?"

Trevor nodded. Killing a human being, no matter how psychotic that human being might be, didn't sit well with him, and had plagued him since he had pulled the trigger.

"It was self-defense. Just as confirmed by the French authorities." Cassandra rubbed his shoulder gently.

"Doesn't change the fact that I killed him."

Cassandra placed a gentle kiss on his shoulder and coaxed him to lie back. He complied, lying on his side and drawing her into his arms. Her warm breath feathered his chest and soothed him back to sleep. If only he could erase that one memory.

★ ★ ★ ★ ★

Cassandra woke to the morning light filtering through the curtains and a warm hand resting on her hip. A soft smile broke across her lips as she rolled to face the source of that warmth: Trevor. His head was turned toward her and an arm bent above his head, framing it on the pillow. Love swelled in her heart as she took in the length of his eyelashes, the five o'clock shadow on his cheek, the soft up and down of his chest as he remained deeply asleep. He lay on his back undisturbed by her scrutiny.

She watched the play of sunlight as it moved across his barely covered body. Her hands itched to follow in its path as it flowed across his skin. She could still feel the imprint of his hand, which now rested between them on the bed. She glanced at it and traced the length of his fingers with her eyes. Her breath quickened and her heart jolted at the memory of those hands touching and brushing over her body not that long ago.

Soft light caressed his face, he stirred, and she moved closer, casting a shadow on him, waiting in anticipation. Cassandra's excitement swelled as his lashes fluttered and eyelids crept open. His sleepy eyes met hers.

She leaned over him and smiled in greeting before she touched her lips to his.

"Good morning," she breathed against his mouth.

His sinewy arms wrapped around her and pulled her close. "Hmm!" he exhaled contently, moving his mouth over hers, devouring its softness. The firmness of his lips sent spirals of heat through her. The harsh, uneven rhythm of their breathing filled the room as they parted and touched foreheads.

After a few moments, Cassandra pulled back. "I can't believe how much I miss you when we're sleeping."

He stared lovingly into her eyes and Cassandra felt the beat of his heart accelerate beneath her hand. "I can try and make up for the lost time. Any thoughts?" A seductive smile spread across his face.

Cassandra grinned down into his dark blue eyes, which always left her with the sensation of sinking in a deep ocean. By the press of his growing erection against her stomach, she sensed exactly where his train of thought was headed, and knew it was on a collision course with hers.

She leaned down again, shading his eyes from the sunlight. As she moved closer, her hair slipped from around her shoulders and surrounded them, closing out the world. She exhaled a moist breath and licked along his lower lip before sucking it into her mouth. Trevor moaned as she released it with deliberate languidness. "Does that give you any insight?"

His eyes smoldered with desire as they met hers and he exhaled deeply. "Yes. Definitely gives me a clue. Can I test a theory?"

Cassandra chuckled and nodded.

Trevor rolled quickly on the bed, inverting their positions, laying the length of his body along hers and spreading her legs with a nudge of his knees. His cock pulsed and grew even harder as she threw her head back, pressing tighter against him. He grasped her wrists, moved them over her head, and held them tightly. He lifted himself to his elbows as he slowly rubbed his body against hers and thrust into her wet, slick channel.

Cassandra inhaled sharply at the contact and arched her back, placing her breasts within reach of his mouth. He swooped down and pulled a dusky nipple into his mouth while his body moved in a slow, easy tempo against hers.

"Faster, Trev!" Immobilized within his grasp, she used her legs to urge him on, circling them around his hips, locking her heels behind his ass. She tightened her thighs and pulled him deeper. "Yes! Love me!"

Cassandra bucked against him with each thrust, with each pull of his mouth and swipe of his tongue on her nipple. Her little cries appeared to rouse Trevor to a peak of desire and override all other thoughts but to give her what she demanded of him, moving faster and deeper into her.

"So close!" she breathed, unlocking her heels and raising a leg higher along his waist to pull him deeper.

Trevor slammed into her, his penetration a mix of pleasure and pain. Cassandra gasped as a flash of heat surged through her veins. He lifted his head and kissed a trail across her chest to her other breast. Capturing her nipple, he clenched it between his teeth and nipped it slightly. "Trevor!" she cried out as he rolled and teased its tip with his tongue.

"I love you," she gasped as she bucked and ground against Trevor, tightening her silky thighs around his hips, flexing her muscles and clamping around him, desperate to drag him with her as the first pulse of her climax flowed through her. "Now Trevor, please!" she cried out for release and, as he loosened his hold on her pinned hands, she was finally free to entwine her hands with his while her body exploded in a downpour of fiery sensations.

Trevor increased the speed of his thrusts as the ripples of her orgasm squeezed his cock rhythmically. "Cassandra!" The familiar sensation of his imminent release radiated through him like an electric shock. He couldn't hold back any longer. It shot down his spine causing him to erupt. He shook with the intensity of it, his gasp and groans echoed in the room as he ejaculated deep inside her.

The intimacy of the moment was more than he could ever have envisioned in his life. Cassandra wrapped her arms around his neck and held on to him as they rode the waves of their climax, savoring the satisfaction their passion had left within each other.

"I love married life."

Trevor felt the curve of her smile against his lips before she commented, "I know, right?" She flexed her inner muscles around his cock, extracting another deep groan from them both.

"Wicked woman!" Trevor exclaimed and rolled off to the side to lie next to her on the bed. The sun's rays filtering through the curtains bathed and licked their skins as their breaths sawed in and out.

"I like waking up like this. Can we give it another go tomorrow?" Trevor laughed, his voice and eyes shining with love.

Cassandra slapped his thigh playfully and rolled her eyes. "Jeez. Insatiable."

"What?" Trevor feigned innocence. "Just because I love, need, and want you all the time? The abuse! Now, come closer, wife," he chuckled, pulling her into his arms. "We still have a time to recover. You wore me out."

★ ★ ★ ★ ★

Dressed casually and ready to go at a moment's notice, Trevor held his cup of tea absently and watched the city stir to life from the large glass bedroom window facing St. Stephen's Green. The sound of rustling sheets caught his attention, and Trevor turned to watch Cassandra.

When her sleepy eyes met his, he saw them sharpen and focus as she rolled to rest on her side. "What's wrong?" she asked as she pushed her hair back from her face.

"Nothing. Thinking." Trevor approached the bed, placed the cup on the side table, and lay beside her. He rested his crossed hands on his stomach as he studied the ceiling.

"There has to be more to it, Trev. You're dressed already. What's up?"

"Devlin called. He's cautious about sending the details we need electronically. I checked his system and agree with him. It's not secure. He sent someone to deliver the info in person. Old style."

Cassandra lay motionless as she appeared to process what he'd just told her. Once she did, she threw the covers off and rose from the bed. "Finally! We're getting somewhere. When?"

"The person handling the delivery is already in Dublin. The meet takes place in thirty minutes by O'Connell Bridge."

Cassandra's expression grew somber as she searched Trevor's gaze. Although they had never needed to use precautions and most of the cases they worked for the NSA to date had involved accessing data and infiltrating computers remotely, Trevor still felt the need to maintain a routine of sorts for both their sakes. Practice always made perfect.

"Just get home in one piece. No side adventures, got it?" Cassandra returned to the edge of the bed and leaned down to kiss him. The sweetness of her kiss left him burning with the promise of more to come upon his return. With a nod, Trevor pushed off the bed and walked to the table beside the window where he collected his messenger bag.

In long, confident strides, he made his way out of the room and down the stairs, two steps at a time, to the main floor. Trevor wondered what life would be like if he wasn't doing what he did for a living. If Cassandra hadn't throttled into his life. Definitely boring. A wide smile spread across his face in anticipation of the thrill to come.

The walk to the bridge was a short one, twenty minutes at the most. He walked out of the house, crossed the street to St. Stephen's Green, and headed north toward Grafton Street. The popular posh street was packed with the usual tourists, vendors, street performers, and the occasional delivery truck parked in the pedestrian-only area. Grafton shops were known for their variety and quality. The fancy, expensive fashion and jewelry stores were open, displaying their precious products to window shoppers. Cafés were filled with the masses looking for their morning caffeine fix and delicious pastries. The street was abundant with spring colors and the fresh smell of coffee and breakfast.

He continued his hike northbound, past Trinity College and toward O'Connell Bridge. His mind swirled with curiosity about the person

Devlin had sent to deliver the information. Devlin's secrecy was a given, considering the possible insider job they were facing. He hoped Cassandra could get a read on the asset and eliminate him from the list of possible suspects. He needed to see this job completed quickly, and reducing the number of suspects would greatly help in attaining that goal. It'd been a long time since they had any solid leads. The intercept George had picked up had breathed new life into their personal quest for answers.

Dublin's streets were full of activity, the norm for that time of the year. Tourist buses parked on the side of the road across from the hotels in the area were a clear sign that the height of the spring season had arrived. The Guinness store was packed as usual with visitors looking for a special souvenir from Dublin—and what better gift than an exclusive pint glass? Trevor grinned as he passed the store and continued his brisk walk to the arranged meeting point. Pulling his phone from his pocket, he plugged the ear buds into his ears.

As he reached the median on O'Connell Bridge, his focus sharpened and he absorbed all the activity around him—a skill deemed critical to his current occupation, and ingrained in him by Cassandra through intensive training. Adrenaline coursed through him, a rush he had wished many times to have had in the past and which had become a part of his life and work of late. Mingling with the morning commuters, Trevor approached Eden Quay and scrutinized the people milling around. Like him, they appeared to be everyday folk going to work, school, or appointments—life happening at full bloom.

★ ★ ★ ★ ★

As soon as Trevor left, Cassandra pulled her hair into a practical ponytail and threw on jeans and a t-shirt. Straightening the bed, she took a moment to shove her face into Trevor's pillow and breathe in deeply. *If only he wasn't such a risk taker.*

She tossed the pillow back on the bed and went into quick action, moving swiftly and with purpose through the house to the kitchen where she made a fresh pot of coffee. The delicious aroma almost made her groan. Cassandra glanced at the clock and her heart skipped a beat. Trevor would be hitting O'Connell Bridge soon. Visualizing the bridge, she knew they couldn't have picked a more perfect spot for a meet and greet. Trevor would blend right in. Nobody would pay attention to a guy standing at a bus stop in the hustle and bustle of the morning commute. She filled a large cup with the dark elixir and took it with her up to the office.

Cassandra's fingers flew on the keyboard the minute she sat at her desk. She established the connection to the Closed Circuit Television control center, tapping straight into the citywide camera network. She located the camera she wanted at the corner of O'Connell Street Lower and Eden Quay where Trevor would make contact. Her heart raced and anticipation filled the room as she waited for him to let her know he was in play. She reached for her cup and sat back against the soft leather of her comfortable chair to wait for his signal.

She didn't have to wait long.

"Cassie, copy?"

"Hold on Trev, just a bit of static." She took a few seconds working the keyboard to filter the signal further. "Try now."

"Can't wait to get back and jump you." His seductive tone came through loud and clear.

"Oh yeah, clear as a bell."

"Almost there. Get ready," Trevor directed softly for her ears only.

Her voice was all business. "Copy."

Cassandra monitored the views of the surrounding area through the CCTV light-rail connections, then initialized the button camera feed. Trevor was holding a book in front of the camera, blocking her view— *The Rolling Stones: The Story behind Their Biggest Songs*. He opened the book so the cover could clearly be seen and pretended to read from it as he continued to scan the area around him.

"Hey, Trevor. Move the book a sec so I can do one last focus check."

Cassandra watched the flurry of activity in front of him as she adjusted the focus. "Perfect." The pages of the book came back into view and, without comment, Trevor returned to his pretend reading.

★ ★ ★ ★ ★

Trevor kept a close eye on his surroundings, covertly taking note of the CCTV cameras positions in the area and thinking how nice it was of the city council to introduce the system in Dublin. Most of the main cities in Europe were rigged with cameras, installed to allow police and transit control to observe traffic and respond to emergency situations promptly. It had become a very useful tool in their line of work. However, it wasn't their only means of surveillance. Echelon was still their main source of data on any project, be it NSA-related or of personal nature.

"Have you heard from George? He never did let us know how the date with Jennifer went."

Cassandra's soft laughter flowed over the link, "Hey! This isn't the right time to be discussing George's love life, Trevor!"

"Okay, okay. How's the tap working? Can you access all the cameras?"

"Yes, sir!" She laughed at his business-like tone. "All cameras are live and accessible. I love the way you tap, Mr. Bauer."

"I'll keep that in mind for later, Mrs. Bauer." He chuckled and returned his focus to the people approaching the bus stop. Time slowed to a trickle as he waited for the asset to show up. Speaking softly, Trevor reached out to Cassandra. "All set. Keep your eyes on those cameras. It shouldn't be long now."

"Okay. I'm ready. So far everything looks clear."

Cassandra kept her eyes focused on the screens. Catching movement in one of the split views, she leaned forward in her chair and in a controlled voice warned him, "Trevor, heads up. Two o'clock. Coming straight at you."

"Already spotted. Thanks, love," he responded softly in his Irish drawl, sending a shiver down her spine.

Cassandra grinned softly at her reaction to him. He would always elicit those feelings from her. *So easy.* Shaking her head to clear her thoughts, she turned her attention back to the business at hand.

From where Trevor sat, he observed a man walking into the opposite end of the bus shelter. He carried a lightweight briefcase and wore a developer's signature attire: jeans and t-shirt. Trevor casually tracked the man as he skirted around people waiting for their buses. When he reached Trevor, the man took a seat beside him and glanced over at the book in Trevor's hand. After their eyes connected briefly, the man deflected his gaze.

A bus arrived and the people in line moved to board it, quickly vacating the shelter. Trevor and the man remained behind. Fidgety, the man stood and walked over to study the bus map posted on the glass wall directly across from Trevor.

After a few minutes, he turned, squared his shoulders, and nodded toward the book Trevor held. "A rolling stone gathers no moss."

The man's tone and expression were full of uncertainty. Trevor lowered the book, giving Cassandra a full view of the man they had now established as being their asset. He replied with the arranged counter phrase: "Sure 'nough, I'm a rolling stone."

Trevor watched as the asset's expressive face changed, becoming almost somber. When he took a step forward, Trevor shook his head and waved him back. "Nope. Stay there. Did you bring the details as instructed?"

The man stopped mid-stride and seemed taken aback by Trevor's order. He had no idea the button camera trained on him was providing Trevor's tenacious wife with a full view of his reactions, allowing her to scrutinize him like a bug under a microscope.

Familiar with Cassandra's love for detail, he was certain she would be making one last critical pass around the perimeter and smiled inside when he heard her over the link. "Looks clear. It doesn't look like he was followed or came with anyone. Turn just a smidge to your left." He did as directed. "Good."

Trevor watched as the asset reached into his briefcase. "Easy," Trevor cautioned him. A face-to-face meeting in their line of work was always risky, no matter how much planning went into it. Being compromised was not an option. But the adrenaline rush in Trevor's veins at that moment made it well worth the risk.

The asset pulled an envelope from the case and, with careful controlled movements, handed it over. Trevor scanned the area to make sure nobody else was paying attention to their exchange before removing the contents from the non-descript envelope—sheets of paper and an unmarked disk.

The man shuffled his feet while Trevor read through the pages, his knuckles stark white from gripping his briefcase's handle. "Don't worry." Trevor glanced casually from the papers to the man. "We have the place covered." The look of surprise on the asset's face on realizing he was being watched was priceless. Cassandra must have thought the same because her soft laughter rippled into his ear.

Trevor lowered his eyes and skimmed the pages. The sheets contained information outlining the data to be retrieved, the importance of it to the company, usernames and passwords, and information regarding the system backdoor. Everything provided was information Trevor was familiar with handling. Trevor reached the last page of the packet and read the note scrawled on it.

Once data is retrieved you will meet Antonín Mucha in Prague. Location and time dependent on data destruction success.

★ ★ ★ ★ ★

Cassandra listened to the exchange and watched the asset closely. Facial analysis had always been one of her favorite subjects during her training at the Farm.

"Wait a minute," she muttered under her breath, pulling up a second screen and rewinding the video capture. "I know I saw something," she continued to mutter and rewound it a second time to scrutinize the man's face.

Cassandra focused on his mouth. His lips were stretched in a tight straight line. Next, she studied his eyes. They were open very wide, the upper lids pulled up while the lower ones were very tense. She advanced the video and froze it again. Both of his eyebrows were raised and pulled tight together. "Trevor, he's afraid. *Very* afraid. He knows something."

Shortly after, Cassandra heard Trevor over the link. "Tell me. Why are you afraid?"

The man's face blanched. "What do you mean? I...I'm not afraid."

"Yeah. And that's why you didn't just stutter?" Trevor chuckled. "You are. Tell me why."

Cassandra commented in his ear, "Trev, I still only read fear...Wait... Hold on." Cassandra noticed that the inner corners of the asset's eyebrows had risen, causing them to slant downwards from the center of his forehead. She leaned closer to the screen and traced the lines of the man's expression with her finger.

"Picking up what appears to be either sadness or guilt."

The asset took a few seconds, as if considering his options, and then spoke to Trevor. "My name is Paul Faber. I'm the lead developer of the stolen project files—now in the wrong hands...." His voice carried a tired, defeated tone.

Within minutes Cassandra confirmed. "Identity verified. I'm going with guilt, Trev. Get it wrapped up. You have what you need."

Cassandra's assessment confirmed Trevor's own instincts and he smiled. Faber let out a huge breath. "So, I can confirm with Mr. Devlin you are taking the job?"

Trevor stuffed the envelope and sheets in his bag. "Yes."

Relief flared in Faber's eyes. Reaching in his bag again, he pulled out a smaller envelope and handed it to Trevor. "Mr. Devlin asked that I give this to you if you agreed to follow through with the job." Trevor took the envelope. Curious to see what other information Devlin had provided him, he looked inside and ran his thumb along the edge of the sheets it contained. Approximately 500 grand in mature US bonds, by his calculation.

Cassandra's whistle came across the feed. "Damn, Trevor, that is a lot of T-bills."

Trevor commented under his breath, "Yep," and quickly resealed the envelope before tossing it back to Faber. Startled, he fumbled and almost dropped it. In a panicked voice he stammered, "But Mr. Devlin said—"

Trevor's voice was velvet-edged and firm. "You can tell your boss this was not part of the arrangement." Money wasn't the reason they were taking on that case. There was only one thing Trevor wanted as payment: his father's notes. "We're done here. I'll be in contact."

Trevor pushed to his feet and adjusted his messenger bag, now containing the key to a new clue in his personal puzzle. He saw uncertainty cloud Faber's eyes again. "Yes?"

"This could have been handled digitally. The information could have been emailed. Why meet in person?"

Trevor considered not responding, but Faber seemed sincerely worried about the fate of his creation, and that made him likable.

"You must know by now there is a good chance this was an insider job. I get why Devlin sent you. As the original developer of the stolen software, your interest would be in recovering and not leaking it. You have the most to lose."

Understanding flooded Faber's eyes. "Who?"

"That's what I've been hired to find out." Before Faber could ask any more questions, Trevor left him standing alone in the bus shelter.

★ ★ ★ ★ ★

With the meeting over, Cassandra took a deep relaxing breath and continued to multitask, tracking Trevor's progress while at the same time saving the data she'd collected to the project file, including the captured video stream from the button camera. All the information on Faber, including body gestures, would be put to use again later when she set up a baseline and ran everything through the facial expression database for further analysis.

Once finished, she leaned back in her chair and swung her feet up onto the desk, crossing them at the ankles. She picked up her conversation with Trevor. "Okay, give. What are we up against here?"

Silence followed and Cassandra could picture his face in her mind. His need to internalize was strong. She could almost hear the wheels turning in his mind. She had been working on breaking that habit of his. "Stop thinking so hard, Trevor. Cough it up."

"The stolen files are the core source files of a new decryption program. I need to analyze the contents of the disk to understand its reach. It might be that Devlin is overreacting. But Faber, being the developer, knows its capabilities and he was scared. I'm thinking it's big."

Cassandra's quick intake of breath echoed through the feed. Her own wheels turned in her head as she mulled over the information Trevor had just shared with her. She dropped her feet from the desk, opened a blank document, and let her fingers fly across the keys as she laid down her thoughts and questions. She and Trevor had a lot to discuss when he got back.

★ ★ ★ ★ ★

Adrenaline coursed freely through Trevor's veins as he made his way back to their house. At the corner of St. Stephen's Green, he accelerated his pace, knowing he was mere minutes from home and Cassandra—his partner in crime, hotter than hell, with a beautiful brain and a wicked attitude to match.

In his rush to be home, he skipped giving her a heads up on his position. Anxious to see her, he strode into the house and climbed the stairs two at time. The exhilaration of fieldwork always put him on edge. Still riding the rush of adrenaline, he burst into the office to find Cassandra sitting at her desk, laptop open in front of her, and still wearing the headset. Startled, she looked at him.

"What happened? Are you—" her question trailed off. She frowned as she watched him stalk toward her with a ravenous expression on his face. "Trev? Why didn't you call in your position?"

He reached for her hand, hauled her from the chair, and led her into their bedroom across the hall from their office. "Not now, Cassandra." With not-so-gentle nudges, he pushed her back until her legs bumped against the edge of the bed and she was forced to sit. He crowded close, his heated gaze capturing hers. "I need to feel you, take you, the way I fantasized on my way home."

A rush of heated color flushed Cassandra's neck and cheeks as his gaze raked her body. A deep sense of satisfaction filled him when she shifted her ass on the bed. He knew she was just as turned on by the way she parted her knees. His cock twitched and grew heavier as he watched her swallow hard and wet her lips with her tongue.

Desire and excitement gleamed from her eyes as she spoke in a breathless whisper, "What are you waiting for?"

Those words unleashed Trevor's desire. He pushed her back against the bed and straddled her thighs, sitting back on his knees and watching the erratic pulse beat out of control at the base of her throat. Holding her gaze, he reached for his pants, working the button and zipper. His voice dropped and his Irish brogue became more pronounced. "I can't wait to be buried deep inside you. Feel you surrounding me, hot and wet."

Without a word, Cassandra nudged him back. Curious, he gave way and moved to the side, following her intently with hooded narrowed eyes. A smile quirked the corner of his mouth as her shaky hands reached for and unbuttoned her jeans. Lust rose inside him to an unimaginable level when she lay back on the bed and raised her pelvis so she could push both the jeans and skimpy underwear off her hips.

Once they reached her ankles, Trevor jerked them off, freeing her legs. The intensity of her gaze burned his skin as he yanked her t-shirt over her head and tossed it to the floor.

Trevor knelt on the bed beside her, pushed his pants down his hips, and fisted his rock-hard cock, now standing at attention. His heart missed a beat and a quiver surged through his veins as his eyes caressed her curvaceous body. "Jezus Cassandra! You're fucking gorgeous."

Cassandra tried to swallow the lump in her throat at the sight of Trevor's long, lean, muscular body. Her stomach and inside muscles clenched in anticipation. "You're pretty damn hot yourself, geek!" Her voice was no more than a broken whisper.

She rested back on her elbows, spread her legs in invitation, and glanced down the length of her body as Trevor moved between her thighs. His eyes mirrored her desire and held hers captive. A shiver rippled along her spine as he guided his cock to her entrance and slid the tip of it up and down along her sex, coating it with her juices.

"Do you feel it? Feel the need?" he demanded as he continued to tease her.

Her heart jolted and pulse pounded. "God, Trevor! Yes. I feel it—need it right now!"

Trevor pushed his hips forward and thrust his cock deep inside her. Cassandra fell back against the bed as she released a soft lingering moan, "Love…me…Trevor."

"I plan to. I will, love."

Initiating a cadence, Trevor supported his weight on his hands and pumped his hips hard against hers. Cassandra wanted more of him. She lifted her feet off the bed, circled her legs around his hips, and pushed her heels against his lower back, pulling him tighter against her. She met him thrust for thrust, circling and grinding her pelvis against his.

Trevor's breath hissed through his gritted teeth. "I love filling you like this, Cassie!"

"Je-zus, Trevor!" she moaned, arching her body instinctively toward him as he increased his tempo. "Harder! Yes!" she breathed, sliding her hands around his thighs and digging her fingers deep in his flesh.

At the same time, Trevor brushed the lace of her bra aside, and pulled a dusty pink nipple into his mouth as he reached down between their bodies, seeking her clit. He pulled, laved, and sucked at her nipple while he rubbed the sweet bundle of nerve endings in a circular motion.

Cassandra's head pressed into the bed as her back arched into him, hands fisting the covers. He knew exactly how to play her, touch her, drive her wild. She breathed in deep, soul-drenching gasps. The gentle stroking of his fingers and the pounding of his cock pushed her beyond thought. Soon her inner muscles rippled around his shaft in her impending orgasm.

"Yes, babe. Come for me. I want to feel you squeezing my cock."

Leaning down, Trevor claimed her mouth hungrily, kissing her hard and deep as he continued his loving assault, their bodies coming together in urgent harmony. She moaned and whispered against his mouth, urging him on.

Cassandra clenched her inner walls, squeezing tight as she sucked and rolled her tongue around his. A swift rush of heat slammed into her. Her entire body tightened and arched from the bed as her climax exploded inside her, forcing her head back and ripping his name from her lips in a scream, "Trevor!"

"Fuck, Cassie girl! God!"

Her body shook with the aftershocks and the pulses of electricity coursing through her, into her sex. Her muscles contracted and clamped down tight around his cock as he continued to thrust deeper and harder into her, pinning her to the bed.

Trevor wanted to bury himself in her over and over until he exploded into his own release, but the need to taste her was stronger. Breaking contact and pulling from her, he slid down her body to kneel on the floor by the bed. He seized Cassandra's hips, yanked her to the edge and draped her legs over his shoulders.

"God Cassie! You're so wet for me, babe. I just want to lick you until you burst again," he whispered as he kissed her inner thigh and sucked her clit deep into his mouth, flicking it with his tongue. He took his time licking and lapping at the juicy folds of her sex.

Cassandra whimpered, threaded her fingers through his hair and grasped it, holding him to her. "Trevor!" she cried out hoarsely in bliss.

"Do you want me to fuck you with my tongue, babe? Tell me."

Cassandra reeled under the rush of sensations flooding her, her body still sensitive from her last release. "Damn, Trevor! Please! I love it when you do…but…I need to feel you!"

Desperate to feel his body against hers again, she lifted her legs from Trevor's shoulders, letting them drop to his sides. She cupped his nape and brought him to her for a hungry kiss that rivaled his intimate one. She tasted herself on his lips, licked along them, and plundered his mouth with her tongue. Trevor crawled his way back up her body, a groan escaping them as their tongues continued to dance along each other's.

Releasing Trevor's face, Cassandra skimmed her hand down his chest to reach between them. Her fingers brushed across the velvety head of his hard cock. Her thumb rubbed across it, massaging the pre-come over and around it before wrapping her hand around his girth. She squeezed him gently as she began to pump her hand up and down along his length.

"Cassie!" he growled against her mouth.

Cassandra felt his cock expand and harden even more in her grasp. "Yes, babe?" she whispered in a shaky voice against his lips. "Please, Trev. Love me. Let me love you."

Her hand was like heaven but, while he loved what she was doing, he would much rather be buried inside her when he came. Spurred by her words, he covered her hand with his and guided the engorged head to her entrance. He rubbed it against her clitoris and a ragged moan escaped her lips. "I want you bad, Cassandra."

Before Trevor's harsh whisper faded, he thrust deep, pumping his groin against hers in a hard tempo, enjoying the sight of his shaft slipping in and out of her body over and over again. A moan slipped through her lips with each thrust. Trevor twined his fingers through her hair, grasped it tightly, and turned her face to his so he could stare in her heavy-lidded eyes and at her plump parted lips. She looked sinfully beautiful. He lowered his mouth to hers, invading it with his tongue.

Cassandra burned out of control, drowning in the sensation of Trevor's grip on her hair, tongue loving her mouth, and cock filling her. She gasped in sweet agony as she moved her legs up around his hips and squeezed her muscles, tightening them around him as he pulled away and relaxing them as he sank back to the hilt. His tongue mimicked his hips, moving in and out of her mouth, twirling and brushing it along the inside of hers before withdrawing and biting on her lower lip.

"Fuck! I love you, Cassie. So damn much."

Swooping back in, Trevor captured her mouth again and her sob filled it as he careened toward release. Her hands reached under his arms to grip his back, nails digging deep as she held him to her. He trailed his lips along the line of her neck to her collarbone as he skimmed his hands along her ribs to her breasts. Trevor flicked the nipples with his thumbs before squeezing and pulling one close to his mouth.

His tongue laved around one of her nipples and his fingers kneaded the other as she arched her back, forcing her breast further into his mouth. The grazing and scraping of his teeth on her nipple triggered another orgasm to rip through her, forcing her body to stiffen and clamp around him rhythmically. Trevor couldn't hold back any longer. "Cassie!" he cried out, giving in and allowing his own release to overtake him. He thrust wildly against her, groaning with each pulse of his cock, each squeeze of her body around him, grasping and milking him to the last drop. Collapsing over her, tired and spent, their breaths wheezed in and out, mirroring the erratic beat of their hearts.

When they finally could breathe again and the racing of their hearts slowed, Cassandra looked at Trevor with a lazy, sated smile on her lips and love shining from her eyes. "So, I take it you feel good about the meeting."

"That was just the excuse. The truth is I just want you all the time," he answered with a wicked glint in his eyes. He rolled over to lie on his back. After a few minutes of comfortable silence, Trevor turned to his side and gazed down at her. "I love you. The great sex is just a bonus to the whole amazing trip we're taking together."

Cassandra cupped his cheek. "So glad I tracked you down. I wouldn't trade this for anything." Smiling softly she leaned into him. "You're stuck with me, you know?"

"I wouldn't have it any other way, love."

Chapter Three

The Mole?

"CASSIE! CHOP, CHOP!" TREVOR YELLED from the office.

"Be right there!" Cassandra grabbed a towel, dried her face, and quickly ran a brush through her hair. "I can't believe he let me sleep in!" she mumbled under her breath as she ran back into the bedroom and slipped into a lightweight dress. Feeling more awake, she hurried across hall to the office where Trevor was already hard at work.

It had been three days since the meeting with Paul Faber; Trevor had been up to his ears in infiltrations, research, and collection of data that would help them pinpoint the origin of the hack that resulted in the theft of MDS's files. Trevor had scrutinized the contents of the disk received from Faber and they now understood the importance of the stolen data.

They had learned that the files in question were actually decryption software that could crack anything encoded with a certain algorithm by exploiting a secret vulnerability. The kicker was that the algorithm in question was the one used by most financial institutions around the world to process inter-bank fund transfers. That meant it allowed access to any bank's system with the pressing of a few keys. The reach and repercussion of the usage of such software was astounding. It could bring the world financial market to its knees. It was the subject of nightmares for anyone in the software development field. Something so powerful could never be distributed at large.

The NSA itself would've loved to have developed such software, have full control of its reach. Instead, it had been the brainchild of a small company on the brink of stardom, and now most likely had fallen into very wrong hands.

Cassandra spotted the cup left by her computer the moment she walked through the door. The addictive aroma of coffee filled her senses and almost brought her to her knees. "Thank the Irish Gods!" Lifting the cup for a slow sip, she gazed at Trevor across their desks.

He raised an eyebrow. "Took you long enough."

Cassandra flashed him a smile as she walked to his side of the office and dropped a kiss on his lips before sitting at her desk. "Hey, you're the one who let me sleep in." She pulled up her notes from the previous day. "So, where are we? Do you have anything new?"

Trevor frowned as he filtered through all the information they had collected about the job. Crossing his hands behind his head, he leaned back in his chair and began to outline what they knew. "Based on the information provided by Faber and George, the data was taken about two weeks ago. Whoever took it erased the data from the server. Thankfully, Faber had copies of the source stored off-site. We also know the potential of the program."

Cassandra nodded in agreement. "Any crook in the world would love to get their hands on it."

"The good thing is the development of the decryption software was not completed when they took it. Maybe they thought they could hire some-one who could easily do that, making it functional in no time. Lucky for us, it isn't that easy. I've analyzed the code. It requires someone with a high-level understanding of parallel computing—not a lot of program-mers with that skill out there."

Trevor watched as she scooted back from her desk, grabbed her cup, and sat on his desk facing him. He could see from the somber look in her eyes that she was deep in thought as she took a sip from her coffee before setting it aside.

"Okay. Who can we trust at this point? Faber is the original developer. We can assume he doesn't want his creation in the hands of criminals, based on the results of the facial analysis. Devlin's out, too. His company would be in financial ruin if the defrauded companies filed suit. Other than that, I don't think we can be sure of anybody." She captured his eyes with hers. "Trevor, we need to be sure what's at stake here and who's involved. We don't want a surprise like France."

Silence filled the air as they both contemplated those ramifications. Cas-sandra and Trevor had met betrayal and unforeseen circumstances on the first case they worked together. Knowing the players in this technological game of hide-and-seek had become a must. Neither wanted to have to go through the pain of seeing the other hurt—again.

Cassandra shook her head and continued, "Hey! What about the logs from the kernel-based keylogger software you installed on all the MDS computers? Did you check the new ones?

He had infiltrated MDS the day he received the details of the case from Faber and installed a keylogger, small programs that gained access and recorded any information typed on the keyboard, on all of MDS's com-puters. The keylogger he had installed was virtually undetectable. It had recorded any input to those computers from the time of its implementa-tion and generated a daily log with the captured data. Trevor never ceased to be amazed by Cassandra's attention to detail. "Get out of my head. I was about to check last night's reports."

Her laughter wrapped around him like a warm blanket. He straightened in his chair and started typing commands to pull up the log files. Although they had full access to MDS's network, which also gave them access to their email server, that wouldn't be enough to track personal communications if the mole avoided using traceable means. "Everybody in IT can read emails. Whoever is involved will use something more inconspicuous, like instant messaging through social media sites. That's why we needed to track keystrokes on every computer." Smirking, he added, "They wouldn't expect their own company to give an outsider root access to their entire network. So much for company privacy policies."

Cassandra watched his fingers fly across the keyboard and chuckled. Trevor looked like a mad pianist, hitting keys, creating magic with his fingers. Under her watchful gaze, he remotely accessed each of the computers targeted and retrieved the logs.

"We have over fifty text files to go through. We can split them between us and be done in half the time."

"Yes, sir!" Cassandra sat back at her desk, eyes glued to the screen, scanning the files for any subtle clue as to who the mole could be.

The keylogger files held details on the applications used, as well as the keystrokes used within each application, such as website URLs, email addresses, and the actual messages typed while using them. It even captured when the backspace had been pressed or letters deleted. Most of the communications were boring emails, some exchanged among the developers and others of a personal nature.

As he read the files, Trevor's sense of humor was sparked by the odd things found in them. He shook his head at some of the content he came across.

Cassandra chuckled while studying her lot of files.

"Did you find amusing stuff in yours, too?"

"Sure did." Cassandra's eyes sparkled with a mix of humor and incredulity.

"Amazing that people still discuss personal things using company computers. They have no idea about what can be restored even from deleted files." He continued with his perusal, scrolling rapidly through them, searching for any unusual communications via instant messaging between someone within the company and an outside recipient.

After several hours of reading mile-long logs, Cassandra's eyes were starting to cross. She rubbed them as she twisted in her chair. "I need a break. My eyes feel like they want to pop out of my head." Her stomach chose that moment to rumble. Trevor's eyebrows rose, making her laugh. "I guess I'm hungry, too." Standing, she stretched like a cat. "Heading downstairs to get us something. I'll be right back."

Trevor's eyes trained on her retreating figure and his heart rolled in his chest. *That's my wife.* He'd never been that lucky. Fate had had a great time mocking him in the past, taking from him the people he loved most—and yet, for once it had actually smiled on him. He sucked in a deep breath and got back to work.

★ ★ ★ ★ ★

Down in the kitchen Cassandra pulled out everything to make quick sandwiches. She'd needed a break from the files and from the apprehension that had been assaulting her off and on since they had taken the case. The mindless task fit the bill. Trevor always mentioned his spidey senses tingled when something didn't jive. She had her own type of sixth sense. The scar on her hip ached again, an indication that things would get a lot more interesting.

With a sense of accomplishment, she lifted the tray and walked back upstairs into the office. Trevor looked up when she entered and grinned at her when she handed him his plate and a pint of Guinness to chase the food down. "Brilliant, love. I'm famished."

She took a bite from her own sandwich and relaxed back in her chair with her feet propped against her desk. "Did you find anything while I was downstairs?"

Cassandra watched Trevor bite down on his sandwich with gusto and nod in appreciation as he chewed. She couldn't help but smile as he swallowed and chased it down with a big gulp of his beer. "That's really good, love. It hit the spot." Trevor tossed the last bite in his mouth and licked his fingers. "To answer your question, no, I haven't. Nothing so far. I hope we can get through this process quickly so we can get to Prague and find out if Mucha has the information I need."

Cassandra's heart twisted in her chest when she saw sadness invade Trevor's features. She immediately dropped her feet to the floor, set her plate aside, and made her way around the desks. His chair creaked under the weight of her hands as she turned it and leaned on its arms. "Patience, love." She placed a soft kiss on his lips and gazed into his turbulent eyes. "We'll find what we need. We will make the meeting in Prague, just as planned."

Trevor exhaled harshly and scrubbed his fingers through his hair. He stared into Cassandra's confident eyes and saw the rock-solid strength and determination that had grounded him in his pursuit of the truth. "I know. I just wish…never mind. Back to work. The faster we ID the mole the better. It's a small company. If we're really lucky, we'll end up with only a few possible suspects." As Cassandra straightened, Trevor trailed his fingers down her arm and gripped her hand, stopping her. "Thank you." She smiled softly in silent acquiescence of the meaning behind his words.

Some time later, Trevor looked up from his screen, satisfaction glowing in his eyes. "I think I might have found something." His voice held a rasp of excitement. "An employee accessed a number of sites with *.ru, .ua* and *.ge* extensions."

Cassandra raised her eyebrows and whistled. "All former Soviet Union countries—Russia, Ukraine, and Georgia."

"Yep. And everybody in this field knows how heavily tied to online fraud those counties are."

Trevor stared pensively at his screen. "How about you do a full background check on this guy? His name is Andrey Tomlin. Check company records on him, too. Need to know if he's a disgruntled employee or something. I'll focus on finishing the last of the files."

Cassandra nodded absently as she jotted his name in her notebook. Working side by side with her had proved to be interesting. He always looked forward to the thrill of having her around during the action. She was definitely a big asset, both behind the scenes and in the field. Cassandra's frown and look of implacable determination as she focused on the background check amused him to no end. *Note to self: find ways to remove that frown from her face later.* While she continued her work, Trevor turned his attention to the remaining logs.

Cassandra was determined to find something that would establish a possible motive. Her fingers pounded a staccato rhythm across the keys as she initiated several financial and medical queries. Next, she opened Tomlin's HR file. It contained some minor disciplinary actions for misuse of company credit cards. *So, Mr. Tomlin, do you have cash-flow issues?*

A little while later, Cassandra eyed the clock on the computer and a wide smile filled her face as she glanced at Trevor. "Done. I packaged it nice and shiny for you. Saved it to the shared drive. He's a suspicious little bugger, as you would say. He may have a love-hate relationship with money. Take a look."

Trevor turned his attention to Mr. Tomlin and the background check she'd compiled. The more he read, the more he felt like there was a good chance they had found their mole. "This is good stuff. If this guy is into something, he has to be communicating with his contact from home as well as from work. He may have curtailed direct communication since the data was stolen. No major money transfers have hit his account yet. He could still be waiting for a payout. We need taps on this guy as soon as possible. I'll get George's take on it tomorrow."

Cassandra nodded. "Between the two of you, no information will be missed." Her muscles ached from the long hours hunched over her computer. She stood and stretched, turning her head to release the kink in her neck. "We've been at it for hours. Are we done for the day, Captain?"

Trevor flashed a wicked grin. "I guess we are done for the day, *a bhean*." The Irish word for wife rolled smoothly off his tongue. He loved saying it. "Let's shut it down." He took her hand in his and led her into the hall. "We'll talk to George tomorrow at the usual time. We can pass all of the details to him then."

The dark curtain of night had descended upon them. The soft moonlight glimmer illuminated the room as Trevor guided Cassandra to their bed. "I can finally start working on getting that little frown off your face." He chuckled at her puzzled silence and cupped her cheeks with his hands. "Don't worry, *a ghrá*. I am sure you'll approve and enjoy my methods." Her sigh echoed in the room has he proceeded to show her.

Chapter Four

Curious George

CASSANDRA'S FOOTSTEPS WERE SOFT AS she made her way to their bedroom. The sight of Trevor standing by the window looking out on St. Stephen's Green, lost in thought, halted her approach. She stood by the door and studied him in silence. His set face, grim mouth, and fixed eyes spoke volumes about his frame of mind. She quietly stepped up behind him, circled his waist with her arms, and hugged him tight before slipping her hands down into his front pockets. Silence descended upon them like a thick blanket as she stood pressed against his back. Whatever was weighing heavily on him she was confident he'd tell her when he was ready.

His concentration implied he was thinking through scenarios regarding the next phase of their current project. As the details of the case filled her own thoughts, they tossed her straight into the memory of Trevor bursting into the room the day of the meet, and the quick, hard love that followed. A slow burn crept up from her chest to her cheeks. Her world had bottomed out in that moment. It had narrowed to only him and the play of his hands and mouth on her body.

Cassandra rubbed her cheek against his back and dropped a kiss between his shoulders. After a few more minutes, his hand drew hers from his pocket and, with a light squeeze, pulled it to his lips, placing a tender kiss in the center of her palm before resting it over his heart. The strong steady beat under her hand was reassuring. Taking his action as a sign that he was ready to talk, Cassandra moved around to face him. She kept her gaze steady and locked on his as she cupped his cheek, his shaved skin soft under her hand. "What's up love?" she asked, rubbing her thumb back and forth where it rested.

Trevor's eyes held a grim determination. "Devlin called. He wanted an update." He flicked his gaze to the street beyond. "I told him everything is still on schedule."

Trevor's hand covered hers again and pressed it tighter against his cheek. She watched a frown crease his brow. "George will be online soon. Hate the five-hour difference. If only we could convince him to move here. We would be able to bounce things off each other easier," Trevor sighed. "But then we would lose the ability to access certain features of Echelon only available to us because he's in Cryptocity. We need to pick his brain and give him what we have so that he can set the taps."

Cassandra drew his attention back to her, searching his troubled eyes for a clue as to what he was really thinking. "When you've worked through it, share what's bugging you with me. Maybe I can help. Two brains are better than one, you know," she teased, hoping to turn his mood. She dropped her glance to the watch gracing her wrist and rose on tiptoes, placing a peck on his lips. "It's almost time for George. I better get everything ready."

She slipped away from him and crossed the hall to their office. Sitting in his chair, she booted his computer. Trevor followed. While she waited for the security login window, she twisted the chair to face him. "Do you think he's made any progress with Jennifer?" she chuckled.

A smile hovered on Trevor's lips and her insides did a small flip-flop. "The way those two dance around each other, they may never get to first base."

Cassandra burst out laughing. "What is it with guys, baseball, and the obsession with bases?" Trevor's wicked smile and wiggling eyebrows melted her insides. She spun to the screen, seeking activity to clear the image of pushing him back to their room and jumping him out of her mind. She swallowed hard a couple of times to dislodge the lump that had formed in her throat. He always had that effect on her. Even after all those months, he could steal the breath from her lungs with just a flash of his crooked smile.

Cassandra squared her shoulders, pulled up the summary of the details they'd captured, and opened the online chat. "Okay. All logged in and set up for the call."

She stood, handing the seat over to Trevor and scooting her own closer. A comfortable silence stretched between them, each lost in their own musings as they waited for George.

Trevor struggled to wrap his head around the next steps to trace the decrypter's location. In the back of his mind, something was niggling at him, making his hair stand on end and his gut clench. Finding the link to the mole had been too easy. Maybe not to an average sysadmin, but to Trevor it had been a piece of cake. Almost as if whoever had taken the decrypter couldn't have cared less if they'd been found. He mulled over the facts, hoping a light would go off, but instead he kept hitting a brick wall. It was seriously pissing him off that he'd not been able to pinpoint the glitch in his theory.

He glossed over Cassandra's notes. The woman could easily get by without taking any—her mind was like an organic file cabinet; but she liked having the notes and records at hand. All details associated with the contact as well as the suspected mole were listed for easy copy and paste. As he read through the background check on Andrey Tomlin the niggling grew stronger—things fit just a little too nicely. Way too easy. The online chat beep sounded in the background. Trevor toggled the window.

Are you there? George had typed on the screen.

Yes. Cassie is here, too. Video call?

Has to be quick today. I have a meeting in about 15 minutes. Something big might be coming our way down the pike.

Not a problem, George. Just let me know if it does and if we'll be needed.

You know how it is when someone wants something yesterday. Oh, wait. That's you most of the time. LOL.

Initiating the video call, George's face appeared on the screen. "Hey, Cassie! Still putting up with this foul-mouthed jerk husband of yours?"

Cassandra laughed, turned her head, and frowned as she looked Trevor over appraisingly. "Yeah. What can I say? He's a keeper. Hot geek, don't you know." She flashed a cheeky grin at Trevor and shrugged. "Just saying."

Trevor shot George a stern look. "Stop ganging up on me or I'll email Jennifer the pictures I have of you from when you came to Dublin and we partied at the Temple Bar."

A clack of teeth sounded as George snapped his mouth shut abruptly, drawing a soft chuckle from Trevor. *The man is head over heels.* George got down to business. "What do you have for me?"

Trevor nodded at Cassandra to take the lead. "Georgie," Cassandra grinned when he scowled at the play on his name. "The MDS project is getting a little sticky." Her grin faded and her expression grew solemn. "We uncovered some interesting information on one employee in particular: Tomlin, Andrey."

Trevor dragged the file into the chat window so George could download the full background check. He watched a crease form between George's brows as he skimmed it.

Cassandra continued with the briefing. "He's single. No current love interests. A fast-tracker within the Company. Used to be a golden boy. That image was tarnished after he was busted and disciplined for corporate credit card misuse. It could have been the catalyst to his involvement in the theft. A good percentage of his personal credit card accounts are maxed out. Possible cash-flow issues. Other than that, he's clean."

George rubbed his chin as he eyed the file. "Still, you never know." His gaze shifted to the camera, "What's this about Russian extensions?"

Cassandra glanced at Trevor. "I'll let Trevor give you the deets on that little nugget. It's his find."

Trevor took over the debriefing and talked about on the many sites Mr. Tomlin was visiting from his work computer. "It's a very weak lead, I know, but so far it's all we've got." He crossed his arms and eased back in his chair. "This is a small company. Not many workers to screen. We had one other potential culprit, but Cassie was able to eliminate him."

"Any clue on the path of extraction?" George's eyes were shrewd and Trevor knew the signs. George's inquiring mind was already working the lead, just as he had.

"It didn't leave the company through the network or I would've found traces of the files being removed via remote access or FTP in the logs. I didn't find any port scans, DNS queries, trace route, or telnet attempts in the logs. No exploits, either."

George's gaze bounced between Cassandra and Trevor. "Sounds like an inside job to me. Someone could've moved the files to an external device and walked out with it."

"That's what we think." Trevor paused, trying to find the right words to express his concern. "The real question is why this was so damn easy to trace."

Cassandra looked at him, her eyes sharp and assessing. "So that's what's been bothering you."

Trevor sighed and nodded. "Why is it that an employee can extract highly confidential data, walk out of the building on a Monday night, and the company not notice it's missing until three days later when the lead developer returns from a business trip and can't find any trace of the files? It's just bizarre. You'd think MDS had better security measures in place."

George nodded and scrubbed his fingers through his hair "Do you think there's someone else involved?"

George hit the bull's eye—the reason Trevor was so puzzled. "There's no activity on his computer to indicate any accomplice within the company. That's why I inputted new keywords in the Echelon library. Keep an eye on it for us, will you? Also, if you can initiate some taps based on the background check Cassie ran, that would help a great deal."

George relaxed back in his chair with his arms crossed at his chest and a smirk like a Cheshire cat curving his lips. "Easy peasy. What do I get in return?" His eyes narrowed speculatively. "You know what I want—"

Trevor sighed deeply. "You're an *eejit*, George. Fine. We'll help you woo your lass. *But*—" Trevor stressed as a grin of anticipation overtook George's features. "No guarantee she'll fall for your ugly ass, even with our help."

George rubbed his hands together, grinning like a child at Christmas. "Hey, something is better than nothing! I'll place the taps and let you know as soon as I have anything." He looked over the top of his monitor and flicked his gaze back to them. "Gotta go."

When the call abruptly terminated, Trevor reached for the mouse and logged them off the chat window.

Cassandra swiveled her chair to face him and frowned as she studied his face. Trevor must have felt her scrutiny because he glanced at her. "What?"

Cassandra searched his eyes and then sighed deeply. "You tell me. Why didn't you mention your suspicions? Did it ever occur to you that I might have had similar questions running around in my head? You should have mentioned it to me, Trev. We could have sounded each other out."

He stared at her sheepishly. "Shite! You're right. Have to remember there is an *us* in the equation, not just *me* now."

"Next time you have one of these gut feelings, spill, okay?"

He took her hand and squeezed it. "Yes, *a ghrá*."

Cassandra squeezed his back. "Don't let it happen again. I have a gun and I *will* use it."

His mouth twitched with amusement and she flashed a wicked grin, chuckling to herself. "Damn if George didn't have the 'I am stalking prey' look at the thought of setting the taps."

She plopped her feet in his lap. "Any thoughts on how we are supposed to help him with Jennifer?" she asked, noticing the rise of his eyebrows. "What? You're my personal footstool. Get over it."

Trevor threw back his head, letting out a hearty laugh. "Glad to be of service."

Cassandra's heart sang on seeing his first real smile of the day.

Trevor took advantage of the little downtime to touch on casual conversation. "Any news from Jessica?"

"Yes! She'll be arriving in four days. I can't wait!"

"It'll be interesting to see you girls in action." He tried to hide his chuckle, but it was an impossible feat. She could see the humor glittering in his eyes.

"You're jealous cause George isn't here to geek out with you. Oh, yeah… George. Where was I?"

Trevor loved watching the wheels spinning out of control in that mind of hers. "I can see you're going to use your big guns on setting up George with Jennifer. I truly hope he doesn't hold me liable for your Machiavellian tactics to hook him up." He leaned back, crossed his hands over his stomach, and looked at her pensively.

"I don't like that look on your face, Trev. It usually means you're up to no good."

He grinned playfully. "What?! Jeez." Feigning hurt, he shook his head. "I wasn't planning anything bad. Just trying to decide on how to properly use your skills on this job."

Cassandra quirked an eyebrow. "I'm listening."

Trevor sighed at her lack of faith and continued. "I'm thinking we should try to secure some video of our Mr. Tomlin. I'll see if I can track something via the building's security system so you can work your magic."

Cassandra's eyes twinkled. As ex-CIA, Cassandra had a wide range of skills. As much as Trevor's instinct was to protect her, he knew she was more than capable of handling herself if complications arose. Monte Carlo had been proof of that. But the apple of her eye was psychoanalysis and how they connected with facial expressions. "More facial analysis?" Excitement and a hopeful glint shone in her eyes.

"Possibly. I was thinking we might need to tap into the CIA tactical video feed. I'm not sure it'll be necessary, though. It'll depend on George and whether or not he comes up with something soon."

Cassandra expelled a soft breath. With George working that case, chances were good he would have new information pretty quickly and she wouldn't have a chance to sink her feet further.

Humoring her, Trevor added, "You mentioned something about a leak the other day?" They had been bantering about the fact she was always wet for him. He craved to validate that claim of hers.

A smile widened across her face and it reminded him of sunshine after a rainy day in Sligo, his hometown. His heart did a little roll in his chest and wreaked havoc on his senses, melting him on the spot. "Or…we could work on something more serious," he said somberly. His words grabbed her attention for a millisecond until she recognized the wicked gleam in his eyes.

Oh, how he enjoyed the way she squirmed under his heated gaze. From where he sat, he could see the pulse pounding at the base of her lovely throat and the dusting of goose bumps along her arms. Cassandra quickly pulled her feet from his lap, crossed her legs, and adjusted her skirt around them before glancing his way with eyes full of false innocence. "Ah…yeah. About that. It's pretty much been a recurring issue since the day I met you. I can't seem to figure out what's causing it."

"Do you need me to get my tool and check it, Cassie girl?" She squirmed some more and he lowered his voice, dragging out his tone and thickening his accent. In a sing-song voice he added, "Would you like me to check it now?"

A flash of humor crossed her face. "Not so fast, geek boy! Assignments have been handed out and work has to be done!" she laughed, pushing back a wayward strand of chestnut hair with a shaky hand.

He loved the way he could clearly affect her with simple words. "Shite. Foiled by my own hand!"

Cassandra looked him over, a wistful gleam in the depths of her whiskey-brown eyes. "Good things come to those who wait, love."

A warm glow flooded him. He wiggled his eyebrows and flexed his fingers, cracking his knuckles. "Then we better get at it Cassie, girl. I'm all for good things."

Chapter Five

Lift off

THE LONG FLIGHT WAS GETTING on Jessica's nerves. She fidgeted in her seat and tried to find a more comfortable position, but the confines of the small space were not very giving. She pressed her elbow against the guy's next to her, but the obnoxious jerk wouldn't share the armrest. Cramped and boxed in, she gave up, pressed her head against the window, and watched the white fluffy clouds outside.

The time difference wasn't going to be easy on her, but each minute spent in Ireland would be worth the trouble. She missed Cassandra and couldn't wait to hug her again. An uncomfortable pang clouded her excitement as her thoughts touched on her best friend. She hadn't been completely honest with her regarding the reason for her prompt acceptance of their job offer and the move to Ireland.

Hell. She hadn't been sure herself as to what drove her to drop everything she had worked for and leave her friends behind to embark on a brand new adventure in Europe—Dublin, to be specific. She had convinced herself that it would be the gateway to broadening her horizons—a new job opportunity, new places to visit and people to meet, maybe new boy-friends to enjoy, all tall, dark, and handsome, with wicked accents. But what appealed to her the most was the proximity to Cassandra. They would have the time of their lives. Well, maybe not so much now that Cassandra was married and only had eyes for Trevor, but she expected they would still have tons of fun working together. She was sure of it.

A niggling feeling still ate at her. Jessica tried to ignore it and sifted through the list of in-flight movies but she had seen them all. She tried to read, but had no patience for the heroine in the paranormal novel on her e-reader. *Another sparkling vampire? Seriously?* Without a distraction, the niggling got the best of her, torpedoing her down memory lane.

Cassandra and Trevor's wedding had been sweet and beautiful. Jessica recalled their conversation that day.

"I predicted you would fall hard, didn't I?" Jessica had bragged as she smoothed Cassandra's veil.

"Yes, you did...never really expect you'd be right, though," Cassandra had smirked.

Cassandra's happiness had beamed through her eyes. She had been far happier than Jessica had ever seen her. Jessica's heart swelled with love for the friend who had stood up for her all those years ago. She deserved hap-piness more than anybody she knew. Cassandra had indeed fallen hard. Thankfully, for the right man. Trevor was her perfect fit in every way. The guy would move heaven and earth for her.

A sad smile quirked Jessica's lips. While she had convinced Cassandra that she was enjoying her single life, the reality of it was, Jessica had been in search of that perfect half for a long time. Unlike Cassandra, who had avoided love and commitment, Jessica embraced it.

She craved the deep dedication, deep commitment Cassandra had found in Trevor. She wanted someone who would ground her, boil her blood, and appreciate her quirky humor. She wanted it all. Damn. If only Trevor had a brother.

The closest thing was an honorary uncle—Stephan. And there it was again…that name. Over the last couple of months, she had tried to avoid thinking about him like the plague. But as hard as she tried, her thoughts always returned to him, time and again. Something stirred in her chest, urging her to make the life-changing decision. The need to know was powerful.

Curiosity was an unreachable itch between her shoulders, one her little research into his life had not eased. She had spent every single night over the past seven months wondering about what had changed her and why she couldn't get *him* out of her system—the touch of his lips, the warmth of his embrace, his fresh woodsy aftershave…his rejection—all etched into her mind since the day of Cassandra's wedding.

Stephan had roused her faster than any other man she had met before and she was driven to figure out what it was about him that affected her so. As far as she was concerned, the only way that was going to happen was to place herself in his path—one of the reasons she'd accepted the job offer and was on that plane. Maybe the constant exposure would desensitize her to him. Wash him out of her system once and for all. She would take back control of her life and again find her fun-loving, confident self. Then maybe, just maybe, she could find the one man who would give her everything and wouldn't leave her wanting for more.

Chapter Six

A Flimsy Link

IT HAD BEEN FOUR DAYS since George had initiated the taps on Andrey Tomlin, and Trevor's impatience had reached new heights. Devlin had called for another update the day before.

"Any news for me, Bauer?"

"Nope. It's not like I can put a gun to someone's head and make them spill where the fucking data is, you know."

"We need you to destroy the information on their servers as soon as possible. If the development of the program is completed—"

"I know of the consequences, Devlin. You don't need to spell it out for me. It's only been a few days. We are talking about hours of transcripts."

"Make it happen, Bauer. Otherwise you won't be seeing the scribbled notes you want."

Mark Devlin was a man on the edge, understandably concerned about the implications around the piece of software his company had approved for development. *And the financial loss it could cause, of course.* Trevor smirked. It didn't surprise him, considering the value of that particular piece of software. Big money was at play. Wasn't that always the case? If the software had been finished under his company's name, Devlin would have had something invaluable under his belt. On the other hand, it would be a tremendous blow if it became known that it had fallen into the wrong hands, resulting in huge losses for corporations around the world. MDS and Devlin personally could be deemed liable for not ensuring the safety of the code leading to its theft, and, in that case, he would be looking financial ruin straight in the face.

"Can't you get to it faster?" Devlin had demanded.

"I have all my resources on it. They'll show themselves soon enough. I'll let you know when we're on the move."

If Trevor could, he would've already handled the destruction of the files, but his and Cassandra's hands were tied until they had a trail to follow. George was like a bloodhound when he was following a lead; Trevor hoped he would sniff it out in no time. For now, they would have to sit tight. But even with knowing from experience these things take time and patience, it wasn't easy being in a holding pattern.

Trevor wanted results; he wanted his father's notes. Way more than Devlin wanted his decrypter out of the hands of whoever took it. The sound of footsteps in the hall brought him back from his thoughts. The aroma of coffee reached him first, followed closely by Cassandra walking in the office with a cup in her hand, her eyes still cloudy from sleep.

Trevor smiled brightly and greeted her, "Good morning, *a ghrá.*" He watched as she sat in her chair, nursing the cup between her hands.

"Damn your cheery self. Here I am, dragging ass," she grumbled.

Trevor chuckled. Gotta love the woman—she was vicious before her first cup.

She took a sip and almost purred. "Hmm. Heaven." Her delight was a turn-on.

"Glad you could finally make it," he teased, hoping to brighten her mood. She leaned back in her chair and continued nursing the coffee, almost as if she hoped its aroma and heat would breathe some life into her. The past couple of days had clearly taken a toll on her humor.

"I spent most of yesterday on facial recognition exercises. Had to get back into the groove, just in case it's needed." She took another sip and moaned. "Plus, waiting on George to come back with news, my brain was about to burst last night." As the coffee worked its magic, she lifted her hooded eyes to meet his. "Good morning, love."

Cassandra had that sensual somnolence on her face every morning; it always tempted Trevor to throw her down and ravish her on whatever flat surface was available. "You, my dear wife, are tempting."

She looked at him over the rim of her cup and smiled sweetly. "What was that for?"

"Nothing in particular. Just stating a fact." He'd never worn his heart on his sleeve the way he did now. Letting his love shine through his eyes, he enjoyed the delectable view as she continued to down the coffee.

Cassandra glanced over the rim and grinned, blowing Trevor a kiss. "So, can I play hooky?" Trevor raised his eyebrows and gave her the look. "Damn. Jeez, it was worth a try," Cassandra sighed deeply. She knew there was no rest for the wicked when they were on the hunt.

Scooting closer to her desk, she readied herself to tackle whatever new assignment they had on queue. As she set the cup aside, she noticed the orange light blinking on the task bar. She rushed to open the chat application and found several messages from George.

Are you there?

Cass?

Trev?

"Hey, it's George!" Cassandra called out to Trevor as she continued to read.

This is BIG! You won't believe what I got.

We need to talk NOW!

"He's jacked about something."

Be here at 14:00 hours your time.

Cassandra's brow furrowed, "Okay, he was one unhappy geek last night." She glanced at her watch. "We have about five hours to kill before he gets to work." A flash of impatience crossed Trevor's face. "Trevor, he has to sleep." Cassandra saw the frown set into his features. He hated waiting. "That's it." She pushed from her chair and stood. "Let's go."

"Where?" Trevor asked surprised.

"Downstairs. Gym. Now."

"Why?" Trevor's amusement was written all over his face.

Cassandra turned and briskly headed for the door.

"Hey!" Trevor called out. "You didn't answer."

She poked her head back in the doorway. "To see if I can still kick your ass! See you downstairs in five minutes. First one down picks the workout."

Trevor's laughter and something that sounded like "payback, lass" followed her across the hall. Within minutes she was changed and racing down the stairs to the basement. She did a happy dance in her head as she walked into the room. She stopped dead in her tracks. *Holy hell!* Trevor was already flowing through a series of stretch exercises. "How'd you change and get here so fast?"

He smirked at her reflection in the mirror. "Clothes were still in the dryer." Trevor tilted his head toward the laundry area. "Voilá. Changed and ready to go." He wiggled his eyebrows. "I win. My choice."

"Freaking cheat," Cassandra mumbled under her breath, moving further into the room, beginning her own series of stretches.

Her narrowed eyes followed Trevor as he walked to the media player, peeved that she hadn't thought of the dryer herself. As the blood-pumping music filled the room, Cassandra felt the heat of Trevor's appreciative gaze tracking her movements from where he stood. She became a little self-conscious as she moved through the warm-up exercises. Glancing in the mirror, she caught the satisfied triumphant smirk on his face and raised an eyebrow. "What? You cheated, that's all." She hated the wide grin that burst across his face at her sulky tone. "But you won. So… what's it going to be?" She pulled her legs together, reached for the arches of her feet, and laid her forehead on her knees. The burn along the back of her thighs invigorated her.

"How about we do some wrestling. We're both good at it."

Cassandra's eyes gleamed with pleasure. She was always game for a good sparring. The last time they had grappled, she had taken him down. Already picturing herself the winner, she moved to join Trevor at the center of the mat. She balanced on the balls of her feet, knees slightly bent and arms hanging loose at her sides in anticipation of his first move. Cassandra eyed the flexing muscles in Trevor's arms as he moved from foot to foot across the mat. *Damn he's hot.* Trevor smirked.

"I just said that out loud, didn't I?" she asked. His widening grin confirmed her worst fears. Cassandra shook her head. *Can't a girl ever get a break?* His smugness fueled her already-burning temper. She faked a grab for his leg. As he jumped out of the way, she hooked her other arm around his neck in a headlock and twisted her body in one single fluid movement so her back was to him.

"Still grinning, babe?" she spoke over her shoulder, tightening her hold around his neck and pulling him flush against her hip.

Before she could force him to his knees, Trevor shoved her arm from his neck, grabbed her shirt in both hands, and swept her leg from under her. She fell with a big "oomph!" to the mats.

Trevor grinned down into her face. "Gotcha!" His hearty laughter echoed in the room.

Cassandra stared up at him in surprise and quickly rolled to her feet back into fighting position. "Yeah, keep laughing, boyo." Wiping her hands on the back of her pants, she watched him closely through narrowed eyes and planned her next move.

They circled each other, looking for a breach in the other's defenses, eyes locked, perspiration coating their skin. Cassandra lunged for his legs. Trevor shoved her hands away, twisting his body to safety. His chuckle filled her ears.

"Really? Still laughing?" she grumbled under her breath. Dropping into a squat she swept her leg out, knocking Trevor's legs out from under him.

A hundred and eighty pounds of lean mass collapsed with a whomp to the floor and a groan filled the air. "Damn!" As he hit the mat, Trevor whipped out his hand, snagged the back of Cassandra's pants, and jerked her to her knees. His move was swift and fluid as he scrambled up behind her and wrapped his arm around her neck in a chokehold. Heart racing in her chest, Cassandra wiggled her hand between his arm and her neck. Covering his hand with her free one, she grabbed three of his fingers and pulled back in a finger lock.

"Fuck, Cassie!" He pushed her from him, shaking his fingers.

Cassandra rolled to her back and a wicked grin covered her face. "Gotcha."

"Shite! That fucking hurt!" he hissed, rubbing them vigorously.

She sat up, leaning back on her hands. "Sorry Trev, did I hurt you? Poor baby! Not smiling now are we?"

"Your little tab is growing, Cassie Girl," he growled and she burst out laughing at the scowl on his face.

Trevor shook his hand in an effort to ease the pain shooting up his arm. The pleasurable game he'd imagined had become a hardcore wrestling match. He faced Cassandra, determined to win now more than ever, and made his move. He charged her and pulled her tight against his chest in a bear hug. She shifted her weight with one leg, throwing him off balance and, as he adjusted his stance, slammed her other knee into his stomach. The air exploded from his lungs and pain radiated to all parts of his body as he crumbled to his knees, wrapping his arms around his stomach. The pain was excruciating. He couldn't breathe. In the distance, he heard her chuckle.

"What the hell?!" he rasped through gritted teeth. "I thought this was grappling, not 'Beat up Trevor' practice. Damn, woman!" She laughed louder and dismissed the threat, turning her back to him. "Okay, that's it! All bets are off now! I am bringing you down!"

Ignoring his screaming stomach muscles, he jumped to his feet, ran at her, grabbing her from behind, and tackled her to the ground, pressing her face-first into the mat with his weight. Cassandra wiggled, kicking her legs and bucking against him. He scissored his legs on the outside of hers, trapping her lower body, and bore all his weight against her back, whispering in a teasing tone close to her ear, "Comfortable?"

Without warning, Cassandra slammed the back of her head against his forehead. His head snapped back and stars crowded his vision. "Fuck!" Rolling to the mat, Trevor lay on his back rubbing the heel of his hand against his forehead. "What kind of training is this? Don't use your dirty CIA tricks against me! Save them for the bad g—!"

Before he could recover, she landed on his chest, pressing him against the mat with her weight while tucking her feet under his legs, preventing him from knocking her off. "You are pinned! And no, the CIA didn't teach me that, Bob did," she smirked with a wide victorious smile.

Trevor dropped his hands from his head and rested them flat on the mat. He took a deep breath and, without opening his eyes, commented with sarcasm dripping from his words, "Remind me to send your dad a thank you note."

Cassandra snorted and took a good look at him. Sweat ran in rivulets from his temple, his mop of hair was damp and mussed, making him look edible. "I'm sure he'll be proud."

Her grin slowly faded when she noticed the red mark marring his forehead. A wash of guilt gripped her and, feeling bad for him, she leaned in to press her lips to the mark, but before her lips touched his reddened skin, Trevor's arms shot out from under her hands and to the side at the same time his hips drove up into her, thrusting her off his chest.

"Shit!" Cassandra yelled as she landed on her side next him on the mat.

In another fluid move, he shifted his hips around toward her and jerked her arm, forcing her flat on her back. He lifted his leg and brought his heel down on her chest. Cassandra's body curved up and she squeezed her eyes shut, anticipating the impact that never happened. When pain didn't radiate through her upper body, she opened her eyes and saw his heel millimeters from her chest.

Her eyes snapped to his, now full of merriment. "Gotcha again."

"Holy hell, Trev! What kind of move was that?"

Trevor leaned over her with a big smile on his face. "You really thought I would give up that easily? I am a geek, Cassie, not a friggin' wimp. It's called the internet and how-to videos."

"Smart ass," she gasped.

He watched as she tried to regain her wits and glanced at the big digital clock on the gym's far wall. They had sparred for a while and killed time. George would be online shortly. Sweat streamed on his skin and he could feel the nice burn in his muscles. Cassandra was a perfect drill sergeant; he had gone from lean to lean mean machine since their move to Dublin. Their endurance training was proving very successful.

Glancing back at Cassandra, he noticed the big sweat stain soaking her shirt between her breasts. It pleased him that their workout had been just as strenuous on her as it had been on him. "How about we call it a tie today? We need to be on that video chat soon." He took in her flushed face and couldn't hold back. "As much as I'd like nothing more than to taste your salty skin and lick you dry right now, I don't think it's a good idea. I'd get carried away and we'd miss our call. We have work to do. Chop, chop!"

The image those words brought to mind sent liquid heat straight between Cassandra's thighs and caused her mind to go blank. She, too, would love nothing better than for him to do just that. The man was definitely skilled with his tongue, in many ways. She grinned back at him and let her eyes travel over his body from head to toe. "Damn, keep those thoughts to yourself next time."

With a deep sigh, she rolled to her feet. "Now that's all I'll be able to think about talking to George." She rested her hands on her knees to catch her breath and wiped the sweat rolling down the side of her face with her shoulder. Cassandra looked up at him. "I don't think we even have time for a shower." She flashed him a wicked grin. "You know how steamy that gets. I'd get carried away and we'd miss our call." She wiggled her eyebrows.

Cassandra observed the calculating look cross Trevor's face and burst out laughing. She shook her head. "Oh, no. No way, Jose! George did not sound happy, and the time for the call sounded non-negotiable."

She straightened and walked over to the laundry area. Retrieving two towels from the shelf, she tossed one at Trevor and wiped her face with the other. "Nice work out, by the way. Tie it is. But I haven't forgotten the cheat move." She flicked his chin with her finger and gripped it, pulling his face down for a kiss before turning for the stairs.

"Hey! You just didn't think of it. You can't tell me you wouldn't have done the same if you had thought of it first."

Cassandra glanced down at Trevor from the stairs. "Yeah, but I didn't and so—" she flashed a knowing smile and threw the towel at him, "—you cheated. I'm heading straight up to get ready. Can you grab me a bottle of water?"

"Yes, ma'am." Trevor wiped the sweat from his neck as he fell in step behind her. The sway of her curvy ass as she climbed the stairs tempted him, sending an electric current of heat straight to his groin. His cock grew hard and heavy with need and he called out in a strained voice. "Grabbing the water. I'll be there in a minute."

In the kitchen, Trevor rested his hands on the counter and hung his head.

His wife would be the death of him, one way or another. He clenched his teeth and sucked in deep breaths, powering through the overwhelming urge to run after her, carry her straight to their room, and lick every inch of her body as he had promised. Once the painful tightness in his groin subsided and he could think straight again, he grabbed two bottles from the fridge.

Back in the office, he claimed the chair next to hers and handed her one of the bottles. His mouth went dry when her lips wrapped around the opening at her first gulp. After downing half the bottle, Cassandra set it on the desk, never once removing her eyes from the screen. "He's not online yet."

Trevor squeezed his eyes briefly and controlled the resurging urge to ravish her then and there. Already in work mode, Cassandra appeared completely oblivious to the effect she had on him. A moment later, feeling more in control but still wanting a taste, he scooted his chair closer to hers. He laid his arm along the back of her chair, leaned toward her, and took her mouth with his. Her damp skin smelled of sweat and gym mats. Such a turn-on. Pulling back just a few inches, he looked into her eyes. "Did I mention I love you?"

She brushed his cheek with her fingers, a soft look graced her eyes. "Where'd that come from?"

"I don't need a reason to let you know how much I care, do I?" The squawk of an incoming call foiled his quest for a second kiss. He straightened in his chair, letting Cassandra answer the call.

George's face appeared on the screen. "Hey! Finally! Been trying to reach you for a while! Where's Trev?"

Moving closer to Cassandra and into the camera's view, Trevor answered, "Here, George. What's up? You sounded pretty excited on your messages."

"I think I got something of interest. It's a flimsy link, but I think it has merit."

"Go on."

"The tap on your possible mole was a black hole there for a while. Not a peep. The guy barely talks to family let alone anybody else. Then yesterday he made a call to a number in St. Petersburg."

George took a deep breath and continued, "I had to get the recording to Jennifer so she could translate it for me, but the dialogue was quite interesting. He talked to a guy about wanting his money and the guy was pretty pissed at Tomlin for calling him. And get this," George added in an excited tone after a brief pause, "He told him he would get the money when the application was fully functional."

"Shite! Bingo! They still haven't completed the development! That's good news. Very good news!" Trevor was pleased. The lack of development on the program bought them the time they needed to pinpoint its location. "You traced the call, right?"

"I've already sent you the coords to the location of the recipient's signal," George answered matter-of-factly.

"Let's keep the tap active and listen in for more details. Tap all the phones and any incoming or outgoing digital communication to and from the source." Trevor frowned. "How much does Jennifer know?"

George eyed him. "I haven't told her much. She doesn't know it was for you. I asked her to keep it between us."

Trevor nodded. "We might need to disclose it to her if we continue to use her as a resource. What do you think, Cassie?"

Cassandra watched the play of emotions cross George's face, transforming his expression from apprehensive to hopeful. She hated to dash his expectations, but her gut told her they should continue to keep Jennifer out of the loop on this case. "Sorry guys."

She opened the email program side by side with the video conference window and checked for the email George mentioned. "If it was one of your cases it would be a no-brainer. But it's not. We still don't know what we're up against or how deep it goes. I think for now she stays on ice." She looked directly at George. "But tell you what, Trevor and I will discuss it and get back to you if we change our minds. Okay?"

Resigned, George sighed. "I hate keeping anything from her, but I understand. So...did you get the email I sent?"

Cassandra opened it as it appeared in the queue. "Yes, it's here." Her eyes lifted to the camera again. "Hey, don't forget to send the transcripts Jennifer translated. Oh! And the source phone numbers."

"Okay, guys. Gotta run. Trev, I'll get the taps on the phones and digital communications set up."

Trevor leaned into Cassandra so George could see him. "Perfect, George. Keep us posted."

George turned his gaze in Cassandra's direction. "Don't forget to get back to me if you change your mind."

"We will. I promise."

"And Trev, I haven't forgotten about my payment."

Trevor laughed and shook his head at his eagerness. "Such a goner, mate. Yeah we'll work on it." George grinned widely.

When the call terminated, Cassandra and Trevor burst out laughing. "I like seeing him that goofy about Jen. It's about time," Trevor commented as he watched her pull up the transcripts.

Cassandra turned her face toward Trevor and flashed him a cocky grin. "You were worse than him, if I recall correctly."

"Goofy? Me? Nah. I was hoping my puppy-dog eyes would melt your icy heart. Look at that! Here you are. With me. It worked," he boasted jokingly.

Cassandra slapped Trevor's arm, feigning hurt feelings. "Icy heart?"

"You have to agree that I had to work my butt off to win your heart. I deserve a reward, not a head butt." He rubbed the sore spot on his forehead where she had hit him earlier.

"How about I kiss it better? Would that count as a reward?"

"Great offer! I'll take it in the shower. We still haven't had one."

She closed the distance between them, their faces so close she could feel the flutter of his breath. He nipped at her lower lip and kissed it softly. "We really should take this to the shower."

"Hmm…" Cassandra cupped the back of his head and sucked on his lower lip before releasing him. "I take it we can now explore that road you were talking about earlier?" She beamed a saucy smile at him. "I seem to recall something about licking me dry…."

Trevor's eyes grew heated as she grabbed his hand and pulled him to his feet. She laughed as she pulled her shirt up over her head. Before he could reach for her she backed away, beckoning him with the crook of her finger. "Come on! Move your ass! We have to be at the airport in a few hours to pick up Jessica."

Chapter Seven

Touch Down

*C*ASSIE! STOP! PATIENCE, GRASSHOPPER! I'M *almost at cus-toms.* Jessica shook her head. Cassandra had been texting her non-stop since she had announced her landing.

Just hurry!

Yes, boss! Jessica chuckled just as her luggage rounded the carousel. "Hold it! Damn it!" Jessica struggled with shoving her phone in her pocket at the same time she leapt for her bag, which had moved past her.

A tall dark-haired man brushed her aside. "Allow me."

Jessica looked up into his moss-green eyes with a relieved smile. "Thank you. My friend would have killed me if I took any longer to get out of here!"

"Hope you friend is a lass," he grinned with a flirtatious glint in his eyes.

"She is a lass, and she's an impatient one at that."

His hand grabbed his chest above his heart and his eyes rolled to the ceiling. "Sweet Mary, thank you for bringing the woman of my dreams into my life."

Jessica cocked a hip and tipped her chin back to look up into his face. "Damn. Does that line ever work?"

"There's always a first," he chuckled in an Irish drawl that reminded her of Cassandra's Trevor. "So, did it work? Have you fallen for my wit and charm?" At the shake of her head and soft laugh, he extended his hand. "The name is Sean. And you are?"

His hand was firm and warm as she took it in hers. "Jessica."

"Well, Jessica. Have pity on a lad and have a drink with me sometime."

Momentarily taken aback, Jessica studied Sean as she retrieved the luggage from his hand. "I wish I could, but I'm fairly certain my friends have plans!"

"Tell you what." He reached his hand into his pocket. "Here's my card. Call me if you change your mind. I would enjoy showing you the hidden delights of Dublin."

As Jessica reached for the card, Sean intercepted her hand, pulled it palm up to his lips, and placed a soft kiss in the center. Replacing his lips with the card, he folded her fingers over it. "Be sure you don't lose that."

Jessica swallowed deeply and sighed. "Are all Irishman like you?" she asked, all the while hoping she would receive the same reception when she connected with him again.

"No, lassie. I am a rare find." His smile was contagious.

The vibration of the cell in her pocket jerked her back to reality. "I have to scoot. My friend will storm the doors down if I'm not out there soon." She pocketed the card. "Thanks again!" she called over her shoulder as she hurried in the direction of customs. Shooting a look behind her, Jessica saw the disappointment written on his handsome face as he watched her hasty retreat. *What's the matter with me? He was right up my alley! Definitely phone-number worthy!*

Twenty minutes later, Jessica exited customs, straight into Cassandra's waiting arms. "Finally! You're here!" Cassandra whooped, squeezing her tight.

Jessica held onto her just as tightly. "Duh! Texted you from the plane. I can see you still haven't learned patience in these past months." She looked around Cassandra's shoulder and spotted Trevor watching their exchange with an indulgent soft smile. "Okay, okay! Step away from the friend. Can't…breathe!" Jessica made an exaggerated gasp for air.

Cassandra burst out laughing and released her. Trevor stepped up, pulled her into his arms in a bear hug, and kissed her cheek. "Welcome to Ireland, Jessica. It's good to see you again."

Jessica hugged and kissed him back. "Thank you, Irish." Looking up at him she winked, "Did you bring me one of you as a welcome gift?"

Trevor gazed down at her and his expression turned serious. "We caught one. Cassie tackled him and I hogtied him. Didn't you see him inside?"

A vision of Sean flashed through her mind. "You are joking, right? Because there was this man—" The twinkle in his eye and Cassandra's giggle snapped her to attention. Jessica shook her head and punched his arm. "Damn. You're such a comedian. You almost had me there."

"I know, eh?"

Cassandra rolled her eyes and hooked arms with them. "Let's go. I'm starved. We'll stop at home so we can drop off your bags and you can freshen up. Plans are to hit our favorite pub for dinner." She glanced at Jessica with concern. "That is, if you are up to it."

"Bring it on. I'm starved, too."

★ ★ ★ ★ ★

The pub was crawling with patrons. Downtown workers, early night crawlers, and the usual tourist crowd made their way through the walls of the Brazen Head, the oldest pub in Dublin. Music played in the background and made the place feel even more magical than it was. Almost a thousand years of history covered the walls. Each picture or item on display took you back in time to when storytelling in pubs was the main form of socializing. Spontaneous bursts of energy resulting in song and dance were commonplace, and that night it wasn't any different.

Stephan absorbed the full impact of the place the minute he walked into the packed room. He loved the Brazen Head and was a frequent patron. Almost every night the pub had something fun going on. The fever pitch was contagious. He smiled widely at the lyrics of the song being performed live. Even the air felt charged with a current of energy.

He followed the movement of the crowd to the back of the room. As he approached, he caught sight of Trevor sitting on the bench against the wall with an arm wrapped around Cassandra, a Guinness in his hand. He changed direction and made a beeline for them, the final stretch to their seating a slow process as he maneuvered through the crowd. He'd never seen the place teeming like that before. *It must be spring in the air,* he thought.

"Trevor! Cassandra! Glad to see you two here! This place is crazy tonight."

Stephan grinned as Trevor disengaged himself from his wife and stood to shake his hand. "Stephan! Good to see you, mate."

Cassandra leaned her elbows on the table and smiled. "No kidding. This place is packed tighter than a sardine can," she snorted. "Glad you came out for air before you got all moldy and stuffy!"

Stephan laughed out loud and leaned down to kiss her cheek. "Cassandra. Always a pleasure."

Trevor took his seat, tucked Cassandra against his side, and pointed to the chair across from him with a tip of his pint. "Join us."

Stephan froze when he turned to take the seat Trevor pointed at and his eyes collided with the biggest, bluest eyes that had haunted his dreams and stirred his blood these last months. *Jessica.* Suddenly bereft of speech, he found himself standing and staring like a schoolboy faced with his biggest crush.

She wore a similar expression of stupefaction on her lovely face. A face that had haunted his dreams and brought to the surface his deepest hopes and wishes. And a reminder he could never take what was once offered.

"Is anybody joining you? I think we can squeeze in if needed." Trevor's comment cleared the haze covering his brain.

Stephan cleared his throat. "Uh…no. Nobody's joining me. I came in for a pint. I'm on my way home. Driving. Alone." *Hell. Where did that stupid line come from?* "I mean…I shouldn't stay long. I just dropped in for a pint before heading home."

What power did she have to make him feel so out of sorts? Apparently all of them—and then some. He hadn't stumbled over his words since his first time with a woman. And considering his age, he should have been long past the point of being made to feel uncomfortable by a woman's presence. Yet she did just that. She brought forward a duality of feelings inside him—the most primal need to take her as his, and the denial, the reluctance to do so knowing the toll that it would take on her. On him.

Stephan could feel Trevor and Cassandra's scrutiny at their exchange, their eyes ping-ponging between him and Jessica.

"You two remember each other, right?" Cassandra peeped in the background.

"Sure do. Hi, Stephan. How have you been?" The surprise that had shined earlier from Jessica's face been replaced by a soft, bordering on devious, in his opinion, smile. Her voice was silken oak and as sweet as he remembered.

"Not bad. And yourself?"

"Hanging in there." Jessica held his eyes in a confident silent exchange.

His throat tightened and he resisted the urge to pull at his collar.

"What's your poison?" Trevor asked as Stephan took the chair next to Jessica's. "It's all on me tonight. We are celebrating!"

Stephan, finally able to break the hold Jessica seemed to have on him, turned his attention to Trevor and met his mischievous gaze. "Just a pint."

He watched as Trevor called the waitress's attention and ordered his beer. He still had that inquisitive quality to him that reminded Stephan of his good friend Conor. They were so much alike. A pang of wistfulness speared through him. Just as Trevor did, he too needed closure regarding the disappearance of his best friend. "What's the occasion?"

"Jessica's move to Dublin!" Cassandra's eyes twinkled and her voice took a higher pitch, excitement spilling over.

Then the meaning of the words took hold of his mind and brought his heart almost to a full stop. "Moving? Here? Oh, right! The job offer." He couldn't sound more pathetic if he tried.

Jessica's smile dimmed. Her eyes took on a sharper quality and pierced the distance between them. "Yeah. That and, as a friend told me, the hidden delights of Dublin."

"I can't wait to get back to the old days."

Jessica's eyes diverted from him to Cassandra and immediately filled with warmth. "I can't wait either, Cassie! It'll be fun!" When she caught Trevor's scowl, she added, "Well…as much fun as work permits."

"You are no fun, Trev," Cassandra teased.

"I'm sure you'll find ways to drive me bonkers with your girlie talk."

"Hey! You and George drive me bonkers with your geek talk."

"I thought that drove you crazy in a good way." Trevor raised his eyebrow and a mischievous glint sparkled in his eyes.

Stephan chuckled at their exchange. Trevor and Cassandra's banter was so fluid and natural. It filled their lives with laughter and made their union unique in the eyes of others. It also made the lack of that sort of connection a sore spot for Stephan. "Come on, you two."

The waitress reached over his shoulder and set his pint of Guinness in front of him, breaking the conversation. The night rolled smoothly after that, aside from the heavy and uncomfortable tension brewing between him and Jessica. He had a pit in his stomach during the entire hour he sat beside her, participating in the conversation without quite knowing what the subject was about, totally focused on and in tune with her own anxiety. He wondered if his was as palpable and if the others were picking up on it, like he was on Jessica's.

When he had reached his limit of self-inflicted restraint, he made his move. "Well…it was nice running in to you all here. Unfortunately, I need to take my leave." Jessica's eyes bore into him.

"So early? The night's still young," Cassandra frowned.

"The night might be young, but I'm sure not."

Trevor burst out in laughter. "Yeah…old man. You talk as if you are ages older than you really are. You need to get out more. That's what you need."

"I really need to go. I have an early day tomorrow." Looking at Cassandra, he prompted, "Call me to arrange that dinner with Terese."

"Terese?" Jessica blurted out, disappointment coloring her tone. Stephan's gaze shot to her and studied her with a curious intensity until she dropped her eyes to her pint glass.

"Stephan's friend. Although I am sure she would love to be more than that," Cassandra joked in reply to Jessica's question.

"Oh." Jessica flicked her eyes to Stephan's. It was as if a light had gone off in them and he kicked himself for even mentioning Terese. On the other hand, it served the purpose. He had to cut the ties that held him captive to Jessica. If that was the only way to put distance between them, then he was taking it.

"Well…I hope to see you all soon. Trev, Cassandra, Jessica." He nodded at them, but before he could move away, Jessica sprang her hand out. He automatically took it in his and the zing that flashed from that touch almost caused him to drop it and shake out his hand.

"Nice seeing you again, Stephan." Sincerity bled from her eyes and words.

"Nice seeing you, too, Jessica." He squeezed her hand, committing the softness of her skin to his memory once more and, turning, made his way through the still thick crowd and to the evening's crisp spring air.

The brief contact affected him as much as their previous one had. No, more. Amplified by months of wanting, craving, and wondering what it would have been like if he had not followed his conscience back then. He shook his head and flicked the devil off his shoulder. He hadn't fallen for the temptation back then, and he steeled himself to maintain that vow. He just needed to avoid seeing her again. He didn't know if he could withstand another shot of the raw need coursing through him from just that one little meeting. He exhaled deeply and set out for his car and out of temptation's reach.

Chapter Eight

Hominess

THE WAITING GAME WAS GETTING to him. The time it was taking to secure crucial details coupled with being cooped up in the house was driving him mad. Trevor's stomach churned with eagerness to get his hands on the decrypter before the people who stole it could finish its development. His mind buzzed with the need to move faster.

Since Jessica's arrival, Cassandra had been able to keep busy showing Jessica the ropes and getting her situated in Dublin. He knew they needed time together, so that had left him with nothing else to do but wait for the taps to bear more fruit.

"I'm going for a walk to the post office and for some fresh air."

Cassandra glanced at him with a questioning look in her eyes. "Want me to come with? Keep you company?"

"No." He walked over and dropped a light kiss on her lips. "I just need to clear my head, *a ghrá*. I won't be long."

"Go. Take all the time you need. Jessica just left to go shopping and settle her banking here. That leaves me plenty of time to handle the last of the background checks uninterrupted. I'm almost finished reviewing the new transcripts. I should be done by then."

"Brilliant, love." Kissing Cassandra's brow, he headed out.

Trevor's mind was crowded with thoughts of the meeting to take place in Prague. The name of the contact was familiar, but he had yet to place him or connect the dots. Maybe the face-to-face with Mucha would trigger a memory, providing him with more clues than the notes themselves. If Mucha was indeed an acquaintance of his parents and possessed information regarding the circumstances of their disappearance, Trevor could close their case in his heart and move on with his life. Move on with Cassandra by his side. Even start the family he'd dreamed of having for so long.

He and Cassandra, both only children, had never discussed having children of their own. The idea was appealing. So much so that Trevor wondered how he'd feel if and when Cassandra found herself pregnant with his child. Delight swelled in his heart and warmth flooded his chest as a visual of her tummy round with their son or daughter filled his mind. He looked forward to the day, but he knew they were in no position to take such a big step at that moment.

Trevor would broach the subject with her once their quest reached its end, no matter what that ending could be. It would be something special to him if, at that time, they could consider relocating to Sligo and to his parent's country home overlooking Ben Bulben. There, they would be able to spend quality time doing things that brought them pleasure, instead of constantly on a drive to find the next clue, the next piece of the puzzle.

Trevor tucked those fantasies in a little corner of his mind and withdrew from his daydreaming only to realize he'd been wandering around for a while. He stood in the middle of the sidewalk on O'Connell Street contemplating what to do next. He wasn't ready to go home just yet. It was shaping up to be a beautiful spring day in Dublin. If he lost himself in the warmth of the sunlight, in the sounds of birds chirping from the trees lining the street, in the mindless excitement flowing from the tourists, maybe, just maybe, his mood would improve a notch.

Distracted within himself, Trevor was startled by a jostle from the side. His head swung to the origin of impact and he found a tourist holding one of the biggest cameras he'd ever seen, looking back at him with a nervous smile. "So sorry, I didn't see you."

"No problem, mate. Nothing broken," Trevor teased, and nodded to the lens on the tourist's camera. "Nice lens. Perfect for wide shots."

The tourist flashed a relieved smile and beamed at the compliment. "I love it. I've gotten some great shots of Dublin. Can't wait to get home to show the family. Sorry again."

With a contemplative look, Trevor watched the man walk away. Talking about the lens had reminded him of something he needed to take care of. But first, he had to face his demons. He turned on his heel and headed in the direction of the Financial District and Brennan Enterprises. He hadn't been there in a few years; he had avoided it since the day he and Cassandra had returned to Dublin, fearing the emotions being there would evoke.

At the sight of the large, imposing glass building, his throat constricted. Taking a deep breath, he pushed through the revolving door. As he reached the other side, the tangy air of the lobby hit his senses. It had not changed in the years since his father's presence had graced its walls. The scent of floral arrangements, the ping of elevators, and the hustle and bustle of the corporate environment bombarded him with memories of the days when he used to visit his dad.

He joined the visitor line and clamped down his emotions. A few moments later, an older security guard approached him. "Mr. Brennan?"

Trevor turned to him with a questioning look.

"You may not remember me—name's Jacobson. You used to come to visit your dad and I would take you up. I recognized you immediately. You are the spitting image of your da."

Trevor smiled. "I do remember. How are you?"

"Fine sir. I take it you're here to see Mr. Connellan?" At Trevor's nod he continued. "You can go straight up. No need to stand in line."

Trevor reached for his hand for a heartfelt handshake. "Thank you, Jacobson."

"My pleasure. Your da was a good man. He's sorely missed."

He watched as Jacobson walked away and blinked his eyes several times to clear the moisture coating them. *Yes, he is sorely missed.* With renewed purpose, Trevor headed up to Stephan's office.

Máire O'Neill sat behind her desk just as he remembered from the last time he had been there, when she was his father's secretary. She looked up and a warm smile spread on her face. She seemed unchanged except for a few more lines of age and wisdom creasing the corners of her cheery eyes.

"Trevor Joseph Brennan! About time you came around to visit. Heard all about your wedding to a lovely American girl."

He hugged her petite frame and a familiar sense of hominess hit him square in the chest. "Good to see you too, Miss Máire."

"What brings you here? I am sure it wasn't to see this old lady."

Trevor's face flushed. He knew he had avoided this visit for far too long. "Is Stephan in?"

"Yes, he is. He's not with anyone at the moment. Just head in," she shooed him on.

Knocking on the door, he walked in and found the man hunched over his desk reviewing the contents of a file. Trevor smiled as he stood by the desk waiting for Stephan to surface. It was a position Trevor remembered well when he was younger. His smile widened when Stephan raised a finger. His version of, "I know you are there, give me a second."

To kill time, Trevor walked the room, looking over the pictures on the walls. One immediately drew his eye; as he stepped up to it, he knew why—it had been taken years ago on the lake. They—his parents, Stephan, and Trevor—had just returned from a great day of sailing. Trevor felt a pinch in his heart as he gazed on their smiling faces. Damn he missed them. Which brought him to the reason he was there in the first place.

A rustling and chair rolling drew Trevor's attention back to Stephan and he moved to meet him halfway. Trevor extended his hand; gripping it, Stephan pulled him into a hug. "Trevor. So good to see you, lad."

Trevor grinned. "You act like we weren't just at the pub the other night, old man."

Stephan scoffed and led him to the guest chairs, taking the one next to him. "It's good to have you here."

Trevor leaned back and steepled his fingers, contemplating the man who had been like an uncle to him.

Stephan's eyes narrowed. "I can see something's on your mind."

With a deep sigh, Trevor held his gaze. "I thought I should come by and check on things."

"It's about time." Stephan studied him for a few moments, then asked, "How have you been handling it?"

Trevor couldn't feign not understanding Stephan's question. He knew him too well. They had been through much together. "Having Cassie with me helps. Some days more than others. But I can't deny it's never going away. At least not until I find out for sure."

"Are you still pursuing that? Even after France?"

"Yes. Not much has come of it. But we won't give up until we find them." His voice lowered. "Dead or Alive."

Stephan nodded and grief colored his eyes. "Is there anything I can do… to help?"

"You are already helping. By not pressing me into taking Dad's place here."

"Whenever you are ready. Until you are, I will keep you up to date. We do need to discuss some new hires I might be handling."

"Do whatever you feel necessary, Stephan. I trust your judgment, just as Dad did." Trevor exhaled a deep breath. "I don't think I can be here just yet."

"Understandable. Keep me apprised of any developments, though. You know your father was like a big brother to me. I need to—" Stephan ran his hand through his hair. "Hell. I need to know as much as you do. If I can help in any way, just say so."

"I understand Stephan. I will. Don't worry." Trevor stood and Stephan joined him. "I need to get going. Cassie will kill me if I don't get back soon. I left her holding the fort."

Stephan grinned. "I can hear her now."

"Gotta love her. I know I do. Woman has me all twisted inside.

The grin slowly washed from Stephan's lips. "That's a good thing, lad."

"I know, eh? Anyway, I should be heading out." Trevor reached out his hand and Stephan once again pulled him in a tight hug, thumping him on the back.

"Give Cassandra my love. We need to get together for another pint soon."

Trevor flashed a mischievous parting grin, "Think you can handle it ol' man?" His grin grew wider when Stephan laughed out loud and turned back to his work.

★ ★ ★ ★ ★

Trevor waved to Jacobson and left the building. Outside he took deep hard pulls of the crisp morning air into his lungs. A weight lifted slightly from his shoulders, and he knew from their conversation that Stephan was not disappointed with him. He felt all the better for it. As he waited to cross the street, a passing tourist reminded him of a little errand he wanted to take care of—one easily handled on the way back home.

The thirty-minute walk to the shop was invigorating, and there was a spring to Trevor's step in anticipation of getting his hands on new toys. Aidan Gallagher, the store's owner, was behind the counter and greeted him with a smile.

"Trevor! Nice timing. I was about to give you a call."

"I know that smile. You're about to relieve me of my entire paycheck today, am I right?"

Aidan laughed and went to the back room returning with a box. "If that amount is your entire paycheck, you have more problems than your addiction to gadgets, my friend."

He placed the package on the counter, opened it with a cutter, and removed a small bubble-wrapped item from it.

Trevor unwrapped one of the small cameras and whistled. "Can you imagine the quality of the images transmitted by this little baby?" He inspected the other cameras in the box under Aidan's watchful eye.

"Is everything as you expected?"

"Yep. Now, just need to find a use for them. When I do, I'll fill you in on how they perform." While Aidan repackaged the small cameras, Trevor reached for his wallet and credit card.

Aidan chatted away as he rang up the purchase. "So where's that beautiful wife of yours?"

"Home and no doubt wondering where the hell I'm at. I need to get my ass back before I find myself grounded."

Aidan snorted and handed a bag with the box back to him.

"I'm off, but I'll be back soon. I want to check out that wide-angle zoom you showed me the other day."

"You're in luck, my man. I still have it. Make sure you tell Cassandra hi for me."

Trevor retraced his steps home. On the way, he stopped at a little bakery and café on Grafton Street. Having been gone a little longer than planned, a peace offering for Cassandra was in order. He had enjoyed the fresh outdoors while she had remained behind, bunkered down in a stuffy house. A twinge of guilt niggled at him. He knew her Cali heart would have enjoyed the walk and beautiful morning. By the time he reached the house, he was juggling a camera-shop bag, a paper tray holding two large cups—one coffee, one tea—and a bag of her favorite pastries and scones.

Chapter Nine

Surprise!

J ESSICA HAD LEFT THE HOUSE with map in hand, but her heart really hadn't been into shopping or handling her financial matters. Sure, she had told Cassandra that was her plan, but it wasn't really her focus. Her mind had been tied up with thoughts of Stephan. Watching Trevor and Cassandra's casual glances and touches were too much to bear. She figured it was best if she made herself scarce for a little while.

She walked out of the Bank of Ireland branch with the paperwork of her brand new bank account. Another step into her new life. Next on the list was some gift shopping. She had promised to send Matt a Guinness shirt as soon as she was settled. That would give her the opportunity to clear her head, organize her thoughts. If only she could stop the image of Stephan's crisp blue eyes from crossing her mind so very often she'd be happy.

Or would she?

Seeing him again after so many months had proven to her that she definitely had it bad. When he had shown up at the pub on the night of her arrival, her stomach had clenched into a bundle of knots and her palms had broken out in a sweat—a schoolgirl's reaction to a crush. As he stood in front of her, larger than life, she was thrown back to the day of Cassandra's wedding and what she had felt that evening back at her house. Nothing had changed. The attraction was even stronger the second time around.

Jessica hadn't expected to see him so soon, and the shock of it had left her in a brainless stupor. The kind one experienced when they were finally close to the one thing they craved most. And, oh boy, had she craved. Now more than ever. She had noticed his unease around her and reveled in the fact that she was the reason for it. She was sure of that. The same realization had dawned on her at his surprised tone when Cassandra commented on the news about her moving there. He had seemed divided between joy and dread—somehow that hurt her.

She needed to see him again. To be sure that the reaction she had caught in his expression before he had hidden his feeling behind a mask of professional courtesy had been real. She needed to know if the burn of their touch still scorched his hand as it still burned hers.

She stared blindly at the shop's window, pondering the information she had been able to glean from that night. Stephan had a woman friend who, based on Cassandra's comment, wanted more from him; however, he apparently hadn't moved forward with that relationship.

It seemed that Stephan was hesitant to commit. Or he had been as affected by her seven months back as she had been by him. Was fear of commitment why he had turned away from her as well? He guarded his feelings so tightly she couldn't quite decipher the hooded looks he threw her way when he thought she wasn't paying attention.

As she glanced at the products in the window display, an idea slapped her upside the head. She fished her cell from her purse and scrolled through the contact list. *Yes!* The word echoed in her mind. "You can run, but you can't hide, Mr. Connellan," she muttered as she hailed a cab.

★ ★ ★ ★ ★

Stepping from the cab, she turned back to pay the driver and then stood looking up at the massive building housing Brennan Enterprises. She had learned Trevor's parents owned the company. Trevor had refused to take his position as the new owner and had handed the reins to Stephan, his parents' longtime friend and business partner. The tall skyscraper was intimidating, but Jessica was up to the task. She shook her head and squared her shoulders as she took a deep calming breath. *Here goes everything. What if he doesn't agree to see me? Hell, suck it up girl. All they can say is no. No harm no foul. At least I'll have my answers.*

Jessica entered the glass turnstile and when it spit her out the other side she took a moment to get her bearings. Her eyes travelled the spacious lobby, soaking up the high-tech feel of brushed metal and glass throughout. They paused on the security desk and on the guards situated like gatekeepers to a castle. With a confident demeanor, she joined the line to check in. Stepping up to the desk, she smiled at the security guard.

"Can I help you?"

"Hi. Jessica Forrester to see Mr. Stephan Connellan."

The guard looked down at his clipboard. "Ms. Forrester. You don't appear to be on the list of visitors for the day."

Jessica, knowing she was about to be turned away, chose a direct approach. "I know. He's not expecting me. I'm a good friend of his from the States and I was hoping to surprise him. Do you think you could ring him?"

"If you're not on the list, we can't clear you."

Jessica leaned on the counter and dropped her voice lower. "Could you please call up to his office? I would hate to have come all this way only to miss him. I'm not staying in the city long and I'm sure he'll see me if you let him know I'm here." *I hope so.*

The guard's expression softened and her hopes flared. "Tell you what.

Have a seat in the lobby. Let me see if I can reach his assistant. He is an extremely busy man, so I can't guarantee that we'll reach him. He might not even be in the building."

Jessica flashed a bright smile. "Thank you so much. I appreciate you trying."

The wait was excruciating. Jessica's pulse raced as she sat in the lobby, thumbing through a tech magazine, praying that Stephan would see her.

The sound of a throat clearing drew her attention and her head snapped up. Her eyes traversed the lines of a well-cut suit until her head tilted back and her eyes clashed with Stephan's deep blue ones. She caught a spark of some indefinable emotion in them just before he shut it down and eyed her warily. Silence spread like a wide ocean between them.

She was acutely conscious of his tall, athletic physique and the rich out-lines of his shoulders straining against the fabric of his charcoal gray suit. His ebony hair was cut short, but was disheveled as if he had raked his fingers through it several times. Her eyes followed the line of his sharp jaw and her fingers itched to feel the prick of the five o'clock shadow hinting along it.

A far-off voice said her name and pulled her from her abstraction. "I'm sorry. Did you say something?"

A faint smile touched his lips and faded away. "Jessica. I didn't expect to see you again."

"Surprise!" Jessica laughed nervously as she stood before him. Even in her heels he still towered over her. She looked up and smiled nervously. "Are you going to let me in?"

A look of indecision crossed his face. It wasn't the reaction she had ex-pected, but one that mirrored the look he wore the night at the pub. Hell, she didn't quite understand what she had expected. Interest? A smile? *Damn it. I have to stop being so impulsive. I should just go. Leave before I lose all dignity.* "Look, if you're too busy I can leave. I just thought…never mind. This was a bad idea. I'll go."

Stephan reached out and caught her wrist in his hand when she moved to walk around him. "You are not the first interruption of the day. Trevor just left not too long ago. Come," he commanded, gesturing for her to join him.

With a hand on her lower back, he led her to the bank of elevators. Jessica's heart tripped the light fantastic as the warmth of his hand burned through her blouse. Her knees grew weak at memory of that same hand skimming bare skin. When the doors opened, he nudged her into the elevator and followed her inside.

The stainless-steel-lined box felt small despite its larger-than-average size. His presence filled every single cubic inch and drowned her in his woodsy aftershave.

Stephan pressed the button for the twenty-fifth floor and then leaned back against the rail with his arms crossed. Irked by his cool, aloof manner, Jessica lifted her chin and met his gaze straight on.

With a sigh, Stephan ran his hand through his hair. "Jessica, how'd you find me?"

A wave of apprehension swept through her and she questioned her impulse again. Mimicking his stance, she leaned back against the opposite rail, facing him. "It was still in my files from when Trevor had me send him Cassie's documents to the company's lawyers."

"Ah. Why are you here?" he finally asked.

Jessica studied him. Up close and personal, he was exactly as she remembered. Her heart fluttered in her chest and the palms of her hands grew damp. His dark hair had the sharp edges of a fresh cut, the gray of his jacket washed his startling blue eyes to a softer shade that melted her insides. She grinned cheekily. "Would you believe me if I said I was in the neighborhood?"

Jessica could have sworn the corner of his mouth quirked, but she couldn't be sure. "I hope you..." The bell chimed for their floor, cutting of her next words. As the elevator doors slid open, Stephan motioned her to precede him. With a deep breath, Jessica stepped onto the floor and looked to him for directions on which way to go. Stephan passed her and led the way down the hall through a set of double doors, which opened to a spacious sitting area.

Corridors extended off it and a receptionist desk lined the back wall. Stephan touched her hand briefly to catch her attention. "I am over this way." He took off in the pointed direction and Jessica scrambled to catch up with his long strides.

"Máire, please hold my calls," he directed the woman sitting at the desk outside his office doors.

Jessica smiled at her as she followed him inside. She studied the large, neatly organized executive office and noticed a few pictures on the walls. Some were of a personal nature. A large group picture particularly caught her eye. Stephan standing between a smiling man and woman, all wind-tousled and grinning widely at the camera. On closer inspection, Jessica recognized the boy with them—Trevor.

A pang of sadness for Trevor's loss slipped into her heart. Looking away, she found Stephan watching her closely. "You have a beautiful office, Ste-phan. It's so…you. It makes Cassie's father's look like a bathroom stall." His mouth twitched and relief flowed over her.

Their eyes locked for a split second and her heart jumped in her chest. The smiles died suddenly and awkward silence lengthened between them. Stephan broke the minute connection by turning and walking around his desk to his chair, almost as if to create a safety barrier between them. Dis-appointment took root in her gut when he sat and occupied himself with organizing the loose papers on his desk.

Jessica's pulse raced and she took a shallow breath to steady herself for the daring move she was about to make. She walked around and stood next to him, leaning her hip against the edge of the solid desk.

Stephan seemed intent on ignoring her, so she reached out and touched him. The muscles of his forearm hardened beneath her fingers, almost as if offended by her touch. She snatched her hand back and clenched it until her nails cut into her palm. A cold knot formed in her stomach. *No way. I didn't come all this way to give up now.* She cocked her head try-ing to catch his gaze and broke the silence. "It's good to see you again,

Stephan. We didn't get a chance to talk the other night. How have you been?"

Stephan's mind was reeling. His collar choked him and a fire simmered in his stomach. It had begun to burn the second he saw Jessica sitting demurely in the lobby. If he had any sense left, he would have dismissed her right there and then, but his determination to keep her at bay had been thrown out the window when their eyes met.

If he didn't know any better, he would think she was enjoying how uncomfortable her presence made him. Being around her was like going shopping at Dunnes with his mother when he was little. He could almost hear his mother's words whispered in his ear. *Keep your hands in your pockets, Stephan. Do not touch anything.* He remembered the craving to touch the toys and articles on display, but he always followed the instructions, always kept his hands in his pockets, even though the need ravaged his insides. Like now.

As he had guided her to his office, he had purposefully avoided any physical contact and realized the stupidity of his decision the minute her humorous smile had spread across her face and flooded her eyes. She looked even more beautiful, her exuberant youth shining through crystal clear.

He tried to make sense of his emotions but couldn't. Being alone with her in his private office was a disaster and, at the same time, a dream in the making. His secretary knew not to walk in unannounced, so there was no chance of an interruption. The temptation to touch her skin, taste her sweet lips with his, feel her puckered nipples scrape his chest again drove him out of his mind.

The devil warred with the angel on his shoulder, and the devil was winning. Hell, the devil was having a fucking field day. What if he took a leap of faith and enjoyed time with Jessica? Explained that he wanted to be in her presence, loved her humor and intelligent conversation. Wanted nothing more than to feel the touch of her skin against his. All without commitment.

The minute the thought crossed his mind he felt like a cur. That wasn't him speaking. It was lust. Pure and simple. His conscience screamed at him. Jessica wasn't the type that would take a fling lightly. At least he didn't see her that way. In his mind's eye, he saw a big shiny ring on her finger and white veils.

She deserved commitment. She deserved someone who would be with her long term, and he knew he wasn't that man. Yet her presence there indicated she was determined to get what she wanted—him. He didn't know whether to laugh or cry at her persistence.

Her question cut through the haze of his emotional confusion and drove him to finally meet her eyes. For a moment, he simply stared at her at a loss for words. "Right. Yes. I'm brilliant, thank you. And how are you enjoying your visit to Dublin?"

Jessica narrowed her eyes. "Haven't started looking for an apartment yet. Cassie said she'd help me when I'm ready."

"So, this job of yours is only temporary?" The thought of her going back to the States and no longer in close proximity to him was almost as disappointing as the shock of finding out about her move to Dublin.

"Oh, no. It's definitely permanent. I'm not going anywhere." She continued to watch him closely as she commented, almost as if she were measuring the impact of each and every word through the expressions on his face.

"I see."

Stephan's heart beat so loudly it could almost be heard in the thick silence that grew again between them. He needed time to think about the consequences of her moving to Dublin. He had believed he could just ignore her proximity, pretend she was still in California, but her visit proved him wrong. Stephan could never ignore her existence. Could never avoid her. Not with having Trevor and Cassandra as common friends. He wouldn't stop visiting with them for the sake of keeping his distance from Jessica.

He needed to rethink his approach. Rethink his convictions. But Stephan couldn't do that with her standing so close to him—so close that her feminine scent invaded him, the heat of her body teased him to reach out and touch her like a moth attracted to a flame. He knew he would get burned with this one, and he wanted to figure out how to minimize the damage of the train wreck he was about to cause. Trying to buy time and create the necessary detachment to investigate his deep-seated fears and resolutions, he stood and blurted out, "Join me for lunch."

A victorious smile curved her lips. "I thought you'd never ask."

Chapter Ten

Score!

THE UNFINISHED ANALYSIS ON PAUL Faber, the MDS employee Trevor had met with, had taunted Cassandra for days. She had wanted to tackle it while it was still fresh in her memory.

After Trevor had left, she'd huddled at her computer, reviewing the video stream captured on the day of the meeting and the notes of the impressions she had jotted down. She reaffirmed her earlier conclusions that there was nothing there to be concerned about.

Cassandra stretched her arms above her head and shook them out to get the circulation moving again. The prickling of the restored blood flow felt as good as finishing everything she had wanted to accomplish that morning.

Cassandra eased back in her chair and rested her feet on the desk while she took a breather. She glanced at the clock. Trevor had been gone a couple of hours, and she still needed to tackle the review of the files George had sent during their last conversation.

A soft smile caressed her lips as she remembered the frown on Trevor's face as he had left—one she always found so damn sexy. If it was still on his face when he returned she would be compelled to do something about it. Vivid images of how she could do just that bombarded her and her face grew warm as a flush crept into her cheeks. *Focus, Cassie.*

Cassandra exhaled a deep breath as she dropped her feet from the desk and dove back into the review of the transcripts. As she read through Jennifer's work her heart rate increased and pounded in apprehension. She could see why George's boxers were in a bunch. It was always a bad thing when Russians were involved. Her days with the CIA had been filled with tidbits of information that could make one's skin crawl.

As she came across names, she took notes and, once finished, began the intelligence work—collecting any pertinent information on all of the names pulled from the transcript as well as the names of persons of interest linked to the phone number in question. Thanks to an anonymous proxy server and a sweet little program Trevor had created to reset and mask their IP address at regular intervals, they were able to do all their poking without being traced.

Confident they were safe, she entered the first few names from her list— Shapko and Pushkar—names mentioned several times in the conversation between Tomlin and the caller.

When No data returned displayed on the screen for both, Cassandra rubbed her face, put her hair back into a ponytail, and tapped her fingers on the keyboard impatiently while staring at the screen. The names weren't flagged in any of the intelligence databases. *They might be small fish.* She crossed them off the list, moving onto the actual caller himself— Sergei Deminov.

Her fingers jumped across the keys as she entered the letters into the search program. With a tap of her pinky, she initiated the scan. While it ran, she toggled back to the transcript.

Within minutes, her eyes were caught by the application flashing on the taskbar. Toggling back to it, Cassandra skimmed the report generated and grinned—the first real one of the morning.

Sergei Deminov was a very naughty boy—someone Trevor would definitely be interested in, based on his activities and connections.

A satisfied smile spread across her lips. *Finally! A real freaking lead.* She returned her attention to the screen and skimmed a few more lines of text, hitting on another name: Vladimir Mikhailov. Excitement gripped her as she paged back through her notes. Mikhailov had been mentioned several times and looked promising. The corner of Cassandra's mouth quirked. The name reminded her of the movie *The Saint* and the lead character's adventure in Russia. *Damn. I love that movie. It has to be a sign.*

She typed Mikhailov into the search field; once the search initiated, it didn't take long for the screen to be populated with details about the man himself. *This just might make Trevor's day.* She copied the information on both Deminov and Mikhailov to the project file and saved it.

Satisfied, she left the office and ran down the flight of stairs to the kitchen. She was starving to the point that her hands were starting to look tasty. She had her head stuck in the fridge looking for something to eat when she heard the footsteps. Anticipation sent her pulse racing: Trevor was finally back.

Cassandra's name died on his lips as he stepped into the kitchen and found her standing by the open fridge. "No need to search, love. Brought you something."

"Perfect timing. I'm starved!"

He placed the bags and cup holder on the counter and handed her the cup with the coffee. He brought his own closer to his nose and inhaled the delicious Earl Grey scent before taking a first sip. "Ambrosia."

Watching as Cassandra closed her eyes and did the same with her Arabian blend, he pulled a plate from the cabinet and set the pastries on it so she could choose her poison.

Trevor's groin clenched when a look of intense concentration overtook her face and her tongue moistened her lower lip. His grin widened when she finally chose a strawberry-filled Danish and took a slow bite out of it.

"Hmm. Really good," she moaned, wiping some of the filling from her chin and licking her fingers.

His cock hardened instantly. He smiled to himself, shaking his head as he pressed his hand against the growing bulge constrained by his jeans to ease the ache.

He was tempted to throw her over his shoulder and run for their room, but they couldn't afford to spend the rest of the day in bed having fun. There was too much on the line. Plus, Jessie could show up any time. He propped his hip against the counter and continued to watch as she delighted herself with his peace offering.

Cassandra nodded at the boxes on the counter and mumbled while chewing the last bite, "So, what do you have there?"

"I stopped by Aidan's shop and picked up the micro cameras I'd ordered last month. The other package is from your dad. The courier was about to knock when I got to the door. No idea what it is."

After brushing the pastry crumbs from her hands, she picked up the package, weighing it. "It's really light." She pulled a sharp knife from the drawer and cut through the packing tape. "He didn't mention he was sending me anything," she commented, setting the knife aside and opening the box. From it she pulled a carefully wrapped intricate pewter picture frame.

Curious, Trevor looked over her shoulder at the happy couple smiling in the wedding picture. He recognized Robert immediately, so the woman could only be Cecilia, Cassandra's mom. The first thing that struck him was that Cassandra was the spitting image of her mother. The second was how quiet she became after unwrapping the frame.

Sensing something was off, he set his cup on the counter and hugged her from behind. She exhaled a choppy breath and her pulse beat rapidly as he placed a kiss on her neck before resting his chin on her shoulder. "She was a beautiful woman, *a ghrá*. You take after her."

"You think so?" Cassandra's chest burned as she gazed at the picture of her parents. Her fingers travelled lovingly over her mother's features. She struggled to recall any memories from when she was a part of her life.

She leaned back against his chest. "I can remember that morning like it was yesterday. I was a little over eight years old. My dad kneeled in front me so he could look into my eyes. I don't think I will ever forget the pain in them. I knew just by looking into his that something terrible had happened. When he spoke, his voice trembled as he told me my mother was in heaven." She paused, lost in thought, reliving that dark moment. "I'd never seen him like that before. I can also clearly remember the day I realized I could no longer see her face, hear her beautiful Spanish accent, or smell the musky scent of her perfume." It bothered her deeply that she couldn't remember more of the happier years. Her voice hitched. "Why would he send this to me now? He cherishes this picture."

Trevor's warm lips caressed her shoulder. "He's trying really hard to make things up to you, Cassie. Maybe he wanted you to have something to remember them by since you're married now, living far from him."

She set the picture on the counter, turned in his arms, and pressed a kiss on his lips. "Do you think it's a sign he's finally moving on?"

"Maybe it is, a *ghrá*," Trevor responded, watching her closely. "Would that bother you?"

"No! I would love him to find someone." Stepping out of his arms, she snagged another pastry and skillfully changed the subject. "Hey, I have something for you. Meet me upstairs in the office when you're ready. I reviewed all the data from George and found something you're gonna find very interesting." Before he could retort, she headed back upstairs. She didn't have time to dwell on the past at that moment. They had more important work to do—work that had an impact on their future.

Trevor took his time following her. He'd observed the frown marring her beautiful face as she left. She needed space and he'd give her some. He covered the rest of the pastries, grabbed the parcel from the counter, and climbed the stairs, making a pit stop on the third floor to store the new cameras with the rest of their surveillance equipment.

When he walked into the office, Cassandra's eyes were glued to her screen.

Sitting at his desk, he pulled up the project file Cassandra had saved. "So, what do you have for me?"

She glanced up and caught his gaze over the monitors. "Sergei Deminov. Russian national."

"Hmm...why is that name familiar?" Trevor narrowed his eyes, searching his memory.

"His connections are shady, to say the least. Appears to be the right hand of a Russian business man named Vladimir Mikhailov."

"Did you say Mikhailov?" Cassandra nodded and Trevor exploded. "Fuck! This is big! The NSA had him on the watch list. He's a well-known Russian mafia boss. An old timer. A thief-in-law."

Cassandra frowned at the term. "Enlighten me. Russia was not part of my directorate."

"A thief-in-law has authority and a high-ranking status within the criminal underworld of the old Soviet Union. Somewhat like the Italian mafia Godfather, but way more ruthless."

"Now that you mention it, I have heard of them. Through Bob. Aren't they considered the elite of Russian organized crime?

"Yes!" Trevor's voice filled with excitement. "Mikhailov is like a Godfather to his underlings; his organization is known for its focus on digital fraud."

Trevor jumped from his chair and cupped Cassandra's face with both hands, pressing a hard kiss on her lips. "The Mikhailov connection is huge! Great job! This guy was involved in several online frauds already investigated by the FBI, CIA, and NSA. He never puts his neck on the line—his group's activities never point to him directly. I am surprised he let this connection slip." Trevor shook his head and began to pace the room. "I think Deminov made a big mistake in hiring a rookie like Tomlin."

A flicker of apprehension coursed through Cassandra. The stakes were getting much higher than she had anticipated. They were turning out to be tied to extremely heavy players. "Damn, Trevor. What are we getting into? What the hell was Tomlin thinking?" She bit her lip, worrying at it as she filtered through potential next steps in her head.

After a few minutes, she leaned forward in her chair. "Considering the Russian mafia controls most of the banking industry there, it's probably safe to say if the decrypter was to be completed in their hands it would be a heyday." She tucked her leg under her and settled back in her chair, moving it from side to side as she watched Trevor circle the room like a caged lion.

She voiced her thoughts as they occurred to her. "Based on the transcripts and the triangulation of the calls, Mikhailov and his people seem to be in the St. Petersburg area. We need to get eyes and ears on his headquarters as soon as possible. Need to be sure George has tapped every single name on those transcripts. Have to find out what else he's got."

Trevor stopped in front of her, quirked an eyebrow, and cracked a smile. "I'm sure he did. Now...breathe, Cassie girl."

On a roll, the thoughts just kept tumbling off her tongue. "Once we confirm Mikhailov's location, can you infiltrate and destroy their servers from here?"

"It will depend on what kind of network he has. If it's something I can do from here then, yes. I don't want to put our necks on the line if we can avoid it."

"Why the hesitation? Cough it up. What's bothering you?"

"Considering who we are dealing with, chances are he has his ass covered."

"And that means?"

"We'll have to be there. Physical infiltration."

Cassandra grew quiet, processing how the infiltration would work. "Maybe we should head there now. Begin close-range surveillance on our own. Tap into George's resources from there." Hearing a low chuckle from Trevor's direction, she tossed him a questioning look.

The grin on his face grew wider. "Damn, Cassie. I love how your mind works. Love you more, but definitely love your brain."

Cassandra felt the heat of the blush creep up from her neck to her cheeks and laughed self-consciously. "Sorry. I got carried away and didn't even let you get a word in edgewise."

Trevor's mouth twitched with amusement. "I agree. We should be there. We'd be close enough to act quickly once we have the location of the files and decide what's needed for the retrieval."

His thoughts filtered back to what he knew of Mikhailov's organization's infrastructure and hoped his network was outdated. If they were lucky, Mikhailov had hired teenagers, who usually weren't as cautious about patching their systems, for the hack job. But he knew that was almost like praying for a miracle.

He slipped back in his chair and stared off into space, considering the risks surrounding the job—and then the reward that would come in the end. Eager to get back to it, he opened the chat application and sent George a quick note.

Send me any current information on Vladimir Mikhailov. This thing goes deep. Find any current tap on him and keep me posted.

Trevor left the application open. Knowing George, he would respond the moment he caught wind of the message.

"Hey, Cassie. We should get things started. We need to book our flight as soon as possible. Do you still have your CIA contacts? Think they might help expedite our visas?"

Cassandra nodded. "Let me see what I can do."

"Okay. In the meantime, I'll update Devlin and let him know we might be on the move shortly."

They both turned to their computers and tackled their tasks in an almost synchronized operation, like a well-oiled machine. Trevor overheard Cassandra making several phone calls and murmuring in the background while Trevor composed the email update to appease Devlin.

A while later, Cassandra turned her chair and faced Trevor, tapping her notepad as she spoke. "Got our visas taken care of. I've scheduled a courier to pick up our passports for delivery to the US Embassy. They're being pushed through the diplomatic queue to the Russians. We should have them within a couple of business days."

"Nice!" Trevor praised her with a big smile on his face. "I am almost done with this report. My stomach is growling. Jessie should be back anytime. Do you want to take a break and start dinner? I will be there to help you in a few."

"Yep. I should give her a call and find out when to expect her or if she's found an Irishman to entertain her already." Her stomach growled as she stood, giving her pause. She glanced over at Trevor and knew by his lifted brow that he'd heard it.

A smile pulled at his lips. "Guess you're hungry, too."

Laughing, Cassandra patted her stomach and walked to where Trevor was sitting. "I guess I am."

"Perfect, I'll be down shortly," Trevor nodded, his attention already turning back to the screen the minute a beep sounded on his computer indicating George had responded to his message.

Chapter Eleven

Childish

CASSANDRA HEARD THE DOOR UNLOCK as she stepped off the last stair onto the first level. Jessica appeared coming up from the foyer a minute later. A fun greeting died in Cassandra's throat at the sight of her friend's flushed cheeks and downright pissed-off expression as she walked toward her, clearly lost in thought.

"Jessica?"

Startled, Jessica's eyes cleared and jumped to hers. "Damn it, Cassie! Don't scare me like that."

"Scare *you*? That scowl is enough to send me running back upstairs for my Glock. What the hell happened? Are you okay?"

"Jeez. Yes, I'm fine. No harm, no foul," Jessica dismissed her concerns with a wave of hand.

"Then what? Someone grabbed the shoes you were lusting after out of your hands or something?"

"Something like that," Jessica huffed, following her to the kitchen where she leaned on the counter. Cassandra knew her too well and could easily unmask her with piercing and observant eyes.

She felt the anger vibrating in Jessica's voice. It was a perfect match to her earlier expression. Something was up and she was determined to find out what had upset her friend so.

Her gaze flicked to Jessica's hands. "Where are your shopping bags? You've been gone *all* freaking day and not one bag?" Cassandra narrowed her eyes and stalked toward Jessica playfully. "Who are you? And what did you do with my best friend?"

Jessica burst out laughing, backing away with raised hands. "Whoa there, tiger." She shrugged her shoulders. "What can I say? I didn't find anything worth spending my precious Euros on. Can't be overspending my savings until I know what my expenses with the new place will be."

Skeptically, Cassandra eyed her up and down before turning her attention to the contents of the fridge. As she rummaged in it, she tossed back, "Uh huh. *And again*, I ask you. Will the real Jessica please step forward?"

Jessica hopped up to sit on the counter and watched Cassandra pop the lids off the containers she'd pulled out from the shelves. As she took whiffs from them, Jessica snorted and Cassandra looked over at her with a raised eyebrow. "What?" she asked. "It's leftover paella. I was just checking."

"How old is it?"

Cassandra paused to think. "Two days…maybe three." Concerned, she blurted out, "Will that kill us?"

Jessica stared at her for a moment and then burst out laughing. "Damn, Cassie. I've missed you."

Working at the counter, Cassandra transferred the paella from the containers to a microwavable dish and, in a fluid motion, placed it in the stainless steel appliance. With a last press of a button, she turned to Jessica, rested her elbows on the counter, and studied her friend for a short time. "So. Spit it out, Jess. What happened to put such a sour look on your face?"

Jessica dropped her eyes and plucked at invisible lint on her skirt. She must have felt Cassandra's undiminishing scrutiny because she sighed and looked up again. After a moment's hesitation, she blurted, "I dropped in on Stephan."

Cassandra's eyebrows rose. "Stephan? Our Stephan? Why would you do that?" The microwave beeped; without missing a beat, she reset it. When Jessica didn't answer, she looked up. The pain that shadowed her eyes gave her pause. A frown creased her brow at the telling expression on Jessica's face. "O—kay. You paid Stephan a visit. Why?" As the paella went through a second round of heating, she pulled a bottle of red wine from the wine fridge encased in the counter.

"The arrogant man—" Jessica caught herself and took a deep breath. Emotion seemed to choke her. She swallowed deeply and started again, still ignoring Cassandra's question. "The arrogant man had the nerve to call me childish."

Cassandra continued to move around the kitchen, still trying to make sense of Jessica's explanations. Her brows furrowed as she grabbed an oven mitt and transferred the dish from the microwave to the counter. "That doesn't sound like Stephan, and it doesn't answer my question, Jessie." In a moment of clarity, Jessica's words cut through her annoyance at her friend's tiptoeing around her question. "Wait. Why would he call you childish for visiting him at the office?"

"Not because of that. We were at lunch. Things were coming along. We were making progress. A woman walked up to the table and started flirting with him. The look she gave me could have pinned a tarantula. When he didn't bother to introduce us, she asked him if I was his niece." Bitterness and disappointment colored Jessica's words, capturing Cassandra's attention.

She pulled off the mitt and set it on the counter. "Jessie, you're bouncing all over the place. What the hell are you talking about? Progress? And the woman actually thought you were his niece? That's funny." Cassandra couldn't help but grin. "What did Stephan say?"

"He introduced me as a friend of the family. That's when I found out the woman was none other than Terese. The same Terese he mentioned at the pub the other night," Jessica steamed as she accounted for the events of the day.

Cassandra's eyes grew intent observing Jessica; her reactions told an interesting story. Knowing Jessica, she might as well listen now, take notes, and discuss later. She was on a roll and wouldn't stop until she had let it all out.

Jessica continued spewing her disdain for the day's events without noticing Cassandra's stare. "Terese ignored me from the moment she approached the table and then looked down her aristocratic blue nose at me," she sighed. "And you know what happens when that kind of thing goes down."

"Oh, lord. You strike back. Snap! What did you say?"

"She asked how I knew Stephan. I mentioned we attended your wedding together and that we had a lovely evening later at my house." Her eyes narrowed. "She had the nerve to ask if my parents were home at the time."

Cassandra snorted and covered her face with her hand. "Damn, Jess. I'm sorry. Terese is actually not a bad person. She cares for Stephan."

"Oh, that's not all, Cassie. As she was leaving, I told her she looked golden for a grandmother."

"Bloody hell, Jess. No wonder Stephan called you childish. Didn't that cross the line a bit?" Jessica was flinging pieces of information at her in such a disparate way, it took Cassandra a while to process what exactly Jessica had said. She glanced at her sharply. "Hold the boat! He was at your house?! When the hell did that happen? And why are you so damn upset about all this? They date occasionally. What's the big deal?"

"On the evening of your wedding. Anyway, she left in a huff and that's when Stephan threw it at my face." Jessica avoided the question a second time.

Cassandra wondered why Jessica was so upset about Terese. Any other time they would both have thought the whole situation a hoot. She studied Jessica, but her face was now void of all expression. *Curiouser and curiouser.*

She was about to begin her inquisition when the sound of Trevor's tread jogging down the stairs reached them. As he walked over to join them, Cassandra looked Jessica dead in the eyes and mouthed, "We're not done."

"Smells good, Cassie," Trevor commented as he dropped a kiss on Jessica's cheek and one on Cassandra's lips.

"Not bad for leftovers. At least it won't kill us," Jessica joked.

Trevor did a double take and Jessica snorted at the concerned look that flooded his face.

"Really? You really think my cooking would kill us?" Cassandra asked, handing him the bottle of wine and opener.

"Teasing, Cassie girl. Teasing," he grinned.

Cassandra carried the platter to the table, calling over her shoulder, "Hey Jess, wanna grab the plates and silverware? Top right cabinet. Top left drawer. *A ghrá,* grab the glasses."

Everyone came together at the table and while Trevor opened the wine, Cassandra dished out the food. Soon they were all kicking back with full bellies, sipping wine, and having an animated conversation about life in Dublin.

Observing Trevor and Jessica's banter, Cassandra's heart swelled with bliss. Her best friend and her husband got on fabulously, and that thrilled her to no end. She couldn't have imagined what she would have done had Jessica, a woman she viewed more as a sister of her heart, had not approved of Trevor.

"Trevor, I heard you paid a visit to Stephan today," Jessica mentioned casually as she took a sip of her wine.

Cassandra shot Trevor a questioning look. "You did?"

Trevor eyed Jessica. "How do you know that?"

"I dropped by his office and he mentioned it. Are you going to start working there?"

"No." Trevor held Cassandra's gaze and took her hand in his. "Stephan will be in charge for a bit longer."

"I thought you were going for a walk, clear your head." Cassandra gazed at him.

"I did, *a ghrá*. The visit to Stephan was part of that. I let him know that I was still looking into their disappearance.'

Understanding and love crowded the concern from Cassandra's eyes. Jessica couldn't help but ask, "Looking into whose disappearance? Your parents'?"

Trevor nodded and Cassandra turned toward her. "That's why we asked you to join us, Jessie. We need to you help us follow up on any leads that we may find. The NSA projects have taken up more time than we thought they would. I could really use the extra eyes and hands."

Jessica sat back in her chair processing what they had just told her. "Wow, I am honored that you want me to help. I promise I will do everything I can."

"I'm sure you'll do a smashing job. You're family, a little sister in a way. Your help will be a godsend."

Jessica suddenly felt overwhelmed by Trevor's confidence. Between the emotional roller coaster Stephan had put her on and the responsibility Trevor and Cassandra had entrusted her with, all she wanted was to curl up in bed and process it all. With a deep sigh, she stood and collected her dishes. "Well, like I said, I will do everything I can to help. Okay, guys. I'm beat. I think I'll turn in."

"Leave it, Jessie. Trevor and I can handle it."

"Night, Jessie," Trevor called after her.

"Sleep well." Cassandra's troubled eyes followed Jessica as she walked up the stairs. Her thoughts revolved around the few consistent pieces of information she had extracted from their conversation. She was so not letting that go.

As Jessica left her field of vision, she returned her attention to the cleanup waiting to be done and met Trevor's questioning eyes. Without much to say, she shrugged her shoulders and began clearing the table. Within minutes, both had everything cleared and put away.

Turning from the sink, Trevor reached for Cassandra and pulled her into his arms. "Still a great meal the second time around, *a ghrá*."

"You were just hungry and didn't know any better." Trevor chuckled. "But it was pretty damn good if I say so myself."

"Ready to relax?" Trevor asked, offering his hand.

"Don't you know it!" She took his hand and followed him into the living room for some much-needed quiet time.

They had created a routine around their habits. Reading, watching the news, and working flowed smoothly in their household as a well-scripted macro.

Trevor relaxed back against the couch reading the latest reports and debriefings George had sent him earlier regarding Mikhailov. Cassandra leaned against his side and he shifted to accommodate her. Draping an arm around her shoulders, he adjusted the tablet in his lap so that he could continue reading.

A comfortable silence stretched between them. As he read, his fingers trailed back and forth along her arm in an instinctive caress. When Cassandra sighed and dropped her head to his shoulder, Trevor's heart did a little somersault in his chest. *This* was what he had looked forward to all his life—the homey, loving camaraderie that his parents had.

A short while later, Trevor surfaced from the documents he had been studying and became deeply aware of Cassandra's hand resting on his thigh, mirroring the lazy movement of his hand on her arm. He had been so engrossed in his reading that he hadn't registered her mood change. His focus narrowed to her hand as her caress became more rhythmic and, without any warning, she cupped him over his jeans.

His attention was definitely captured by the warmth of her hand on his hardening cock. Without hesitation, Trevor set his tablet aside, cupped the nape of her neck, and pulled her to him, claiming her mouth. She tasted of spices and wine. Needing more of her, he thrust his tongue past her lips, exploring its sweetness, teasing her tongue into an exotic dance. His groin twitched as she joined him in the wicked game, sucking his tongue into her mouth, and a groan rumbled in his chest at the flush of desire that burned through his veins.

"Shite, woman. Where did that come from? Not that I'm complaining, but…" he muttered against her lips.

Cassandra laughed softly. "Do I need a reason?"

She couldn't hold back the smile that tugged at her lips or the way her heart slammed against her ribs as she gazed down the length of him. She gave his growing arousal a slight squeeze and cupped his cheek with her free hand, the light stubble from the day's growth felt rough against her palm.

Trevor watched her intently as she brushed her thumb across his lower lip. The sight of him was too tempting. He squeezed his eyes shut and whispered, "Cassandra."

A thrill riding the tail of an electric current shot through her and she replaced her thumb with her mouth, holding his lips hostage, licking and nipping. He turned into her, slid his hand from her nape to her hip, imprisoning her against his body.

A soft moan welled up from her chest as he deepened the kiss, his hands roaming over her shoulders, down and along her lower back, making her squirm. A surge of heat washed over her, leaving her weak in the knees. Out of breath, she pulled back from the kiss, slipped from his arms, and stood on not-so-steady legs next to the couch, smiling down at him.

"A nice soft bed is calling our names this time, babe." Tugging him to his feet, Cassandra led him to the stairs. "Besides, if Jessica caught us I am sure she'd be struck blind."

"Shite! Only a week here and she's already put a cramp in my style," Trevor chuckled, admiring her ass as he followed her up the stairs to their room, shutting the door behind them.

Air hissed through his teeth in appreciation as Cassandra turned from the edge of the bed to face him and reached for the hem of her shirt, pulling it over her head. Taking her cue, he yanked off his own and tossed it to the floor. Her hair cascaded over her shoulders, framing her beautiful face as she unbuttoned and, ever so slowly, shimmied her jeans off her curvy hips and down her long, shapely legs.

Trevor's hands froze on his own button, his gaze snared by her golden skin and the tiny swatch of lace panty barely covering the thatch of hair at the V of her thighs. She caught his eye and with a raised eyebrow nodded toward his jeans, which he quickly chucked, springing his erection free. A soft gasp escaped her and he grinned.

"You went out commando? All day?" Her questioning voice was low and sultry.

The heat flooding her eyes scorched him from his chest to his knees and his heart flipped in his chest as a saucy, sensual grin tugged at the corner of her mouth. He stalked closer, covering her tempting breast with his hand and holding her eyes as he sank his fingers in her hair.

Tightening his hand around the back of her neck, he pulled her firmly toward him until they melted into each other, skin to skin, trapping his rigid shaft between them against the soft skin of her belly. His fingers kneaded her breast and his thumb rubbed across her nipple in lazy circles as he claimed her mouth, sucking down the needy moan escaping her lips.

Cassandra wrapped her arms around Trevor's neck, cupped the back of his head, and sank deeper into the kiss. Her head rolled back on her shoulders as his lips trailed along the slender column of her throat to the pulse beating rapidly under her skin and back up to the shell of her ear.

Her mouth became dry, her control slipped. With a deep shuddering breath, she pressed against his shoulders and stepped back, but his hand tightened at her nape holding her in place. "Trevor! I want—"

"No, *a ghrá.* Not this time. I want to make you scream tonight, taste and suck you like never before. I need this…we need this."

His words sent a shiver of longing racing down her spine and her thighs trembled in anticipation, chasing all thoughts but of him from her mind. All that existed was Trevor and a deep-seated need to feel the weight of his body against hers, inside her. She sought his mouth again and covered it with hers in a deep, wet, open kiss. Her hand glided between them, gripping his hard silky erection, the other skimmed down his back to his ass.

Cassandra's nails dug into his skin and her tight grasp around his shaft made him want her even more, but his need to give was bigger than his need to take. Trevor broke from her touch and slid down her body, tracing a path of soft kisses on her ribcage, waist, and hips, until he kneeled in front of her.

He trailed his wet tongue along the elastic band of her panties, hooked his fingers in the fabric on both sides, and slid them down from her hips, kissing the unveiled soft satin skin. Nudging her back against the edge of the bed, she fell upon it, and he slipped the panties past her feet, leaving her bare under his heavy-lidded gaze.

Holding eye contact, Cassandra spread her legs in invitation. With a deep groan rumbling in his chest, Trevor spread her folds with the pads of his thumbs. She was all pink, juicy wet, and his mouth watered for a taste of her. He inhaled deeply, savoring the scent of her desire, and then swooped in, covering her tender flesh with his mouth, sucking her clit into it, and flicking it with his tongue. She gasped in shuddering draws of air at the contact of his tantalizing tongue pressed against her. Releasing her clit from that sensual kiss, he lapped at her folds, her sweet juices flooding his taste buds.

"More…Trevor…please!"

His alternating between long, languid licks and short little flicks turned her gasps into a drawn-out tormented groan, a heady invitation to take his fill. Her body squirmed beneath his tongue and his own screamed for him to take her and drive toward his release, but still, he waited. He wanted—needed—her to scream his name, to come in his mouth before he allowed himself the satisfaction of burying his cock in her tight heat.

He nudged her legs further apart, pushing her thighs up and back with his forearms as he spread her folds again, thrusting his firm tongue in her wet slick sheath, mimicking the rhythmic moves his hips would soon repeat.

"God, Trevor!" Cassandra's hips bucked against his mouth and her belly tingled as one of his hands skimmed up her ribs, along her stomach, and cupped her breast. A needy sigh eased from her lungs as his tongue continued to thrust inside her and his fingers brushed across her sensitive nipple. A soft pinch sent a flare of electricity straight to her womb, causing it to clench and her clit to ache. Sensations bombarded her—his fingers plunging deep inside, the pad of his thumb and tongue grazing her throbbing clit.

Her body trembled and she shifted her hips, craving more. "Shite Cassandra! So hot, so wet! Come for me, *a ghrá*," he demanded harshly. Cassandra's inner muscles clenched in response and her thighs tightened, riding the first waves of her oncoming orgasm.

"Trevor!" she cried out as it ripped through her entire body. Trevor groaned and latched his mouth on her clit, sucking hard and fast. Her body bowed from the bed. "Too much love!" she sobbed, throwing her head back, riding the wave. Spent, she fell limp to the bed. Her chest heaved and she gasped for breath, shivering in the aftermath. "Oh my god, Trevor! That was amaz—"

"We're not finished yet, Cassie," he breathed against her thigh, kissing it tenderly. "Remember I said 'scream like never before'?"

"But—"

"Nope. Not even close. You can to do better than that," he murmured, pressing a hand on her stomach and stopping her from sitting up. When he felt her relax, he gripped her by the waist and pulled her ass closer to the edge of the bed.

She lifted and draped her legs over his shoulders as his finger slid inside her still-quivering sheath. With a soft pumping motion, he added two more, filling and stretching her.

"Trevor..." His name was a long whisper spilling from her lips, but he still wanted more. He wanted her to forget all her inhibitions and scream. He primed her with his fingers now coated with her slick juices, driving hard and deep. His cock twitched and grew painfully hard when her half-mast eyes filled with heated love and desire met his. He held her gaze and, in slow deliberate movements, slid his fingers into his mouth, sucking her wetness from them.

Her lips parted and her head leaned back. "Ah..."

Her taste rolled over his tongue and his cock surged. "Heavenly," he whispered, leaning down to take her with his mouth. "I want you to come in my mouth again. Do it for me," he urged, penetrating her with his tongue again. Her muscles quaked, her hips rolled into him, her heels dug into his back, pulling him tighter against her.

Her fingers threaded through his hair, taking hold as she rode his mouth. "Oh...oh!" she moaned. "I'm coming!" she cried out as her knees clamped against the sides of his head.

He dragged his tongue over her clit in a long lap and flicked it, forcing her back to arch and her head to press back against the bed. A quick nip at her clit tossed her over the edge.

"Trevor! Yesss!" she screamed, tensing, tumbling over into a second release. Chest heaving, she fell boneless to the bed.

Trailing kisses up her thigh to the soft skin of her abdomen, Trevor commented in a rough voice, "I think we can proceed now."

Flushed and trembling, Cassandra lifted her head and looked down at Trevor, who had a wicked smile on his face. Her wide eyes collided with the devious glint in his, making her mouth go dry. She rose to her elbows and stammered, "You think we can proceed now? What the hell does that mean?"

Trevor crawled onto the bed over her, forcing her to fall back on it. He took his time tasting the rest of her—licking along her stomach, pausing to swirl his tongue in her navel, and trailing it along her ribs to the tender underside of her breast. A hiss escaped in a soft whisper and her mind went blank as he pulled her nipple into his mouth, stretching and sucking it hard. Reaching between their bodies, she circled his shaft with her fingers, moving them up and down his length before twisting slightly while rubbing her thumb across its crown. She wanted to give him as much pleasure as he had given her—her heart demanded it.

"No, Cassie. Not this time. This time I want inside." He shifted his hips, pressing his rock hard erection tight against her.

"You mean like this?" Her breath was moist against his lips as she rubbed the head of his shaft against her wet entrance.

"God! Yes! Like that," he groaned.

Encouraged, she guided him closer until his crown slipped just inside, and then she tightened her muscles around him. "Cassandra!" he cried hoarsely, forcing her knees to her chest and driving his shaft hard and deep inside her heat in a fluid thrust.

Trevor's breath came in harsh gasps as he buried his cock to the hilt, her clenched muscles a fist around him. His mind swirled with the pleasure of being surrounded by her and, after so much constraint, he felt ready to burst. He started the cadence, thrusting and withdrawing from her in a fast beat. Her mewls and groans pushing him to the brink, the force of his thrusts slapping his balls against her ass cheeks.

Her legs shifted to cradle his body against hers and lifted to meet each thrust. He grasped her bottom lip between his teeth and sucked it. Her moan flowed into his mouth as he covered hers in a deep kiss. He pumped deeply, grinding against her nub, and a fire kindled in his chest and spread through him, burning him from the inside out. Her taste still filled his senses with delight, reminding him of how beautiful she had looked as she had screamed his name in ecstasy.

"Fuck! You feel so good, babe!" Her inner muscles quaked around his shaft, warning of a new release rushing toward her.

"Trevor—you're killing me!" she screamed, arching her body into his, hands bunching the covers as she careened toward her climax.

Her inner walls rippled around his shaft, surging him toward his own release. He gathered her in his arms as his balls tightened and a twinge shot through the base of his spine, sending him headlong into a mind-blowing eruption. His hips thrust out of control as he spilled deep inside, her muscles flexing around him, milking him dry.

Cassandra wrapped her arms around Trevor and held tight as they rode it out. Her muscles continued to spasm, wringing another surge from his cock. Lifeless, they collapsed and held each other as their bodies began to cool and their breath returned to normal.

She tucked her face against his neck and breathed him in, whispering, "I love you." Humorously, she added, "At least we made it to the bed this time. I think it was beginning to get a complex!"

"I love you, Cassie," he chuckled, smiling at her jest. "I don't think any room in this house can complain about being ignored, *a ghrá*."

"Well the good thing is, Jessica's eyes have been saved. I'm not sure what she would have said if she had stumbled on your white Irish ass sticking up in the air!" Cassandra snorted. "Oh, hell. I do know! She would've snapped a picture and posted it on the internet under the caption, Irish Butt Dance."

He burst out laughing and, with a groan, pulled out of her. They scrambled under the covers and he gathered her back into his arms, slipping a knee between her legs.

A knock on the door startled them both just as they were settling for the night. "Hey you two! Not to be blunt, but your house was not made with visitors in mind!"

Cassandra stifled a giggle against Trevor's chest, whispering, "Oh my god. See? We did almost blind her!"

"Shush!" Trevor chuckled before swallowing his laughter and clearing his throat. "Go away, Jessie!"

"I can't even tell you to get a room! You are already there."

They both listened closely as she walked away and burst out laughing again before falling into a sated silence.

Chapter Twelve

A Rock and a Hard Place

CASSANDRA WOKE TO A DARK room and Trevor's warm body wrapped around hers. It was a position that she never got tired of and never would. She snuggled closer and tried to fall back to sleep, but the earlier conversation with Jessica kept playing over in her head. A creak sounded above them and Cassandra heard the soft pad of Jessica's feet on the stairs and past their closed door. She checked the time. Two in the morning.

She gently slipped out of Trevor's arms and from the bed. Pulling on her robe, she left their room, closing the door gently behind her, and headed downstairs in search of Jessica. She found her friend sitting in the living room staring off into nothingness.

"Hey, Jess. Couldn't sleep?" Cassandra plopped herself next to Jessica and rubbed her leg soothingly.

"No. Just too much going on in my head, I guess."

Cassandra tucked her legs under her and turned to face her friend. "Does it have anything to do with Stephan? We never really did finish our talk."

Jessica shook her head but didn't elaborate.

"Come on, Jessie. What the hell is going on? I'm your best friend, for chrissake. Never once, in all these months, have you mentioned that Stephan had been to your house. What the hell is going on between you two?"

Jessica rested her head back against the couch and exhaled sharply. "Hell, Cassie. I have no idea."

"Why don't you start with the wedding? The last I remember, Bob had offered you a ride home."

Jessica rolled her head to the side and glanced at Cassandra. "With all the goodbyes and well wishes you must have missed Stephan offering to take me instead. I said yes."

Cassandra pondered a moment and a wide grin spread over her face. "Shut up. I'm remembering now. After the vows, I caught you watching Stephan. I almost said something to you. Damn. I also remember seeing a shit-eating grin on your face when I looked out the rear window as we drove away."

Jessica shook her head. "Jeez, Cassie. Don't have a coronary. Trevor would have my ass on a platter."

She burst out laughing and grabbed Jessica's arms, giving her a little shake. "Spill! What happened, woman?!"

"Okay, okay. Damn. No dismemberments, please," Jessica laughed, and then sobered. "Stephan drove me home. I don't know what happened, Cassie. There's something about him." Jessica caught herself and scrubbed her face with her hands.

Cassandra turned fully to face her. "Well?"

"He drove me home and walked me to the door. The next thing I know

I'm inviting him in for a drink. He was hesitant but said yes. Once the door closed...."

Jessica went on to retell the story. When she was finished, Cassandra couldn't hold her astonishment. "Oh. My. God. Jessie!"

★ ★ ★ ★ ★

It was way past midnight when he stepped into his house, straight into the soothing arms of darkness and silence, after a loud night at the Brazen Head. Stephan had avoided going home for as long as he could. He watched the whole football match between the Shamrock Rovers and Shelbourne at the busy pub. Part of him hoped Trevor, Cassandra, and their guest would show up for a pint, but they never did.

The house was kept pristine by his housekeeper, who stopped by a few times each week to make sure his clothes had been sent to the drycleaners and to leave prepared meals in the fridge that could be easily heated when the mood swung him. He didn't need much. At that moment, the only thing he wanted was to drown in a bottle of whiskey.

What started as a way to get his head wrapped around Jessica and what to do about the gut-wrenching feelings he had for her turned into a bigger wreck than he had expected. He padded to the liquor cabinet and pulled out a tumbler and the 25-year-old Bushmills he'd bought as a gift for Robert James. The circumstances justified his actions.

He loosened his tie and collar, tossed his jacket onto the back of a chair and, carrying the glass and bottle, made his way to his office. He dropped in his chair and released a long deep breath. He was emotionally shattered. Stephan took the cap off the bottle and poured a generous draught in the tumbler. The plan on his return from the States to erase Jessica from his memory by going out with other women had so backfired.

For the last nineteen years, he had buried himself in an emotional hole— living only for and through work. When he took the job at Brennan Enterprises, his friendship with Conor and Maeve had grown into a camaraderie beyond the workplace and he began to live again, but still refused to dip his feet in the dating pool. He'd decided to stay away from that field and was remaining true to his resolutions. It was the only thing that had kept him sane so far and he wanted to remain so. Meeting Jessica at the rehearsal dinner had thrown his resolutions into a tailspin, and him back to his youth.

He swirled the amber liquid in the crystal glass and brooded, letting images of the day play back in his mind. The hurt in Jessica's eyes as she left him at the restaurant haunted him. He chugged the full-bodied whiskey in a long gulp. The smooth liquid slid down his throat and burned a path of fire that bloomed into warmth in his chest. It was a good burn. He poured himself another to chase the cold and emptiness inside—a coldness that had intensified since the day he'd met Jessica. That innocent offer to drive her home had ballooned into so much more. The whole set of events careened through his mind like a runaway train. He leaned his head back on the chair and his thoughts were hurdled to California and to that day, just as they had done so many times since then.

When Trevor introduced her as Cassandra's best friend and their eyes met for the first time, he was taken aback by the intensity of her gaze. It had been like standing in front of a wrecking ball and receiving the full impact of its blow.

From that moment on, he could feel her eyes lingering on him when nobody was watching. He could almost feel the caress of her gaze on his skin, stripping him from any preconceptions of how a young woman should behave. The truth of the matter was that she aroused him to no end. But it was a road he couldn't allow himself to travel. So, pushing the pro arguments to the farthest corner of his mind, he excused himself and left at the first opportunity.

He felt the burn of her fixed stare on his back and a string of disappointment wrapped around his heart. He couldn't ignore that she had touched him in a way nobody had touched him before. That was all the more reason for him to keep his distance. He had had his share of heartache in the past. He could definitely do without a repeat.

That night, he tossed and turned. His deprived mind swirled with thoughts of her. He pictured what it would be like to be with her, to have her heat surrounding him, tightening around him as she screamed his name in release. He couldn't contain himself, and hers was the name that escaped his lips as he stroked himself toward his own release that night.

The next morning, on the day of the wedding, a duality of feelings swam under his composed surface. Half of him was ashamed for having such thoughts about a woman young enough to be his daughter, reinforcing the fortress around his heart and steeling him against the hammering of her influence during the day. But the other half, the treacherous half, craved, wished, and wanted everything that was Jessica.

The wedding went off without a hitch. Aside from the more covert looks she gave him through the day, his focus was on Trevor and Cassandra, as it should be. It was only after the wedding, when they all stood around saying their goodbyes, that on impulse he offered to drive Jessica home.

Robert turned to her when they were making arrangements to leave. "Ready to go? I'll drop you off."

Before Jessica could respond, Stephan blurted out, "I think you live close to my hotel. Can I offer you a lift?"

She hesitated, leaving him to think that maybe her attention had a different meaning, one he had not identified. "Lift…? Oh…ride, right? Sure." She stumbled over her own words, blushing at the confused look he threw her.

The drive to her home had been made with a few casual words of conversation and tons of electricity passing between them. He parked in front of her townhouse and turned the engine off. He squinted in the bright sunshine reflecting off the hood of the car as he turned to face her and collided with her clear blue eyes focused on him with a mix of curiosity and humor twinkling in them. The air in the car was a livewire of attraction within the confines of the small space. His eyes strayed to her mouth and she parted her lips as if she could feel his gaze caressing the soft skin of her full lips. He wanted to touch them more than he ever wanted anything before.

"Will you walk me to the door?"

He frowned at her comment, since that was something a date would do. It took him a few seconds to organize his thoughts. "Of course."

He climbed out and rounded the car to help her. He then followed her to the front door, keeping a safe distance from her, insulating him from the sensual aura she exuded. It evoked the mating call of yesteryear, leaving him wanting to thrum his fists against his chest to gain her attention and privileges. He shook his head. What the hell was he thinking? He wasn't Tarzan and she sure as hell wasn't Jane. The faster he could deposit her safely indoors and leave, the better off he'd be.

Jessica rummaged through her purse and pulled out her key. Smiling brightly at him, she cocked her head in a graceful feminine way that would knock any man to his knees at her feet. He was no exception. "Thank you for the ride. It was really nice seeing you again. I'm sure we'll be seeing more of each other, now that Cassandra is your pseudo-niece."

The reminder of the age difference wasn't purposeful, but it hit the spot. He shied away. "If you ever come to visit her in Ireland, I guess we will see each other. I don't come to the States often and have no reason to come back to California."

A small cloud billowed across her eyes but quickly dissipated. "Well, then you have to give me the pleasure of enjoying one last drink with you, since I won't be seeing you again until my first visit to Ireland. It might take a while. How about you come in and have a drink or a cup of tea with me? I am curious about Brennan Enterprises and the technology you develop there."

The reference to business caused him to pause. Maybe he misinterpreted the whole thing. Maybe, all this time, she was just curious about the business, the products he helped develop as interim president of the company. He didn't know whether to feel disappointed or relieved. But that gave him an excuse to stay a little longer, soak up more of her, her presence, her scent. To capture images of her in his memory. "My flight leaves tomorrow, so I'm in no rush. I'd be happy to join you and discuss what we do at Brennan."

She unlocked the door and he followed her in. The minute the door closed behind them, the air shifted and became charged like that of an oncoming electrical storm. She turned, and when their eyes locked, it was as if a billion kilowatts had been delivered straight to his cortex. As they stood face to face, wickedness filled her eyes, carrying the promise they had delivered the day before—a promise of caresses along his body that had driven him to a painful arousal.

One minute they were simply staring at each other—her eyes travelled to his *mouth and her tongue moistened her lips as if she could taste him on them. In the next, she pushed him against the wall, wrapped her arms around his neck, her legs around his hips, and captured his mouth in a hard kiss.*

His mind went blank, devoid of any coherent thought but the taste of her, the feel of her against him, the heat of her skin against his. He dug his fingers into her hair, cupped the back of her head, and took control of the kiss. A moan escaped her as she reached between them, fumbling at the buttons of his shirt. Mouths sealed together, they pulled and tugged at clothes, removing layers until skin met skin. She flung her bra over her shoulder and bared her breasts—soft skinned, pink-tipped nipples, engorged with desire for him—to his eyes.

Their frenzy paused for a delicious moment as he took in their beauty and, almost reverently, covered them with his hands. A deep moan vibrated low in her throat. "I want you." Her eloquence triggered another onslaught of urgency. Mouth on mouth, tongues swirling, dancing, her hands touching his chest, cupping his face, combing through his hair. His blood coursed hot and fast in his veins and he felt alive. More alive than he had imagined to be, more alive than he had dreamed.

He grabbed her by her hips and pressed her against him, the bulge in his pants a clear demonstration of what she did to him. Her little moans and sighs with each touch and nip of his teeth drove him beyond any clear thought. He was so close to losing himself in her allure.

And then, she slipped her hand inside his slacks, circling his cock with eager fingers. The shock of her touch snapped him from his dreamy state. He realized how far they had gone, how much damage he had done. He thrust her away from him, keeping her at arm's length. Taking a deep unsteady breath, he leaned back against the wall, heaving and trying to regain control of himself and his thoughts.

"Stephan?" Her desire-laden eyes widened and filled with questions.

"No."

"But—" Her eyes showed the tortured dullness of disbelief.

"No, Jessica. We can't be." His voice was strangled, raw. There was nothing

left to be said. That single sentence said it all.

Pain filled her eyes and his heart by proxy. He grabbed his scattered clothes and slipped into his disheveled shirt as he struggled to open the door. He kept his eyes averted. A single look could have destroyed his determination to leave. Without another glance, he walked out and closed the door behind him. He all but ran to the car, leaving behind the best and worst thing that had ever happened to him.

Stephan downed another gulp of whiskey and set the glass on the side table. He was a dumbass of the biggest kind. He had done wrong by everybody in his need to keep his heart safe. He'd used Terese as a buffer, in hopes of dimming his memories of Jessica, to find solace by taking a safe road, one with no fiery emotions involved. But Jessica's colorful and vivid image couldn't be erased from his mind. In fact, the distance of the last months had enhanced his fantasy. The little taste he'd gotten only left him wanting more of her, like a thirsty man who had been given a sip of water and left to wander parched in the middle of a desert.

The best thing to do was to walk away, let her think the worst of him, hate him if she would, but he couldn't. Stephan knew he was between a rock and a hard place. "Fuck!" He raked his hair with his fingers and, resting his elbows on his knees, dropped his head in his hands.

His mind went through all of the items on his emotional fuck-up list. He had loose ends to tie off with Terese. He had to make it up to her somehow, smooth things for the sake of the friendship they had developed over the last months.

Most of all, he had to find a way to deal with Jessica. First, he had to stop lying to himself. He wanted her. He inhaled a sharp breath at the realization. Was he willing to move forward with it, knowing where it would end? Could he train himself to withstand the blow when it came down to it? All for the opportunity of enjoying her presence and the pleasure of her body? It didn't take him long to understand that he had crossed that line long ago. He would risk it all. He just wasn't sure his heart would survive the impact this time around.

Chapter Thirteen

Rage Inside

IN THE EARLY HOURS OF the spring morning, the streets of St. Petersburg crawled with the commuter crowd. The brisk northern cold air still lingered, forcing people to huddle in their winter coats for a little longer. Puffs of hot breath mingled in busy bus stops as ruddy-cheeked Russians found their way to work.

The café was a bustle of activity as patrons stopped in for a quick morning coffee or roll. It was a luxury still limited to the privileged in a country that had seen many changes in the last twenty years. From deep-rooted socialism to an emerging capitalist market, Russia was growing fast and taking giant footsteps on the playing field.

Yet corruption still reined free and, based on the growing influence of the criminal underground, was not close to coming under control anytime soon. The old country had its homegrown flavor of the mafia. It was spiked with the hardest vodka one could find. Throughout the decades, the government had initiated several projects to handle and control fraud and corruption within its thick walls. Each had failed at some point or another and morphed into the next-best idea.

The new country had become a capitalist version of the old. The gap between the rich and poor had widened, and those left with very little option on how to survive each and every day were easy pickings for the bigger fish.

Nikol Petrovna took a last drag of her cigarette and flicked the butt to the sidewalk. The server clicked his tongue and gave her a disgusted look. She shrugged. It was a nasty habit, one she had struggled to abandon many times in the past. What used to be a two-pack-a-day habit was now down to a stick. Her cravings surged each time she went undercover and she used that one a day as a relaxation moment, time to put her thoughts in check. Considering she had very little time to relax and let her guard down on a regular basis, she'd be damned if she would let anyone spoil her one vice. When she achieved her goal she could quit. All of it. The force and the habit. But until then, she would do what had to be done to keep her sanity.

She lifted her cup in the direction of the server and raised her eyebrows. At her demand, he retrieved the carafe and refilled her cup. She nodded and wrapped her hands around it in an effort to absorb its soothing warmth. The cup was overly hot to the touch, but the burn was better than having icicles for fingers.

Over the rim, she stared at the file spread out before her. Her eyes hardened and her mouth tightened into a grim line. She intently traced the features of the man in the mug shot on the dog-eared page. His features were as familiar to her as her own fingerprints. Very much so. For the last five years she had kept tabs on him. Followed the progression of his features over the years—each new wrinkle, each new crease added to her memory bank.

Rage flooded her insides, fizzing and bubbling like lava. A rage that had burned deep in her soul for a long while. An inferno that had grown over the years since her mother confided her story. It had taken years in the service for Nikol to reach that point, years as an underling, years of careful planning, pain, and abuse among the filthiest underground organizations peppering the country. But now, everything was within her reach. *He was* within her sights. Finally.

She glanced at the crystal face of the Mondavi watch gracing her wrist. "Fuck!" she murmured under her breath.

She would be cutting it close. She flipped the page of the file and grimaced as the deep steel-gray eyes stared back at her. Sergei Deminov was an unexpected complication. She studied his image. It was nothing like him. The mug shot was placid, just a snapshot of a second of the man's life; it did not translate the heinous aura that bled from him. Up close and personal, the six-foot-two Siberian was a force to be reckoned with.

He was also a womanizer—she had seen women fawning over him in nightclubs. Granted, some would consider him handsome with his chiseled cheekbones, broad lips, and tight muscular body sculpted during his many stays at state-run prisons. But she knew better: he was a monster. Her mouth filled with the raw and bitter taste of bile each time his slimy hands touched her. His interest and possessiveness was a surprise even this early in the game. She hated how he often stated that she was the perfect fit for him. That she was as hard and cold-hearted as he was. What scared her most was that he could be right.

So far, she had been able to fend off his sexual advances, but he was becoming more demanding and forceful. That was fine with her, because now that she had him hooked, he would unwittingly help her accomplish her goal faster—he was her ticket into the organization. The reason she had been put through the most grueling hazing those last few weeks. She was determined to pass the initiation and be welcomed into their den even if it meant….

She shook her head, not willing to dwell on those details just yet. Her thoughts bounced to the latest test. Last night's activities had been distasteful, but a necessary evil. Had she failed, she too would be floating in the river, dancing with the fish. She had prevailed, had pulled the trigger with no remorse. The bastard Sergei had taken her to interrogate had been a traitor, and doubly so. A traitor to the organization she was trying to infiltrate and a traitor to the organization she was accountable to.

Anatolii had recognized her while he had huddled on the concrete floor before her, a bloody pulp of a man after the beating and cutting Sergei had delivered. When she had stepped from the shadows to take her turn, she had seen recognition in Anatolii's eyes as they bobbed from her to Sergei and back again. A sly look had invaded his narrowed calculating eyes, a gleam of revenge had filled them as he had squared his shoulders confidently—the scum had been about to rat her out.

Without hesitation, she had pulled the Heckler & Koch from the waistband at her back and swung her arm from behind her, shooting him dead center in the forehead. "Fuck!" Sergei had yelled. The weight of a hard right hook had smashed into her jaw, causing her head to snap back under the impact. She had fallen to the ground, barely conscious, but had steeled herself to face Sergei's anger. "You fucking bitch! We needed him."

Nikol had schooled her features and wiped the blood from her mouth with the back of her hand before pushing herself up from the warehouse floor. She had glared at him maliciously as she casually holstered her gun at her waist. She had wiped her hand against her thigh, defiantly crossed her arms at her chest, and shrugged. "He bored me."

Her tone had been neutral, masking the fury boiling inside her. It had taken a huge amount of control—a control she'd exercised and mastered over the years—to keep her from whipping out her gun again and wiping Sergei from existence.

A gleam of lust had flooded Sergei's cold gray eyes. He had grabbed and jerked her into his arms. It had taken everything in her being not to react to that rough handling. His hands had harshly outlined the curves of her body encased in fatigues and a tight-knit turtleneck before palming her breast and squeezing it hard. He had buried his face at her neck and bit the tender flesh, murmuring, "I love a woman with a masochistic streak as wide as mine."

The memory sent a shudder through Nikol's entire being. His attentions had become more intense with each month she had been around him, but she was willing to put up with it for now. Let him think his actions thrilled her right up until the moment she put a bullet in his head. And she would. There was no question about it.

The blaring honk of a car pulled her back from her dark thoughts and she gathered the files, shoving them into her backpack. Nikol tossed a few notes on the table, pulled the hood of her jacket tight around her, and headed out for her appointment—a briefing with her superiors.

She knew they would hold her accountable for Anatolii's death. At least until right about the time they read her complete report, which was already typed and waiting in her backpack to be handed off. It should be a short meeting.

Traitors and snitches weren't tolerated, especially in post-Cold War Russia. Anatolii had been a first-class weasel responsible for the deaths of two of their best operatives in the past few years. Luckily, she had been able to identify the source of the leaks and take him out without compromising herself.

Walking briskly, Nikol cut through an alley and headed in the direction of the stone building located just a few blocks away on Suvorovsky Prospekt. She hated that building. Had hated it since her first day there. She followed procedure. Made sure she didn't have a tail and then cut through another shadowy alley. One could never be too sure. Sergei was still weary of her and tried to trip her up at every opportunity.

The pungent stench of rotting garbage and sharp tang of urine invaded her nose. The tart aroma didn't bother her anymore. It was life in the city—so different from the small-town farm living of her childhood. She reached a recessed door and glanced around before ducking through it.

The ringing of phones and the loud buzz of conversation assaulted her ears. Unwilling to walk through the maze of cubicles and by the dispatch desk, she fled to the stairwell and jogged up three flights, bursting through the door on the fourth floor. Shoving the hood from her head, Nikol moved through the desk-infested floor with hurried purpose, ignoring the snide remarks tossed her way. Names like "slut" and "bitch" followed in her wake. She didn't care what they thought of her. The means didn't matter. The end did. And she would get to the end she wanted.

When she reached her destination, she turned to the room at large and gave them all a one-finger salute as she entered the conference room.

"Petrovna. Sit." Colonel General Stanislav Olegovich's familiar voice was stern and cold.

On entering the room, she cleared all expression from her face—but that didn't ease the pounding of her heart, which was beating loud in her ears. She unzipped her jacket and shrugged her backpack from her shoulder as she approached the chair positioned in front of the long table behind which three men sat motionless. That routine was getting old. Had she been a man, she wouldn't have been called before the inquisition.

She saluted them and took the appointed seat, setting the backpack at her feet. Back straight and hands folded respectfully in her lap, she waited. The three men were silent.

The Colonel General had his eyes buried in a file and didn't bother diverting his gaze from it on account of her arrival. The second man, senior police officer Eduard Alexandrovich, refused to look her in the eyes, as if by doing so her darkness would contaminate his soul. However, the third, Grigori Maximka, had no such affliction. His eyes bore into her like a laser-guided missile. Nikol squared her shoulders, held his gaze, and sneered. After a while, he averted his gaze. She almost chuckled inside. Wimp.

Nikol glanced at her watch. Time was slipping by and she couldn't— wouldn't—be late for her next meeting. The silence in the room was thick, cut only by the sound of the shuffling papers. She grew weary of waiting. The Colonel General must have sensed her agitation, for he looked up from the papers with profound irritation coloring his stare.

"Explain yourself," the Colonel General frowned at her.

"Sir?"

"The body of Anatolii Svyatoslavovich was pulled from the river early this morning. Informants fingered you and Deminov."

Maximka jumped to his feet, planting his hands on the table as he leaned forward and darted her with his words. "You are not fit for this job. You let a comrade die!"

"Sit down, Grigori." The Colonel General turned his head to her. "Report."

Nikol relaxed her body back against the chair and spoke without remorse. "He was a traitor. The bastard was responsible for the deaths of Taras and Semyon. He compromised their cover. His leaks were the reason they were killed."

"This is ridiculous," senior police officer Alexandrovich scoffed. "He was a stellar detective. An honorable man."

Nikol pinned him with her stare. "Not only did he rob from the mob, but he was about to compromise my own position within the operation to save his neck. He was a greedy bastard. A corrupt one."

She reached into her pack, pulled out her report, and tossed it on the table. "It's all there. I shot him. He was about to seal my death warrant. I couldn't let that happen. My role within the secret service is more important than his life ever was."

Senior police officer Alexandrovich dragged the file to him, glanced over it, and slid it to the Colonel General. Maximka sputtered. "I don't believe you. You are a rogue who needs to be put down. You're a turncoat. You don't work for us. You are cold-blooded killer and the mob's bitch."

A flush crept up Nikol's neck at the accusations flung in her face. With extreme control, she stood, crossed to the table, and splayed her hands on it, leaning until her face was inches from his.

Her voice was low and she smiled smoothly, hiding her rage. "You can call me a cold-blooded killer, but my actions have been for the success of this mission. You are the ones who put me in this position. I walk with death every waking moment, while you sit on your bureaucratic ass in your safe, puny office." She fought her own battle for restraint as Maximka's jaw clenched and eyes narrowed. She leaned in closer until they almost touched nose to nose. She could see the accelerated pulse on his neck and dilated pupils. Fear. *Perfect.* She couldn't stop herself from whispering humorously, "You're soft. You would never last in the world you have assigned me to."

"Take your seat, Petrovna." Nikol's head snapped at the Colonel General's directive and she backed away from the table with hands out before her.

"My deepest regrets, sir." A quirk of a smile appeared at the corner of his mouth and disappeared just as quickly.

She turned to her chair, but, instead of sitting, grabbed her backpack and shrugged it on. "You have my report. It's all there." She eyed them dryly.

"We are not finished with you, Petrovna," Maximka bit out, frustration seeping from his every word.

"Oh, but you are." Her attention focused on the Colonel General. "I'm late for an interview with Mikhailov." A smug expression overtook her face. "We're there, sir. By this evening, I'll be a member of the inner sanctum." Nikol turned on her heel and strode to the door. With her hand on the doorknob, she turned back to the room and saluted her superiors. "It has been a pleasure."

Once back in the hall, she skirted the room and ducked into the stairwell. Flying down the stairs, she burst into the alley and back out onto the busy city streets. She mingled with the passersby as her thoughts focused on the upcoming meeting, wondering what she would be up against. *Let the games begin.*

Chapter Fourteen

Old Connections

CASSANDRA'S THOUGHTS SPUN AS SHE sat at the kitchen counter chewing on the end of the highlighter in her hand. A map of St. Petersburg lay open on the counter, several suitable apartments, hotels, and suites now marked on the grid. They had to finalize their plans regarding the location for their base of operations in Russia.

She looked out the window and soon lost focus as her thoughts pulled inward, marveling at how stressed she was—a new feeling for her. She was compelled to ensure the location they chose was the best choice from a strategic standpoint. If not, considering who they were dealing with, their lives could be endangered—and that was not a risk she was willing to take.

Returning her gaze to the printouts, she ran down the list of apartments and amenities, color-coding them with highlighters based on strict criteria. Once that task was completed, she opened her notebook and checked the to-do list she had created earlier. Next in line: CIA central and her buddies to see if there was a safe house in the vicinity they could use for back up.

Trevor climbed the stairs to the main level, wiping the sweat from his face. He had just spent the last couple of hours completing the workout routine Cassandra had spec'd for him. The workout was grueling, but he enjoyed the results. Catching sight of Cassandra in the same position he had left her in—at the counter with printouts spread all over the place—he observed that the frown of concentration marring her face had grown deeper.

"How's it going? Any luck?" Popping a quick kiss on her lips, he walked by her to the refrigerator for a glass of water.

She looked up from her papers. "Have some possible good choices for apartments. I'll list the ones I feel are the best options so we can look them over later."

"Whatever you see as the best choice is my choice. You're the expert strategist here, remember? I'm just the geek." He grinned and Cassandra chuckled as he quenched his thirst in big gulps. "Any news on the visas?"

She nodded and proceeded automatically with her military-style report. Another ingrained reaction. Cassandra had been raised, by her father, an ex-Navy Seal, under strict military code, and would quite possibly never lose the stiff habits developed during her upbringing; but Trevor was sure as hell doing his best to change that.

"Our passports should be here by tomorrow."

He approached her from behind, spun her around on the stool to face him, and kissed her deeply. When he broke from the kiss, she frowned. "What was that for?"

"Just wanted to know what military speak tasted like," he chuckled, releasing her abruptly and walking swiftly toward the stairs. He was in dire need of a shower and he knew it. "You're welcome to join me in the shower if you like, milady," he smiled wickedly at her as he jogged up.

Cassandra's head reeled from his kiss. She shook it, grinning at the sound of him thumping up the stairs. His unexpected kiss had left her mouth dry. No way would she be joining him. She knew fully well where that would lead, and she had phone calls to make. Phone calls she preferred to make on her own. She had a backup plan in mind that she needed to set in motion, but for that she would require Nathan's help. Cassandra gathered the printouts, her notebook, and a glass of iced tea, and carried everything upstairs to the office.

As she passed the bedroom, she heard Trevor whistling in the shower. Another grin spread across her face only to fade as an image of him wet and slick flashed before her eyes. Heat crept up her neck and she pressed the cool glass to her cheek, hoping to ease the need.

Back at her desk, Cassandra logged in and stared at the screen, searching for the nerve to reach out to her old friend Nathan Nelson. He still hadn't accepted the fact that her heart belonged to Trevor, and their contact had been spotty at most since the day of the wedding. Cassandra knew he was keeping tabs on her based on conversations she had had with her father, but still she hoped at some point he would move on. *Just freaking bite the bullet!* She took a deep breath to center herself and opened a chat window. His status was set to offline so she typed a quick message.

Hey, Nate. Let me know when you can pop in. Ears if possible. I have a huge favor to ask.

The response was immediate. His status turned online and a call request popped up on the screen. She accepted promptly.

"Cass," Nathan's deep voice came over the speaker, startling her.

"Hey. Damn, that was quick. I wasn't expecting you so soon."

"I just walked in and caught your message. What's the favor? Need a plane ticket home? Tired of the Blarney Stone?"

Damn. Straight to the chase. "Nathan." He must have gotten the hint when she used his full name in a chastising tone instead of the casual nickname she used to call him.

"Shit." He exhaled a deep breath. "What do you need, Cass?"

"Okay, Nate. I'll make this quick. Trevor and I have to travel to St. Petersburg—"

"What the hell are you going to Russia for?" Nathan's voice lowered, "What is he up to now, Cassie?"

"We have a business opportunity we can't pass up, Nate."

"So where do I come in?" His tone simmered with unvoiced anger.

Cassandra swallowed hard. She really needed his resources and knew she had to tread lightly. "You, of all people, know how I always like to be prepared in case something goes south. I just need a backup plan in case foreign businessmen become targets for any reason while we're there. Can you help me?"

"Fuck, Cassie. I don't like this one bit. First Paris, now Russia? What kind of business is he dragging you into that you need a contingency plan? Last time you were shot. If anything happens to you this time… he's dead," he bit out.

"Nathan. Stop that shit! All I need to know is if you can you help me. I need access to a safe house in the area. Inactive. No host."

Nathan grew silent and, after another dragged-out intake of air, began clacking on his keyboard. She pictured him scrolling through databases searching for the right real estate. The silence was unnerving to her. "Do you have something?"

His fingers paused and returned to drumming on the keys several times before he spoke again. "There is a location. A farmhouse outside of St. Petersburg. The host was transferred to South Africa and they haven't found a replacement."

He gave her the address and coordinates, which she immediately cross-referenced with the accommodation options she'd listed earlier. The dots were connecting nicely.

"What are the access protocols for the house?"

The creak of his chair reached her ears. "Damn it, Cass. I could get nailed for this."

"We'll probably never use it. It'll just be reassuring to know it's there." Desperate to do everything in her power to keep them safe, she played her trump card: "You owe me."

Silence filled both rooms. She imagined that he, too, was recalling that afternoon, some years back, when she'd saved his pretty ass. "Give me this and we're even."

"Hell. This is your lucky day. Consider it done. I am doing this for you. Not for him. Hear me?" he spit out snidely. "I'll email you the security codes tomorrow. And Cass, *don't* make me regret this."

Cassandra was slightly taken aback by the viciousness of his response. She loved him like a brother and the tear in their friendship was an ache in her heart. She had hoped that they would be able to patch things up, but more and more it looked like that wasn't about to happen any time soon. "I'll keep an eye out for the email. I assume it will be encrypted?"

Before he could answer, the squeak of door hinges and someone stepping into his office flowed over the speakers, followed by silence when the call was abruptly disconnected.

Cassandra stared at the chat window and sighed heavily when his status turned to offline again. All she could do was wait and hope he would follow through.

She closed the window and turned in her chair to find Trevor leaning against the door frame with narrowed eyes. "What the hell was that about? What does the Hulk want? He has no right to speak to you like that, Cassie."

Her mouth quirked at the nickname. "I called him to find out about available safe houses in or near St. Petersburg. He's emailing me the access code for one we can use."

Trevor's hands itched when he had heard Nelson's voice over the speakers. It irked him that Cassandra still made overtures to the bastard. Nelson made his feelings for Cassandra clear when he had declined the invitation to their wedding. Trevor knew he still harbored feelings for her and hovered like a vulture waiting for their marriage to fail.

Trevor moved to his desk and sat. "What else? That was a lot of talk just for access codes." He hated coming off boorish, but couldn't help himself.

Cassandra must have noticed the tone right away, but instead of being upset about it, the corners of her mouth twitched with humor. "Jealous much?"

"What do you expect? The guy is like a dog with a bone. It's been almost eight months since our wedding. When will he give up? I know he hasn't given up on you. Hell, I've witnessed it firsthand." Trevor couldn't believe the jealousy that flowed through him like a freight train. He knew she was his, but the fact Nelson was still sniffing around pissed him off. Royally.

Cassandra's smile grew wider. "Trevor, you are being, as you call, an '*ee-jit*.'" She stood and climbed into his lap. His arms automatically wrapped around her waist as she pressed her lips possessively against his and combed her hands through his hair. "I love it when you get all Alpha Geek on me."

Trevor captured her mouth again in a deep kiss and moaned as her tongue rubbed against his. A moment later, she whispered breathlessly, pressing her forehead to his, "We can't…otherwise nothing will ever get done. We have stuff to do."

"You sure have more self-control than I do," Trevor sighed as she scooted off his lap and returned to her chair. A twinge of satisfaction appeased him, seeing the glazed look of desire in her eyes. *Definitely mine*, he thought, turning to his screen.

Messages from George had arrived overnight and Trevor hoped he had good news regarding the taps he'd placed on Vladimir Mikhailov. He planned to spend the day reviewing the background checks and reports he already had at hand and reacquainting himself with the Russian's operation. Once they had a good handle on his infrastructure, it would be easier to determine the infiltration procedure.

Trevor preferred to get in and out of their servers remotely and not risk their necks—Cassandra's neck—needlessly. But if the server was a standalone, then the only way to erase any possible hint of the software from it was to physically infiltrate the location and zap the server with a data destruction tool or worm. Excitement filled him at prospect of the task ahead and he grinned widely at his wild streak.

Cassandra must have caught the grin and understood the reason for it. "Ah, hell. I can see the Techboy's gears turning."

Trevor glanced at her. "Oh yeah. I am so going to enjoy leaving them a little gift—servers that can be used as doorstops."

Trevor's grin took her breath away—all boyish and sexy at the same time—and his excitement beat at her, bringing a smile to her face. But, with all his enthusiasm, apprehension at the prospect of an on-site physical infiltration gnawed at her.

So many things could go wrong. A dropped connection, changes in the target's routine, an unforeseen alarm or alert system. Cassandra sucked in and exhaled a deep breath to ease some of the tension building in her gut. *Well, that's what backup plans are for.* She picked up her notebook and ran through her to-do list again. Damn. Guns! She sat back in her chair and chewed on the tip of her pen as she weighed their options. "Babe, think weapons."

Trevor's fingers paused on the keyboard and he looked at her across the desks. "Okay. Thinking weapons. Would rather think geek, but thinking weapons." He wiggled his eyebrows. "Are we talking light sabers? I want red."

Cassandra shot him a serious look. "Sorry. No can do. There's been high demand for them. All sabers are out of stock. I tried hiring Obi-Wan to build you one, but he's booked solid. Convention schedule is hell on his Force."

Trevor burst out laughing and shook his head at her cheeky grin.

"Seriously, though. We can't take weapons with us. But we should have something when we are there just in case." Cassandra turned back to her computer. "Damn. I should have discussed weapons with Nate." Trevor began muttering up a storm—she heard something that sounded like *"Eejit"* escape his mouth at her mention of Nathan's name and she chuckled.

With the safe house address in hand, Cassandra traced escape routes back to the few locations left on her list. Those had been reduced to just a small number by then; within minutes, she zeroed in on the location that provided them with the best possible outcome in an Escape & Evade scenario—E&E as it's called in the CIA.

Without hesitation, she filled out and sent the tenancy agreement as well as credit card information to book the place. They still had the second-best option available as back up, but she hoped to get the one she had her sights on. At that moment, a thought hit her. "I just remembered something. I think Bob has a friend in St. Petersburg who also runs a security agency. Let me check to see if maybe he can help us."

After a quick glance at the clock, she reached for her cell. "I think I can catch him before he leaves for the office." She put the phone to her ear and leaned back against her chair.

On the third ring, Robert's voice flowed over the connection. "Hello?"

"Hi, Dad."

"Cassandra! Everything okay?"

"Yes, Sir. Everything is perfect."

"Is everything okay with Trevor?"

"Trevor? Yes, he's good."

"Did you get the picture?"

"Yes, I got the picture—but I have a bone to pick with you on that one when we can talk longer…"

He peppered her with questions. "Have you received the wine I sent?"

"No, the wine hasn't arrived yet."

And still the questions kept pouring in. "Dad—" she burst out laughing when he continued with his drilling. She tried to get his attention again,

"Dad!"

"What?"

When he settled, she added, "I need a favor."

"What kind of favor?" His tone was cautious.

"Trevor and I have a business meeting in St. Petersburg."

"Russia?"

"Yes, Sir. Russia." He flooded her with new questions to which she gave quick replies. "No, Sir. We should be okay. That's why I'm calling. Does your friend Boris Kostas still run his security agency there? No Sir, we don't need a security detail. But…do you think he can set us up with a few Glocks and Sigs or something similar plus ammo?"

"That's my daughter. The apple doesn't fall far from the tree."

Amusement and pride surged through her when Robert praised her fast thinking and preparedness. "Well, you're the one who always told me to be prepared for anything."

"Let me get a hold of him. It'll give me an excuse to talk with him. It's been awhile since the Old Russian Hound and I talked, but I don't think it'll be a problem."

She nodded at Trevor and smiled, adding, "Okay. I'll email you the deets. We're on a tight schedule, so I'll need to know by tomorrow."

"I'll contact him as soon as I get it. Oh and Cassie? Tell Trevor 'Hi' for me—and that if anything happens to you again, I am coming for him."

"Thanks, Dad." A snort of laughter broke loose and Trevor glanced her way. Grinning at him she responded, "I'll let him know." After a brief hesitation, she added, "Love you."

Silence settled over the connection before he responded, "I love you too, Cassandra."

"Bye, Dad."

As she set the phone down, she could feel the weight of Trevor's eyes drilling into her. "Well?"

"He said he'll get a hold of him. He hasn't talked to Boris in quite a while and this will give him an excuse to talk with him. He doesn't think it'll be a problem. I'll email him the address in St. Petersburg as soon as we have a firm location."

"Anything else? You seemed awfully amused by something he said."

She smiled. "No. He said to tell you hi and to keep an eye out for the wine." She stifled a chuckle at her father's words. No need to worry him needlessly about Robert gunning for him. They would get the job done without a hitch. With the weapons issue dealt with, she moved on to flight schedules.

Trevor watched his wife return her attention to the screen as if nothing had happened, but he knew there was something left unsaid. Her little smirk spoke more than words and he was positive that she was playing with him. With a shrug he let it go, but began planning what sort of persuasion tactics he would use to extract the hidden details from her. *Later.*

During her time with the CIA, Cassandra had been one of the top strategists and, with her ability to read facial expressions, a real asset to her team. Her psychology background gave her an added edge, allowing her to analyze the targets as well. His woman had many talents for sure. Trevor knew she worked all angles in her head, planned for any possible scenarios. He also knew she missed the thrill of the field, the adrenaline rush coursing through her veins, and the satisfaction of a task completed.

That she had joined him on his personal quest was icing on the cake for both of them. He thought back to the past summer, meticulously calculating the odds of the circumstances that had brought them together. He was definitely a lucky man. Trevor shook his head in wonder and focused his efforts on the minute details he could extract from the reports he'd reviewed, while Cassandra tackled the preparations for the trip with free rein to run with what she saw fit.

Mikhailov's connections and importance within the Russian Mafia were clear. But something didn't sit right. Thieves-in-Law, or Vory as they were called in Russia, had been prominent in Russian society since the early 1900s. Their power had been declining with the larger influence of capitalism in Russia and as better educated criminals found other lucrative ventures, namely digital fraud. However, for some reason, Mikhailov's group seemed to be flourishing and gaining notoriety. The more Trevor read, the more it became apparent something was definitely up.

The fact that Mikhailov still ran free was an indication that the NSA still didn't have a clear, full picture of his activities; otherwise they would've been all over him like a wet rag. Trevor could smell something foul.

The sound of the Imperial March and Cassandra's snort cut through his concentration. "Damn, that cracks me up every time, Trevor."

"What? It's perfect!" Trevor chuckled. "I'll get it."

He headed downstairs and opened the door to find a courier standing on the stoop with a brown envelope in his hands. "Mr. Bauer?"

Trevor smiled back and nodded, "Yep. That would be me."

The courier collected his signature, handed him the envelope, and took off. Trevor checked the sender's name as he made his way back to the office.

"Who was it?" Cassandra called out.

"The passports are here," he commented, handing her the envelope.

"Wow! They pushed those through faster than I expected!" Cassandra pulled the documents from the envelope and efficiently checked each visa, making sure all was in order. She looked up with a wide grin on her lips. "Damn. I love it when a plan comes together. As soon as I can get our location confirmed we're all set. We can leave anytime. I'll let Jessie know later."

"I assume that means we can now book our flights?"

"Yes."

Trevor could tell he'd already lost her to flight plans and itineraries. He loved the "I will conquer the world" expression that overtook her as her thoughts turned deep and gears cranked in her head. He was sure whatever she had planned for them would meticulously fit their needs when the time came.

"Back to work I go." His words fell on deaf ears. She waved him off and he returned his attention to the transcripts. The more he could learn from them before they left the better. He also needed to compile a small list of the critical equipment they would need to take with them on the trip. Aside from their laptops, which were a given, a small directional microphone and other surveillance equipment would be required. His little list included a serial keypad hacker, a little electronic tool kit, small Maglite flashlights, and other small odd pieces of equipment only he could appreciate.

He made a mental note to retrieve them from the storage room before Jessica returned from apartment hunting. He threw a quick glance at Cassandra. She was deep in her notes. A heavy frown creased her brow. "Let me know if you need my help with anything. You know—bouncing ideas, any input, body massages." He waited to catch her reaction to his little tease. The quirk at the corner of her mouth was a telltale sign she was paying attention to his rant. "Ha! Gotcha."

She chuckled. "Incorrigible and bored, I take it?"

"Well. Trying to lighten up the mood a bit. Most days I have enough dark thoughts for both of us, *a ghrá*. I prefer when you don't have a deep frown like you've been wearing for a while now."

"Just getting things done." Cassandra's matter-of-fact tone didn't fool him.

Trevor knew she was calculating every single move they would make in Russia. "You know you can't control every minute or action while things are developing, right?"

She sighed and turned her eyes from the screen, staring into his with disconcerting intensity. "I know, love. Don't worry. I just want to make sure we're both safe."

Sneaking a peek at him, she could see the tension etched in his face, matching the concern in his voice. The man took more risks than a Navy Seal when he was on the hunt, and she had to be on her toes. The sound of an incoming email drew her attention. Quickly clicking on the application, she saw the email confirmation for the small studio apartment she had booked.

"Hey! We just received confirmation on the apartment." A satisfied grin spread on her face. "Well, a studio really. But it's perfect. Wi-Fi internet access, located on a main drag, close to two metros and—" she flashed a grin, "—it has a supermarket next door." She took a small breath before continuing with her dissertation on the place. "It's pricey, but well worth it for the location."

"Secure?"

"Very. We'll receive the entry codes via email no later than tomorrow."

"So, now you're booking the flights?" His excitement was like a child's at a playground.

"Yes, I am. You can pack your toys now." With a grin, Cassandra toggled to the travel site she had bookmarked and finalized the bookings. She also sent Robert an email with the address so he could pass the information to Boris. A satisfied sigh filled the room as she sat back. Just a few more items to check off her list and they were off to Russia.

★ ★ ★ ★ ★

Stephan's hand hesitated briefly before he picked up the phone and pressed the sequence of numbers he'd memorized. He had reached a decision on how to handle things. It was time to face the music. The call rang five times—five of the longest rings of his life—and, for a moment, he thought it would go unanswered.

"Hello?" The transition from ring to the greeting that followed filled him with anticipation.

"It's me."

"Stephan?"

"We need to talk." He was straight and to the point.

"What do you want to talk about?"

"Not over the phone. I'd like us to meet."

Silence stretched until the feminine voice asked, "When and where?"

"Brazen Head. Tomorrow at eight?"

"I can be there," she said softly.

"I will see you then."

"Good night, Stephan."

"Good night." Stephan disconnected the call and leaned his head back against the leather seat. That was a decision that couldn't be put off any longer. He had stalled long enough and hoped the outcome would be a mutual understanding.

One day. Just one more day to get this weight off my shoulders. "Fuck!" he breathed out harshly.

Chapter Fifteen

The Race

"D O YOU HAVE EVERYTHING YOU need?" Trevor asked as Cassandra came down the stairs. Standing in the foyer beside their luggage, he took mental note of the equipment they were taking with them—all easily justifiable as business-related and tied to their cover as data recovery specialists interested in expansion to Russia, a hot market for their services.

Cassandra gave him a droll look and he bantered, "Okay, I get it. Note to self. Never ask Cassie if she has everything she needs when she's the one who planned the trip to the last microscopic detail."

She laughed. "Damn right! And just as a clarification, yes: I have everything we both need." Shaking her head, she retrieved her laptop case and handbag from the entry table. As she was about to head to the front door, the sound of Jessica's light tread running down the stairs stopped her in her tracks.

Jessica reached the bottom and launched herself at Cassandra. "Hold up! You can't leave without giving me hug!"

Cassandra was filled with amusement. "You mean one more hug. You've been saying goodbyes since I told you last night about the trip to Russia. I bet the hugs are just a cover. You really can't wait to get rid of us so that you can have the place to yourself."

"The hugs are real. But I have to say with you both gone, I just might finally be able to get some uninterrupted sleep!"

Cassandra's hearty laughter filled the room. "Sorry about that. I...ah... sometimes I can't contain myself."

"Sometimes? I might have to upload your household's soundtrack to the internet one of these days. Oh my god, I can just imagine the number of hits it would get. The newest rage touted on all internet news channels."

"You wouldn't dare!"

"Just kidding!"

Cassandra scrutinized her friend and noticed that her smile didn't quite reach her eyes. "Jessie, are you really okay with us taking off like this? I know it's short notice, but it's an opportunity we can't pass up."

"Definitely. It'll give me a flavor of what it's like to have my own place in Dublin," Jessica reassured her.

"Are *you* okay?" No other words were needed. They both knew to what Cassandra was referring.

Jessica smiled and hugged her again. "Yes and yes! Get on with you or you'll miss your flight."

Holding Jessica's hand, Cassandra stepped back hesitantly. "You have our numbers. If anything happens, you need to talk, vent, scream, you call me, hear me? You can also catch me on chat after we're settled."

Her friend burst out laughing. "I'll be fine. I swear. Everything's great.

I'll be checking out some of those apartments we found in the paper. No worries. I also have the paperwork you piled on me to keep me busy."

Trevor walked back into the house. "Okay, all loaded. Ready to go, a *ghrá?*" he asked as he pulled Jessica into a big hug. "Be good, lass. If you need anything, call Stephan. He'll be able to help you out."

Jessica and Cassandra glanced at each other at Trevor's mention of Stephan. She let the comment slide.

He took Cassandra's hand in his and led her through the door to the car. Cassandra cast one last worried look and waved at Jessica, calling out, "Love you. We'll be in touch. Remember what I said!"

"Yes, mom," Jessica joked, but the smile dimmed in her eyes as she waved them off.

Cassandra watched her walk in and close the door as Trevor merged into the late afternoon traffic. Jessica's reaction to Terese was not proportional to her nonchalant description of what existed between her and Stephan. Cassandra knew Jessica would come clean about what really was going on between the two of them when she was ready. Until then, short of beating it out of her, she would have to wait patiently for the whole of it, just like Jessica waited for her own disclosure about her feelings for Trevor.

★ ★ ★ ★ ★

The house was eerily quiet as Jessica closed the door behind her and walked upstairs to the homey and welcoming guest room. As much as she loved being around Cassandra, and as welcome as Cassandra and Trevor made her feel, Jessica knew she was intruding on the newlyweds' bliss.

Cassandra had helped her search through apartment listings and narrow the list to a few in neighborhoods that Trevor had said to be brilliant. Jessica smiled at the use of the word. Definitely not one heard stateside, and definitely not in California. Her plan, while her friends were away, was to find her own digs.

Once she'd secured her new place, she would focus on her personal dilemma. The reason she was in Dublin in the first place. Should she persist in reaching out to Stephan? That question kept prodding her since her arrival in Ireland. When she had made the decision to cross the pond and test the waters with Stephan, she knew it would be hard, but she never expected the obstacle in her path to be her age.

Could that really have been the reason he'd run like a bat out of hell from her house that evening? She knew there was something special between them, knew that he was not indifferent to her, even though he was holding her at arm's length.

Her heart twisted in her chest and a chill raked up her spine when her thoughts turned to that afternoon in the restaurant. He had voiced his opinion about her behavior then. It had even appalled her. Could she change his opinion? Granted, she had been snarky, but didn't they say all is fair in love and war?

She froze as that thought penetrated her self-awareness. Did she love him? Really, really love him? Jessica's heart beat erratically, her breathing rushed in and out of her in hard pulls. Lightheaded, she sank to the edge of the bed and hung her head between her knees. She wanted him. That was a given. Just thinking of him warmed her inside. She craved his hands on her breasts, the feel of his weight pressing her against silky sheets, his velvety hardness buried inside her.

She fell back on the bed and started at the ceiling. Seeing him again proved that she wanted more. She wanted to share the little things with him—grocery shopping, laundry, bad days at work, laughter. She wanted to confide her innermost thoughts to him and have the same in return. That was no crush. It was something bigger, deeper. That was growing into a much larger ball of wax.

If she decided to pursue his attention, was she ready for the heartache if things didn't turn out the way she wanted? The words she had spoken to Cassandra months ago came back to haunt her. *Go with the flow. Do not overthink it. Let your hair down and enjoy the moment, it will be what it will be. You don't want to miss out on a good thing. What if he's the one? If you don't try, you'll never know. Search your heart. Take a chance.*

Isn't that what she had been doing? That and many other questions populated her mind as she moved off the bed to head out. She grabbed her purse and gathered her jacket from the chair. As she did so, a card fell on the floor.

Jessica picked it up and turned it over—Sean. The image of the gorgeous Irishman she had met at the airport brought a smile to her face. She tucked the card in her wallet as she made her way downstairs. Apartments were waiting to be viewed. Stephan would have to wait till later.

★ ★ ★ ★ ★

Silence lingered in the car until Trevor's questioning glance cut through the haze of her thoughts. "I'm worried about Jessica."

Trevor took her hand in his and squeezed it. "She'll be fine. She's one tough cookie. Probably just off balance from the move." As if knowing she needed something else to occupy her mind, he changed the subject. "So…did you get the codes from Nelson?"

She turned in her seat and watched Trevor as he drove. She loved watching his eyes tracking everything in front and behind him. Always vigilant. Always aware. She felt a ripple of mirth knowing the reaction he would have to her next comment. "Yes. The Hulk delivered on his promise."

Trevor shot her a glance and all but growled, "Cassie…."

She burst out laughing. Catching her breath, she wiped tears of laughter from her eyes as she continued, "Anyway. To answer your question, yes, I have the codes. The house is located in Vyborg, a thirteenth-century city about two hours by train from St. Petersburg. Basically, once we're settled my plan is to secure one-way train tickets that can be used on any given day. Just in case…." Unconsciously, her brow furrowed as her mind systematically ran through the E&E checklist.

"Cassie?"

"Huh?"

"Lost you there, Cassie girl."

"Sorry. Was just going over everything in my head again." She gave herself a mental shake. "Oh, Bob emailed late last night and said the meeting with Kostas is set for some time next week. He'll contact us to let us know exactly when he'll be stopping by to bring us a housewarming gift." She tossed a saucy grin his way. "Hopefully some nice toys."

"I'm sure you have everything worked out in that brilliant mind of yours. Looking forward to the toys. It's always a big turn on seeing you armed and dangerous. Totally hot," he grinned back at her in devilish amusement.

They cleared security without issues. Their passports were heavily stamped with visas from many countries, proof of business dealings abroad and added credibility to their excursion to Russia.

The business lounge offered comfort and amenities as they waited to board their flight. Trevor had his laptop open in seconds flat after they took their seats. "George sent me new transcripts. Got them while you were packing. Haven't had time to review them yet."

Cassandra glanced at him as she opened her own laptop. "Just let me know if you find anything I should be aware of."

Trevor reached out and touched her face. "Do you have a headache, or is that frown caused by the speed of your thoughts crashing inside your skull?"

She laughed and shook her head. "Only you would come back with such a question. I am fine, really. Just crashing thoughts, as you put it." Indeed, her thoughts were crashing—around Jessica. If she didn't know better, she'd swear that her friend had fallen for Stephan in a bad way. She hadn't mentioned it directly, but Cassandra had a gut instinct about it. She could read the signs, having lived that denial herself.

When their flight was called, they gathered their things and proceeded to the gate. As Cassandra led the way, Trevor observed her confident posture and the energy around her. She mesmerized him. She had since the day she walked into the NSA fuming and ready to take him down. Trevor smiled at the memory as he followed her onto the plane. He stowed their carry-ons and took his seat beside her for the long trip ahead of them.

They'd spent the whole week gathering the latest intelligence on Mikhailov and had learned enough of his mode of operation and digital fraud activities to have a good idea of how he intended to use the decrypter—a scary thought all on its own.

He leaned back in his seat and watched Cassandra looking out the small window at the landscape as they finally began taxiing. As usual, she appeared calm and collected. Yet he sensed that little familiar turbulence below the surface. He knew better. She was the duck that you see floating serenely on the water but whose little feet were paddling furiously out of sight.

During operations, he knew her mind kept going miles a minute, calculating, weighing, measuring, even when she had already planned everything to the last detail. He smiled softly at the memory of many other times they'd worked the leads on his parents' disappearance and he'd seen that same focus and determination on her face. Each and every time, Cassandra had behaved exactly the same way—unsettled. And each time made him love her more, if that were even possible.

His eyes caressed her figure and lingered on her shoulder where she sported a souvenir from their last brush with death. She had another from her stunt with the CIA—an op gone bad, but it was the one on her shoulder that had the power to bring him to his knees—a gift from a psychopathic killer, and one that had been intended for him. Inhaling deeply, Trevor worried that they were headed straight into a rockier situation in Russia. He quickly dismissed that dark thought. Focus on the positive. That had always been his motto.

He reached for her hand as the plane accelerated for lift off. At his touch, she turned to face him, a smile finally curving her full lips. When the seatbelt lights went off, he lifted the arm that kept them apart, allowing Cassandra to snuggle closer, lean against him, and tuck her face in the hollow of his neck.

"I gather you don't want to work right now, either?"

"Nope. Too comfy. Just want to stay right here like this."

Trevor draped his arm around her shoulders, bringing her closer. He rested his head back on the seat and closed his eyes, just enjoying the moment. But his thoughts bounced to the last set of transcripts George had sent them. They still had to establish the course of action they would need to take based on visual surveillance of the location where Mikhailov's developers worked and where his servers were housed. They would handle that once they were settled.

They were so close to achieving their goal he could almost taste it. It was a race against the clock, and they were both determined to win.

Chapter Sixteen

Surrender

THURSDAY NIGHTS WEREN'T AS BUSY as Fridays and weekends at Stephan's favorite pub. The busy place transformed into an intimate environment, more suitable for the private conversation that was about to take place. Stephan stepped toward the back of the great room and selected the farthest table from the door. It was cozy, secluded, and away from the noisy bar.

He sat facing the entrance. He wanted to see her when she walked in. Although the last few days had somewhat solidified things in his mind, he was still unsure of the outcome of this little talk—things were sure to take a turn that night, regardless of the outcome.

The waitress popped in at his table for the second time, asking if he wanted something to drink. He waved her off again. He didn't want a drink. He wanted his mind clear when the conversation took place.

Impatient, he flicked his wrist and looked at the time. Five past eight. *Is she going to stand me up?* His brows creased at the thought, but, as his eyes were drawn to the entrance, his insides twisted in knots. *She* had arrived.

She stepped further into the pub and, in that very moment, he knew he had made the right decision. Stephan watched her eyes casing the room, searching for him. When they collided with his, his heart rate accelerated, his breathing became deeper, and his groin tightened. A smile swept across her face and the ingrained confidence that had drawn him to her sparked in her eyes. He was doomed and he was fairly certain she knew it. The public place had been a smart choice and would ensure they dotted the i's and crossed the t's without succumbing to the deep pit of attraction their proximity created each and every time.

His gaze held hers as she crossed the room toward him. There was an inherent sensual quality to her walk that affected him like a well-aimed arrow, straight through his being.

He stood and pulled out a chair for her as she closed the distance between them. Before taking the chair, without a second of hesitation, she placed a kiss on the corner of his mouth. That simple gesture sent his pulse careening and left him momentarily speechless.

Once she was seated, he reclaimed his chair across from her. Their eyes locked and the air buzzed with electricity with that one look.

After a charged moment, she broke the silence. "Hello, Stephan. I have to admit, I was surprised to get your call. I never thought you would even keep my card after the incident with Terese. So…what's this all about?"

Stephan studied Jessica, traced the line of her delicate neck, the curve of her lips with his eyes. She parted her lips as if his visual caress was somehow palpable to her. Just as she had done before.

There was no more denying that he wanted her. Stephan couldn't fight the need to be around her, with her. He couldn't avoid something that had already happened—his surrender to the emotions she dug from deep inside him.

"I wanted to apologize for my behavior the other day at lunch."

Jessica sighed heavily and sat back in her chair. "You're not the only one who should apologize. I reacted badly to the whole incident with Terese. Your lack of introduction between us, the red cape she waved in front of me loud and clear. You were right. I did behave childishly. Hopefully I didn't cause any problems between you. That was never my intention."

He frowned. *Is she dismissing me?* "No. What I mean is, Terese and I… we had an understanding." Talking about Terese with Jessica felt wrong somehow. But if they were to move forward, he needed to clear the air.

Jessica raised an eyebrow at his choice of words. "Understanding? What type of understanding?" Then a knowing look covered her features. "Oh. Is that what they call it here?"

"Call *it*?"

"You know, 'friends with benefits.'" Jessica used her fingers to reinforce the quotations around the words.

Stephan smiled, catching the implication, but the glint in his eyes showed he wasn't quite light-hearted about it. "Yes. Terese and I agreed to see each other on those terms."

A shadow of a frown briefly marred her brow and then disappeared as she schooled her features. "Why am I here?"

Stephan leaned over the table and took her hand in his, holding tight when she tried to pull back. Her breath hitched at his touch. He caressed her soft skin on the back of her hand with his thumb, and held her gaze. "I think you know why, Jessica. We've been trapped in this journey since the moment I left your house last year. It was only a matter of time before we encountered each other again. Isn't that why you're here in Dublin? Here with me now?"

Her eyes darkened. "I made no secret about my feeling for you, Stephan."

"I know. You said so."

"Enlighten me. Honestly, I'm not sure what you want from me. What are you trying to say?"

"Fuck, Jessica!" Stephan raked his fingers through his hair. "You know damn well I want you, too."

Jessica's eyes latched on to his and searched them. "Are you saying what I think you are?"

"Before we go any further, I want to establish a few guidelines." To him they were more like rules of engagement.

"Guidelines? Such as?"

"We need to agree that when it ends, we will part ways as amicably—as Terese and I did."

"You ended things with Terese?" Jessica's eyes widened.

"I don't date multiple women simultaneously, Jessica."

A smile spread on her face. "I guess that's a good thing. I don't share well, either." Her smile dimmed slightly when understanding set in. "Ah. You want us to be 'friends with benefits.'"

Adrenaline shot through Jessica's veins and her pulse raced out of control. When she stepped into the Brazen Head, she had expected the worst after his curt phone call. Her heart had ached for days after her encounter with Terese and his dismissal. Her pulse continued to race as she considered his words carefully. He was just trading partners. To him it was just sex. He wasn't offering more. Definitely not what she wanted from him.

"Do you have any questions or anything to add?"

Jessica managed to reply through stiff lips, "Why would you have a termination clause for something that hasn't even begun?"

"We both know that's not true, Jessica." He held her gaze and a flash of electricity speared her, proving his point. "I've been battling my reaction to you since the first time I set eyes on you."

"If that's the case, why did you run? Why did you leave that night? Why the distance these last few days? I've all but thrown myself at you!"

"Let's be honest here. There's a huge age gap between us. Terese thought I was your uncle for chrissakes."

"That's bullshit. Terese saw your interest in me and mine in you. Women have a sixth sense—a radar in our brain that clues us in on these things. She considers you to be hers. You may think you were only friends, but she definitely wanted more. She wanted to embarrass me in front of you. Obviously, by your reaction, it worked. It was a well-executed maneuver, I might add."

"If that was the case, then she was truly misguided. I never led her to believe there was anything more between us. That's beside the point. How old are you? Twenty-six? Seven? I am old enough to be your father."

"You're wrong. You're just right for me." Jessica's mind spun out of control and she needed a moment to gather her thoughts. Being so close to him wasn't helping matters. She looked around and asked, "Where's the ladies' room?"

Stephan paused as if trying to decide whether or not to let her go. He then took a deep breath and pointed. "That hall to the left."

She placed her napkin on the table, avoiding his gaze. She wasn't sure her eyes wouldn't give her inner emotions away. Stephan rose and helped her out of her chair. "I'll be right back."

Jessica felt the weight of Stephan's stare on her back as she walked away. It was a heated and longing caress that made her skin tingle. In the empty restroom, she leaned her hands on the sink and stared in the mirror. Her heart banged so hard against her chest that she thought she'd need a defibrillator soon.

Jessica absorbed the implications of Stephan's words. Here was what she wanted—him. But she wanted so much more. As far as she was concerned, he was her endgame. And now her goal was partially within her reach. Should she accept his offer? Would it be enough for her?

I can't breathe! Jessica ducked her head and splashed cool water on her cheeks. She patted her face dry and looked in the mirror, seeing her decision reflected in it. Tossing the towel, she took a deep breath and headed out to join him again.

Stephan rose to his feet and pulled her chair out for her once more.

Seated, she composed her features and looked him in the eye.

"I agree to your terms. For as long as you'll have me," Jessica added.

Stephan closed his eyes and smiled softly, savoring the sound of her words. *If only they were true.* He knew from experience that eventually she would grow restless, want much more than he could give her, and then she, herself, would walk away from him. But he had made peace with that. The last few days had forced him to rethink his old convictions. He would no longer deny himself what little he could have.

He wanted her. He had lusted over her for months and, since her arrival, it had become painfully obvious to him that she had snared him good and proper. For the sake of his sanity, he had to set a limit in his mind. Maybe exposing himself to massive doses of her would help him build some resistance, sate the thirst that threatened to consume him.

But lusting and loving were two different things. "I need to be sure you understand that when I say it's over, it's over."

A glimmer of hurt filled her eyes but she covered it up with a smile. It took all of his strength not to call it off there and then.

"I understand." She paused briefly and added, "And accept your terms. But you have to remember it is a two way street and accept it if *I* decide to end our agreement."

Stephan squeezed his eyes shut as relief and pain stabbed him simultaneously. Pain at knowing that at some point she would want to end it. He opened them and his gaze collided with hers. There he found the same desire, the same need that had been pooling inside him since the day he first laid eyes on her.

He stood abruptly and offered her his hand. "Let's get out of here."

Jessica stood with him and placed her hand in his, reveling in the feel of his skin against hers as they walked out of the pub. She followed him, blind to her surroundings, her pulse loud in her ears, her heart jumping for joy in her chest.

She almost had to run to keep up with his long strides, but the smile never left her face. She was heaving by the time they reached his car from the surge of anticipation that flooded her with every step. Her stomach was in knots as he opened the door of the elegant sedan and helped her in before taking his place behind the wheel.

Stephan appeared as calm and confident as ever. The only thing betraying his emotions was the slight tremble of his hands and the sight of his clenched jaw as he turned the engine. Jessica kept her eyes glued on his profile, allowing her gaze to trace the straight line of his nose, his chiseled chin, and strong arms hidden under his well-cut suit. She had touched the skin under the rich fabric before and her fingers itched to do so again.

The drive was short and charged with an expectant energy that flowed between them. She grinned when Stephan pulled up in front of an elegant Victorian house similar to Trevor and Cassandra's. She should have known he would live in a house and not a glass-and-steel box.

Stephan rounded the car to help her out, and the gesture brought back the images from the other time he had done the same, back in California. The gentle touch of his hand on her lower back was laden with promise. Her breathing accelerated at the recall of his palms cupping her breasts and the reverent look on his face. Jessica wanted him to look at her like that again. She wanted his hands and mouth all over her body. She couldn't wait to do the same with his.

Stephan turned the soft lighting on before he closed the door behind them. Jessica absorbed her surroundings. That house was so like him— conservative but comfortable. Sturdy wood furniture and warm colors painted an interesting picture, one she hoped to explore more closely as they spent time together. She hoped to uncover clues as to what made him put restrictions on their relationship.

It was the tone of his voice that gave her hope. The hesitant tone in which he had delivered his restrictions left her doubting whether he really meant them. It was almost as if he was trying to set the limits in his own mind, set the limits for himself. Drawing a line in the sand regarding how far he would take it before he pulled away.

Despite respecting his wishes and understanding that a relationship could only be carried forward if both parties put in the same emotional investment, his limits only served to intrigue and entice her more. A challenge. Jessica would show him how wrong he was, drive him to the brink, make him break his own rules, and compel him to dismiss the boundaries he, himself, had established.

Her stomach churned as he closed the distance between them. She felt the heat of his body as he stood behind her. His breathing deepened and each expelled breath feathered hot across her shoulder, bringing shivers to her skin. She swayed back against him and he groaned at the first contact. Leaning down, he traced the column of her neck with his lips and nipped her earlobe.

A shrill of desire coursed through her. "Stephan…." She turned to look up into his face, and the heat she found in his eyes fanned the flames burning in hers.

"I want to savor this, Jessica. Slow this time. No rush."

His words wrapped around her chest and squeezed tight. Each poignant syllable pulled at her insides and sent a twinge through her entire body. She held his gaze and nodded. "Me too."

His hand slid down her arm and clasped hers. He guided her up the stairs, turning the lights on as they walked into a large bedroom suite. The warm, masculine, solid furniture was also present there. A massive king-size bed dominated the sparsely decorated room. He drew her to the edge of the bed and, cupping her face, pressed his lips to hers.

Heaven. His mouth on hers felt like heaven. The initially chaste kiss gradually intensified into a heated dance of swooping tongues and nipping teeth, ragged breathing the only sound heard in the room as they tried to control the wild fire burning between them.

For the second time, her fingers struggled with his buttons, but this time there was no frenzy. She savored the moment as he had said, taking it slow. Once she opened his shirt and cuffs, she smoothed her hands under his shirt over the skin of his stomach and chest, pushing the fabric off his shoulders until it slipped past his arms to the floor. Her eyes travelled over his bare chest, following the trail of soft hair down his abdomen to the waist of his slacks. Heat flooded her cheeks at the sight of the bulge straining against his pants.

Stephan tipped her chin up and locked eyes with her for an interminable moment. She leaned forward and, maintaining eye contact, pressed her lips to his chest seductively.

"Don't do this," Stephan whispered harshly.

"Don't do what?"

"Eat me alive with your eyes."

She chuckled softly. "Is that what I'm doing? Eating you with my eyes?"

"That's what it feels like. I can almost feel you touching me."

"Welcome to the club. I have always felt the touch of your eyes on me."

"I want you to feel much more than my eyes on you," he rasped as he began unbuttoning her blouse. Soon, it joined his shirt on the floor. His eyes trailed the outline of her lacy bra with fiery intensity before he commanded in a hoarse tone, "Take it off."

Without hesitation, she unclasped the front of her bra. When the silky lace parted, baring her breasts, he reached out with unsteady hands and slid the bra straps from her shoulders and down her arms. Stephan indulged in the lovely sight before him. Her skin creamy, her nipples erect and puckered from the sensual tension coursing between them. That alone almost brought him to his knees, and sent a surge of blood straight to his aching cock.

His gaze caressed her exposed skin, tracing the curve of her breasts and the valley between them. "Beautiful. Just as I remember. Just as I've dreamed of." He reached and pulled her closer. "This time I want more."

They bared themselves to each other, each removed layer was one step closer to the complete intimacy they sought, and once all clothing had been discarded, he drew her into his arms. He held her snug against him and groaned at the contact of skin against skin, her beautiful breasts against his chest, pebbled nipples scraping his skin, driving him mad.

Jessica absorbed all that was Stephan. Her eyes soaked in the defined abs, the taut skin. The dusting of hair she had followed to his waistband before now travelled south and surrounded his erect cock. The knowledge she was the reason for his quite impressive arousal set off an intense warmth low in her stomach.

His hands slid to her ass, cupping it and lifting her higher. "Wrap your legs around my waist." She complied and a moan burst from her lips when he leaned down and took a turgid nipple between his teeth, gently rolling it with his tongue before sucking it deep into his mouth.

Another gasp escaped her and she gripped the back of his neck, holding him to her as he sucked on it in long, lingering pulls. One of his hands splayed at her back, pressing her closer so he could take his fill. He kissed a trail across to the other and gave it the same attention, swirling his tongue around her areola and circling her nipple with his teeth.

Stephan's hands reverently cupped her breasts, pressing them closer together, and with a moan, his tongue and teeth alternated between each— grazing, teasing, and pulling on the sweet hard puckered buds with little nips. A deep moan escaped Jessica's lips. Her body pulsed in little jerks with each little tug of his teeth. A wet heat bloomed between her legs and her inner walls contracted at the worshipful look he gave her.

Lowering her onto the bed, he raised himself on all fours, hovering over her, watching her with hooded eyes. "You are beautiful."

The desire in his eyes fanned the fire burning low inside her. She needed him filling her, thrusting inside her. The urgency that had plagued her months before returned in full. They would have time for foreplay once they had quenched that thirst parching her throat and lips. "Take me."

Stephan groaned and swept down, taking her mouth in a hungry kiss. He slid his hand firmly over her ribcage and hips and further down between her welcoming thighs, moaning into her mouth at what he found there. "So wet for me."

"For you. Only you," she breathed in a husky whisper.

Perspiration beaded on his skin with the effort to contain himself from taking everything he wanted from her. His cock twitched, begging to dive into her heat. In a moment of clarity, Stephan pulled back from the kiss and reached into the box on the nightstand. He kneeled between her creamy thighs and tore at the foil packet. His hands shook as if he was a teenager on his first encounter.

Jessica covered and stilled his hands with hers. With a soft smile she took the packet from him. "Here. Let me."

Stephan's heart jumped in his chest and his muscles tightened when she unwrapped the condom with steadier hands and positioned the thin sheath over the crown of his cock. Circling her fingers around his girth, Jessica unrolled it down along its length. When he was fully encased to the root, she lay back and extended her arms to him in invitation, one he couldn't refuse.

He shifted his weight and settled between her legs again, locking eyes with her. She responded to his unspoken question with a confident gaze and he surrendered to her siren call. In a smooth, slow move, he plunged deep inside her, to the hilt. Their breaths hitched and a soft gasp spilled from Jessica's parted lips as their bodies melded together.

Stephan held still and rested his forehead against hers as her arms snaked around his back. She shifted her hips and Stephan pushed forward with a moan, pressing his weight against her, pinning her down, speaking through clenched teeth. "Don't move. Give me a second. I want this to last and I am too close to the edge."

Jessica had waited too long to finally have a taste, a true taste, of him. Her body ignited at his words, sending a burning heat straight to her clit, tugging at her inner muscles, which pulsed along his length.

Stephan moaned and surged deeper. "Jessica!" he groaned as she met his thrust, arching her body into his. She was gorgeous: the sheen of sweat glistening in the dim glow of the lights, the blush of color flowing from her neck to her cheeks, the tight rosy buds of her nipples taunting him to taste more of her.

He dipped his head and pulled one of the tempting tips into his mouth, sucking it deep in tandem with his thrusts. Jessica's head fell back, pressing against the bed. She lifted her hips and ground tight against his groin as her hands moved to her breasts, cupping and lifting them. "Oh, Stephan—" she gasped out in a long breathless moan. "I'm so close! Don't stop!"

Jessica sobbed under the pressure building inside her. She was divided between the need to reach her release and the need to relish more of him. Pressing her foot to the bed, she rolled them and inverted their positions, forcing him onto his back. As she straddled him, his hand gripped her hips and guided her back over his rigid erection. Their groans filled the room as she impaled herself on him. At the deep penetration, a spear of pleasure jagged its way across her.

Jessica bowed her back and leveraged her weight on her knees and hands, initiating a sensual dance, pulling from him then descending again, impaling herself to the hilt. Her heart thrummed in her chest as Stephan's thumb covered her clit, pressing and rubbing against it.

She's tight. Oh, God. So tight. Stephan's heart raced out of control with each ripple, each squeeze of her sheath around his cock. Her breasts bounced as she rode him, each sway of the rounded pink-tipped mounds robbed the breath from his lungs. He raised his torso from the bed and wrapped his arms around her waist, latching his mouth to a sweet nipple. He sucked and pulled at it with his teeth while her body rocked against him in undulating waves.

Stephan brought her down to him and captured her mouth with his in a hot, wet, tongue-thrusting kiss. Holding her tightly against his chest, he pumped his hips in a rapid succession of thrusts, flesh against flesh.

"I'm coming!"

"Yes! Do it for me." His command was rewarded with her release. The quakes of her orgasm around his cock propelled him into his own. He came crashing into a mind-blowing climax while she rode him to the brink of reality, fisting and milking him to the last drop.

Her orgasm descended upon her in hot waves, flowed through her, and dropped her boneless and spent on top of him.

She lost track of how long they stayed entwined in each other's arms, still joined. It was much more than she had expected. *He* was much more than she had expected. His hands caressed her lower back in circular movements, bringing ripples of desire to the surface again. She was not alone. His cock twitched to life inside her once, twice.

"Already?" Mirth colored her tone as she lifted her head from his chest to face him.

He had the most relaxed expression she'd ever seen, and a smile quirked his lips.

"We *have* wasted a lot of time. Lots to catch up on."

"I'm so with you on that one."

A deep laugh echoed in the room as he rolled them again, setting her on her back and breaking their connection.

"Hey! I thought we were catching up."

"We are," he grinned, reaching for the box on the nightstand again, pulling out another condom.

"Ah." She smiled, anticipating another mind-blowing orgasm in the near future. She was fast becoming addicted to him. *Definitely addicted.*

"This time, exploring the benefits of foreplay is in order, something I regretfully ignored the first time around." There was a trace of laughter in his voice.

"By all means, explore away," she quipped.

Sheathing himself again, he crawled back and locked eyes with her. "As you wish." His voice broke with huskiness as he slid down to the juncture of her thighs.

"Stephan—"

Chapter Seventeen

Venice of the North

U PON THEIR ARRIVAL IN ST. Petersburg, they collected the rental vehicle at the airport and made their way to the apartment overlooking one of the many canals in the beautiful Russian city. St. Petersburg wasn't called Venice of the North without reason. Its beautiful architecture and imposing monuments were a feast for the eyes. Cassandra admired the view from their car while Trevor juggled traffic with the expert help of his GPS.

Once they unloaded the car, Trevor helped Cassandra with setting up their little base of operations.

"You mentioned there's a store nearby?"

"Yep. I marked it on the map I printed before we left. It's tucked in the front pocket of your laptop case."

He retrieved it and took a minute to look it over. "We need some basic staples for the morning. I'm going to get some things before it gets too late. Are you okay here?"

"Yes, sir." She made fun of his stern tone. "By the time you get back we should be up and running. Just remember the most important thing on your list."

"How can I forget your fuel? Besides, I want to survive this job in one piece."

"Trevor Joseph! I am not that bad without my morning coffee."

He pulled her into his arms and dropped a peck on her lips. "Not bad at all."

Cassandra chuckled and waved him off. "Just go, you oaf." Her laughter followed him as he left the apartment.

Standing by the window, Cassandra kept her eyes on the street below and watched as Trevor strode toward the store. The warm sunset rays glowed through the window. Any other time, she would have enjoyed sharing the view of the canal with Trevor, sipping a nice wine, whispering naughty promises in his ear.

She could see it so clearly in her head: the sunlight caressing the sharp angles of Trevor's face, enhancing the deep ocean blue of his eyes, touching his cheeks and lips as it faded behind the buildings; the crimson shimmer of the wine glass in his hand as he lifted it to his lips, softly kissing the rim as he drank from it. The sensuality of the scene pulled at her insides.

She would enjoy the view of him, follow the lines of his trim, muscular body, love the way his navy blue shirt matched the color of his eyes, fitting him just right. His legs, encased in slacks, would be a feast for her eyes as they hugged his thighs and tightened across his ass as he moved.

She shook her head to clear the fantasy. It dawned on her that with each passing day his hold on her heart grew tighter and tighter. Turning from the sunset now hidden behind the buildings, she found Trevor leaning against the doorframe, watching her closely.

"Trevor! You startled me. Didn't hear you come in!" Noticing his hands were empty, she shot him a questioning look. "Did you pick up anything at the market?"

"They are on the counter. I called out to you when I got back but you didn't reply, so I came looking for you." With a lift of his chin, he pointed at the window. "What caught your fancy out there? Sneaking a peek into an apartment across the street?" A wicked glint sparkled in his eyes.

The heat of a blush crept up her neck and flooded her cheeks. *Busted.* In an effort to compose herself, she walked to the laptop and turned it on. "Nothing really, I was just thinking about the case."

"Hmm." Closing the distance between them, he traced the blush along her cheek and down her neck with the back of his fingers. "I can see that it was nothing," he grinned before kissing her softly on the lips. "Care to share?"

"Share what? My to-do list?" She turned her attention to the laptop's screen, feigning innocence. Her heart was a wild drum in her ears as Trevor stepped up behind her. The weight of his hands dropped on her shoulders. His lips touched just behind her ear and trailed kisses along the curve of her neck, leaving a dusting of goose bumps in their wake. His hand brushed down the side of her body and around her ribs to cup her breast.

A soft moan slipped from her lips as he pulled her back snug against him. She all but melted into him as he licked a path back up from her shoulder to her neck, sucked her earlobe into his mouth, and licked along the shell of her ear.

"God, Cassie, I need you," he whispered, his hot breath tickling her ear.

Her stomach clenched and her insides pulsed at his words and she shift-ed, turning into him. Her lips hovered close to his but, as they were about to kiss again, the sound of an incoming message echoed in the room.

"Fuck!" Trevor whispered harshly.

"Damn it," she breathed longingly against his cheek at the same time.

"It's George. He has the worst timing ever!" Trevor complained. "I'm seriously rethinking our agreement to help him with Jennifer."

"Yes. Something to be considered," Cassandra laughed softly before kissing him hard on the lips. She took the chair at the table, pulled the laptop closer, and toggled to the chat window.

Are you there? Hellooooo!

Trevor came up behind Cassandra and watched as she initiated a conversation with George.

Here. What's up?

George replied instantly. *Have you already started the recon?*

Trevor shook his head at George's impatience. "Tell him we'll be starting recon tomorrow."

Trevor paused as she typed his response. When she reached the end of the comment he continued as she typed.

"I am also going to attempt infiltration from outside again. See if I'm lucky this time and can find a way in without having to put my ass on the line. Ask him if he has the location under watch."

Cassie fingers did a quick step across the keys, posing his question.

All under watch, guys. Steady stream of people at all hours. Sending you more satellite footage and the latest transcripts of the calls made and received by Mikhailov's phones as well as emails. Will be in contact once I get more for you.

His response brought a satisfied grin to Trevor's face. George was precise and attentive to detail. If there was something to be found, he would definitely find it.

George's contact, while brief, had taken long enough to interrupt the magic that had built between him and Cassandra earlier. Attention was diverted irrevocably to the task at hand and the job ahead.

Trevor took stock of the apartment. The small living room had a tiny dining table and a desk, which Cassandra had set up as workstations before he had gone out. Since she had laid claim to the table—by the look of her files already organized on it— he took the desk where she'd set him up and hunkered down to business.

He opened a shell connection and conducted a search for an access point into Mikhailov's servers. That initial attempt would be the least intrusive as possible. Even if someone analyzed the firewall logs, it would show as a port scan—not worthy of a red flag.

There were many possible sources of vulnerabilities in any system. The key was to find the easiest and fastest way in. Trevor knew there was little hope that Mikhailov wasn't wise enough to have his servers severed from the outside world. With his involvement in digital fraud came the knowledge about the many ways hackers found their way into a network. He would have secured his own by now. He performed a Network Enumeration, the first step to an external penetration test using the series of Internet Protocol numbers listed on file for Mikhailov's servers. Those IP addresses worked as home addresses on the internet; they identified a connection exactly as a house was identified by a street name and number. He stared at the network discovery with the knowledge that he would eventually hit a brick wall. *It would be stupid to have some of the best hackers in the world on your payroll and not secure your own network properly.*

Testing the connection to see if it was live, he made sure he stayed under the radar of an intrusion detection system by randomizing the test. Cassandra, knowing him well, left him alone as he dove deeper into the network. He found a live IP and initiated a trace route—a very tedious process, but it would identify any possible way in as well as which computers were accessible within the network.

His mind swirled through the several options he had available at that point. Triggering a quick vulnerability analysis, he scanned the network for open ports and for the list of applications running on any of the network's computers to compare with available vulnerability lists. A good system administrator would know to patch all holes and follow all security guidelines. He was sure Mikhailov had hired the best, but he had nothing to lose by trying.

Even a fully patched operating system could become vulnerable if one of the many installed applications was not properly updated. Hoping to take advantage of any pitfalls in the system, Trevor inputted command after command, fingers flying over the keyboard, to reach his target. Using a less-known exploit, he finally gained access to the remote system. "Oh yeah!"

Cassandra looked up at him with a smile on her face. "I knew it wouldn't take you long."

"I'm not there yet. I'm not sure if this is the network where the decrypter is stored. If it is, then he needs to hire a new sysadmin," he scoffed as he continued his search.

Installing tools on the system to enable remote control, it didn't take Trevor long to gain full access to one of the machines. Using the list of files names provided by Paul Faber, he initiated a full network scan looking for them. Although he knew the chances of getting a hit on any was slim, disappointment bloomed in his chest when the scan turned up zip. *Fuck!* His blood always pumped faster whenever he was heavy into infiltrations.

Frustration punched him hard in the face. Trevor cracked his knuckles. It only meant one thing: Mikhailov's servers were disconnected from that network, severed from outside access. Hackers called them standalone boxes—a server which had limited access and was directly connected to a few desktops, sometimes with only one main access point, and no access to the web.

The only way to reach the server was through physical access to one of the connected computers. "It looks like the Lion's den it is." He spoke softly, but Cassandra must have heard him because the expression on her face was in tune with his—filled with determination and stubbornness. *She was meant to be mine.* "We need to figure out how to get in."

"What do you have in mind?" she promptly asked.

"No clue right now. I'm sure they are armed to the teeth and their security system is guaranteed to be top of the line. We're going to need to be inventive on this one, *a ghrá.*"

Cassandra raised an eyebrow. "Trevor?"

"Nah. Don't fret. Nothing too crazy." He turned around in his chair, sporting a frown and tapping his lip with a finger as thoughts circled wildly in his head. "Do me a favor, will you? Try to find out how Mikhailov hires his developers and hackers."

Her eyebrows shot up. "What the hell are you planning this time, Trevor?" A twinge of concern colored her voice.

"I think I know exactly how I'm going to gain access to their server."

"I have seen that spark in your eyes before, Mister. Spill!" Cassie ordered him with a stern tone.

Trevor shook his head and turned up his smile a notch. "George said there's a steady stream of people in and out of the house. Could mean they have shifts, which in turn could mean they are always in need of good developers and hackers." Trevor paused, watching her digest the information.

"Trevor Bauer, hacker for hire?" Her tone was almost incredulous.

"Well, you'll need to find me a better name," he joked.

Cassandra's eyes opened wide as understanding flooded them, and he knew she had landed on the same page.

"Yep. I'm going in the easy way. Through the front door."

Chapter Eighteen

Exit Strategy

THE SOUNDS OF LIFE STIRRING in the apartment complex—a door slamming, little feet running, and moms calling out to their children—pulled Cassandra from sleep. It took her a moment to register her surroundings and the fact that she and Trevor were not at home in their own bed.

Stretching like a well-rested cat, she felt a slight twinge along her spine, reminding her that long hours spent in front of the computer was a body killer. Making a mental note to step away from the computer more often, she reached over and flicked Trevor softly on the nose. "Wake up, sleepy-head. Time to get to work!"

She turned on her side and leaned over him, kissing him gently on the lips as his head turned her way. His sleep-glazed eyes opened slowly and a smile glinted in them as awareness set in.

"Good morning!" she greeted him as his arms reached around and pulled her into a tight embrace.

"Good morning, *caoimh-leannán*." His brogue became heavier as he called her "sweetheart" in Gaelic. It sent shivers coursing under her skin. He dropped a kiss on her lips and yawned. "What time is it?"

Relaxing against him, she rested her head on his shoulder and lazily glanced at the crystal face of her watch. "It's almost seven-thirty. We need to get moving. We have a lot of prep to get done."

He tightened his arms around her in a hug, took a deep breath, and slowly expelled it. "Yes, *a bhean*. No rest for the wicked. Just give me a sec to clear my head."

Smiling softly at being called "wife," Cassandra turned her face into his shoulder and placed a kiss there, giving him the time he asked for. Time to recoup after the long hours he had put in since their boots hit the ground in Russia. Cradled in his arms, she watched the rise and fall of his chest, listened to the morning bustle of taxis and buses driving along Fontanka, the street just outside their window. St. Petersburg was a busy city and they were smack in the thick of it.

As Trevor drifted in and out of sleep, Cassandra began to grow antsy. Unable to relax any longer and anxious to get started, she kissed his cheek and slipped quietly from the bed.

Stepping out of the shower, she ran through a mental checklist, reviewing what they needed to do that day. She had left the cameras' battery packs to charge overnight. The ball was in Trevor's court to set up their transmitters and receiver. She splayed her hands on the sink and her head dropped forward as she tried to contain the anxiety churning in her gut. The understanding that Trevor would soon be knee-deep in hell rushed over her. It didn't sit well that she would be on the sidelines, unable to have his back up close and personal or help if something went south. All she would be able to do would be to sit back and listen. Be his eyes and ears.

Pushing those thoughts to the back of her mind, she padded back to the bedroom. Careful not to disturb him, Cassandra watched Trevor for a brief moment as he continued to doze. Last night she had fallen exhausted into bed, but he had stayed up, combing through the information George had provided.

All she could remember was glancing at the clock when the bed dipped and his arms wrapped around her. It had been around three in the morning when he had pulled her back against his chilled body, tucking his face in the curve of her neck before he had dropped off to sleep. *I'll give him fifteen more minutes,* she decided as she pulled on a pair of low-cut jeans and one of Trevor's button-down shirts.

Standing by her makeshift desk, she booted the computer and checked for new emails from George and Jessica, but there was nothing there.

The sound of rustling covers drew her attention. She turned and leaned her hip back against the table, watching as Trevor dropped his legs over the side of the bed and scrubbed his face with his hands.

Disappointment clouded his face when he spotted her. "You're already showered and dressed."

"Have you seen how small the damn thing is?" she countered. "There is no way my ass is sticking out while you hog the water."

"I'd have kept you warm, Cassie." His voice dropped in tone and his brogue thickened as a wicked glint filled his eyes.

"Yeah, yeah. You, my love, are a shower hog and we both know it."

Laughing, Trevor tossed back the covers and rose, heading to the washroom. The view he offered as he walked away brought back recent memories of another morning not too long ago when he afforded her the same nice view of his delicious ass.

He was still a wonder to her. Thanking the fates that brought them together, she headed to the kitchen and snorted, remembering a line from a movie: "Java, java, java." Coffee was definitely in order.

As the coffee brewed and the kettle heated for Trevor's tea, she returned to her laptop and began running through a series of checks to see what systems, aside from CCTV, were out there that she could tap. Once they had a sense of Mikhailov and his henchmen's routines and had captured some still images for facial recognition, they would be able to track them through the cameras located around the city.

When the shower cut off, Cassandra headed back to the kitchen and poured Trevor's tea along with her coffee. She turned when she heard the slap of his feet on the tile and almost dropped the cup at the sight of his lean, muscular hips encased in a towel. Not the typical-sized bath towel from back home, but a much smaller one. The skin of his thigh and the hint of other promises took her breath away. "Should I get you a camera, Cassie girl?"

"What?" she asked, slightly dazed.

"That way you can carry it with you everywhere you go."

"What?" She looked up at him and caught the gleam in his eyes. His words finally sank in. "Shit, Trevor, get dressed."

His face glowed with humor as he took the cup from her hand. "Here, let me take that. Can't have the wife burning herself."

She rolled her eyes and grabbed her coffee before following him back into the studio area. She settled back at her laptop and concentrated hard on keeping her eyes on the screen while listening to the rustle of clothing as Trevor dressed. Within minutes, out of her peripheral vision, she saw him walking barefooted her way.

Damn. I really love that look on him. She was definitely not giving him that tidbit of information. The joking and teasing would never end.

"Good morning, again." Trevor dropped a kiss on the top of her head before walking over to the desk. He set his cup beside the computer and booted it up. "So, where are we?" His eyes were riveted on his screen

"I've just started my tour of St. Petersburg through their CCTV cameras."

"Do we have good quality imagery of the house?"

She shook her head. "No, we'll need to plant the cameras as soon as possible if we're to get those pretty mugs for ID purposes."

"I plan to take a quick trip later at night. Do we have all of the equipment ready?"

Cassandra gave him the eyes—eyes that said, *Really? You need to ask?* He raised his hands in defense. "I know, I know. You always quadruple check everything.

She was barely able to keep the laughter from her voice. "I guess you're forgiven."

He logged on to the satellite imaging system—a feat accomplished with a few well-placed backdoors—and patted himself on the back.

"What the hell was that about?"

Seeing the amusement in Cassandra's eyes, Trevor laughed. "A geek affliction. It's usually accompanied by a 'Damn, I'm good.'"

Cassandra snorted and he shrugged, returning his attention to the screen. High walls hid the large well-kept grounds from view to any outsider. Zooming in closer on the surrounding area, he took note of the locations he wanted to plant the surveillance cameras for the best frontal view of the house.

They needed to get this job rolling before Mikhailov found a way to finish the decrypter. That thought was first and foremost in their minds. If finished, they wouldn't be able to stop him from wreaking havoc with the powerful tool he would have under his control. All the blame would fall on Mark Devlin, the client, and MDS, his company, once the source of the decrypter was traced back to them. A nightmare in the making.

Having spent most of the night reading through the latest transcripts and monitoring the house for more details, Trevor was confident they were on the right track to accomplishing their goal—even with the added complication of having to infiltrate the organization physically. He pushed from the desk and walked over to the equipment case. He picked up the cameras and hooked up the battery packs. Placing them at the selected locations was the only thing left on their surveillance checklist.

Setting aside the exact number of cameras needed for that night's excursion, Trevor double checked each by switching them on and adding their individual signal to the receiver for a quick test. Cassandra had been thorough, as always. She had already set the range to the correct distance between Mikhailov's house and their own little pad.

Connecting the receiver to his laptop, Trevor verified that the cameras were live and working. Once he had cleared that up, he attacked more mundane activities—checked his email and reported the latest developments to Devlin to keep him informed and out of their hair.

Cassandra pushed from her desk and stretched her back. "Time for some recon of the area. We need to get those tickets taken care of."

"Good timing. I need some fresh air," Trevor grinned at her as they gathered their jackets and headed out the door. Taking her hand in his, they walked out of the building onto the sidewalk facing the river.

The nearby metro station was a short walk from the apartment. They made their way there at a casual pace, enjoying the sun and the brisk cool breeze blowing from the canal. At the station, Trevor purchased the tickets, communicating with the cashier in fluent Russian.

"How many languages do you know?" Cassandra asked him as they exited the station.

"I have a thing for tongues." Trevor's expression was serious, but the humorous glint in his eyes betrayed him.

"Don't I know it," Cassandra's laughter sang in the air.

A couple head-over-heels in love on a romantic getaway in St. Petersburg. Anybody watching them would reach the same conclusion. It did help that they were indeed in love—that part was no pretense. But instead of viewing the area as tourists would, they both took mental notes of their route, the places around them that could be useful exit points, and distances to and from the metro stations. It gave them a visual to go with the details of the contingency plan they would be reviewing later.

"We should have the debriefing after the cameras are placed so that we both know what the alternate plan and the exit strategy are," he said softly, for Cassandra's ears only.

She nodded and responded in the same quiet tone, "I have it all ready for you."

"For us," he corrected her.

"Yes…for us. And we are having the debriefing *before* you head out. Not after."

Noticing the determination in Cassandra's eyes, Trevor acquiesced. "Yes, ma'am."

At his poor imitation of a Texan accent, she shoved him jokingly, then wrapped her arm around his waist as they set course to their home away from home.

★ ★ ★ ★ ★

"I am starved," Cassie commented as she assembled generous ham-and-cheese sandwiches for both of them. Taking their plates, they sat at their desks and returned to the task of reviewing the operations' details. The satellite imagery had provided them with the in-and-out pattern of the people frequenting Mikhailov's mansion. Some parked their nondescript cars as far from the enormous house as possible and walked the distance to the front gate. Others drove flashy sport cars and parked them directly out front, or were given access through the gates. An interesting observation of the working class and the high society mafia comingling in the same house.

They just needed the close-up surveillance for some handy pictures to ID the faces of the pawns in the game. Once they had a list of names, Trevor could have George tap into their communications. Soon the whole paint-by-numbers picture would be completed. Then, and only then, could they move forward with the infiltration plan.

With Trevor sitting beside her, Cassandra pulled up the details gathered for the debriefing. "Are you ready, Freddy?"

"Sure thing, Cassie girl. Better to get it done now, as you said."

"I'd rather you know it before going out, as a precaution."

Used to the debriefing procedures, she jumped right in. "Here's the rundown. The safe house is located in Vyborg, close to the border of Finland—a plus if we need to leave the country in an E&E. It's about two hours by train from St. Petersburg. Damn, if we were here for pleasure I would have suggested we visit. Bucket-listed it. Anyway—"

She pushed her hair from face impatiently while looking at the metro map displayed on her laptop monitor. "I actually have two exit scenarios. One uses the Blue Metro Line called Parnas, and the other the Red Metro Line called Devyatkino."

No longer feeling Trevor's presence at her shoulder, she glanced around the room and found him back working at his computer. "Oiy!" she called, and whistled to get his attention.

Startled, Trevor's head shot up and he rubbed his ear. "Damn, Cassie. Could you have whistled any louder?"

"Eyes on me, Trev. I know you feel you're invincible and we've never had to fall to plan B, but we have come close on a couple of occasions." She narrowed her eyes. "There is always a first."

He raised his hands and headed over to her. "Okay, okay! I'm all ears… hands…tongue…?"

Cassandra rolled her eyes, not falling for his boyish charm. She was very serious when it came to his safety.

"I was listening!" Trevor exclaimed, catching her frown.

Cassandra sighed deeply and returned her concentration to her monitor, mentally visualizing the routes as she described them to Trevor. "First route, the Blue Line. Wherever we might be, we need to make it to the Blue Line section of the metro, which ends in Parnas. If something happens and you are here at the studio, use the Metro Station in Sennaya Square."

She caught his eye. "That's the one we bought the tickets from, remember?"

"Yes, *a ghrá*," Trevor answered quickly, leaning over her shoulder and pointing at the map on her screen. "That station has three metro entrances—Sennaya Ploshad, Sasskaya, and Sadovaya."

She grinned up at him. "I should've known you'd make note of all of them. Once you come to the end of the line, take the bus to Vyborg. If you need to get off the metro sooner, count the stations to Udelnaya."

"Why count stations?" Trevor asked in a snarky tone.

Cassandra rolled her eyes and her mouth quirked with humor. "Don't remind me. I know, I know. Just another picture in that camera you have for a brain."

"I knew it! You think I'm a genius!" His laugh was deep, warm, and rich.

"Damn, could your head swell any bigger?" she murmured, concentrating on the map and tracing the route on the screen. "Get off there." Cassandra tapped on the RR Udelnaya stop. "Once off the metro, all you need to do is catch the train to Vyborg." She dragged her finger across the screen and rested on the Red Line. "The same holds true for this route, except it ends in Devyatkino. From there you can take the same bus. Your other option is to get off at the Finlandsky and catch the train to Vyborg from there."

She retrieved the two sets of tickets from the desk and turned in her chair to face him. "Tickets for each of the lines," she said, raising the two bundles in each hand. "Each set includes a metro, bus, and train ticket. I have my own." She pulled hers from her back pocket showing him. "You know the drill, but I am still going to say it. Keep these babies on you at all times." She watched him shove the tickets in his back pocket and her heart skipped a beat while she mentally crossed her fingers. *I hope we won't need them…ever.*

With the debriefing behind them, Trevor concentrated on the placement of the cameras. Cassandra's expression was closed as she watched him grab a backpack from the equipment case and place the small wireless cameras and relay transmitter inside it.

"Do we have zip-ties?"

She reached into the desk drawer and pulled out a clear plastic bag of black zip-ties. He raised a brow and smiled at her organization as he continued the task, adding a small tool kit and the magnetic strips to the mix, along with the ties. He tested the backpack's weight and whistled softly. "Amazing technology. Hardly weighs anything."

"Yeah…for the price we paid for those puppies they better be lightweight. More importantly, they better work," she chimed in.

"Don't worry, Cassie girl. They will. Do you have the receiver set to receive the signal once I've enable the cameras?

Cassandra's hands flew over the keyboard, opening the video surveillance software. "All set," she replied matter-of-factly, and walked to the same case.

She removed the small two-way radio set and military-grade tactical throat microphone. "Here." Handing him the microphone, she set the frequency on the radios.

Trevor set it on the bed and slipped his legs into a pair of soft-shell black pants made of extremely flexible material. He jerked off his shirt and strapped on the microphone, adjusting it at a comfortable spot on his throat. Once satisfied, he pulled on a form-fitting black turtleneck. As he crossed the room to the desk, he tucked the transportation passes Cassandra had given him earlier into one of the many pockets.

"Can you give me a hand with the cables?" She stepped around him and reached under his shirt. Her fingers skimmed his back as she tugged at the cables, drawing them between his shoulder blades. Her warm touch on his skin sent a shiver through him and his cock twitched with interest. Trevor squeezed his eyes tight, trying to rein in his desire and put some distance between them as he finished getting ready.

"I'm a go." He stood by the door, pushing his arms into his Under Armor jacket, as Cassandra approached him with one of the two-ways and a black knit cap. A frown marred her beautiful face and her eyes were somber.

"I don't like that you are going in naked. No fire power," she said softly, her eyes narrowing as she handed him the radio first, watching as he connected the microphone cable to the unit, turned it on, and slid it in the side leg pocket of his pants.

"It'll be fine, Cassie. I'm just setting cameras, not heading to a gun fight."

Cassandra moved closer, and, as she set the knit cap over his head, he wrapped his arms around her waist, hugging her tight against his body. He claimed her mouth in a hungry kiss, thrusting his tongue deep in her mouth, nipping her lower lip. "Something to keep in mind while I'm gone." He released her and opened the door. "Keep your eyes on the screen and open the channel as soon as I leave so we're in contact at all times."

"Aye, aye, Captain." Her heart raced and she found it hard to breath in the wake of that searing kiss. Her eyes followed his every movement as he slung his backpack over his shoulder and walked out.

Chapter Nineteen

Big Dogs

"TEST. TEST."

"Crystal," he responded in a soft voice.

"Copy. Oh, by the way. Payback. Just saying."

His laughter flowed through the signal. She nudged the bantering aside and switched back to business. "Let me know when you get close and which cameras you're setting as you go so I can check each signal."

"Roger," Trevor replied, keeping his senses fully attuned to his surroundings as he crossed the street, heading toward the bridge across from their apartment. At a fast clip, he continued southbound, crossing paths with couples walking hand in hand and with a few pedestrians making their way in the opposite direction. The early spring nights in Russia were brisk, and warm puffs formed into the cold air with each breath he took as he walked the dimly lit streets. "Almost there. ETA, five minutes," he advised Cassandra as he turned onto Zagorodny Prospekt, only a block away from Mikhailov's mansion.

"Report." He heard Cassandra's request loud and clear through the earpiece.

"Chill. It's only been what? A nanosecond since the last? Still no activity. All clear. Will report again once there."

Hunched over the laptop, Cassandra's fingers drummed a staccato rhythm on the desk. She was anxious to get that over with. She knew Trevor would get the job done smoothly and quickly. It was the outside factors that concerned her most. Yes, they had some preliminary data regarding the activity around the mansion, but people changed routines and they really didn't have an up-close and personal on the security measures around the place.

Based on what they knew, that night at the mansion should be unusually slow, with minimal activity, which was the reason Trevor was on his way there—but you just never knew. Cassandra rubbed at the scar on her hip and whispered into the two-way, "You have the transport tickets on you, right?"

"Yes, Cassandra. I have both sets of tickets," he answered indulgently.

A smile tipped her lips at his use of her full name. "Copy. Too anal, I know. Just had to check."

Turning onto Mikhailov's street, Trevor's adrenaline spiked and, with a casual gait, he continued his journey until he reached the area in front of the magnificent mansion. Its façade was traditional Russian and regal. Intricately carved wooden trim crowned big windows, which were illuminated by soft light. A creepy sensation slithered along his spine as he stood in the shadows, observing Mikhailov's nest. The imposing property, protected by high walls and iron gates, rose in the darkness and held a stately air, in complete opposition to the nefarious activities taking place inside.

Across the street from the mansion was a small public park, a perfect hiding spot for the transmitter. "I'm in position. Keep an eye on the receiver," he spoke quietly into the microphone.

"Copy. Ready when you are."

Trevor took one last look around to be sure he wasn't being watched, and slipped into the wooded area. Within minutes, he found the ideal place for the transmitter—a metal lamppost positioned in the middle of the small garden, surrounded by thigh-high bushes. The best hiding spots are the ones in plain sight—one of the several lessons he'd learned geocaching, a high-tech treasure hunt game he and Cassandra enjoyed regularly back in Ireland.

Kneeling by the post, he eased the backpack from his shoulder, retrieved the transmitter, and mounted it to the base of the post using the magnetic strips. To any passerby, the transmitter would appear to be a part of the electric component of the post, making it virtually invisible.

He pressed the switch. "Transmitter in place. Active. On to plant the eyes."

Cassandra checked the meters on the laptop and watched the signal from the transmitter flood the bar. "Check. Transmitter online."

Before Trevor exited the garden, he scanned the gates for any cameras that Mikhailov might have. *Bingo.* "Copy. Setting camera one now."

As each camera was set and turned on, their images began displaying on the screen and the feeds were automatically saved to their external hard drive. They were also motion activated, transmitting data only when activity was detected. That meant they could run the surveillance for hours on end without running out of disk space.

Cassandra became lost in the flow of activity and jumped slightly when she heard Trevor's devious chuckle ripple through the connection. "Damn it, Trevor. I know that laugh. What the hell are you up to?!"

"What?! Can't a guy have a little bit of fun on the job?" His voice held a rasp of excitement.

"Why is it that when you say 'fun' I hear 'trouble'?"

His voice held a hurtful tone. "No faith, whatsoever, in my skills."

She guffawed. "Yeah, yeah."

"Okay. About to set last camera."

Trevor checked to be sure that the coast was clear before he left the cover of the trees and sprinted for the sidewalk across from the park. He hugged the wall as he pulled the last camera from his pack. Staying out of view of the security camera he'd spied earlier atop the gate's side pillar, he used the intricate design of the wrought iron gate as a ladder to reach the camera. Its location was ideal to record the faces and license plates of cars arriving at the gates, and its angle prevented any peripheral activity from being recorded. *Eejits made it too easy.*

At the top, he swung a leg over the rounded edge of the gate, balancing himself to keep from falling on his face as he reached from behind for the encased camera with both hands. He carefully attached their micro-camera and battery pack to the top front edge of the casing.

His voice was hushed and cartoonish: "Oh, grandmother, what big eyes you have! The better to see you with…."

Cassandra's snort of laughter traveled over the audio link.

"Oh, you liked that, didn't you?"

"Just because I laugh at your jokes, doesn't mean they're good, you know." Her voice oozed disdain and he could picture her rolling her eyes.

He kept tabs on the surrounding area as he adjusted the position of the micro-camera. He switched it on and gave Cassandra the last signal. "Let me know if this one has a good angle."

After a few moments, her voice exploded over the link. "What the hell?! That is from pretty high up. Really good view, but really high up! How the hell did you accomplish that one, Trevor? Hold on a second. Where *are* you right now?!"

"Setting the cameras?" He feigned innocence.

"Get your ass out of there on the double!" Anxiety bled through her words.

Her fear beat at him. He sobered immediately. "I'm on my way down; I'll be out of here in no time, Cassie."

Trevor swung his leg back over the gate. Suddenly a deep growl blasted his ears and a heavy weight slammed against the fence, knocking him from his perch. "Umpf!" he exclaimed as he hit the sidewalk. Pain seared through his entire body. His vision dimmed and ears grew muffled as he exhaled in shallow breaths to ease the radiating agony. The low menacing growls and barks from at least two dogs penetrated his haze. *Move your arse, man!* he grimaced to himself, rolling instinctively up against the wall into the cover of shadows. Sucking in a deep shaky breath, he held his position and tried to regroup.

"Trevor! Report!" Cassie's frantic voice demanded in his ear.

Winded, he couldn't squeeze out the words to comfort her. A commotion inside the gate forced him to press tighter against the wall, hoping his dark clothing would help as additional camouflage.

"Trevor! Report. Now!"

"Here!" he gasped out with a groan.

A voice behind the wall yelled. Trevor smirked. The guard blamed the dogs' barking on a stray cat.

Someone else cursed at the dogs to shut up.

"I would like that, too, thank you very much!" Trevor mumbled to himself as he completed an internal assessment. The pain was fading and, although nothing seemed to be broken, he had landed on his back and on the small toolkit box in his backpack. *That's going to smart in the morning.* Confident he hadn't blown his cover since he wasn't kissing shoes or facing gun muzzles, he finally responded to Cassie's frantic requests.

"I'm okay. Just sore. All cameras placed. I'm heading back."

"If you think you can just scare the crap out of me and walk home like nothing happened you are very wrong, mister." Cassie's voice, although steady, was now seething with anger. "What the hell happened out there, Trevor!?"

Trevor checked his surroundings, crawled closer to the gate, and popped his head around the corner of the wall to check the house. Again, loud growls echoed in his ears and the gate shook under the weight of a body butting up against it. The dogs were right in his face, doing what they were trained to do—guard the property.

"Dogs, Cassie...*big* dogs happened." He pushed to his feet and leaned back against the wall. Concern worried at his heart and, to avoid leading a possible tail directly to Cassandra, he decided to take the longest route back.

He headed in the opposite direction from which he had arrived. "ETA, seventeen minutes."

Cassandra immediately picked up on the change of plans. "Why seventeen? Why not the twelve it took on the original route?"

She was like one of the freaking dogs behind the gate chasing him for answers. He sighed. "It's all okay, Cassie. Just taking a different route back. I will explain when I get there."

Cassandra continued to badger him. "Oh, damn straight you will! What the hell were you thinking, climbing the fence to plant the camera up there?" She interjected, "Mind you, it was truly brilliant, but that's not the point! You can't let yourself get carried away and lose perspective of the goal here, Trevor!" Her implication left an ache in his chest.

"It was just the perfect location to get the shots we need of both the people and license plates of cars arriving at the mansion," he commented quietly as he briskly walked around the block and to the street that would lead him to the bridge and back to Cassandra. The risk had been great, but Trevor didn't regret a minute of it. It was a necessary one to get what they needed. Still smarting from the fall, he limped, listening to the concern and anxiety coloring Cassandra's voice as she ranted about how reckless he had been and how she was going to kick his ass when he got there.

The connection had gone quiet as he approached the building and he wondered what it would take to get back on her good side and out of the doghouse. Entering the code, he limped up the stairs and entered the apartment. Cassandra stood right at the door, her flushed cheeks a clear sign of her anger toward him at the moment.

"What the fuck, Trevor?"

As those words hung in the air, his thoughts narrowed to her, her flushed face, the anxiety in her tone, and the pulse beating out of control at the base of her throat. Without a word, he kicked the door shut, dropped the pack to the floor, and roughly hauled her into his arms, seizing her mouth in a hot, searing kiss.

Cassandra's stomach churned. Her throat was so tight she could barely breathe, let alone speak. Her anger was directed both at Trevor for taking risks and at herself for knowing the risks—handling the risks—and still dying inside each time he did. How had she ever let him have so much control over her heart? It was as if he'd chipped away the ice and nursed the flames that now engulfed it.

A part of her wanted to grab him and hold on tight, happy he was back in one piece. But the part of her ruled by anger twisted in his arms, trying to push him away, unwilling to set aside the emotions that ate at her. Her efforts were thwarted by his tight hold, the press of his body against hers, and his relentless kiss determined to conquer her anger.

Under his assault, her struggles subsided and she sagged with a sigh of relief at having him back safe in her arms. Soon, it was washed away in a flood of desperation fed by the last couple of hours filled with pent-up worry and an overwhelming need to feel every inch of Trevor's body against hers.

Cassandra returned his demanding kiss with one of her own, pulling at his jacket and searching for the zipper until her groping fingers landed on metal. She quickly unzipped it and pushed it open, desperate to touch him. She groaned at the feel of his heat beneath her hands before sliding them up and pushing the jacket off his shoulders. Trevor held the kiss, sucking at her lips and tongue while shrugging the jacket off.

Their tongues continued to dance as her hands pulled the turtleneck from Trevor's waistband and slid underneath it, brushing up along his chest, loving the feel of his skin hard and quivering under her touch.

Trevor's chest heaved as he tried to suck in lungfuls of air; brushing her hands away, he yanked the sweater over his head and tossed it to the floor. Cassandra's impatient hands dropped to his pants and made quick work of his button and zipper, releasing his hot pulsing cock into her grasp. He groaned and squeezed his eyes shut. "Damn it!"

He quickly toed off his shoes, kicked free of his pants, and jerked Cassandra's sweater up over her head, forcing her to release him.

"Shite, Cassie!" he breathed out throatily at the sight of her breasts, already bare to his gaze. "All day? No bra? Fuck me!" he exclaimed, resting his forehead against hers.

A sensual grin broke along her lips as she reached down once again for his cock, taking it firmly in her hand, squeezing it gently as her other hand moved to rest at his waist, urging him closer. A deep groan reverberated in his chest and his hips thrust into her grip.

Their heat mingled, skin melting against each other when they finally touched chest to chest. A shiver shimmied up her spine as their lips sought and found each other. Cassandra's heart thrummed against her chest and her emotions got the better of her. She pulled back, giving his cock a little jerk. "Damn it, Trevor! You drive me crazy with the chances you take!" she whispered harshly against his mouth, giving his cock another gentle tug to make her point.

His hand covered hers since she had him hostage and he quietly whispered, "Shush, *a ghrá,*" before taking her lips roughly in another wet kiss, sending quivers of heat to pulse at her clit.

Drawing in a ragged breath, Cassandra dove deeper into the kiss, never wanting it to end, exploring his mouth as if for the first time, loving and savoring the taste of him, so unique and stimulating to her senses. She tried to throttle the dizzying current racing through her as Trevor ravished her mouth and moved them toward the bed. Wrapping her legs around his waist, her soft curves molded to the contours of his lean body. Only the fabric of her jeans separated her skin from his heat. "Trevor my jea—" Before she could finish her sentence, she was thrown onto the bed.

As she gasped for air, Trevor quickly grabbed her jeans and panties, roughly jerking them from her. He joined her on the bed, covering her body with his and capturing her hands above her head. They both stilled. His eyes, gleaming brightly with love and desire, gazed down along her body before returning to meet hers, which mirrored the same need.

Someone had told her once that in a couple's relationship there is always one that loved more than the other. Cassandra contemplated that statement as she took in his tight muscular body, the lines of his abs, and his rigid cock pressed against her belly. Her mouth went dry. Snaring her eyes again, Trevor leaned closer until all she could see was the seriousness that had crept into his stormy blue eyes. "Know this Cassie. I'll always come home to you. Always find you, no matter what."

It was then she knew the statement was false. They loved each other just as deeply and equally. A miracle really, considering neither had been seeking love when they'd found each other.

She swallowed deeply, searching for words to convey her thoughts. "I know. But this is me, the consummate worrywart. I just found you. I don't think I could stand losing you." She turned her head, breaking their gaze as she sucked back her emotions. Who knew he would have such a daredevil streak? It wasn't the first time—and she was positive it wouldn't be the last—he'd put himself out there.

Trevor released one of her hands, gripped her chin, and turned her face to him. "I know, *a ghrá*. That's what I love about you. So hard and efficient when you need to be, and yet so soft and yielding to me." His voice turned to a whisper as his lips pressed against hers. "Two sides of a coin. Both such a delight," he continued as he trailed kisses across her eyes before returning to softly tease and coax her mouth.

Trevor kissed Cassandra, hoping to ease the worries and the tension of the last couple of hours. He nipped at her lower lip and continued to taunt her until they engaged in a deep, open kiss. She moaned as he ground his hips against hers. The full extent of his desire pressed between them, rubbing her mound.

"I love you, Cassandra," he breathed into her mouth.

"I know." There was a mellow quality to her voice as she spreads her legs wide, cradling him between them and nesting his throbbing cock at her wet folds. A groan rumbled through his chest as his firm head touched her hot slit. Trevor stared into her eyes and whispered, "I want you so much."

Cassandra's heavy-lidded eyes glistened with moisture as she held his gaze. "You have me. Love me, Trevor."

As those words passed her lips, she thrust her pelvis upward, sheathing his cock, and instinctively his hips pushed forward, driving deep inside her. They both moaned in pleasure at the joining of their bodies and began moving against each other in a give-and-take of love and deep devotion. Supporting his weight on their clasped hands and his knees, Trevor slowly withdrew almost fully before driving swiftly back inside her wet core again and again until her moans grew ragged.

"Harder!" her raspy and broken voice begged. Trevor used his knees to push her thighs wider apart and slid one of his hands down between them, reaching for her sensitive nub. His touch sent electric tendrils through her body, making her tremble, and he felt the first quakes of her approaching release.

"Touch me," she moaned again. He increased the rhythm of his thrusts as he pressed his thumb on her clit, rubbing it in the alternating circular and side-to-side motions he knew she loved. Her breathing became ragged and loud and she bucked underneath him. Releasing her hands, he caged her as he leaned down and sucked her pebbled dusky nipple deep in his mouth.

Cassandra's fingers combed through and grabbed handfuls of his hair, holding his head to her breasts. He took his time nibbling and sucking on each as he drove his cock in and out of her hot wet channel in a slow cadence, engulfing himself in the heat of her and the sweet taste of her skin.

Her body arched toward him and he took her offering hungrily, pulling more of her breast into his mouth, kneading the other gently with his fingers. "Oh, Trevor!" Her sigh was a slow exhale of breath urging him to continue his ministrations.

Light rhythmic squeezes around Trevor's shaft alerted him that she was spiraling faster toward release, and he felt a need to take her higher—make her scream his name, say she was his. That she would always be his.

"Wrap your legs around me, Cassie," he urged her. She locked her ankles against the small of his back, pressing him closer each time he thrust into her. Their bodies collided and ground incessantly as he plunged into her heat. "Cassandra—" Her name flowed from his lips with reverence as he increased the speed of his pumps, and soon they were both lost in each other, lost in pleasuring each other to the fullest. Grinding and writhing, rubbing and touching the other in places they'd learned would bring them closer to their mutual release.

Her inner muscles exploded in spasms around him and her breath came in long surrendering moans. "Ah...."

Her body tensed and a twinge pricked his lower back. They were both so close. Her name left his lips in a victorious yell as they set each other ablaze. "Cassandra! God!"

"Yes! Trevor!" Her sheath squeezed him repeatedly, massaging, and milking him until, spent, he collapsed on her. He lay his head beside hers, face tucked at the sweet curve of her neck, chests heaving at the exertion, hearts beating a mile a minute.

After a few moments, Cassandra's humor bubbled against his ear. He lifted his head to face her and found a pair of mischievous eyes staring back at him. "What?"

"Little Red Riding Hood? Really!?"

He laughed out loud and mimicked the voice again, "But, grandmother, what a dreadful big mouth you have! The better to eat you with..."

Her laughter rippled through the air. "God, you're insane and I love you."

Trevor rolled to the side and cradled her tight against him, brushing her brow with his lips. Her breathing grew shallow as she began drifting into sleep. "I love you, too, Cassie," he repeated her words softly as she slid a leg between his and wrapped an arm over his chest.

Chapter Twenty

Bruised Ego

TREVOR'S GLANCE CUT TO CASSANDRA. She held the steaming cup of coffee between her hands as if it were an anchor. He could tell by the shadows in her eyes and the blank stare directed at her laptop's darkened screen that her thoughts were in turmoil.

His adventure the night before had left his body achy and stiff. He felt as if he'd been passed through the wringer and spit out to dry. Earlier that morning he had assessed the damage to his back in the small bathroom mirror. The bruise sustained in the fall was taking on an ugly hue—a dark purple brand, rectangular in shape, taking a place of honor right smack between his shoulder blades. He grimaced at the thought of what Cassandra would say when she finally set eyes on it.

Since they had gotten up and jumped into work, she had avoided his gaze and all conversation. That was the first time since the day they'd met that

Cassandra had been truly angry with him. The last months had been a rollercoaster of activity and adventure. They had gotten themselves into hot water before, but that last brush with the unexpected had shaken her badly and he couldn't pinpoint why.

The silence was killing him. He missed the laughter and camaraderie they shared. Unable to handle the silence any longer, Trevor turned to face her and blatantly stared at her until she closed her eyes to avoid his gaze.

"You scared me last night," she murmured.

"I didn't mean it. I'm sorry if I did." Trevor tried to rationalize. "You do know that what we're doing has risks. I can't guarantee I won't be harmed in the process. Neither of us can. You always knew that. Have you changed your mind? Do you want us to go home?"

The bitter taste of uncertainty filled his mouth and he wondered how he would move forward if she decided she'd had enough of his personal quest. A fist squeezed his heart at the thought of the choices he would have to make. As much as he was driven to find out what happened to his parents, he wasn't willing to proceed with his search for answers if it meant destroying his relationship with Cassandra.

"Why would you think I'd want to quit over something so asinine? I'd never quit looking for them, Trevor. Neither will you." She paused and he exhaled the breath he'd unknowingly held. "It's something you need so you can move on…we can move on." His wife was a wise and perceptive woman, even when angry. At that moment, he thanked the fates again for all the events that had put her in his life.

"To be honest, I think I was more frustrated than scared, sitting here, hands tied and unable to back you up. That daredevil sitting on your shoulder has become a permanent fixture." She shook her head and a small smile tugged at the corner of her lips. "It scares the shit out of me sometimes. We're still working blind here, Trev. We don't have a solid handle on the routine at the mansion." She turned to look at him at last and held his gaze. "And you were up there. What if someone had driven up to the gate or left on foot from the property? What if you had fallen inside? Damn it, Trevor. You would have been dog meat for sure. No pun intended," she blurted out.

Understanding her reasons didn't make it any easier for Trevor to take them. "I'll be putting my neck on the line again soon…are you sure you can handle that?" he asked her directly. No point in using half-truths or soften the reality that was to come.

"I'll be fine," she responded with a deep sigh. "I get the risks. I've lived those risks long before meeting you, and knew the risks when I finally accepted the fact that you were going to be a permanent part of my life. But that doesn't mean I can't give you shit for stupid antics like the one on the gate."

Her tone and the look in her eyes clearly indicated she wouldn't be forgetting his little stunt any time soon, and would definitely find ways to remind him of that— every chance she got. "Please tell me you won't retaliate with another workout. Please, please don't turn me into Chuck Norris."

Cassandra stared at him with a blank expression on her face and, after a moment, shook her head and burst out laughing. Her humor quickly faded to a grim slash of lips and she booted her computer. "Nah. I called Bob instead. Once we finish this assignment, we're heading to the States. You've been enrolled in Bob's buddies' Navy Seal Boot Camp for Geeks. His motto is, 'We'll knock the geek out of 'em and some sense in.'"

It was Trevor's turn to stare at her. Bob's Navy Seal buddies were forces to be reckoned with, as Trevor had discovered upon their return from Paris. They were take-no-prisoner kind of guys. First-person shooter games were most likely modeled after those guys' MO. "What the hell, Cassie? You did what?!"

Cassandra ignored his question with a shrug and switched gears on him. "What do we have from the cameras?"

Trevor grimaced. "You'd better be joking." The glitter in her eyes gave him his answer and his heart settled in his chest. The tragedy of his early death had been averted.

Glad she was ready to get back into work, he filled her in. "We have several files from last night. Why don't we go through them?"

"Sounds like a plan," she answered, a trace of laughter still lingering in her voice.

Over the course of the next several hours, they combed the footage they'd collected. The activity from the cameras showed several so-called employees entering and leaving the mansion. Running the data from the feeds through facial recognition programs and pairing it with trivial information, such as license plates, helped them identify some of them.

Trevor pulled up George's latest email reporting the activity from Mikhailov's phone conversations. He sent back a reply, attaching the information they had compiled and screen captures from the surveillance videos with instructions to initiate some extra tapping on the new players.

George should be able to cross-reference the new names and their phone numbers with any previously recorded incoming or outgoing conversations sourced from the tapped phones in the mansion and from known associates of Mikhailov's. Their hunt had grown into more than just a little game of hide-and-seek.

Chapter Twenty-One

Salted Bread

IT HAD BEEN FIVE DAYS since the cameras had been set, and they were finally getting the big picture of Mikhailov's operation. Cassandra came up for air and rubbed her eyes. Reading through the new transcripts was a tedious but necessary evil. She glanced at the clock and couldn't believe how time had flown. "Trev. Kostas should be here any minute."

Almost as if on cue, the intercom buzzed. Cassandra pushed away from the table and, as she moved past Trevor, brushed her hands across his shoulders. "That should be him."

Cassandra hit the button on the intercom on the wall by the door. "Yes?"

"Cassandra Bauer?"

"Yes?" she responded cautiously.

"It's me, Kostas."

"Kostas! Right on time. Come on up." She buzzed him in.

When a knock sounded, Cassandra opened the door and came face to face with none other than the Russian her father had fondly spoken of when she was younger. Although he was about the same age as Robert, Boris looked older than she expected, with his salt-and-pepper receding hairline and slightly heavier physique.

"Cassandra! You were expecting me, no?"

"Kostas, welcome. Please come in." She fully opened the door and Kostas walked in with a big smile on his face and a large bag dangling from his hand.

"Cassie! Daughter of my good friend Robert. I am so pleased to meet you at last." He glanced sideways as Trevor joined them at the door. "Ah, this must be your husband."

He gave them both bear hugs and handed the bag to Cassandra. Taking it, she was surprised at how heavy it was. Peering inside, she found two of the largest round loaves of bread she'd ever seen. She shot Kostas a questioning look and a flash of humor lit his eyes. "You're wondering about the bread?"

She opened the bag wider so Trevor could see them.

"It is a Russian folk custom, honoring the emperor and empress when they would pay a visit to a village." Kostas smiled and continued, "During their visit, the merchants and gentry of the area would present their guest with a round loaf of bread piled with salt as a sign of hospitality. We also give this gift to a new couple to wish that they always have the necessities of life, and as a housewarming gift to wish that their pantry will always be full. So you see, my gift, how do you say in America? Kills two birds with one stone? Housewarming, and, since you are newlyweds... well, you see."

Pulling the round loaves from the bag and setting them on the table, Cassandra urged Trevor to test the weight of one of the loaves and suppressed a giggle at the surprised look on his face.

Trevor cleared his throat and glanced at Kostas. "How dense is your bread? Should I be afraid?"

Kostas's eyes took on a sly gleam and a mischievous grin spread across his face. "Ah, this is a good question," he countered in heavily accented English as he reached for one of the loaves, pulled out a pocket knife, and carefully proceeded to cut into it.

Intrigued by his actions, Trevor and Cassandra moved closer. Suddenly Trevor burst out in a deep belly laugh, his twinkling eyes shot her way. "Oh yeah, Cassie. Definitely be afraid."

"What the hell are you guys going on about?" Her gaze bounced from one man to the other. "The guns are in the bread? No freaking way," she quipped, joining in the laughter as Trevor scooped the two standard issue P-443 Grach handguns from the cavity. "Damn. I was kind of looking forward to eating that bread," she added, crestfallen.

Kostas's grin grew even wider and he gave Cassandra a hug. "Your father said you would appreciate the gesture. I cannot wait to let him know how well it worked."

"Oh man, we will never hear the end of that one for sure," she laughed, releasing him. "You must stay awhile. Would you like something to drink? Coffee? Tea?" She tossed him a saucy grin. "Vodka?"

"Just a cup of tea for me, Cassandra," Kostas guffawed.

She glanced to Trevor. "I'll have the same, *u ghrá.*"

Trevor led Kostas to their sitting area while Cassandra left the two to their devices and headed for the kitchen.

Trevor leaned forward, resting his elbows on his knees. He casually studied Kostas, trying to read him before broaching the subject regarding the little employment opportunity he had in mind.

Kostas broke the silence first. "So, how do you like St. Petersburg?" The question hung in the air for just a brief moment before he added, "Not that you are here to see the many beautiful sights it has to offer."

"What makes you think that?" Trevor was wary of the comment.

Kostas relaxed back in the chair. The vibe Trevor caught from him was more of a viper ready to strike at any moment.

"Not many tourists call for the type of delivery you did unless they were here for something other than pleasure."

Trevor took stock of Kostas. Weighing his options and finding no other, he prompted, "I have a little issue that I think you might be able to help me with."

Kostas smiled. "I will do my best to help. Anything for Robert's daughter and her husband. Robert is like family to me."

Trevor's eyes narrowed speculatively. He wished Cassandra was there to observe Kostas's facial expressions. "I need connections...or to appear to have connections so I can get inside a very secure place here in St. Petersburg."

Kostas's smile grew wider. "There is *secure*. And there is secure," he teased. "I know a lot of people. What is this place of yours?"

Trevor flashed a smile at his implication but treaded with caution, watching him carefully. "What if I were to ask you to find me a way inside Vladimir Mikhailov's mansion?"

Kostas's smile faded instantly and the glint in his eyes transitioned to one of disbelief. "Did you say Vladimir Mikhailov? You are joking, yes?"

"Not joking." Trevor considered what to tell him. Honesty was the only way to go. "I need access to his servers. I've tried to infiltrate them from outside but I can't. The only way is from the inside."

All color bled from Kostas's face, leaving behind a pallid mask. "You know what you ask is a dangerous proposition." His tone was serious and the smile of minutes ago, a lost memory.

Trevor nodded. "I'm well aware of the risks. But it's something important to me...to us. No other way around it. I *need* to complete this job."

There was a pensive shimmer in the shadow of Boris's eyes as he studied Trevor. "What exactly is this job you speak of?" he asked as his eyes narrowed, boring into him as if trying to ascertain what his and Cassandra's real purpose in Russia was.

"Mikhailov has something in his possession. Something he stole from my employer." Trevor wasn't going to disclose the details regarding the job nor the personal reasons behind it. "All I can tell you is that I need to destroy Mikhailov's servers."

A cold, hard, calculating look filled Kostas's eyes, now narrowed to slits. "Does Robert know why you are here?"

Cassandra returned from the kitchen at that moment, carrying a tray holding the tea and cups. "No, he doesn't. We would like to keep it that way," she said as she set it on the coffee table.

A thick silence engulfed the room as they studied each other. Kostas leaned forward in his chair. "You already have something in mind, I'm thinking?"

"Yes, indeed." Kostas waited patiently for Trevor to continue. "We know Mikhailov employs hackers. He might be in need of a skilled one." Trevor paused, allowing Kostas to absorb the full impact of the request. Kostas was as sharp as he appeared and didn't miss the boat.

"You really want me to throw you into the shark tank," he chuckled in disbelief.

Trevor nodded and glanced briefly to Cassandra as she moved to his side and rested her hand on his shoulder in support and solidarity. "I won't go into detail as to why, but I need to do this. I would like you to trust me when I say it's important. Can you help us?"

Kostas appeared lost in thought, possibly weighing the merit of Trevor's words. Words of a man he had never met before.

Trevor sensed Cassandra's anxiousness in the squeeze she gave his shoulder as they waited for Kostas's reply. They both understood that if he didn't agree to help them, it would take them longer to achieve their goal. They would lose precious time building connections on their own in order to get a foot through Mikhailov's door.

Kostas exhaled deeply. "I will see what I can do. I will keep this between us. Robert will kill me if he finds out that I help to put you two in danger. Know this: I will advise him if I feel it is for the best."

Cassandra squeezed Trevor's shoulder a little tighter this time. "We are indebted to you. Thank you, Boris. We can call you Boris, right?" Cassandra asked Kostas sweetly.

"Of course you can!" he smiled widely, standing and extending a hand to Trevor, who grasped it in a tight handshake.

"Give me a few days to get this figured out. I have connections that can help, but I need to find the right way to approach them about this." Kostas's lowered voice and cautious tone caught Trevor's attention. It was almost as if Kostas thought someone would overhear their conversation.

"We'll sit tight until we hear from you."

Kostas squeezed Trevor's hand tighter and draped an arm around his shoulders in a close hug. "You better keep her safe and out of harm's way," he whispered in Trevor's ear, and then spoke louder, "In the meantime, enjoy St. Petersburg."

"I definitely will." Trevor's response addressed both of Kostas's comments, and from the knowing glance he shot him, Trevor knew the double meaning was understood.

Kostas released him and pulled Cassandra into a tight hug. "I will bring a proper loaf next time."

Cassandra laughed and placed a kiss on his cheek. "Thank you, Boris. For everything."

With quick words of goodbye, Kostas left. Trevor locked the door and turned to Cassandra. "One step closer." *But at what price?*

Chapter Twenty-Two

Roots

ASLIGHT BOUNCE ON THE mattress woke Jessica right before a muscular arm wrapped around her waist and a warm body spooned against her back. A smile spread across her face as memories of the nights spent in Stephan's arms engulfed her.

The stirring of life tucked between her thighs caught her attention. Her breath hitched in her lungs when his hand slipped from around her and began a sensual trail of fingertips from her knee to her hip. When she didn't react to it, a sharp intake of breath sounded behind her. His cock stirred against her ass cheeks again and she almost giggled at his impressive control.

They did have a lot to catch up on and they were sure up to the challenge. Stephan had been a total surprise to her. Once he had surrendered to their attraction, their physical relationship had unfolded in unexpected ways. He was a domineering and bossy lover, and she adored every second spent complying with his every demand. The first days had eased the sexual frustration and hunger they both had been plagued with since their taste of each other in California. Their first weekend together had been especially satisfying, spent in mutual exploration, learning everything there was to be learned about each other. Their second even more so.

The urgency had lessened, but not the attraction and desire. Those were growing with each simple touch, each gesture, each word. And with it also came the understanding that she wasn't infatuated. She had a good old-fashioned case of unadulterated love for Stephan. Jessica had told Cassandra that she would know when she fell in love, that it would hit her square between the eyes. Jessica was smarting from it. She pictured herself growing old with Stephan. She saw a life with him beyond just desire and sex.

With each day, she had started to spend more and more time with him, in his arms. They had fallen into a comfortable routine of sorts, having breakfast together, which usually consisted of two cups of coffee for him and whatever she could scavenge in his pantry, before they both tackled work. Cassandra had left Jessica a few tasks aside from housesitting. Their data retrieval business was booming. She had a few prospective clients to call back and gather preliminary information on their cases later that day.

Stephan's breathing deepened behind her and Jessica shifted her hips and rubbed her ass cheeks lightly against his cock. He groaned softly, still not taking that sensual wakeup call any further. She decided to take matter into her own hands. Draping one leg back over his muscular thigh, she reached down and, positioning his cock, pressed her hips against his, impaling herself on his hard, pulsing shaft.

"Fuck!" Stephan cried out at the swift move, driving deep.

It didn't take long before he got the drift and began moving inside her, slowly, lovingly. His hand glided to cup her face and turn it to him. He took her mouth gently, reverently, nipping, teasing, until he plunged his tongue between her lips. She took him in, reveling at the swell of her heart, the heat growing low in her belly with each thrust.

"Touch yourself."

The commanding tone didn't leave any room for refusal. Not that she would anyway. Her hand traveled low to her engorged clit and wet folds. Her fingers fanned the fire burning with each push of him inside her. "Oh God, Stephan!"

It didn't take them long to burst into their release. Stephan wrapped his arms around her from behind and tucked his face in the hollow of her neck, holding on tight until their breaths quieted. He then broke contact and rolled from the bed. Once parted, she took notice of the condom and giggled.

Stephan followed her eyes to his crotch. "I was hopeful."

"No kidding. We both know I'm weak when it comes to you. It was a sure thing."

A smile spread across his face but didn't quite reach his eyes as he walked to the adjacent bathroom. She heard the water running and waited for him to come back, showered and ready to start his day.

Stephan spent weekdays buried in business at work. He dressed for the job and she loved watching him shrug into well-cut suits each morning while she lay naked and burning for him under the covers. He looked amazing, and carried an aura of power whether he was naked, voicing his commands to her, or dressed in Armani, commanding the boardroom.

"You clean up well, Mr. Connellan."

A smile quirked his lips and he gave her the look. She loved that "don't tease me or else" look and the promises it carried. She knew that once the day was over, once the sun had set over Dublin, she would return to his house and be fulfilled again. Taken into his world, his arms.

"Busy day ahead?"

"Yes. I have a couple of appointments to view apartments. Narrowed the search to a few. I don't want just anything and, thankfully, I don't need to rush my decision. Trev and Cassie haven't told me when they'll be back, but it doesn't look like it'll be anytime soon."

"What exactly are they doing in Russia?" Stephan asked while tying his tie.

"Data retrieval for a client." Stephan raised his eyebrows. "Cassie hasn't said much about it, only that it was something they couldn't pass up and she would fill me in when she got back. From her last message, it sounds like everything is going like clockwork."

He removed the suit jacket from the hanger and eased it over his shoulders while her eyes travelled over his body, measuring, recalling. "Don't." A smile twitched across her lips at his reprimand. "You are a dangerous little vixen, Miss Forrester."

"One you would love to discipline this very moment for being naughty?"

He stalked to the edge of the bed, leaned over, and caged her between his arms. "It's amazing how well you can read my mind." Placing a hard kiss on her lips, he nagged, "Move it. I can't take any more of your tempting looks. I have meetings I can't miss today."

He strode out of the room, leaving Jessica breathless and longing to tempt him more. She got out of bed and stretched. An ache in muscles she didn't know existed greeted her. The soreness between her legs was something she could appreciate. They had been very active since their first night together. She should really buy stock options of the brand of condoms he used. Jessica was sure she would make a tidy profit. Her mouth quirked with humor as she retrieved her clothes from the night before and dressed.

The trips back and forth between Trevor and Cassandra's home and Stephan's were becoming a drag. Granted, she had work to do and plants to water, but it would be nice if she could at least make the trip in fresh clothes. Maybe she could just bring a couple of things over to Stephan's. Small things—a pair of panties, a toothbrush.

She walked to his closet and opened the doors. His suits and matching dress shirts were perfectly organized by color—blacks, dark blues, grays. She caressed the fabrics and buried her face in their softness, breathing in his tantalizing scent, and a liquid heat pooled low between her thighs.

Jessica shook her head at her fancy and opened another set of doors. She found two empty sections. Perfect. She would bring a few things, leave them there the next time she was over—which seemed to be every night of the week. With a new spring to her step, she left the room to join him in the kitchen. Her mouth watered at the delicious aroma of coffee wafting at the top of the stairs.

He handed her a cup when she walked in. "I was thinking I could help you with your apartment hunting."

"What do you mean? I thought you were busy."

"I can't today, but if you'd like to reschedule, I can take the day off tomorrow and help you with the viewing. I can also advise on the locations."

"That would be a relief. I actually feel a little lost without Cassie to give me pointers."

"Then it's settled. I will reschedule my meetings and join you. If the ones you have lined up don't pan out, we can start looking again. Find one closer to me."

His words slammed her heart against her chest. The promise in them, alluring. "That would be a definite plus."

He left his cup on the counter and casually dropped a kiss on her lips on his way to the door. "Will I see you tonight?" His tone implied it was more of an invitation.

"You bet." She watched as he left and, with a deep breath, collected her purse from the couch. Their relationship had gone from zero to a hundred in less than two weeks. If she wasn't enjoying it so much, she would have a case of whiplash from the speed at which they'd moved. Their arrangement was settling into comfortable routine. The clause was still a sore spot, but one Jessica could handle, especially with the attention and care he had shown her.

Stephan was a dichotomy at the best of times. He had pushed her away sternly and surely, only to pull her to him faster and tighter than anything she could've imagined. Jessica still hadn't figured out what had driven him to reject her back in California when the proof that he wanted her was so obvious. If she ever had doubts about his interest in her, they had disappeared shortly after their first night together. And his interest wasn't limited to the physical realm either. He enjoyed her company. She could feel it in the relaxed way in which he behaved around her and how he sought her out.

Jessica stepped out of Stephan's house into the bright morning sunlight and waved for a cab. Next thing on her list—a car. It would give her more freedom and make life way easier, another step toward her new future. She was there to stay.

★ ★ ★ ★ ★

Stephan slipped behind the wheel of his sedan and cupped his cock, pressing his palm tight against it to ease the ache that had built under Jessica's watchful sultry eyes. They had burned him with their intensity as he had dressed. His desire for her hadn't diminished. The more he tasted her, the more he craved her—to the point that he was beginning to second-guess ever entering into their mutual understanding. She was under his skin, embedded in his senses. He smelled and tasted the musky sweetness of her all the time. Their parting, when it happened, would be more painful than he ever envisioned.

He had been a fool to believe that the understanding would give him control. Place her in the same category as the others, as Terese. A comfortable relationship without a driving need to be with each other, one he could orchestrate to his and her mutual satisfaction. He had definitely been a fool.

Jessica was neither Terese nor any other woman he had met or dated before for that matter. She was uninhibited where he was concerned, a perfect match for him in every way. There wasn't a day that went by that he hadn't wanted to know how she spent her day, who she talked to, what her opinion about some random subject was. There wasn't a day that went by that he didn't want to spend it enjoying the warmth of her smile or the heat of her body.

She had grown roots inside him and they delved deep, as if searching for the softness in him, feeding off his need for her. Shaking his head, Stephan took a deep breath, turned the engine, and pulled into the morning flow of traffic, resigned to the fact that Jessica would be on his mind for the rest of the day.

Chapter Twenty-Three

High up the Totem Pole

T REVOR HATED THE SMALL LAPTOP screen, especially when he needed a number of windows open simultaneously. At home, he had the luxury of a triple-screen sweet set-up, which allowed him to have as many applications running side by side as needed; but Jack II's screen was way too small for that. He had to either squish the windows to almost slivers or toggle back and forth, which was a pain in the ass.

He had the split screen with the cameras' views to one side and the text editor to the other as he kept an eye on the mansion's movements while he screened another set of transcripts he had received from George. Whenever movement was detected, the little cameras would go live and send signals to their receiver, which in turn activated the recording and the view on his screen.

Trevor caught movement on one of the cameras but thought nothing of it since the mansion had been a true revolving door during the day, and even some nights, since they had set up surveillance. He was about to return his attention to the transcript when something snared his attention.

His heart accelerated and his brows drew together in a puzzled frown. "What the fuck?!"

Cassandra turned in her chair to face him. "What happened?"

"I think I just saw Boris walking into Mikhailov's mansion," he commented in a baffled tone.

Cassandra scrambled to his side while he accessed the file. Opening the video file with the sequence recorded minutes earlier, they watched a replay of a black Mercedes with tinted windows rolling up to the gate and stopping for security clearance.

Cassandra scribbled down the plate number picked up by their little camera on her notepad and continued to watch the scene play out with Trevor.

"Son of a bitch!" Trevor exclaimed as Cassandra cursed under her breath when the car's window rolled down and the driver's face came into focus. That was definitely the same man who had shaken his hand and hugged Cassandra in their apartment days before.

They watched in disbelief as Boris Kostas waved at the mansion's security camera once cleared and drove through the gates. They figured, in his line of work, Boris would have connections. Trevor just hadn't expected him to have connections that high up the totem pole.

"What the hell does this mean?" Cassandra blurted out.

"I don't know. But having this little tidbit of information might come handy. We need to watch our backs."

"Can we just tell him we gave up on the idea? Maybe try to find another way in?"

"Too late for that now. He knows we want in that mansion. Any infiltration would be directly linked to us in the time it took to say supercalifragilisticexpialidocious."

Her expression changed and became almost somber. "So what do we do now?"

"We continue our surveillance. Gather details on the people inside for when the time comes. And we wait. The transcripts are vague, but so far no sign that there is any development of the software taking place."

"Okay, then. I'll leave you to it while I work on identifying the new players from last night's captures." Including the woman she'd observed entering the mansion earlier that morning. There was something about her that intrigued Cassandra. Something in her walk, her face.

Trevor nodded absently and Cassandra returned to her workstation. She stared blankly at the monitor. Thoughts swirled through her head. *Is Boris on the up and up? Is he batting for the other team? Does Mikhailov know about us? Has he put Trevor's life—and my life, for that matter—in danger?*

She sat back in her chair, folded her arms across her chest, and chewed at her lip, deep in thought. *Does Bob even know about his activities?* Cassandra's father prided himself on being a good judge of character. Robert had kept in contact with many friends who had covered his back in his Navy Seal days and who on some occasions had even saved his ass.

She'd heard the stories of Kostas's exploits and how they had met in the mid-eighties when Robert worked a security detail during Russia-US cooperation agreement sessions. Glancing over at Trevor, she saw speculation clouding his expression.

"Hey, babe?"

"Yes?" Trevor's attention was focused on the screen, a frown still creasing his brow.

"I'm dropping a line to Bob to see if he can shed any light on Kostas."

Trevor turned his narrowed eyes to her. "Don't disclose what we saw just yet."

Friend or foe? That was the question. Cassandra was careful with her words as she composed the email.

Hey Dad,

Just a line to let you know we are in St. Petersburg and prospects look promising. You should see Trevor in action. Boy, does that man know how to work it. He reminds me of you, all determination and no nonsense.

By the way, met Boris Kostas this past week. It was great to finally meet the man behind the stories I'd heard so much about over the years. Let me tell you, he lived up to expectations—larger than life and full of surprises. Not sure if you've had any contact with him recently, but he did mention he would be telling you the story of our little housewarming gift and his creative wrapping.

If not, suffice it to say he brought the gifts we discussed earlier in two large, hollowed-out rounds of salted bread. A tradition, he said. The bread, not the surprise inside. It still gives me a good laugh. Trevor caught on first. Me? I was more interested in the salted bread. It's a shame it had to go to waste.

Trevor enjoyed meeting him as well. Later he asked me the details of your friendship with him. If he was married, had a family, what did he do before establishing his security company, etc. I realized I didn't know anything more than how you first met. Quickly shed some light, will you, so I can get Trevor off my back? You know how curious he is about people and he is hounding me to freaking death.

Looking forward to hearing from you when you read this.

Love, Cassandra.

Cassandra took a deep cleansing breath and hit send. Hopefully her father would get back to her with more details so they could paint a better picture of the man.

Glancing at Trevor, she watched him working quietly, fingers strumming over the keys. She could tell his mind was humming, processing everything they'd captured that day, and she was sure he was dissecting Kostas in his mind.

Kostas was still foremost on her mind as well, invading her thoughts at every turn. Cassandra's eyes rested on the notepad where she had written down Kostas's license plate. Following Trevor's example, she dove back into work. She began tapping her resources to find out more about him. Because of the danger he posed to Trevor, good old Boris had just become her personal target.

Chapter Twenty-Four

Trial by Fire

NIKOL'S POSITION WAS TENUOUS AT best. She had finally infiltrated Mikhailov's organization, but the pig had no use for women aside from as bed warmers. He had been brutal in his attempts to break her. She had steeled herself for such a confrontation and withstood his verbal and physical abuse. The bruises she sported on her body were badges of honor as far as she was concerned. It still hurt to bend or sit, but she never let them see her sweat.

Her fortitude had almost been her undoing. Mikhailov had even less use for strong women, but Sergei insisted that she would be useful. Eventually, he had approved her introduction to the organization. Sergei had put her through all sorts of hard exercises, trying to find any vulnerability he could use against her, but she had remained strong, focused on the final reward of that mission.

Nikol knew that many more of those exercises would happen along the way to test her loyalty. The problem with thieves and criminals was that they were always betraying one another, which in turn fed the paranoia among them.

She walked into the lavish mansion only to be greeted by Sergei, who grabbed her unceremoniously by the arm. Pain radiated from his grip as he dragged her to the basement she knew too well. A sharp sting of fear slashed through her. She was familiar with the uses and agony the instruments and torture devices decorating the walls could inflict. She had seen the results of their use. Her heart dropped to her stomach. *Fuck! My cover is blown.* Understanding finally penetrated her panic when she noticed a young man tied to a chair, sobbing.

Her glance shot to Sergei and a gleam of satisfaction filtered into his cold eyes. A parody of a Cheshire grin curved his mouth and he nodded with his head toward the man. "Are you ready to play, little Nikol?"

Nikol swallowed hard, relieved that her cover had not been blown. But her relief was short-lived, replaced almost immediately by sorrow. Sorrow for the fate of the man tied to the chair. Nikol took a step back, placing some distance between them. She cocked a hip, crossed her arms over her chest, and eyed the man. "What has he done?"

Sergei snickered slyly, "It is what he hasn't done."

"Hasn't done? What does that mean?"

"Vladimir hired him to do a job based on the special skills he bragged so proudly about. He could not finish the project. Said it was impossible. Even after he assured us he could do it. That his programming skills were top-notch. He lied. Now—" Sergei shrugged, "—he dies." The last words flowed from Sergei's lips in a soft breathy voice. He was a ruthless bastard who took great pleasure in others' pain and suffering. His profile definitely had not done him justice. Compared to the real devil, the man in the file was a pussycat.

Nikol struggled to keep a grip on her emotions. She wanted, needed, to help the man, a young programmer she had seen around the mansion a couple of times before who appeared to be no more than twenty or so.

His sandy blond hair hid his face, his head hung dejected between his shoulders. The knees of his jeans were scuffed as if he had been dragged to the chair to which he was tied. Blood from the many cuts on his face along with sweat and tears dampened the front of his Duran-Duran t-shirt. Her heart ached for him and his fate. A fate she couldn't prevent. Not without putting everything she had worked for and her own life at risk.

Sergei pulled a cigar guillotine from his back pocket and closed and opened it several times. The loud click of metal echoed in the room. The young man's head snapped up and his eyes grew wide. His arms jerked, his fingers gripping the arms of the chair to which they were strapped. His frantic eyes darted to Nikol, a silent plea in them. Nikol shoved the sympathy from her expression and schooled it, looking coldly down on him. She fisted her hands and pressed them against her thighs to mask their shaking.

Realization that she would be of no help must have hit the man, because tears began to stream down his face as Sergei approached him. "Please! No! Don't do this! Let me try again. Maybe I missed something. I can do it! I swear!"

"You had your chance. You didn't deliver. Now you are mine." Sergei stalked him, taunted him with slaps to the head. He leaned close to his ear and lowered his voice to a whisper, but Nikol could still hear his words. "Now, we play."

Sergei grabbed the programmer's hand and imprisoned his fingers, spreading them and then placing one through the ring. The young man's screams and Sergei's joyous laughter bounced off the walls as the boy's finger fell to the floor and blood spurted freely from the wound. After the third finger, the young man passed out.

"Fuck! That's no fun," Sergei cursed, slapping the man awake time and again before moving on to the next finger, cutting them one by one.

The physical damage Sergei inflicted upon him was grizzly and, at times, Nikol herself almost threw up from watching it. The bitter, acid taste of bile coated her mouth.

A metallic tang wafted in the air and filled Nikol's nostrils. She raged inside at the invisible ties binding her hands, preventing her from going to the young man's aid. A price to pay for getting one step closer to her goal. A price to stay alive. A price that would stain her soul for a long time to come.

Nikol's pulse jumped to her throat and choked her when Sergei cleaned the cutter, kicked the fingers aside, and retrieve the sledgehammer from where it leaned against the wall. Bile pushed up her throat at the sight of the cut off finger that had rolled to a stop next to the toe of her shoe. She worked hard to hold back her protest, but Sergei must have heard it because his head and eyes snapped to her and pinned her. "Do you have something to say, Nikol?"

She took a deep breath and held it before blowing it out slowly to calm herself. Moistening her mouth, she chose her words carefully. "You're making a nasty mess, Sergei. I am not cleaning it. I am bored; can I go?"

Sergei's eyes gleamed with dark, deadly promises as he continued to hold her gaze and gestured her to join him. She sucked in a breath and moved to his side with a casual gait.

His bloodied hand grazed her breast, leaving a smear on her blouse. She cringed inside and swallowed the retch that squeezed her throat. The bulge in Sergei's slacks said a lot about the man. He was getting off on the torture. Before he could take her hand, she took a step back.

Sergei's eyes narrowed to slits. "Run away while you can. I know where to find you."

As he swung the sledgehammer above his head and she turned to leave, a loud ring sounded in the room. With a curse, Sergei dropped the sledge-hammer and fumbled with his cell phone, pulling it out of his pocket, and answering it.

"Yes sir." He pocketed the phone and pierced her with a deadly look. "We are needed. Company."

"Right." As Nikol turned for the door, Sergei's hand snaked out and grabbed her hair, twining it in his fist and pulling her to him.

Tears filled her eyes at the pain. He brought her face close to his and bit her lip. "Don't think this is over. We will play later."

He released her abruptly and strode to the door. Nikol shot a look of regret at the young man. No matter how hardened life had made her, that was one scene and one person that would haunt her to her grave. Sergei was even more dangerous then she knew. She would need to tread carefully if she wanted to survive this mission. But more than just a job, her own personal quest was at stake, and she wouldn't rest until she reached her goal.

★ ★ ★ ★ ★

Boris drove through the gates of Mikhailov's mansion and parked in the circular driveway as usual. He had a good standing with the Vory boss, and he wanted to keep it that way. It paid to have connections in the right places—and in Russia that meant organized crime. He'd built a reputation, and even though he was a minor player, he could hold his own against the best of them.

Boris's services were essential to the mafia boss. His security business was the perfect cover to allow him access to security equipment and firearms as needed. That had made him a popular figure in Mikhailov's circle. It was a dangerous game, but one he played well.

Walking through the mansion's door into the vast lavish foyer and onto the sitting room beyond, Boris admired the lovely frescos on the walls and the many art pieces spread prominently around the room. Carefully illuminated alcoves exhibited precious items in a subtle but efficient display of wealth and power.

As he admired the art—a familiar past time while waiting for Mikhailov to show up—he heard footsteps echoing on the marble floors coming toward him. Turning to the origin of the sound, he watched as Mikhailov, his right-hand man Sergei Deminov, and a new player, a woman, walked into the room.

Boris casually addressed Deminov with a nod and noticed his shirt was speckled with something dark; the woman, who stood stoically next to him, also had smears on her blouse. Boris was taken aback by the hostility that pierced him from across the room when their eyes briefly met.

"Boris." Mikhailov's greeting distracted him from studying her further.

Boris extended his hand for a firm handshake while maintaining eye contact with the Vory boss. Having known him for some years, Boris had learned to respect the man's business mind as well as his viciousness. One thing was certain: one did not mess around with Vladimir Mikhailov. He asked Mikhailov in their mother tongue, "You mentioned that you needed to talk to me. What can I do for you, my friend?"

Mikhailov's smile faded as he appeared to remember the reason for Boris being there. A hard edge sharpened the gleam in his eyes. "The usual. I need more ammunition. My men used a little bit more...effort...than necessary when taking care of a swine for me a couple of weeks ago." Mikhailov's eyes were cold and unforgiving. Whoever that swine was, it was someone who had not been smart enough to stay out of Mikhailov's business.

"That is not a problem. How many rounds do you need?" Boris asked without hesitation.

Deminov interrupted, his voice filled with authority, "As many as you can bring us."

Boris frowned but didn't question Deminov's request. Nothing good came from questioning him. "When do you need the ammunition?"

The woman stepped forward and ignored the sharp warning glance Deminov shot in her direction. "As soon as possible. Is that a problem for you?" Her voice shimmered with barely checked disdain.

Boris inhaled deeply. For some reason this woman targeted him. He scrambled to calculate when he could have the ammunition delivered, and also how to approach introducing the subject of Trevor's request. For people in his field, it was all about the return investment for helping someone else. In this case, he expected a big favor from Trevor in return for putting his neck on the line.

Tension filled the air. Boris knew that broaching the subject of Trevor at this point in the conversation would be overstepping his bounds.

Mikhailov was furious about something or at someone, and things could definitely take a wrong turn under his current temper. The reference to the "swine" had sent a chill down Boris's spine. Letting sleeping dogs lie, Boris answered, "Give me a few days. I should have the ammunition for you within the week." He exhaled softly. "Is that all?"

Silence swirled around them as Mikhailov studied Boris's face carefully; his stare raked on his nerves like nails on a chalkboard. He squirmed inside but hid his discomfort, keeping a tight rein on his emotions. Displaying emotions would leave him open to the piranhas standing before him. Living among the Vory was like living in a jungle full of predators. At the first scent of fear or blood, they took one down quickly and effortlessly.

Mikhailov seemed to reach a decision. Narrowing his eyes, he said casually, "Now that you ask…I'm in a tight spot." He took his time capturing and holding Boris's gaze as if trying to peel back the layers of Boris's skin. It didn't matter that Mikhailov had known him for years. They all knew a wolf could hide in sheep's clothing. Trust was a hard commodity to come by.

Mikhailov knew many people, both legit and underground, who could possibly solve his current dilemma, but this time Boris seemed to be in the right place at the right time. After holding Boris in suspense, he spoke. "I need to find a good replacement for my software developer."

Boris was stunned. It was exactly what Trevor wanted. A fast-track to Mikhailov's computers. The opportunity dropped in his lap sounded too good to be true. *Was it a coincidence? Has Mikhailov been watching me? Is he aware of Trevor and Cassandra's intentions? Does he know of my visit with them?*

Too many questions swirled in his mind, prompting Boris to choose his words carefully. He studied Mikhailov's reaction as he probed, "I gather that the need for a developer was a result of your 'swine' problem?"

Mikhailov showed a hint of a smile, one that enveloped his face in a cruel mask. A deep satisfied chuckle rumbled from Deminov's direction. "You gathered correctly. Let's just say that I don't tolerate animals in my house," he continued in the same dark and calculating tone, holding Boris's eyes. "If they think they can turn on me and go on with their lives, living off my hard work, they are wrong!"

Boris's gut told him it was time to bring the conversation to an end and leave as quickly as possible before all that was left of him was speckles decorating Deminov's shirt. His only relief was that he knew from his dealings with the Vory over the years that Mikhailov was just asserting himself before making Boris privy to high-level information. Information he would kill to keep under wraps.

"Why me?" Boris needed to confirm his assumption that he was about to be introduced to a higher level of the Vory hierarchy.

Mikhailov's right-hand man cocked his head and narrowed his eyes. "You don't want to do Vladimir a favor?" His tone conveyed that he would like nothing more than to show Boris why he should accept the recruiter job.

Boris struggled to mask how tense he was. "Of course I will help. I just want to know why I am to receive this…honor," he responded in a steady voice, managing to keep any sarcasm from coloring it.

"You have proven yourself many times, Boris," Mikhailov praised. "The Vory code has been threatened by weak links for many years. We used to be the absolute power. Now we are riddled with traitors, turncoats." Boris could finally see Mikhailov's wheels turning. He now knew he had finally made it to the top. "We need strong key players, and you know people. You have your own ass to cover and you keep your mouth shut. A perfect fit."

Excitement rippled in Boris's blood. He'd waited several years for this, the opportunity of a lifetime: access to Mikhailov's inner circle. "I am very honored by your trust, Vladimir." Taking a deep breath, Boris asked without fear, "What can I do for you in regard to the computer person you need?"

Just as Mikhailov began to give Boris the requirements, one of his runners—a young man Boris recognized as having just joined the mafia and who made trafficking deliveries for the organization—walked into the room and froze like a deer caught in the headlights when he encountered the silence and the four people staring back at him. "I am sorry, sir," the boy stammered. "Forgive me. I had no idea—"

Mikhailov interrupted. "I can see that." His temper flared at the abrupt interruption of his business dealings with Boris, the illusion of the businessman gone in a second, and in its place, the ruthless man he truly was.

Mikhailov stalked toward the young man. As he drew closer, the boy's eyes grew wider. Without any notice, Mikhailov pulled a small Makarov pistol from his pocket and shot the boy in the fleshy part of his thigh. Boris watched unfazed as the boy screamed in pain, doubling over to hold his wounded leg while Mikhailov stared down at him. "Learn not to wander around," he said in disgust. "Sergei!" Mikhailov called to his right-hand man.

Deminov immediately made a phone call and soon a knock sounded on the door. Two men strode in. They bee-lined straight to the writhing boy on the floor, each grabbed him under an arm, and dragged him, like a sack of potatoes, out the door, leaving a trail of blood behind.

"Piece of shit got my floors dirty," Mikhailov said, as if he'd had no part in how the blood came to be there. He walked back toward Boris to continue the conversation. "Where were we? Ah, yes. The programmer. I need someone who can finish developing a piece of software I recently acquired."

Boris mirrored Mikhailov's stance. He had seen much worse posturing in his many years in the business. Mikhailov wanted to show who was boss, flexing his power and demonstrating how short his tolerance was. *Short? Hell, it is almost nonexistent.*

"Let me see what I can do. I will call you once I have someone who fits the bill." To give Trevor's name right now would sound too eager. He would play the game, letting Mikhailov grow anxious to get a name, any name. "I have some contacts that might be able to help," he added.

"I am sure you do." Mikhailov held his gaze with burning intensity as he extended his hand for another firm handshake before leaving the room.

Mikhailov's last words stressed his expectation of the outcome. It had become Boris's trial by fire. Deliver, or else.

Chapter Twenty-Five

Pardon Me As I Check My Shoe Mic

M IKHAILOV WAS A VERY CAUTIOUS man. It was a given, considering his line of business. Reading the extensive profile Cassandra had put together on him with Jessica's help, Trevor noticed there were no living family members on record. The file listed a wife deceased twenty years back. Her death, an unsolved murder.

His gang was rumored to be one of the most vicious in operation, but the police had never been able to prove his involvement in any of the many murders or high-profile fraud cases he'd supposedly orchestrated.

Tracking the mastermind of the theft and gathering all they could about his operation was crucial, but Trevor felt the need to learn more about him as a person before sticking his neck into the pit. Mikhailov's history was fuzzy. Beside the fact that he had been born in Glazov, there was not much available about him. Very humble origins. Working-class parents. His trajectory from a child to ruthless mafia boss was marked by several incarcerations. With each visit to the slammer, he advanced to bigger and heavier crimes.

They had focused too much on his operation, how he conducted his business, and had forgotten to study the man behind it all. After spending a couple of hours going through the detailed report and George's latest transcripts, he was anxious for the meeting to take place. The more Trevor read, the more he understood Mikhailov, but not enough to decode his frame of mind. Aside from being a vicious mafia boss, he was a man who had been pushed by unexpected events in his life to be what he had become. Maybe the result was caused by the grief, by the guilt of not having been there to avert disaster. Of not having been close to say goodbye. Trevor became lost in his thoughts. A heavy feeling crowded his chest. He had also lost people important to him under circumstances he could only hypothesize as violent. Strangely, he felt a connection with Mikhailov.

★ ★ ★ ★ ★

A loud ring echoed through the apartment. When it continued unanswered, Cassandra looked around and realized Trevor was nowhere in sight. She pushed from her desk and tracked the sound, at last finding the phone by the teakettle, where Trevor must have last set it during his many excursions for tea. The man had been sucking it back like candy since the little surprise they'd captured on the surveillance feed.

Trevor entered the room as she glanced at the number and answered the call.

A brief silence followed before a male voice came across the connection. "Cassandra? This is Boris Kostas."

"Boris! How are you?" Cassandra's gaze shot to Trevor and she raised her eyebrows as she walked over to where he stood.

"I am well. *Very* well, actually." Deep satisfaction emanated from his heavily accented voice. "Can I please speak with your husband?"

Cassandra didn't like the cheery sound of Boris's voice or the little laugh akin to what she imagined one would sound like having won the lottery. "Here he is," she said as she put the call on speakerphone.

"Hello, Boris. Hope you have good news."

Not knowing Boris's game had become a hindrance to the whole operation. Before the little eye-opener a few days ago, they had only one source of concern—Mikhailov. Now, with Boris in the picture, it had become harder to gauge who to trust. Trevor felt like they were walking on eggshells at all times. They needed to pin down whether he was an asset or a drawback.

"Yes, I found a way inside. It means meeting Mikhailov himself." Boris's tone was jovial.

"Mikhailov? When?" Alarms rang in Trevor's head.

"On Monday." Boris paused for a few seconds before adding, "At the mansion."

The location took Trevor by surprise. Mikhailov must be either desperate or softening up if he was allowing newcomers into his den so easily. That, or Boris had more influence in the Glazov, Mikhailov's organization arrogantly named after his birthplace, than they'd ever imagined.

Trevor took a deep breath. Holding back his suspicion, he fished for more information. "How did you manage that feat?"

His reaction seemed to amuse Boris. "Secrets of the trade, son."

Too many secrets.

As they talked, Cassandra became absorbed with the details on the identities of the mansion's regular visitors. Some of them were small businessmen, like the banker who had left the mansion pulling at his collar and sweating buckets. Or the financial institute director they had seen leaving the mansion with blood dripping from his ear and wearing a glazed look as if he'd escaped the jaws of death.

Others were just "employees" who worked there. Several, as she'd found, were your typical run-of-the-mill hacker—young, vulnerable, and otherwise unemployed. Her final objective was to compile a profile of each employee to give Trevor an advantage once he made it in.

Trevor continued to address Boris over the speaker. "So, what's the deal?"

"He wants to meet you. Decide for himself if he can trust you."

I should be the one worried about who to trust, Trevor thought. "He's a smart man." His voice dripped sarcasm.

Boris proceeded, oblivious to what they knew of his connection to Mikhailov. "A very smart man. He knows how to keep his business under wraps."

"Will it give me access to the computers?"

"Yes. He is desperate to get his hands on a skilled developer. You will need to prove your worth if you want to become his new one. I cannot help you there. It will not be easy. His last one left the project…unfinished."

The whole story was too good to be true. Just a few days after their discussion and they already had a way into the organization? With the potential of full access to the servers? *What were the odds?* "Why can't I shake the feeling that there's more to the story than just the fact you have contacts in the right places?" Trevor's voice was smooth as velvet, yet edged with steel.

"Just be glad the fates conspired to help your cause. *And* I never said I was doing this for nothing. I will have a favor in return."

And there it was—the catch. "Go on."

"I will tell you once you are cleared. No point in telling you now without knowing if Vladimir will hire you for sure."

"What's my story? You didn't tell him who I really am, right?" Concern hit Trevor square in the chest. What if Boris had given his real identity to Mikhailov? What if Cassandra had been put in danger as a result?

"Of course not! He would kill me first if he knew I am consorting with someone who has close ties to people like Robert James, an ex-Navy Seal, and Cassandra, ex-CIA. That would guarantee us all bullets to the head.

I have as much to lose as you do." Boris's disposition turned sour, clearly offended by Trevor's insinuation.

Before Trevor could respond, Boris continued. "You are the son of a good friend of mine. Recently emigrated from London to his parents' home country. A skilled hacker and software expert. Looking for opportunities in the new digital Mecca. Since you couldn't find a job that paid you what you wanted, you decided to try other avenues for securing an income. You are not opposed to taking a job that is not legitimate, as long as it pays well," he said sarcastically.

"Got it. Do I have a name?"

"Mark Ivanov."

"Will I need papers?"

"I will take care of that when the time comes."

"Okay, then."

"I will call you if things change, but otherwise, prepare to meet the man."

"Will do."

Trevor killed the call and turned to Cassandra. Excitement shone in his eyes and bled into his voice. "This is it, Cassie."

Cassandra watched the play of emotions flow across Trevor's face. She wanted to grin at him and his boyish glee sparked by the knowledge that he would soon be jumping into the fray, testing himself against the Russian bear. But she balked at the idea of Trevor behind the mansion's walls with only Boris as his backup. The same Boris whose voice oozed satisfaction just a moment ago.

Deep lines of worry appeared between Cassandra brows. "This is way bigger than what we originally thought. You are not just going in covertly with a 'wham-bam-thank-you-ma'am' approach." Her voice was low, edged with concern. "In order to do what they need you to do, you'll have to live and work among them for longer than just a visit. Chances are it'll take days, maybe even longer, for you to get access to those files. You've never done something like this before, Trevor. This is new territory. There's no way you're going in there without real backup. No way you're leaving me here without ears." She shook her head and smoothed her brow with both hands. "No freaking way." Her lowered voice held a silken thread of warning.

Trevor walked over to her and caressed her cheek with the back of his knuckle. "I agree with your assessment, Cassie. But you are wrong. You *will* have ears. I have an idea that will keep you informed of what's going on while I'm in there."

Her frown deepened and he tucked a stray tendril of hair behind her ear with a mischievous grin. "Good thing I read everything I could find on Russian intelligence," Trevor commented as he turned and walked to his suitcase. He could feel Cassandra's eyes tracking his every move as he pulled out a pair of loafers and returned to where she was sitting.

She shot him a confused look. "You need to get off the tea. You're making no sense."

He laughed, put the shoes on the table, and retrieved a few small pieces of equipment from the other suitcase. "Patience, grasshopper…you'll see."

Setting a small microphone on the table beside the shoes, he grabbed one of the loafers and unceremoniously pried off the heel. "Trevor! Those were a gift from me!" He watched her closely, waiting; suddenly her eyes brightened with understanding as the meaning of his words and actions finally clicked. She got where he was headed. She got him.

"Oh man. The old microphone-in-shoe KGB trick?" She smirked and shook her head at his ingenious idea. "Nice touch. Can I help?"

Trevor knew she'd planted more bugs than she could count in the past, so he immediately handed her the shoe. "Do the honors."

"We're going to use Russian techniques against Russians. That's so wrong on so many levels. But so…you," she laughed softly as she inserted the transmitter in the heel.

While she worked on it, Trevor set up the relay transmitter they had hidden outside the mansion to receive the shoe's signal.

Cassandra replaced the heel and handed the shoe back to him. "Here you go, Agent 86. Looks like instead of, 'Pardon me while I get my shoe phone,' you'll be saying, 'Pardon me while I check my shoe mic.'"

Trevor burst out in rich laughter as he took the shoe from her. Cassandra's humor cut through some of the tension that had hung in the room, and Trevor realized for the umpteenth time how well they worked together. It was a well-choreographed dance. He checked the signal from the microphone; it came across loud and clear on the computer.

"Are you sure I'll be able to hear you?"

"You should have a clear reception. No worries there."

He was fairly pleased with himself, so she enjoyed the moment with him. "Oh Max! It's marvelous."

Trevor snickered at her *Get Smart* references. Suddenly feeling the weight of the many days over the keyboard, Trevor straightened and stretched his sore back. His body still felt the ramifications of the fall; he ached all over.

Looking over at Trevor, Cassandra felt his exhaustion beating at her. From the way he was seated, she could tell the bruise on his back bothered him. All she wanted to do was fall into bed and sleep cradled in his arms. Her own exhaustion beat at her. Barely able to keep her eyes open, she closed her laptop. "I am out. If I look at one more piece of surveillance, I swear I'll go blind." She walked to him and rubbed his shoulder to get his attention. "Come on, babe…it will still be there in the morning—and then some. Let it go for a couple of hours. Come to bed."

Releasing a deep breath, he stood to follow her. "I guess you're right."

Lost in their own thoughts, without a word they moved to the bed, stripped, and climbed under the covers. When their heads hit the pillows, they both groaned and lay there enjoying the sensation of stretching out after sitting long hours in the uncomfortable chairs.

With a deep sigh, Cassandra rolled and curled into Trevor.

"Hey, I meant to ask if you've heard from Jessie," Trevor yawned as he wrapped an arm around her shoulders and pulled her snug against him.

"We talked briefly when she sent over the information she researched for me. She said that Dublin is great and that she's having the time of her life." Cassandra's tone was unsure.

"Isn't that a good thing?" Trevor chuckled. "Of course she's having the time of her life. Pubs…Irishmen."

Cassandra snorted. "No. For some reason I don't think she's partying hard. She sounded…I don't know how to explain it. Something's different. Something happened and I just can't put my finger on it."

"Well, we better not walk in on somebody else's white Irish ass keeping her company on our couch when we get back." His humor rumbled in his chest and she could feel his silent laughter under her palm.

"Oh my god, Trevor. That is *so* wrong."

"What? Just saying. Besides, any guy applying to date Jessie has to go through my seal of approval. She's like a little sister to me now."

Cassandra laughed out loud as she snuggled closer and slipped her arm around his waist, already feeling the fingers of sleep tugging at her eyelids. She could hardly wait to see Trevor behaving like the protective brother in the near future. It sure as hell would put Jessica's panties in a bunch.

★ ★ ★ ★ ★

Heart racing, Cassandra ran into the alley, trying her best to lose the tail she'd picked up about two blocks back. Looking down at her cell and the GPS application on the screen, she took a left, a quick right, and then sprinted all the way down the block to cross the next street. Once there, she glanced over her shoulder and saw she still had a buddy.

"Fuck!" she cursed under her breath, drawing a startled look from a passerby. *Can't shake him.*

Not wanting to draw attention to their base location, she ran for the metro station only two blocks away from her. Her heart raced, sweat beading down her back as she weighed her options. If she could get there, she could fake catching a train and double back to the apartment unnoticed.

She caught a glimpse of the tail reflected on the window of a store she passed. The tail—a man of slight build, just under five feet tall, wearing a black trench and sporting a black fedora—looked familiar to her. Her pulse surged. *Do I know him?* She picked up her pace and, reaching the metro, jogged down the stairs.

As luck would have it, there wasn't a line at the booth. She dropped some notes in the slot and pointed to the first stop on the map so the attendant would know what ticket she needed. Her Russian was spotty at best and she didn't have time to mess around. The woman took forever to print the ticket.

"Come on, come on, come on!" she mumbled under her breath as her hand tapped on the counter and she threw glimpses toward the top of the stairs. Just as the tail's loafers and trench coat came into view, she snagged the ticket out of the attendant's fingers without waiting for change and took off for the platform.

She moved at a brisk pace until she reached the stairs to the second entrance. A flow of commuters crowded the platform, making it impossible for the man to catch up with her. Her stomach turned in knots as she waited for her chance to get out of there. Just as the train barreled into the station, she sprinted up the stairs in the opposite direction of the flow of people boarding. Cassandra hoped he had lost sight of her in the commotion. She sucked in gulps of brisk fresh air as she reached the street and ducked into the nearest store—a bakery.

Her breath came in quick gasps as she bent over, resting her hands on her knees. Sweat ran down her temples in rivulets as she straightened and pretended to shop, looking over the pastries on display in the window, giving the illusion she was looking to purchase something, all the while keeping an eye on the metro's entrance. A flash of black appeared in her peripheral vision. *Shit!*

She hid from sight and watched her "buddy" exit the station. His eyes scanned the surrounding area, head turning rapidly from one side to the other, looking for her. Catching a better glimpse of his face, her mind stumbled. She recognized him! "What the fuck?!"

Cassandra's eyes snapped wide open as she sprang up in bed in the darkened room. Her heart filled her throat, beating wildly, making it hard to suck in air. Sweat coated her brow as she shoved her hair back from her face.

What the hell! Cartoon characters? A freaking nightmare with Boris Badenov from *Rocky and Bullwinkle? Really? Damn, Cassie, get a grip.* As she waited for her pulse to slow its frantic pace, she took it as a sign she wouldn't be getting any more sleep until she dug deeper. Slipping out of bed, she mulled over the meaning of the dream.

Shivering in the dark room, she noticed the time on the clock: three in the morning—the witching hour. "Figures," Cassandra muttered as the last cobwebs of the dream fell away. The need to find out more about Boris pounded in her head as she moved to the table and booted up the laptop.

Trevor was deep asleep, undisturbed by her sudden awakening. She shifted the laptop so that the glow from the screen wouldn't wake him. Checking her email, she found two—one from her father and the other, oddly, from Nathan.

Cassandra opened Nathan's first. It held an update regarding the house they were interested in "renting." *The premises are still available for the next few weeks. No tenants have reserved the location.* She grinned. She had to give him credit. He had been inventive in passing on that bit of information regarding the safe house. As she continued to read, a frown creased her brow when she saw the closing: *Think of me.* She rolled her eyes and moved on to her father's email.

She mentally crossed her fingers and hoped for answers to her questions about Boris Kostas. As she read, her hand stilled and her focus moved inward as the names—Boris Kostas, Boris Badenov, Boris Kostas, Boris Badenov—formed a continuous loop in her mind, hammering at her until suddenly, things made sense. She fell back in her chair shaking her head. *Holy hell! Boris Badenov was Boris Kostas.*

His favorite quote, "It's good to be bad," brought shivers to her skin. The sneaky little Russian cartoon spy she'd seen on the old reruns of *Rocky and Bullwinkle* sometimes engaged in his own schemes, like the episode where he wanted to start his own organized crime gang. Was her sixth sense trying to tell her something? Either way, it was time to get Jessica and George to work their magic.

Chapter Twenty-Six

Quiet Before the Storm

TRADITIONAL RUSSIAN MUSIC PLAYED SOFTLY in the background as Boris nursed a glass of aged port while relaxing in his comfortable recliner. He was enjoying the calm before the storm when a call rang through to his cell phone. He suspected who the caller was. One more reason to have ignored the first call to the house phone earlier.

Boris's tone was sharp when he finally answered the call in his mother tongue. "You should not be calling me. Especially not now."

The familiar voice laughed and, with a hard edge, answered in kind, "Skittish, are we? Should I remind you who the boss is?"

"What do you want?" He wasn't up to games. The events over the past days were snowballing. To top it off, he had become the focus of Mikhailov's latest henchman—or henchwoman, to be exact. He pictured the woman in his mind. There was something about her....

The caller's casual, unhurried response drew him from his musings. "You have not called in a while. I just thought I would check on you. I do not want you to think I have forgotten you. I am watching. We are always watching," Boris's boss continued. "Do you have the information we need?"

"Not yet." Boris was treading very carefully. It had taken him almost ten years to get this close to Mikhailov. "Do not ruin it by meddling. You will get what you need. Soon. I will make sure of that." Boris's tone was confident. He would get his hands on the information the man on the other side of the call wanted desperately.

Russian organizations took each other out regularly. Betrayal among rival gangs was common, even within the gangs themselves. What made the Russians exceptionally ruthless wasn't the violence, but the willingness to turn members, hand them over to the police or rivals if the situation called for it. Flipping the weakest to cover their ass and pay their way out of the hole. Boris knew his way out of holes. He had used his connections in the past to help Mikhailov avenge his wife's murder, and now that "good deed" was finally paying off.

He never thought it would take so long for Mikhailov to take into account the services he had provided and finally bring him in, but the man had become more suspicious and cruel over the years, as if the loss of his wife had created a violent progression that was getting worse each year—catapulting Mikhailov into the annals of brutality, extreme even for the Russian mafia.

"When?" the man demanded.

Boris sighed. "I do not know for sure. I will know more tomorrow." He paused and added, "Do *not* call again. I will call you when *I* have what you need."

Boris disconnected the call before the man had a chance to retort and took a long sip from his glass. The smooth sweetness of the port coated his tongue and relaxed him as he considered what he would have to do. He had gotten used to living a double life. Boris missed his old self, the one who could laugh and enjoy the small things. When had he lost that part of him?

Alina's face crossed his mind and he tried to push back the memories of her, to no avail. Alina. His long-lost love. A sigh burst from him at the thought of her. He swirled the glass in his hand and took another long pull of his port, all but shooting back the rest of what remained in the glass. A nice warmth filled his chest, but didn't reach his heart. She'd left him when she could no longer handle his dedication to his activities and the associated hazards that had come with it.

If only he'd had the insight into his life then that he had now, he would have made different choices. *Would I have, really? Would I have given it all up for her? Followed her to the ends of the earth. Gone wherever she had wanted to, as long as she would stay with me? Would she have stayed then?* That part of his life was water under the bridge. He would never know for sure. Boris exhaled a deep sigh and set the glass on the side table. It was time for bed. He would catch a few hours of sleep before he had to brave the storm.

Chapter Twenty-Seven

You Belong to Me

CASSANDRA CURLED INTO TREVOR AS the first tendrils of consciousness pierced her. Laying her head on his shoulder and wrapping an arm around his waist, she stared off into the darkness. Her thoughts focused on the danger he was about to face and how he would be at the mercy of a lethal Russian mafia leader.

What concerned her most was that he wouldn't have anyone whom he could completely trust to watch his back. The microphone in the shoe was fine and dandy, but it would only give her ears. Without eyes or a way to communicate directly with him, there wasn't much she could do for him if trouble ensued. A war of emotions raged inside Cassandra and her mind worked overtime again as she ran through different scenarios in her head, but couldn't formulate a single viable backup plan. Her old fears were back with a vengeance; loss, a devil rearing its ugly head again.

If only they had a better handle on Boris, they could determine whether or not he could be of help within the mansion's walls. *Boris.* Her thoughts tumbled to Robert's good friend. *He's a good man,* Robert had asserted in his email. *I wish I knew that for sure, Dad,* she berated in her head. But until she could eliminate all of her doubts about his motivations, he was one of them.

Feeling once again somnolent, she tucked her face in the crook of Trevor's neck and inhaled his clean, warm, musky scent as she drifted at the edge of sleep. An hour later, the glow of the new day crossed her eyelids, rousing her. She stretched and, as she opened her eyes fully, her gaze collided with Trevor's sparkling blue ones.

"Good morning sleepyhead." He dropped a kiss on her nose. "It's time to get up, *a ghrá*. Boris will be here any minute."

Instantly alert, Cassandra swung her legs over the side of the bed. "Damn. I don't know what happened. One minute I'm awake, ready to get up, and the next you're calling me sleepyhead. This is not good. I have things to get done before you leave."

Scurrying, she dressed in jeans and a sweater, hurried to the bathroom, and emerged, feeling more like herself. Stepping into the kitchen, the smell of coffee engulfed her senses, her mouth watered at the thought of a hot cup in her hand and caffeine in her system.

Trevor smiled and handed her a cup. "Something to jumpstart your brain."

Cassandra took the cup he offered and grinned. Closing her eyes, she savored the delicious scent invading her nostrils. "Heaven."

While Trevor took his turn in the bathroom, Cassandra moved to the closet and pulled out the contingency bags. She double-checked each to be sure all was in order—tickets, passports, ammo, clothing, necessities, food staples, and water—before setting them by the front door.

She popped her head in the bathroom and her eyes connected with Trevor's in the mirror. His gaze expressed loud and clear the conflicting feelings that were also churning in her chest. Trevor held the contact a moment longer, a lifetime of words spoken in a blink of an eye, before he returned to shaving.

Cassandra's pulse was a livewire of activity, beating out of control. She wasn't ready to face what the day had in store. She booted her laptop, her focus turned inward, the wheels in her head in constant motion. She needed to contact George and Jessica and have them tap Boris. Dig into his past, find any skeletons hiding in the closet—a closet her father apparently hadn't explored.

The computer beeped; as she glanced down, she realized her hand was rubbing along her scar, which didn't necessarily make her a happy camper. *That can't be good.* The scar—a gunshot wound sustained years before—had become a sixth sense of sorts.

The pad of Trevor's approaching steps drew her attention. He was dressed for the meeting in a dark gray pinstriped two-piece suit and a blue shirt that intensified the blue of his eyes. She glanced at his hands as she took her first sip from her coffee and noticed he didn't have his usual cup of tea in his hands. "What, no tea? Who are you and where is my tea-toting husband?"

Without even the smallest quirk of a smile, he responded, "No time, Boris is due any minute."

"Right." She sensed his need to get straight down to business and switched gears. Sitting in front of her laptop, she initiated the graphic interface of the sound equalizer they would use to record the incoming signal from the shoe's microphone.

"Are we good?" Trevor looked over her shoulder at the screen.

She watched as the wave modulation registered the high and low tones of his voice. "Yep. We're good," Cassandra confirmed out loud, more as a reassurance to herself. They were okay, they would be okay. *Damn it. Since when had she become such a whiner? Maybe the question should be, where's Cassandra Bauer and what have I done with her?* She struggled to understand why she was emotionally all over the board.

The aspects of their projects were nothing new—surveillance, analysis, and planning were all second nature, and they had been working together for several months like a well-oiled machine. *So why am I getting so emotional?* Where had the no-nonsense-get-it-done-take-no-prisoner Cassandra gone?

She turned her head and watched Trevor as he finished his preparations for the meeting. Since giving her heart to him, her outlook on life had changed. He'd taught her to have fun, loosen up, and relax, her strength as deeply rooted as ever before. After a quick self-assessment, she realized what was different—very different: the stakes were higher. Trevor's life was on the line in a way it had never been before.

Her determination to keep him safe was equal to his own to keep her out of the physical infiltration and danger's path. Fortunately, she was determined to find a way to keep them both safe. Once Trevor walked out the door, she would secure resources for all the information she could get regarding Boris. That information could be the ticket to getting them out of Russia alive.

The ring of Trevor's cell was a double-edged sword—dread for knowing it was Boris calling him and relief in knowing it would take them one step closer to going home. On the second ring, Trevor answered.

"Yes? I will be right down. Give me a minute." Trevor disconnected and met Cassandra's gaze. "He's waiting downstairs." He cupped her face with his hands and placed a soft, gentle kiss on her lips. Cassandra froze briefly, then wrapped her arms around his neck and took charge, deepening the kiss, sliding her tongue between his. He moaned and allowed himself time to enjoy her taste before gently pulling her arms from around his neck. He stared into her eyes and stepped away. "I will see you in a couple of hours," he said with quiet emphasis.

Cassandra's heart squeezed tight as she watched him walk out the door. What she wouldn't give to go with him. A deep breath escaped as she steeled herself for the day ahead.

She turned her attention to the screen and double-checked that the sound recorder application was receiving Trevor's signal. Turning up the volume, she heard Trevor enter the car and ask Boris, "Any special instructions?"

"I can hear you loud and clear, love," Cassandra whispered under her breath, knowing full well he couldn't hear her. She knew it was early in Fort Meade, but she couldn't wait any longer. With their dialogue low in the background, she called George. While it rang, pulled up the file she had thrown together on Boris.

"Cassie. What the hell are you doing calling at this ungodly hour?" His exasperated tone brought a smile to her lips.

"I know. I'm sorry. I needed to talk to you. Are you alone?"

"What do you think? Duh! It's two freaking o'clock in the morning."

Cassandra chuckled at his vehemence. "I guess you haven't been using the romance cheat sheet we sent you?" she snorted.

George sighed heavily. "Working on it. I'm a quick study. I'll catch up. So what do you want, crazy woman?"

A frown creased her brow and the smile died. "You may just be right about the crazy bit."

"What's up? I can hear it in your voice. Something wrong?"

"Nothing to worry about. I'm working a hunch. Do you have a pen and paper?"

"Yep."

"Okay, take this number down."

George repeated it back to her. "This looks like a phone number. Whose is it?"

"It belongs to a friend of Bob's. His name is Boris Kostas. He's helping us with getting access into Mikhailov's den. I need you to trace this number and send me the call records on his phone and any other number that has called him within the last month."

"Cassie, what the hell is going on?"

"George, just get it, okay? I'll fill you in later. I have to run. Don't forget, as soon as you can do your magic."

"Cass—"

Cassandra disconnected the call and placed another, this time to Jessica. When the call to the house went unanswered, she rang Jessica's cell.

"Hello?" Jessica's languid voice answered on the second ring.

"Jessie? It's Cassie. I just called the house. No answer. Where are you?"

"Cassie! Everything okay?"

Cassandra picked up on the avoidance to answer her question, but the timing wasn't right for further quizzing. "I need you to handle something for me. Can you take notes?"

"Hold on. Let me get something." Cassandra heard a rustle and, shortly after, Jessica came back on the line. "Okay. I'm ready."

Cassandra recited a few strings of numbers.

"Okay, got it," Jessica confirmed.

"The first one is the license plate of Bob's friend, Boris Kostas, who is helping us. Bob wasn't able to shed much light on his background. Boris owns a security business here. The other number is his bank account. I'm looking for any large deposits. I was able to get hold of a transaction report, but I didn't see a lot of activity on it. Can you see if you can find more? Maybe another account? I have a gut feeling there is something more…hold on…"

Cassandra honed in on the conversation and observed Trevor and Boris's arrival at the mansion through the camera feed. She heard Boris talking to someone at the gate through the audio being picked up by Trevor's shoe.

"Jessie, listen. I have to go. I need any information as soon as you get it."

"I'm on it. I'll let you know as soon as I find something."

Once she hung up, Cassandra returned her attention to the feed and her heart dropped. They were in the mansion. Trevor's lowered voice came over the speaker. "Have you been here before?"

★ ★ ★ ★ ★

Jessica tossed her cell and notebook on the nightstand. She slipped back under the covers and turned into Stephan. His arms wrapped around her and pulled her close.

"Who was that?" he asked in a groggy voice.

"Cassie."

"Everything okay?"

"Not sure. She wants me to check someone. Go back to sleep—you have a few more minutes." Jessica snuggled closer and closed her eyes.

★ ★ ★ ★ ★

Trevor sat back and stretched his legs, trying to gauge Boris's mood as the Russian pulled smoothly into the flow of traffic. Boris had picked him up in his luxury sedan—the same Mercedes he had used in the captured surveillance video from days before. The man appeared at ease and unaffected by the fact that he was about to lead him into the lion's den. "Any special instructions?"

"Keep your jokes to yourself, and whatever you do, don't smile. Russians do not trust smiles—especially not Mikhailov," Boris answered sternly, and continued, "Let me do the talking. I will translate the negotiation for you."

Keeping his fluency in Russian under wraps had been a joint decision made with Cassandra, something that could give him an edge later on. Trevor nodded his agreement to Boris and gazed out the window for the duration of the drive. He straightened in his seat as Boris approached the gates and lowered the tinted window, allowing the camera to register his face. A voice came through the speakers in Russian, "Name?"

"Boris Kostas. Mikhailov is expecting us."

Trevor focused his gaze ahead of him, scanning the mansion grounds, taking note of certain landmarks inside the property that could come in handy later if he needed to find his way out. The mansion's grounds were opulent, but not overly so compared to pictures he had seen of some mafia bosses' homes. The Russian mafia loved to flaunt their power and money. Mikhailov seemed to be an exception, preferring a more understated appearance.

The voice over the speakers came back after a couple of minutes. "Who is the guy?"

"None of your business. Report to Deminov that I am here with the boy."

Trevor turned his face away to hide the fact that he had understood their conversation and pretended to study the mansion's façade.

With a quick acknowledgment, the security detail ended the conversation. Moments later, the gates opened and Boris guided the car up the circular driveway to the house, parking in front of the tall double door.

"Get out," Boris ordered Trevor in English.

Trevor complied without argument. Boris circled the car and took the lead as they headed to the front door. A young man opened the door and gestured for them to walk in. Boris moved casually through the lavish foyer and into the sitting room where they were directed.

"Have you been here before?" Trevor asked under his breath, studying Boris's expression.

Boris's mouth tightened to a grim line and he ignored Trevor's question. He walked further into the sitting room and stared intently at the door opposite to the one they came in, balancing on the balls of his feet, apparently expecting a horde of orcs to come rushing through.

As if on cue, several men and a woman entered the room. Trevor immediately recognized many of the faces he and Cassandra had captured on video. One of the men was Mikhailov; the other, close at his side, was his henchman, Sergei Deminov. The surprise was the dark-haired woman standing behind Deminov. He had seen her enter the mansion before, but didn't think she was part of the posse.

Boris approached Vladimir Mikhailov with an extended hand and Mikhailov returned the handshake, unceremoniously pulling him into a hug. Trevor observed Boris's body stiffen on contact only to relax again during the traditional exchange of three kisses on the cheeks—a common exchange among close friends and family. *Are they that close?*

Trevor was shocked at their familiarity, and quickly schooled his expression, maintaining a somber mask of respect, just as Boris had instructed him. He watched Boris closely, and out of the corner of his eyes noticed the woman observing them just as intently. He would consult with Cassandra later and figure out who she was. They needed to determine when she had joined the game and what her role might be.

A heavy sensation of being scrutinized claimed Trevor's attention. Turning his eyes to Mikhailov, he found his trained on him, looking him over from head to toe, taking his measure, studying him. He was being dissected alive. Mikhailov held his gaze and riddled Boris with questions in their language. "So...this is the boy." The term "boy" hit a nerve with Trevor, but he gave no indication of how it riled him.

"Yes. This is Mark Ivanov. He is eager to help you." Boris's words were clipped.

Mikhailov's smirk was unnerving. "Can he speak Russian?"

"Not much."

The smirk transformed into a wide smile. "Good." Mikhailov turned and addressed Trevor in English. "Ivanov, how do you like Russia so far?"

"I find it very...welcoming, even though it's been a bumpy ride." Memories of the fall from the fence and his bruised back came to mind.

"Bumpy ride?" Mikhailov frowned, questioning his choice of words.

"Yes. The lack of opportunity for a foreigner in my field is appalling."

"Ah!" Mikhailov exclaimed. "Everything in Russia is about who you know. Connections are worth their weight in gold."

Trevor sensed Boris monitoring their word exchange carefully, ready to intervene if Trevor stuck his foot in his mouth.

"What are you doing in Russia and why do you want to work for me?"

"England's employment market for programmers is down the tubes since the financial market collapsed last year. A friend of mine told me about opportunities in Russia. And since I had family connections to the country, here I am."

"Even if the job is breaking the law?" Mikhailov scrutinized him with narrowed eyes.

"As long as I am not caught red-handed," Trevor shot back. A true statement. Trevor used his skills to take down those who broke the law. Mikhailov's possession of the decrypter had the makings of a worldwide financial crisis. His attention focused on the large numbers of victims Mikhailov's use of the decrypter could leave in its wake.

Mikhailov cocked his head and said in a droll tone, "Prove it."

Immediately Trevor's mind went on alert. *Prove it? What does he mean by that?* Before he could think through the possibilities Mikhailov added, "You will hack into a bank, for me. Now."

Trevor realized right away that having him hack into the bank was not a test of his computer-related knowledge—hacking didn't have much to do with the program development skills he knew were needed—but a way to test his loyalty and his true interests regarding the mafia boss's organization—whether or not he was too squeaky clean to join the "family."

The challenge rattled Trevor. He was all for crazy adventures, but hacking into a bank and wreaking havoc on innocent people were not things he relished or took lightly. But it was a chance he had to take; otherwise, Mikhailov would suspect he was not as thrilled about joining his organization as Trevor had led him to believe.

"No problem. Piece of cake. Just tell me which bank and what you want me to do once I'm in."

Mikhailov waved to one of his men, who left the room only to return with a laptop in his hands, which he handed over to Trevor. Opening the laptop, Trevor realized it was already running and that a shell account—a user account located on a remote server and his open door to the bank—had already been set up.

"Come to papa. You're happy to see me, aren't you my little beauty?" Trevor's humorous side reared its head while he waited for the bank information. Mikhailov handed him the bank's servers' Internet Protocol numbers—the information he needed to try a brute force attack on their system—and a bank account number. Memorizing the numbers, Trevor used the shell account to trace any vulnerability in the system. Banks in Russia didn't appear to have the same server security or intrusion blocks that the Western banks had. That made it easier for him. He infiltrated the server using a buffer overflow hacking tool, which forced the target host to execute the code he specified. He gave himself owner permissions and acquired access to the whole server remotely—it was the same as if he was physically sitting in the server room at the bank.

Next, he quickly located the application used to access clients' bank accounts. Running it, he found the account associated with the number Mikhailov had handed him. Trevor couldn't help but feel smug at how easy it had been to get in, even though he knew it was wrong to do so. A smile spread across his face. Without checking the account's details, he looked up and met Mikhailov's eyes. "Now what?"

Mikhailov seemed pleased with the results. "Transfer thirty million rubles from that account to this one." He handed him another account number in the same bank.

Trevor concealed his surprise at seeing who the holders of both accounts were. Guilt had weighed heavily on his shoulders when he thought he would be hacking into some innocent person's account. He had planned to go back and return the money to the original owner once he and Cassandra were out of harm's way. But now, knowing the target of the hack was another mafia boss, the guilt lifted.

Mikhailov was playing with fire. Stealing from Pavel Zarev, leader of the largest mafia organization in St. Petersburg, was one hell of a three-alarm. It all made sense now. It seemed clear that Mikhailov vied to take the top bear position in the underground world and wanted to send a message to the Tambov gang, Pavel's organization. Taking the money was a show of power, control. Yet it could quite possibly start a gang war and drop them all in the middle of bloodshed. *Holy shit!*

Trevor's mind raced a mile a minute as he transferred the money between the accounts. Boris joined him and looked over his shoulder at the screen while he finalized the transfer. "Done!" Trevor announced with a cocky smirk on his face.

Boris's eyes opened wide and he glanced at Mikhailov. "This is madness."

Trevor feigned consternation at Boris' statement. "Why?"

Mikhailov surprised them all by chuckling. "I have long suspected the Bogàtstvo Bank's security to be laughable, but I never thought it to be this bad. Here is the deal, Ivanov. You showed no scruples at hacking into the bank and taking money that belongs to Pavel Zarev."

Boris sucked in a sharp breath at the mention of the name.

"You now belong to me. As long as you do what I need you to do and keep your nose out of my business, I won't slip your name to Pavel as the thief who took big money from his bank account." Mikhailov's face displayed a mix of cruelty and satisfaction.

Trevor hadn't expected this turn of events. He couldn't have imagined that Mikhailov's purpose with the "test" was to tie him to his organization in such a way that if he tried to remove himself from it or betray his trust, he would be dead meat either way.

It was a smart move, really. He'd killed two birds with one stone: confirmed Trevor's willingness to work by testing his morals and ethics, and at the same time tied his hands by making it impossible for him to sell his services to the competition without dying in the process.

"How about payment? What do I get for my effort?"

"One million rubles on delivery."

More than a year's salary for a developer in Russia. "Very generous of you. I guess that would be fair for the trouble."

Mikhailov smirked at Trevor's comment and directed Deminov, "Move all the assets immediately." The henchman nodded, turned on his heel, and left the room, followed by the woman.

Mikhailov returned his attention to Trevor. "I am sure you would approve the transfer of my assets to another bank, since this one seems to be so vulnerable."

"I definitely approve," he replied sarcastically.

Mikhailov turned from Trevor and spoke to Boris in Russian, "He'll do. Have him come here tomorrow morning. I will assign someone who can speak English to show him what needs to be done."

Mikhailov took Boris's hand in a tight squeeze, indicating the meeting was over, and dismissed them. Boris turned for the door and Trevor swiftly followed him, noticing a last penetrating look Mikhailov shot his way. The man was truly a snake.

Silence enveloped them as Boris shifted the car into gear and maneuvered through the gates, away from Mikhailov's property, without a word or look in Trevor's direction. A few minutes later, while negotiating the traffic on the busy streets of St. Petersburg, he finally broke the silence. "You, my friend, are in deeper than you wanted to be," he sighed. "He wants you there tomorrow morning. Make sure you're on time. Keep your humor and your cocky smirks to yourself and you might leave the place in one piece."

The extreme seriousness of Boris's words brought reality crashing down. Trevor never imagined his search for answers would get them into such a deep mess. It was one thing to track and retrieve stolen data, but it was another entirely to tangle with the bosses of two Russian mafia organizations.

Trevor's expression grew solemn and he blew out a deep breath. "I know. I'll try my best not to say anything stupid. I can't promise it won't happen spontaneously, though."

Boris grinned for the first time that day. "You are a nutcase, Trevor Bauer."

"Cassie tells me that all the time," he grinned back.

Trevor relaxed for the first time after spending a tension-filled hour in Mikhailov's presence. "I appreciate your help with the meeting today. It's nice knowing we have a friend here."

Boris chuckled. "I told you I wasn't doing this for free." It dawned on Trevor that Boris was humored by his naïve belief that he would do them a favor out of the goodness of his heart.

A frown furrowed Trevor's brow. "What do I have that you could possibly want?"

Boris laughed out loud. "Oh, it's nothing you have yet." He slid his glance toward Trevor. "But it is something you will be able to get for me once inside."

Trevor's frown grew deeper, searching for the meaning of his words. "Get for you?"

"Yes. When you are inside, you will make copies of any files containing Mikhailov's contacts, his runners, his sources for the contraband he runs to many countries. I want it all. Including the bank account numbers you used today."

Trevor's eyes narrowed and the hairs on the back of his neck stood on end. "What do you need them for? It's not as if I can walk out of there alive if they catch me smuggling a hard drive in my pocket. Do you know something I don't? You and I both know they will be watching me closely."

Boris's smile turned into a big grin. "I recommend you find a way to do it. I put my neck on the line for you. In Mikhailov's words, 'you belong to me.'"

His frigid tone chilled Trevor to the bone. *What the hell? Did he just threaten me?* Thoughts raced through his mind. Inhaling deeply, he looked ahead and noticed they were nearing the apartment. "Sure. Fine." The tension eased from Boris's shoulders and his hands relaxed their grip on the wheel. "But I have a condition."

Boris eyebrows raised in disbelief. "I don't think you are in the position to create conditions."

Trevor cut him off and plowed ahead. "I need you to make sure Cassie leaves Russia unharmed if anything goes wrong."

Boris grew still at the mention of Cassandra's safety. Pulling up to the front of the building, he parked and killed the engine. "I will do it for Robert and for you." He turned to look Trevor directly in the eyes. "She is a good woman. Do not let her go. You will regret it if you do."

Trevor's frown deepened, puzzled by Boris's cryptic comment. At the same time, relief coursed through his veins knowing Cassandra would be taken to safety if things went awry.

Trevor nodded and exited the car. Standing on the sidewalk, he watched as Boris disappeared into traffic. *Damn!* It was in that moment that he realized Cassandra was well aware of his little discussion with Boris. She would have overheard the entire conversation through the shoe micro-phone. She was privy to the mess they were in without him even having to tell her. *Cassandra.* He drew a deep breath, raked his fingers through his hair, and headed inside. *Let the games begin.*

Chapter Twenty-Eight

Promises, Promises

J ESSICA JUGGLED THE TAKEOUT BAG and her purse as she unlocked the door to Stephan's house. After spending the day tied up with Cassandra's curious request for a deep profile and background check on Boris Kostas, she was looking forward to enjoying a nice dinner and a quiet evening with Stephan.

She dropped the bag on the counter and ran upstairs for a quick change. More and more her personal items were finding their way to Stephan's closet. Although he hadn't said a word about it, she had caught him eyeing her things and wasn't sure what to make of the emotion she had seen in his charged, troubled eyes at the time.

Back in the kitchen she set the small table instead of the larger one in the formal dining room for the two of them—it was more intimate that way—and turned the oven to pre-heat so she could slide the lasagna in, timing it for his arrival from work.

As she pressed the last button, the phone rang and she scrambled for it, catching it on the fourth ring.

"Hello?" she answered breathlessly.

"I was about to hang up and call your cell." Stephan's deep voice sent a ripple of sensual awareness through her.

"I just got here. I'm getting dinner ready. What time will you be home?" She cradled the phone between her ear and shoulder as she carried the lasagna from the counter to the stovetop, readying it for when the oven beeped.

"That's why I'm calling. Not any time soon. I've been rather distracted of late—" A chuckle rumbled over the phone, "—and need to compensate by putting in some extra hours. There's a specific project that needs my attention."

"I hope you haven't been annoyed by the reason for your...distraction," she quipped back.

"Not at all." His tone deepened. "It's been the best weeks of my life."

Goose bumps formed on her skin at the warmth and promises held in his words. "I'm glad. It's been the best time of my life, as well." Loaded questions crashed and tumbled in the silence until she prompted, "Should I go home?"

His reply was quick. "No. Stay. I should be home in a couple of hours."

Her heart fluttered with joy at knowing he wanted her there, in his house, waiting for him. *Home.* His house had begun to feel more and more like hers also. "I'll wait."

"See you soon."

Jessica hung up the phone and turned off the oven. Stowing the lasagna for later, she leaned against the counter and considered what she could do to fill her time until he got home. TV or a good book weren't enough to keep her attention for long. After almost two hours of aimlessly walking around the house, fluffing pillows, straightening perfectly angled paintings, and re-organizing tidy cabinets, she'd had enough.

Her thoughts turned to Stephan cooped up in his office buried in reports. She pictured him hunched over his desk, the knot of his tie loosened, his dress shirt unbuttoned, displaying a peek of his skin and the soft layer of hair on his chest. She grew hot at the thought and mischief invaded her mind immediately.

Without hesitation, Jessica jogged back upstairs for another change of clothes. Picking up her purse and grabbing the keys to her new car—one of the many items Stephan had helped her select and purchase, items that solidified her stay in Ireland and closer to him—she headed out into the brisk night.

★ ★ ★ ★ ★

A rap on the door tugged Stephan's attention from the papers he'd been staring at blindly for the past twenty minutes. The last few weeks had been surprising and very enjoyable, but had left a mark and he was paying the price.

The project in front of him was important to the business. They had just experienced the loss of one of the programmers and were falling behind in the software's development. He needed to focus, but he couldn't shake Jessica from his mind.

Frowning at the interruption and expecting to see one of the night security guards doing his rounds, he called out, "Come in."

Instead of the guard, Jessica's head popped in. A big smile covered her face and glittered in her eyes. "Surprise!"

He couldn't help the smile that curved his lips reflecting his pleasure on seeing her there. "Someone got impatient."

"You know me too well, Mr. Connellan." She deliberately locked the door behind her and approached his desk with a lazy sway of her hips.

"How did you manage to get through security?" His eyes didn't leave her figure, watching her like a predator watched his prey.

"John was downstairs. The guard I met the first day I called on you for a visit. He remembered me."

"Ah…another caught under your spell."

"Hey, anything to get up into the tower. I needed to rescue my prince."

The brightness of his smile faded at her comment. "You shouldn't be here. The whole reason why I'm here is to focus on work. Definitely not happening when you're around." His mouth quirked with humor. "You are way too eager, Miss."

"I am. What are you gonna do about it? Punish me?"

"I might." His words were playful, but the meaning was not as his tone took on a dark, dangerous, raspy quality.

"Promises, promises."

Stephan considered the glint of mischief in her eyes. Their relationship had progressed over time and they were embarking into a new phase of discovery. One in which they could expose their most intimate fantasies. Jessica had hinted at some. He, in turn, had kept a tight lid on his, treating her like a fragile, porcelain doll. She wasn't taking that treatment lightly and pushed his buttons all the time, almost as if knowing that if she stuck to it, he would eventually cave to his deepest desires.

His reaction was immediate. He stood and walked around the desk to where she remained motionless, waiting. Threading his fingers in her short blonde hair with one hand, he cupped the back of her neck and covered her mouth with his. There was nothing tender in the kiss as he plunged his tongue in her mouth, taking the kiss deep, hard.

His fear and anger at a future without her blended into that biting kiss and took away the restraint of the last couple of weeks. His hand tightened in her hair and on her neck as he allowed her to experience all of him, his desire to take and keep what he had conquered.

He broke the kiss and turned her, swiftly pressing her to the edge of his polished mahogany desk. Her hands fell on the surface and she glanced over her shoulder. "Stephan?"

His arm swept the papers, pen, and phone aside. "Bend over." There was a biting edge to his command. It wasn't a request. It was an order.

"But—"

"Do as I say, Jessica." He followed his command with a press of his hands between her shoulders, forcing her closer to the desk.

Jessica's heart raced out of control and a liquid heat flashed through her. She anchored her hands on the smooth polished surface, but his firm push made her hands slip and pressed her chest down against the desk. The cool wood felt refreshing against her heated cheek. Her breath hitched, knowing her skirt had inched up her thighs as she bent over.

She held her breath in anticipation, unsure where the little play was going. Jessica jumped when his fingers skated up the back of her thigh and slipped under her skirt, trailing lazy circles across her butt cheek. The brush of his fingers soothed her and she breathed out a soft sigh, sinking further against the desk.

She raised her head and tried to catch his eye. "Steph—hey!" she cried out as her tender skin throbbed from a sharp slap. She tried to straighten and turn from the desk, but Stephan pinned her thighs against it and pressed his weight on her. A hard slap burned across her other cheek and she gasped.

His warm moist breath caressed her ear and his voice shimmered with barely checked passion. "I said I might have to punish you," he whispered, running his tongue along the shell of her ear and nipping it before lifting off of her. Jessica's throat tightened with excitement and her breath came in shallow gulps of air. Heat surged in her veins and straight down to her throbbing clit.

Her breath caught as a warm wetness spilled between her thighs, soaking her panties. Jessica thought she had died and found heaven. The few lovers she had experienced were young, gentle, and sweet. Although she appreciated the gentler side of a man, she had always craved more—a man who would take it a little further. She had fantasized about that. Many times. Jessica had never voiced her wishes then or now. Yet Stephan

seemed to be attuned to her thoughts and gave her what she desired—
something primal, darker.

Her heart almost stopped when his firm hands brushed her waist and the
curve of her ass. She jumped at the touch of his palms as they glided up
the outside of her thighs, hooked her panties with his fingers, and yanked
them down to her ankles.

"Step up." Jessica complied and Stephan freed her from the tiny swatch
of cotton.

"Spread your legs." Jessica hesitated. "Now!" he rasped.

Shifting her stance, Jessica followed his demand. Cool air wafted up her
bare legs, sending a shiver crawling up her spine. She was very aware of
where his warm, firm, persuasive fingers touched her skin as he pressed
one palm on the small of her back and the other smoothed over her skin,
inching closer to the heat at the juncture of her thighs.

The soft feel of Jessica's supple skin under his fingers was tantalizing.
Leaning over, he kissed the back of her neck as his fingers slipped inside
her already wet sex.

"So wet. You seem to like being punished, Jessica," he moaned in her ear,
rocking his fingers in and out of her slick, tight channel.

"Only by you," Jessica panted breathlessly against the surface of the desk.

Her words and the outline of his hand on her now rosy heart-shaped ass
broke the dam Stephan had built around his control. Undoing his belt
and zipper with one hand, he freed his cock. He positioned himself at her
folds, and with one fast, deep thrust, buried himself in her heat.

They both moaned as his cock stretched and filled her, her welcoming
flesh enveloping him whole. "You feel good, so good," he breathed out
in a rough whisper.

Jessica's stomach clenched. "Stephan!" she cried out, grinding back
against him as he thrust again, harder, slamming her against the desk. She
loved the feel of his muscular frame pressing against her back. A shiver of

need ripped through her. She reached back for him, digging her nails in the hard skin of his hip and held tight as he pumped into her.

"Stephan, I want to feel you deeper!" she breathed as they strained toward each other, his hips colliding with her ass.

With a groan, Stephan gripped her hips and jerked her against him in rhythm to his thrusts. Jessica sobbed and leveraged her hands against the edge of the desk, pressing back against him. He wrapped an arm around her waist and fisted her hair with his other hand, pulling her against his chest. "God, you're so hot," he whispered against her ear as he rocked tighter against her.

Jessica reached her hand up to cup his neck and arched her body from him, taking him deeper. With a growl of lust, he pushed her down on the desk and pinned her with his weight. Stephan increased his tempo and changed the depth of each plunge.

Faster and harder, his hips pumped until they almost pushed the desk out of its place. His fingers dug deep into the smooth flesh of her buttocks. Her long drawn-out moan was an electrical current that travelled straight to his cock. His heart felt like it would burst from his chest. Wanting the moment to last a little longer, he changed pace, moving his hips in a circular motion, and he couldn't resist—he delivered another sharp slap followed by a gentle caress to her reddened curves. Her body reacted to it by pulsing and squeezing him tight and she cried out, "Stephan… please…I need—!"

Stephan couldn't resist her pleas. Increasing his tempo and moving one hand underneath her, he pressed his thumb against her nub, circling and massaging it as he took her from behind. She moaned in pleasure, her voice a thick sensual drawl. He felt his cock harden even more. "It feels so good inside. You're so fucking tight. I can feel you squeezing me!"

Jessica's heart raced and her breathing came in short gasps. Her body began to tremble as the first threads of an orgasm danced under her sensitized skin. She gripped the edge of the desk and pushed her ass up hard against him. She pressed her forehead into the desk, enjoying the rough feel of his fingers circling and rubbing her swollen sensitive flesh.

"Stephan!"

Jessica quaked and seized around his shaft tightly as the burning heat of an orgasm hit her. With a shuddering breath, she released the desk and covered his hand with hers, guiding his touch against her clit. Her spine arched and she ground against him as a silent scream ripped from her in a burst of air. When she could finally breathe, she gasped out, "Now Stephan! Please, I need to feel you lose control!"

Gripping her chin and turning her head toward him, Stephan took her mouth in a deep, searing kiss, sucking on her tongue as he continued to piston his hips into hers. He could feel her inner muscles squeezing him tightly, rhythmically drawing him closer and closer to his release.

Jessica broke the kiss. "Oh, God!" She slammed her ass back against him giving her room to reach between them. She cupped his balls, squeezing and rolling them between her fingers.

Her touch threw him over the edge. His release shot through him, hot and scorching. "Jessica! God!"

Jessica shuddered with a second orgasm, her contractions caressing his shaft, milking him as he pushed into her with every pulse, every spurt. Spent, they collapsed onto the desk. A fine sheen of sweat covered their brows as his body caged hers. He held her tight as their breaths sawed hard in and out of their chests.

When Stephan's brain finally jumpstarted into gear, it felt as if a pit had lodged itself in his stomach. Had she really enjoyed their moment, or, when her own sense came upon her, would she run for the hills? Suddenly he was uncertain and unsure how to open a conversation. The smell of her luscious skin still enticed him and he shifted to move off her. Before he could pull out, Jessica tugged his hand to her mouth and placed a soft kiss in the center of his palm. Relief flooded him and the ache in his stomach eased. A gentle chuckle rippled past his lips while he trailed long lingering kisses on the back of her neck to the spot just between her shoulder blades.

Jessica squeezed his hand. "What's so funny?"

Stephan pulled out from her and helped her from the desk and into his waiting arms, capturing her mouth in a deep kiss, tasting, licking, and nipping every inch of her mouth. Jessica's heart collided with her ribs at the intensity of the kiss and her arms wrapped around him, holding him tight. Coming up for air, Stephan rested his forehead against hers.

"That, little missy, should have taught you a lesson. I can see I misjudged you once again. You *are* a little surprise."

Jessica flashed a wicked grin and brushed her fingers across his jaw. "Have I told you how naughty I was earlier, alone in your room?"

His eyes glittered with interest. "Let's go home. You need to show me what you did so I can exact the proper punishment."

Her grin widened and her eyes sparkled. "Promises, Promises."

Chapter Twenty-Nine

Off the Hook

EITHER THE SOUNDS OF TRAFFIC from the street below nor the hum of voices from the other apartment units could soothe or dampen Cassandra's worry. She sat at her desk and stared blindly at the dark screen of her laptop, holding her usual cup of coffee, after Trevor had left for his first day at the job. The warmth cupped in her hands was not enough to chase the chill that had burrowed into her chest.

Her mind burned with the memory of the events from the day before, reviewing and picking apart the conversation she had been privy to, the same way a scientist studies a nasty strain of bacteria. Even though she was confident Trevor could bluff his way with flying colors, her gut still clenched at the element of danger still uncharted when dealing with combustible individuals like those in that room.

As she had listened in, she had paid careful attention to voice intonations and other details that would give her a better idea of who they were dealing with. The majority of her focus had centered on her new target: Boris. She had listened to the entire meeting and had captured her observations—the unspoken anger that threaded through Mikhailov's voice, Boris's caution, Trevor's cockiness, and the eeriness that oozed from Sergei when his clipped tone pierced the connection. Her sense was that the mafia boss and his henchman were pure evil, without an ounce of guilt or remorse. Her greatest disappointment had been her inability to ascertain more of Boris's intent.

The searches she'd conducted while the meeting had taken place had also come up empty, and George and Jessica hadn't yet contacted her with any additional findings. Cassandra had to admit that Boris intrigued her. There was very little to be found on him. She had been able to track down copies of both military and police force records; his honorable discharge from the military validated her father's praises. She uncovered information showing that, a number of years later, he had retired from the police force and started his own security business similar to Robert's. It was a couple of years after opening the agency that Boris' name became linked to Mikhailov's.

What Cassandra had not found was the event that had brought the two together in the first place. It had to have been something major to instill the sense of trust Mikhailov had demonstrated during the meeting—trusting in Boris' referral of Trevor and allowing him to watch the bank transaction take place.

Boris' comments around what he needed from them in return had been the biggest surprise. "Great favor," she scoffed. His use of the mafia boss's words *you belong to me* as his own threat to Trevor had left her blood frozen in her veins. Cassandra knew in her gut it would be something tricky, but she never imagined it would have Trevor toeing the line with danger so intimately.

The unhappy turn of events weighed heavily on Cassandra's shoulders and she wanted to get a handle on what they could be up against. "You never know when these things will bite you in the ass," she muttered as she initiated a search on Pavel Zarev, the new player Mikhailov had so strategically placed on their game board. Data available on Pavel and his organization was fairly easy to access, and the file she'd created grew by the minute.

Trevor would be interested in seeing more on the mafia boss he had inadvertently shafted. Zarev's organization was an even bigger monster, more diversified than Mikhailov's. He had deep ties with major banks, oil companies, and other considerably sized entities, as well as a member of his gang in the local government.

"Talk about having your finger in every pie. Pavel could start his own bakery," she mumbled.

Cassandra's pulse jumped when a flashing light appeared on the application bar. She opened the chat window and found a message from George.

Cassie, I think I'm onto something. Still digging. Hang tight.

Her shoulders slumped slightly in disappointment. She had been hoping for more. Something that would get her closer to figuring out what Boris was up to. Hanging tight was all she seemed to be doing lately, and she chafed at the bit.

Will be waiting, she responded, hammering the keys.

Cassandra had no time or inclination to wallow in frustration. While she waited, she went into action. Calling up the video feeds from their own surveillance cameras, she searched for any frontal views of Boris. She planned to analyze the footage, find any possible hook on him, but to no avail. There were no useable shots.

Trevor's voice boomed over the speaker and Cassandra's eyes darted to the video feed on her screen. He had reached the mansion

★ ★ ★ ★ ★

The invigorating chilly morning wind greeted Trevor as he walked out of the apartment building. He lifted the collar of his wool coat and braved the rain on the short walk to Mikhailov's mansion. Standing by the iron gates, he pressed the button above the speaker and waited until a voice demanded in Russian, "What do you want?"

Trevor answered in kind, pretending to stumble over the words any new-ly arrived immigrant would know, "Hello? I was told to be here today. Mark Ivanov."

The speaker went silent. A few minutes later, the gates opened and he sauntered up the drive to the front door. He spoke, just loud enough for Cassandra to hear, "So far so good, *a ghrá*. Hopefully, this will be a walk in the park."

The door opened on cue with his approach. Deminov stood inside and nodded at Trevor, speaking in heavily accented but clear English, "In-side." The order was given in a cold, severe tone.

Deminov slammed the door shut behind him. Standing in the foyer, he noticed another man immediately behind the henchman.

The second man extended his hand in greeting. "Hello, my name is Dmi-triy Vlasov. Vladimir asked me to show you the computer room and explain the rules."

"Nice to meet you, Dmitriy. I'm Mark." He grasped his hand in a firm shake. For a split second, Trevor felt welcomed to the place, an illusion destroyed when Deminov shoved him from behind and gave him a full pat down. Trevor stood motionless, arms outstretched, in wide stance as Deminov checked every single inch of him for weapons. He felt molested to a certain degree. Trevor froze when Deminov patted his back pocket and yanked out his ticket bundle.

"What is this?"

"Sightseeing tickets?" Trevor grinned, his humorous tone hiding the in-ner agitation at having the E&E tickets taken from him.

Deminov scoffed and shoved the bundle back. Once he was satisfied Tre-vor wasn't packing or carrying any other devices, he nodded at Dmitriy and slipped off down the hallway. Dmitriy directed Trevor with an ex-tended hand in the opposite direction. He continued his dissertation in fluent English, not the least bit affected by Deminov's rough handling of Trevor. "No cell phones are allowed, no pouches, or anything you can use to take components out of the room. Things are tight here after a developer was caught stealing hard drives."

Trevor nodded. "That sounds reasonable." Addressing Dmitriy lightly, Trevor tried to assess his role and level of dedication to the organization. "You speak English perfectly. Have you just recently arrived in Russia?"

Dmitriy glanced at Trevor, his face beaming at the compliment. "I was born in England to a Russian mother and English father. I speak both languages fluently." Dmitriy artfully avoided answering the second question.

Considering how quickly Deminov had left him in his hands, Trevor guessed he had been there a while and held some level of trust within the Glazov. They continued down a long hallway to the back of the mansion toward what appeared to be a solid core steel door, in front of which one of Mikhailov's soldiers stood guard.

Guarded entrance. That was an unexpected turn of events. Trevor had anticipated he'd be working in a simple computer room with easy in-and-out access. The whole operation was becoming a big-ass onion full of deep and intriguing layers.

At Dmitriy's nod, the man pulled a key ring from his pocket and unlocked the heavy door. As soon as the door opened, Trevor instantly knew Cassandra was going to freak. At a glance, he had a fairly good idea what the security measures were for the computer room. Hoping to give Cassandra a heads up, he commented, "Damn, this is *off* the hook."

The door slammed shut behind them, and the lock clicked; the bolt slamming home echoed loudly in Trevor's ears. The image of Cassandra's panicked expression when she realized communications had been severed burned him. He could only hope that she had caught his double meaning.

★ ★ ★ ★ ★

Cassandra couldn't move. Couldn't think. Darkness crowded her vision and an electrifying shudder reverberated through her. She shook as fearful images flooded her and an acidic tang reached up her throat. When her mind and body finally reconnected, her numb fingers fumbled across the keys, double-checking the feeds. *Shit! Okay. Chill. Think.* Panic rioted within her. She took a deep cleansing breath and licked her lips nervously. *Okay. He didn't say the words. Good sign. Or is it?*

She drew her legs up and hugged her knees as thoughts careened from one possibility to another. *Damn, this is off?* What did he mean by that? Frustrated and anxious, Cassandra scrubbed her face with her hands and, pulling it back, tied her hair in a knot at her nape. *Stick to the plan. Hold tight. If he doesn't show by midnight, I'll head for the safe house as planned.*

Chapter Thirty

Lifeline

DMITRIY EYED HIM CLOSELY. "THIS computer room is totally isolated from radio waves. Nothing can be transmitted from down here. No cell signals and, as I mentioned, no radio frequencies of any kind can penetrate these walls."

Trevor pushed his concern for Cassandra to the back of his mind; there was nothing he could do for the moment. He needed to concentrate on the tasks at hand—the files and his life. He schooled his features and maintained a casual, unconcerned visage as his adrenaline spiked in reaction to the thoughts exploding in his head. That room was another layer of the onion. *Fuck!*

Dmitriy lead the way down into a surprisingly vast, empty room. Trevor observed a long, narrow table off to the side shoved against the wall and peppered with several computer workstations. He was puzzled by the lack of users and by the mainframe—a very large and expensive computer, capable of supporting hundreds, even thousands, of processes simultaneously—inside a glass-paneled temperature-controlled room taking up most of the right end of the lab. Opposite the mainframe's glassed room was a large metal cabinet.

Trevor frowned. The size of the operation caught him off guard. This wasn't the sign of a small criminal mind but something more complex. No wonder Boris had his sights on Mikhailov. The mainframe staring Trevor in the eye was the most surprising part yet in the "I Spy in Russia" game into which he and Cassandra had stumbled.

"The loo is here." Dmitriy pointed to a door immediately to the right of the stairs—practical if one didn't want employees wondering around the house, sticking their noses where they shouldn't. "Home sweet, home," Dmitriy voiced sarcastically as he led Trevor to the workstations. "You can use this one," Dmitriy indicated one of the computers and moved off to take his own seat at another.

"Where is everybody?" Trevor asked, taking ownership of the machine.

"Who?"

"Come on, Dmitriy. Anyone in the programming business with a little bit of hacking skills knows Mikhailov has a finger in online fraud." Trevor used widely known information to chat him up. "I don't have to be a rocket scientist to know that, considering the size of the mainframe and the mentions he made during our conversation yesterday, he has to have others under his thumb."

Dmitriy narrowed his eyes. "You see too much. It can get you in trouble." He paused just a moment and added, "They're in a separate area of the house. You won't be working with them."

"Okay, then. Better this way. Fewer distractions." Fewer eyes on him. Perfect, actually. He stretched his hands and fingers in front of him and dove in. The system was already logged on, so Trevor took his time, thoroughly checking and inventorying the programs installed and the applications available at his fingertips.

"The files you'll be working on are located on the external storage drive under a folder named 'Koschei,'" Dmitriy chuckled; "A poetic reference to the Russian mythological creature that can't be killed." Dmitriy observed as Trevor located and checked the contents of the folder. After a long pause, he commented, his tone full of curiosity, "You don't look the type."

Assuming an air of innocence, Trevor countered, "What type? Geek type?"

"No, criminal type. You do know who you are dealing with here, right?"

Trevor was still interested in how deep Dmitriy was in bed with the organization and eyeballed him. "I had no choice. I needed this job. How about you? You don't seem the type either. For one, you smile an awful lot for a Russian."

Dmitriy chuckled halfheartedly. "Vladimir is my uncle. If that's what you wanted to know."

The news confirmed Trevor's suspicions. He would need to watch his back around Dmitriy. Although he didn't look much like the stereotypical vicious mafia type, he was family, and blood spoke louder when push came to shove. "I was just curious as to how you got here. Why aren't you working on the program? You seem to know your way around computers."

"My knowledge centers on hardware and network engineering. Not so much into programming, but enough to be dangerous." He spread his arms, embracing the room. "I set up the entire network for the mansion."

What he said explained a lot. Dmitriy appeared to be knowledgeable about what he did. The network, and specifically the mainframe, was secure and isolated from the outside world. Trevor studied him a moment and then it dawned on him. Dmitriy was the reason Trevor found himself in that position. The security he'd placed on the network had made it impossible to be accessed remotely.

"That makes this a fully standalone network," Trevor commented, almost to himself.

"Yep."

Trevor probed in an attempt to assess the capabilities of Dmitriy's creation, "You do have backups of the files, right? I don't want to make a mistake without having something to restore to."

"Of course. But I didn't want to run the risk of having remote backups. Sensitive information can easily be taken the minute you open the network to remote instances. I do have a hot backup of the disk running twice a day." He continued with his description of his work, beaming with pride at what he'd created.

Trevor had to agree, his work was quite something—tight security, standalone server, single backup on-site. Very secure and extremely convenient, especially because he had to copy the files requested by Boris and erase the whole damn thing in one fell swoop. "Yeah, I hear you. Nice job, by the way."

Dmitriy smiled openly at the praise, his western education bleeding through.

"The entire network is—" Trevor's gaze wandered to the mainframe in the corner of the room, "—quite impressive."

A look of satisfaction crossed Dmitriy's face.

Trevor glanced at the time and was surprised at how fast it had gone by. It also reminded him of how long he and Cassandra had been out of touch and how worried she had to be. He was comforted by the knowledge that no matter the situation, she was a stickler for details and wouldn't deviate from the plan.

★ ★ ★ ★ ★

An eerie silence pulsed in the room. Since the morning hum of life in the apartment building and the conversation on the feed had subsided into quiet, worry burned a hole in her stomach. *Is he in danger right now? Is he alive?* Twitchy, with anguish crawling under her skin, Cassandra needed something to occupy her thoughts.

Her eyes lit on Boris's file still displayed on the screen and it spurred her decision. She grabbed her cell from the desk, dialed Jessica, and put it on speakerphone.

While it rang, Cassandra pulled up the satellite link and inputted the address she'd acquired from Boris's driver records.

"Hey Cassie!" Jessica's voice flowed out of the speaker on the fifth ring.

Keeping her eyes trained on the screen, Cassandra replied, "Jessie, I thought I was going to have to track you down again."

While she talked to Jessica, an image appeared on the screen. Zooming in, she observed the small house with well-groomed gardens, surrounded by low fencing. The black sleek sedan she had come to know so well sat in the driveway.

Jessica laughed. "What's going on?"

"I'm calling to see if you'd made any progress on the research on Boris Kostas."

Cassandra snagged a screen capture of the house and added it to Boris's profile. Movement on the feed drew her attention back to the image and she watched a person moving from the house to the car. Adrenaline raced through her veins as she zoomed in closer and discerned Boris. *Gotcha! Guess you're taking a passenger you didn't count on.*

"He's kind of squirrelly," Jessica continued. "Not much available on him other than what's on public record. Military records, police, opening his own security business."

Cassandra listened with half an ear as she watched the car pull from the driveway, following its progress back into the heart of the city.

"Cassie, did you hear what I said?"

Finally, the car came to a stop and disappeared into what looked like a parking structure.

"Yes, Jessica. Sorry. Just checking something out here. I already know all that. Did you check for bank accounts? Off-shore?"

"What do *you* think?" Cassandra could tell her friends eyes had just rolled in her head.

Her fingers danced along the keyboard, accessing the CCTV system they'd tapped earlier, hoping that once Boris stopped she could track him through the city. Locating the cross streets, she quickly found the right corner. A few minutes later, Boris appeared on foot, heading south. *Yes. Mine!* Cassandra's heart pounded in her ears and a new surge of adrenaline pumped through her veins. She was on the hunt.

She turned her focus back to Jessica. "Jessie. Didn't mean to jump you. It's just that things here are not a clear cut as they are in the States and Western Europe. I'm just covering our bases."

Although Cassandra's thoughts were never far from Trevor, tailing Boris made her feel useful. She followed his path, saving snapshots of him whenever his face was visible to the camera. Later she would try pulling a clearer image from them for her analysis.

"I get that, Cassie. I'm doing my best, you know," Cassandra's attention was caught by the snippiness in Jessica's voice.

Cassandra kept one eye on the camera feed and turned her attention to Jessica. "Jessie. What's going on? You sound different. Is everything okay? Have you moved into your new digs? I saw the pictures you sent. It looks great."

"Not yet. I get the keys the beginning of the month. Stephan has been helping me wi —" Her voice cut off abruptly.

"Stephan is helping you with...?"

"Nothing. With you gone I asked his opinion on the place before I rented it."

"And?"

"And nothing. End of story."

Cassandra wasn't convinced her friend was being open with her by her evasive tone. "Jess. It's me, Cass. What's going on? Why do I get the feeling there's something more to it?"

She tracked Boris's progress and watched him turn into a restaurant. *Damn it.* He came back into view again in the large glass-paneled front window standing before a man with dark hair sitting at a table for two. Her heart beat like a drum against her ribs as she focused on their blurry profiles. They appeared to greet each other before Boris took the chair across from him.

"Did you hear me? Cassie?!"

"What?"

"I asked you how Trevor and you are doing. How come I don't hear him? You guys are always working me over tag-team style each time you call."

Cassandra's breath hitched and she took a minute to collect herself. "He's running an errand. He…he should be back any moment."

"Cassie? You're hiding something."

"Look who's talking, Jess. I'll find out what's bugging you even if I have to shake it out of you when we get back."

"Wow, you should see how my legs are shaking. Not!"

A deep belly laugh bubbled from Cassandra's lips. "Damn, Jessie. You don't know how much I needed that. Hey other than the apartment, has Stephan checked in on you?"

"I…I haven't seen or heard from him recently."

"Trevor asked him to keep an eye out for you on penalty of death. Strict instructions to chase off any bold guys sniffing around you. He said you're like a little sister now. That whoever wants to date you will have to go through him. Lucky you!" Cassandra scoffed. Silence filled the airwaves.

After a moment, Jessica's halfhearted laugh flowed through the connection. "Well, he'll be damned surprised."

"What?" Cassandra asked.

"Anyway. I need to go. I'll send you information on Kostas as soon as I finish my search."

"Okay, Jessie. Talk to you—" Cassandra eyed her cell on the desk as the call abruptly disconnected. Talking to Jessica had taken her mind off her problem, but it also left her worried about her friend's strange behavior. Raising hell about it would have to wait. She didn't have time at that moment.

Sighing, Cassandra turned back to the computer. The pictures she'd saved of Boris's date weren't stellar, the majority of them fuzzy or at the wrong angle.

Taking a chance and hoping for the best, she ran the facial recognition software against them. The pictures weren't clean enough for her program to locate the needed markers. *Damn cheap CCTV cameras!* Anxious to know more about Boris's new connection, she zipped the files and dropped them in an email to George with a note asking him if he could try his luck at enhancing them and identifying the person of interest.

★ ★ ★ ★ ★

"So…what happened to the other developers who tackled this project before me?"

Dmitriy's eyes never left his screen. "Some fired. Most dismissed temporarily. Others dismissed…permanently." He paused and then added, "None of them were capable of handling the coding required."

The chill of an unspoken threat crept down Trevor's spine. Dmitriy seemed to be giving him a sensible tip to fulfill his side of the deal or else.

Turning his attention back to the computer screen and opening the file in the compiler application, Trevor continued to search for ways he could get the data out of the room. The more he thought about it, the more it seemed it would be as hard as smuggling gold out of Fort Knox. Looking over the data on screen, Trevor narrowed his eyes. If the purpose of having him tackle the decrypter's programming was to ensure the program was fully functional as soon as possible, why would they restrict his access to the data set? "I thought Mikhailov wanted this program finished fast."

"He does. Why do you ask?"

"Why would he only release parts of the data for analysis instead of the full data set? I can't provide him with what he needs if I don't have full access."

The sound of door locks being turned and footsteps coming down the stairs interrupted his speculations. Dmitriy whipped his chair around, his expression wary. Trevor looked toward the stairs and observed Mikhailov as he entered the room. His eyes zeroed in on him.

"How is the work going?" he asked without niceties.

"Just started on it. Can't say much based on what I saw so far," he responded quickly.

Mikhailov's eyes narrowed to glittering slits. "How long before it is finished?"

"Hard to say. With the piecemeal you seem to be giving me? Months," Trevor shrugged, a disguised challenging tone coating his voice.

Anger flared in Mikhailov's eyes. "You said you were good."

"I am. Very good. But I can't work my magic if you tie my hands. I need access to the full data set, not crumbs."

"I was not born yesterday, Ivanov. I was betrayed by more than one of your kind."

"Then I guess we are done here. I need the money, but the way this is going it will be months before I see the end of this project." Trevor knew he was pushing the envelope, but he had to buy time and needed to be able to verify the deletion of the whole data, not just parts of it. He leveraged on Mikhailov's desire to have the program ready to use. "Dmitriy, can you escort me to the door?" Dmitriy drew in a quick breath and shot a worried look at his uncle.

Mikhailov's took a step forward. For a brief second, Trevor thought Mikhailov would burst into a rage, punch him. Anger swirled under his cold blue eyes, hands fisted, but then he contained his turbulent emotions. Trevor was almost certain the Vory boss had realized he could be his one chance to achieve what he wanted.

Trevor looked him in the eye. "A full-time programmer would take at least a month to complete development. Including testing. I can finish it in half that time. But only if you give me access to the files I need."

Mikhailov shifted his gaze to Dmitriy and nodded his head back at Trevor scoffing, "The boy is cocky."

Dmitriy chuckled nervously.

"Confident," Trevor shrugged.

Mikhailov observed him for a while. Just when Trevor thought he had crossed the line to the point of no return, the Russian bear spoke. "Agreed. I will give you access."

A rivulet of sweat trailed down his back and his pulse beat wildly. In his head, Cassandra was hissing at his recklessness, putting his life on the line for a piece of software. Trevor released a shallow breath he hadn't even realized he'd been holding. His stubbornness could indeed come in handy sometimes. A cocky grin began spreading across his face; Mikhailov wore a matching one. "But…you are now my guest."

"What do you mean, 'guest'?" Trevor struggled to put a lid on his panic.

"You cannot leave the mansion. You stay here for as long as it takes to finish the development."

"I can't just stay here. That would mean for at least a couple of weeks. I have no clothes, nothing with me."

Mikhailov checked his nails and commented casually, "If you leave, you are gone forever. You are mine. Remember? I assure you, if you decide to leave, Pavel will be happy to make your acquaintance."

Just when Trevor thought things couldn't get any more complicated, he was in the thickest mess he had ever thought he could find himself. If he left, he would forfeit his claim to his father's notes, leaving the decrypter and the fate of the financial world in Mikhailov's hands. More importantly, he would put Cassandra at risk. If he stayed, it meant days without her take on things, her voice of reason, her soothing logic. Days away from her. It would be the first time they were apart since their wedding.

However, it would also give him the opportunity he needed to retrieve the files Boris had demanded.

Realization was a lighting strike in his head. A knowing gleam shone from Mikhailov's eyes. He knew damn well he had Trevor hogtied. "No need to worry about clothes. I will take good care of you. In the meantime, enjoy my…hospitality. My humble home is now yours."

The man was a hair short of psychopathic. Trevor's greatest concern now was for Cassandra. If he didn't find a way to contact her, she would put the E&E plan in motion, and that would be a total fuckup.

Mikhailov cocked his head and asked, "How long have you been working?"

Surprised, Trevor checked the time. "Give or take, some eight hours."

Mikhailov raised an eyebrow in Dmitriy's direction while still addressing Trevor. "I hope you were fed appropriately, your needs taken care of?"

Trevor turned his gaze to Dmitriy's wide-eyed one. "Yes, he has been extremely generous. My appetite tends to disappear when working. In this case, I was too engrossed in the code, I guess…the hazard of being a geek."

"Come," he gestured. "You need to eat good Russian food. Hearty, as they say in the West."

"But…I just need a sand—" Trevor shut his mouth, catching the subtle warning in Dmitriy's eyes and rethought his words. "I mean…sure…I am actually hungry."

Mikhailov smirked and turned for the stairs, expecting him to follow. "Now, Ivanov."

The underlying threat of "move your ass or else" spurred Trevor to follow him up the stairs and out of the room, with Dmitriy close at his heels.

★ ★ ★ ★ ★

Cassandra uncurled her body from the computer and stretched the kinks out of her shoulders and back. She was surprised to see that darkness had invaded the room. *Still not a peep.* Slumping in her chair, she rested her head back to wait.

She felt like she was watching Trevor's teakettle, waiting for it to boil. The more one watched, the longer it took. The same was happening with the audio wave bars on the graphic equalizer. The more she stared at them, the longer the cone of silence continued.

Sighing deeply, Cassandra leaned forward in her chair, resting her head in the crock of her arm on the desk. She closed her eyes and drifted on the edge of exhaustion as she willed the silence away, but silence was a bitch who refused to cooperate. A hiss of static buzzed through the speaker. She lifted her head and stared at the bars, willing them to move. Her heart raced, her throat tightened, and her body grew tense in anticipation.

Her heart skipped a beat when they fluctuated slightly. *Come on, come on. Be him!* Suddenly the sound of door hinges and voices came across the feed, including the voice she had been yearning to hear—Trevor. "I'm still impressed by your thoroughness in locking the lab down, blocking all radio waves."

Shit! The signal had been blocked! A small sob escaped her lips. Cassandra was overwhelmed with relief. The knowledge that he was alive and well filled the hole in her heart dug by the silence of the last eight hours. His voice reverberated over the laptop's speakers, making her warm inside again. She heard chairs scraping along the floors and cutlery sounds amongst lively conversation. It appeared Trevor was Mikhailov's guest for dinner at the mansion. She was impatient for him to be home, but it seemed that would not be happening for a little bit longer.

★ ★ ★ ★ ★

Trevor and Dmitriy followed Mikhailov to a big dining room. Trevor hoped his covert message had reached Cassandra and prevented her from deploying the E&E prematurely. Trevor scrubbed his fingers through his hair in frustration. It was inevitable. He would be Mikhailov's guest of honor for some time. *Cassie isn't going to like that one bit.*

★ ★ ★ ★ ★

Cassandra's stomach grumbled; since it appeared the dinner would be a long one, she turned up the volume and went to the kitchen for a bite. She scavenged some lettuce and ham from the fridge, frowning at Trevor's grocery shopping skills, and pulled a sandwich together. Back at the laptop, she listened while she ate her makeshift dinner and grumbled. *Bugger! He's probably having a nice hot, hearty Russian meal while I'm stuck here eating this pathetic sandwich.*

Half the conversation was impossible to follow. It was in Russian, a language she had yet to master. Every once in a while, questions in English were tossed Trevor's way. His life in England, did he have a family, all deflected with ease. It was near the end of dinner that a comment had her sitting up in her chair. "Dmitriy will escort you to your room." *Hell!*

★ ★ ★ ★ ★

After the meal, Dmitriy showed him to the small room, and, with a quick wave, left him to make himself comfortable. As if that was possible. He was in jail, with no defined end to his sentence.

When the door was pulled shut, Trevor tested it: sure enough, it had been locked. He slumped on the bed. Raking his unruly mop of hair with his fingers and inhaling deeply, he tried to center his thoughts. He would find a way to get out of it. For both their sakes.

Trevor hadn't been able to pass any direct information to Cassandra during dinner. He had to have faith she had heard at least enough of the conversation to grasp the predicament in which he found himself. Now, locked up in his temporary cell, he had time to think and explain. He kicked off his shoes and stripped down to his boxers, carefully folding his clothes and placing them on the chair. Reaching down for the shoe with the transmitter, he set it on the small table next to the bed.

He flopped to his back on the small twin bed, his feet dangling off the end, and crossed his hands behind his head, the tightness in his chest a dull pain he couldn't ignore. It choked him once, twice. Struggling to keep his voice steady, he began, "I don't know if you are listening right now, *a ghrá;* if not, at least everything I say is being recorded and you'll hear it soon enough."

Cassandra's heart bottomed out, listening to the mix of anger, fear, and love coloring his deep voice. "I'm listening, babe." She raged inside that he couldn't hear her. Almost as if hoping to send any sort of comfort through to him, her fingers traced the jumping bars on the graphic equalizer interface on screen as his voice filled the silence in the room. The cool smoothness of the screen was a harsh reminder that it wasn't Trevor's face she touched.

Numbed by the absoluteness of their situation, Cassandra fought back the tears that threatened to choke her. He was alive and well; that was what counted. "Come on, Trevor. Tell me what's going on in that head of yours." Her voice was an echo in the small lonely apartment.

Trevor's insides constricted, uncertainty filling him. Squeezing his eyes shut, trying his best to keep his voice from faltering, he paused to search for the right words. "I'm sorry, *a bhean*. I never thought our first time away from each other would be under these circumstances. I always pictured you taking off with Jessie for one of those girly spa weekends, leaving me behind to fend from myself. Instead, we are knee-deep in this fucked-up situation."

Trevor stared blindly at the ceiling. "If you haven't figured it out by now, I have been sequestered until the development is complete. It was either this or…. Anyway, Mikhailov is one paranoid bastard. Sees betrayal around every corner. So, here I am. Here we are."

He sighed deeply. "The room I'm working in is insulated. All signals are attenuated and there is no way to transmit from there. That's why you didn't hear me today, and why you won't hear me while I'm down there for the days to come. I'll find a way to send you little signs of life, to stay in contact. Let you know I am okay. Don't, I repeat, *don't* deploy E&E unless I give you our signal. As soon as I figure out how to get the files out of here, I'll let you know."

"You have every right to be pissed off right now. But this was the only way. I miss you, *a ghrá*." He shut his eyes tight at the sudden pang in his chest. "It might be silly for a grown man to be shaken the way I am right now, but I feel lost without you. When did you become such a big part of my life? Probably the same moment I faced your angry stare for the first time. I promise you. I'll find my way out of here and back to you, Cassandra Brennan."

He'd hoped the intentional use of their true last name would help convey his innermost feeling. He would finish this job. He would get back to her. How to make that happen was on what he now had to concentrate his energy.

His voice was tender, almost a murmur; it sliced through her like a hot knife. Cassandra's heart ached and it felt as if a hand had closed around her throat. They were crazy. Just as she held his heart, he owned hers—from the moment she had set eyes on his crooked smile and unruly hair that day in the NSA bullpen.

"I miss you, too," she said out loud, holding back the tears when he called her by her true last name—one she held dear to her heart.

A thought burst into his head. "Ah hell, Cassie. Does this mean that you'll be shipping me to that training camp thingy you teased about?" His attempt at humor was short-lived. The day's developments weighed heavily on him. "Okay. I need to get some shuteye. I'll catch you tomorrow. Remember. Don't panic when you don't hear me during the day. I love you, Cassie girl."

The cold isolation of the room beat at him. Turning on his side, Trevor stared at the shoe, his lifeline to Cassandra, and yearned for the warmth of his wife's body, the scent of her skin. Edgy, he searched for a comfortable position on the hard mattress. He had a long and restless night ahead.

★ ★ ★ ★ ★

At the mention of the boot camp threat, laughter spilled from her lips. Damn. Only he had the power to do that to her. Make her laugh at the worst of times. "I love you too, Trevor."

Cassandra grabbed her laptop and took it to bed, setting it on his pillow. She stared at the audio receiver software opened on her screen, her lifeline to Trevor. The heat blowing from the laptop's fan across her cheek was a poor substitute for his touch. Moisture filled her eyes until the pool of tears grew too heavy and trailed down the sides of her cheeks. Her breath came in shallow gasps and a heart-wrenching sob filled the room.

Burying her face in her pillow, Cassandra gave into the tension that had been building all day, letting all her anger, anxiety, and fear soak her pillow. The silence over the connection was a black hole sucking everything that she was into it.

Flopping onto her back, Cassandra stared at the ceiling illuminated by the glow of the laptop. She felt helpless. No backup plans for this one. If push came to shove, she would go in, guns blazing, even it if meant.... She squeezed her eyes shut. No. She was confident Trevor would take care of what he needed and would find a way out.

She drew in a deep, shuddering breath. She didn't have time to be an emotional wreck. He was taking care of business, and so would she. Hopefully, George and Jessica would have information for her in the morning, including the enhanced images of the man Boris had met with earlier. Trevor was stuck, so she had to sit tight. Be prepared to receive any information when he could get it to her.

Cassandra rolled to her side, pushed the laptop to Trevor's side of the bed, and pulled his pillow tightly against her, inhaling his musky scent. "No doubt about it Trevor, I'm kicking your ass," she mumbled against the smooth cotton. Her last waking thought before drifting into a fitful sleep.

Chapter Thirty-One

Fingers Everywhere

FYODOR PUSHKIN SAT IN HIS very aristocratic and elegantly decorated home library. The smell of tobacco permeated the air as he took another drag of his cigarette and poured another shot of vodka—Russian Standard, one of the best and most expensive vodkas available in Russia. The walls were covered in family pictures, the shelves lined with the classics—Gogol, Tolstoy, and Dostoyevsky, among many others—neatly organized by literary periods. The library was his oasis of tranquility, where Fyodor came to escape.

Unfortunately, he was there not to be soothed by the familiar environment, but was instead waiting for updates on the people Boris had mentioned during their quick conversation at the restaurant that afternoon. Boris had been quite angry at being forced to a face-to-face meeting, but he hadn't taken no for an answer. He had wanted to look Boris in the eye when discussing his involvement with Mikhailov.

Boris had again affirmed that he had everything under control and that he would get what he needed from Mikhailov. Furthermore, that he had enlisted some help in the form of two new friends. He stressed that they were *his* people and to be left alone.

Unbeknownst to Boris, the couple had been placed under close watch since the day he had paid them a visit at their little apartment by the Fontanka River. It has been quite useful to also have eyes on Boris, because he was then observed transporting the same man to Mikhailov's mansion several days later.

During the years that he'd held his position, he had learned that no matter how much you trusted someone, you still had to be cautious about the ones closest to you. Boris had proven to be dedicated and useful. Very useful indeed. But it didn't mean that Boris wasn't playing his own game and using their connection to his advantage behind his back.

One would say Fyodor was a cynic, but he preferred to call himself a realist. It was twenty-first-century Russia after all.

The Russian mafia had eyes, ears, and fingers everywhere they could. The rule of thumb was, the more influence and contacts one had, the more powerful one became; the more powerful one became, the richer they grew. To those who had very few emotional attachments, money was everything.

At midnight, the phone rang and Fyodor answered on the first ring, *"Da?"*

The voice on the other end of the call responded in Russian, in a very calm and precise manner. "The man left the apartment in the morning. Alexei followed him to Mikhailov's mansion. He arrived at ten thirty. He has not left the mansion since."

"What about the woman?" he prompted.

"The woman is still in the apartment. Lights are on right now." The summary was given in a clipped tone. By the sound of it, the people assigned to the surveillance detail had been bored to death watching those two.

"Keep them covered. Report any new developments," he ordered, and hung up.

Boris had assured Fyodor he was going to get his hands on what he needed, told him to be patient. He was just trying to make sure that happened, his own way.

Fyodor leaned back against the chair, downed the shot of vodka in one gulp—its burn an old friend chasing away the cold of uncertainty of Boris's loyalty—and took the last drag of his cigarette. Snuffing it out, he walked out of the library to his bedroom for a short sleep. Duty called early every day.

Chapter Thirty-Two

Crumbling

"**W**HAT DO YOU THINK?" JESSICA held the cushions up for Stephan's scrutiny. "Red or green?"

He compared the color against the creamy tone of her skin and made his choice. "Red."

"That's what I thought, too." She dropped the green back on the display and picked up a matching red one.

Stephan indulged in the familiarity of the moment. Buying items for Jessica's new apartment, helping her select new clothes, and even the occasional grocery shopping trip mattered to him. He had never felt so alive. She brought light and laughter to his world where shadows and silence once reigned.

He observed the woman who had been the center of his thoughts long before they came to be partners in bed. The sex was more than good. Her vitality and impetuous behavior made for unforgettable nights... and days. But that wasn't what kept him tied to her like an anchored boat. Everything about her made sense. Everything she did, every gesture, every crazy comment, every deep laugh they shared made him want more of her.

The only time he was ever close to being that happy was when Layla.... *Where the hell had that come from?* Time had reinforced the barriers around his heart, suppressing all thoughts of her. Her name had always been a source of painful recollections in the past, but somehow, for the first time, he didn't feel the usual twinge of pain or the fist around his heart.

"I think I have all I need."

"And then some?" he chuckled at her enthusiasm.

Stephan followed Jessica with his eyes and warmth ignited in his chest at the sight of her contagious smile. *How had they gotten to that point so fast?* He frowned. He had dropped all his defenses and allowed her to stroll into his life, but Layla's name had been a grim reminder of what was sure to happen, given time. The memory of that last day with Layla filled his mouth with the bitter taste of bile. At least this time around he knew what to expect.

Gathering her purchases, Jessica approached him. "Do you think we have time to grab a bite? I'm starved."

"When are you not starved?" he joked, taking the bags from her. "Allow me."

Jessica hooked her arm around his as they walked toward the exit. They were good together. Her youth and lively personality gave him a sense of what had been missing from his life for so long. If only he could hold onto that. If only it could be just the two of them, nothing more. He was immediately struck by the selfishness of his thought. She deserved more. Much more. He had no right to stop her from achieving what she wanted and dreamed of.

As they drove to a nice restaurant near the store, he considered telling her everything, letting her decide their future. Uncertainty gripped him again when he considered the repercussions. She was smitten. She wanted to be with him. He knew what her answer would be, but that didn't change the fact that later down the road she would resent her decision. She chose that moment to brush her hand along his thigh, another comfortable gesture he so wanted to keep all to himself. He glimpsed at her, her smile a mile wide. Lately, Stephan had lived with dread churning in his gut. The more she meant to him, the more he waited for the axe to fall.

At the restaurant, once seated, Stephan leaned on the table and gathered her hand in his. It was just a way to maintain contact—touching her was one of his many pleasures. His eyes traced her features, committing each expression to memory. In that moment, he realized he couldn't speak up just yet. He would give it time. Let their relationship grow stronger and then, selfishly, he could leverage on that to keep her. "Have you heard from Cassandra and Trevor?"

"Actually I have. I've been working on some research for Cassie. Almost finished with it. She wanted it yesterday. Bossy woman. But it has been a bear of an assignment. Not a lot of information readily available, and it has required some digging." A deep frown marred Jessica's brow. "I'm a little worried. She mentioned things are different there and she wants to cover her back, whatever that means."

"Well, I am sure everything is fine. They would contact us if they were in trouble. At least I hope they would."

"I'm sure they…would." Jessica's eyes were drawn to the couple walking in the restaurant.

The wife, heavily pregnant, tugged the hand of a little boy. The husband helped her to her seat and sat the little boy in his highchair. Laughter drifted from their table. The woman pulled toys from a bag and set them in front of the toddler and the little one pounced on them with a squeal of delight.

Stephan followed Jessica's gaze to the happy couple. The sight of them propelled him back in time.

"Marry me, Layla," he asked her after another night spent at the pub with their friends. They had been living together for a couple of years and she had deflected his proposals several times before.

"Why do we need to be married to enjoy each other's company?" she responded with the same old litany she always did when he asked.

"Don't you want to live happily ever after with me?"

"I already am! We don't need a piece of paper to prove that."

She had again talked him out of it. Back when he was in his early twenties, Stephan had loved Layla in a young and careless way, so on par with his impetuous behavior. Looking back, he should have been happy she hadn't accepted it, considering what went down not long after that. He wouldn't have wanted to make her wait the four long years required by law in Ireland before she could get what she wanted—what he couldn't give her. Although he could rationalize the clean break between them, it hadn't make things any easier to accept. That day had forged him into the man he was now. That day had taught him a lesson in selflessness, but had also made him unable to relinquish control over his heart, over his relationships.

Jessica was caught up in watching the family of three, soon to be four, sharing a casual lunch. At one point, the woman jumped in her chair with a little gasp and then giggled with excitement as she grabbed for her husband and little one's hands and placed them on her distended belly. After a few minutes, rich laughter filled the room as they all shared the magical moment of the baby's kicks against the palms of their hands. Jessica couldn't hold back a wide smile when the toddler cried out, "Again, again. Mama, make him do it again."

The boy snared Jessica's attention. A sweet little imp with a thatch of dark hair and sparkling innocent blue eyes, a typical Irish child. The whole scene left her wondering what it would be like to have a family of her own. To be the kind of mother hers had been—loving, caring, always ready to kiss her boo-boos better. She sighed deeply and prayed she would be a good mother when the time came. For now, she was content with her lot in life and, selfishly, she wasn't ready to share the man of her dreams. She wanted to keep him to herself for a little while longer. She couldn't ask for more.

Stephan watched the whole train of emotions cross Jessica's eyes and wanted to scream, bang his fists against the table, punch a wall. *Too early! I haven't had you long enough! I need more time.* But he knew it was inevitable, he knew he couldn't prevent what was coming next. He knew she would eventually want what that couple had. Layla's memory creeping up on him at this time had surely been a bad omen. The tightness in his chest—that tightness you had when you knew something bad was about to happen—had dogged his heels for days. It was like witnessing a train wreck, unable to contain the disaster, unable to help those trapped inside.

He sat there blank, hollow, shaken, watching the scene with the young family unfold and absorbing its effect on Jessica. Lost in his misery, he didn't realize she'd turned her attention back to him. "Are you okay?"

The weight of her hand on his and her words drew him back to their world. "Yes." Deflecting the attention from himself, he asked, nodding at the menu, "Have you decided?"

"I'm divided between the fish and the stew. Both sound delicious."

"How about we get one of each and share?"

A happy grin spread across her face. "That sounds good!"

After their orders were placed, Stephan masked his feelings and made it through the rest of the dinner on the tail of false pleasantries. The tenderness Stephan witnessed in Jessica's eyes earlier had been like a serrated knife to his heart, shredding as it sliced its way through him, leaving a crumbling mess behind. He needed time alone to think, regroup. Time to deal with the decision he had to make on his own, for her benefit. On the way back home, he detoured in the direction of Trevor and Cassandra's address.

Jessica frowned as they pulled up to the restored Georgian house across from St. Stephen's Green. "I thought we were going to your house. Why are we here?"

"I remembered at dinner that I have to meet a client later over drinks.

Purely business. I'm sorry, I should have said something earlier. I don't know how late the meeting will run. I figured you would be more comfortable here instead of bored out of your mind waiting for me at my place."

Jessica's heart sank; she could smell an excuse from miles away. She had spent hours waiting for him at his house before. What the hell just happen? What had changed?

"Are you sure? I mean—"

"I am sure. I don't know what time I will be back. I will call you tomorrow." He avoided her gaze as he exited the car and rounded it to help her.

At the front door, she hesitated before opening it. As she was about to cross the threshold, he pulled her into his arms, cupped her face with tender hands, and took her mouth hungrily. His spicy taste flooded her system, the smell of his musky aftershave invaded her senses.

Stephan's warm touch called for her to pull him in and have her way with him. Jessica's heart strummed erratically in reaction to the hint of longing and despair she sensed in that kiss. Jessica reached for him, desperate to return to the love and happiness she had felt only moments ago, but he broke the kiss and stepped back, exhaling a deep shaky breath.

"Stephan. I don't understand." When he didn't elaborate, her heart sank to her stomach and her arms dropped at her sides. "Call me tomorrow?" She noticed he hesitated for a millisecond.

"Yes. Tomorrow." His thumb softly caressed her cheek as he leaned down and gave her a quick peck on her lips. "Go in. I don't want to leave you outside."

She walked into the house and turned to watch his retreating back as he made his way to the car. She caught the look of regret that clouded his eyes as he shot one last glance in her direction before he drove off into the cold dark night. That look sent a trail of ice inching up her spine, chilling her to the bone.

Chapter Thirty-Three

Hellish Days

THE DAYS AFTER BEGINNING HIS not-so-solitary confinement in the mansion had dragged. Trevor was treated well, but was still a forced guest there. Dmitriy had offered to go to his house and pick a change of clothing for him, but he lied, saying his girlfriend was supposed to be out of town that week and, expecting to have gone back home that first night, hadn't thought to get the keys when he left that morning. Dmitriy didn't pursue it and provided Trevor with a couple of changes of clothing. Although they were a tight fit, they would suit him for the short period he planned on being there.

"You'll need to handle your own laundry though," Dmitriy had laughed when Trevor thanked him for the loan.

"No worries. I'm housebroken." He hoped to make Cassandra laugh with his comment. Let her see that his smart-ass self was still thriving under the stress of the situation.

Trevor had spent the previous few days divided between finding a way to remove the files he needed from the servers and continuing the development of the decrypter to keep Mikhailov off his back. He didn't want to give him any reason to "dismiss him permanently," as Dmitriy had put it.

The decrypter was quite an impressive piece of work. It drew him in, and the excitement at the challenge of unraveling it pushed everything else to the back of his mind as it absorbed all his attention. Days spent under the grip of the code made his confinement a little easier to take. He was totally intrigued by its complexity and filed a mental note to contact Paul Faber, the decrypter's creator, to discuss it in detail.

Aside from that, Trevor spent each moment out of his makeshift cell in deep observation of the people and the network, searching for vulnerabilities he could use to his advantage. Each person, each pawn in the hierarchy of the organization, was becoming very familiar to him as he observed their interactions during the time spent among them, listening to their conversations. They spoke freely in front of him, unaware of his understanding of their mother language.

Dmitriy had been drawn to him, possibly because of the shared expatriate status and the fact that they were two oddities amongst the violent members of the Glazov. They had spent each day almost glued at the hip. Dmitriy never left his side unless it was to use the small bathroom, which was causing a complication for Trevor. Dmitriy was never far enough, nor gone long enough, to allow him access to the server for the time he estimated it would take to pull the files from it.

"I am hungry. Are you up for lunch?"

Trevor frowned. It was early, but it would give him another opportunity to provide Cassandra with a glimpse of what was going on. "Sure."

They made their way to the enormous kitchen, where long tables were set to accommodate the many people living in the mansion. As they sat and waited to be served by one of the kitchen maids, Trevor noticed Dmitriy's intense interest in one referred to as Tatiana.

Trevor had seen her in the kitchen before. A shy young woman, she was efficient and mostly kept to herself, completing her duties without complaint, even under the crudest treatment by some of Mikhailov's henchmen. Dmitriy followed her with hooded eyes, a poor disguise for the attention he gave her.

"Spasibo," Dmitriy thanked the woman, continuing to track her movements as she served Trevor.

Trevor repeated the word when she placed the plate in front of him. He had to agree, the food smelled appetizingly good. He took a long whiff of the generous serving of steamy meat and vegetables and settled in to eat, all the while keeping close tabs on Dmitriy.

"So...does she know you love her?"

Dmitriy's wary eyes shot to Trevor's. "Why would you say such a thing?"

"Been there, know that," Trevor shot back. "So does she?"

Mikhailov's nephew glanced back at his plate and pushed the meat around with his fork. His shoulders curved slightly and he gazed over to the counter where the woman in question was busy serving others as they trickled into the kitchen.

"I'm not sure. We met for the first time a number of years ago when I was sent here for a short visit. I haven't been able to get her out of my head since. I remember it clearly. Tanka was puttering around the kitchen getting ready for an evening meal. I startled her and she dropped a knife. When it fell, it sliced her finger. I offered to look at it, and when our hands touched...."

Trevor studied him and understood the unspoken words. Dmitriy was definitely taken by the woman. He probably hadn't even realized he used the affectionate version of her name in his retelling. "Why don't you say something?"

"She's shy. I've been taking my time in courting her."

Trevor took a bite and savored the hearty meal. "How's that working for you?"

Dmitriy dropped his fork on his plate and rested his elbows on the table. He shot a covert glance in Tatiana's direction. "It has taken me a year to get her to even laugh at my jokes. We have slowly become friends. I believe my efforts are paying off. The last few months she has begun to warm up to me. I think…I don't know for sure…but I think she now has affection for me."

Trevor could not imagine having had the patience to wait that long for Cassandra. He had wanted her the first time he had set eyes on her, and had pursued her relentlessly. Thank god she had come around in those first short months. Trevor clapped Dmitriy on the back. "I am glad it is working out for you, my friend. There is nothing better than loving a good woman."

Dmitriy cocked his head. "You sound like you speak from experience."

"Just wistful. Thinking of holding a beautiful woman in my arms again soon." He flashed a cocky grin. "Hard to do when you're locked down."

"You have that right." Dmitriy turned his head in Tatiana's direction, lost in thought.

★ ★ ★ ★ ★

Over time, Trevor had stealthily wormed his way into the mainframe. The massive server contained hundreds of folders. It would be impossible to remove the entirety of its contents without having access from the outside or access to a portable storage unit. Based on what he'd uncovered, there was no way he could get it all done in one day. At least not via a flimsy remote connection.

The micro thumb-drive he had absconded in the hem of his pants his first day on the job wasn't large enough to hold all the files in one single swoop, either. Even if he limited the copy to text documents only, it would take days to do a full backup of the files, considering the little time he was left to his own devices in the underground room.

The size of the data housed on the server puzzled Trevor. *Why would a mafia boss have so much data on a standalone server anyway?* Intrigued, he had checked the contents of a few folders. They contained mostly logs of some sort and documents that appeared to be lists of names, records of payoffs, bribes, businessmen owned by the different organizations, black-mail—you name it. There were also massive databases with user details that could be sold to spammers and online criminals alike.

Mikhailov's hacker network had been prolific. *Hackers.* Trevor had not been able to infiltrate the mainframe from the outside, and hadn't considered burrowing his way out since he had no access to the outside world from there. If he could establish a connection to the outside, he could push the files out, a batch at a time.

Dmitriy walked in after his usual mid-morning cigarette break and sat at his computer. He toggled to the browser, searching for hardware parts. "I don't understand why we have to buy piece-of-shit computers when we can afford top-of-the line desktops."

"Getting what you paid for?"

"Yeah. Two of the desktops upstairs are dead in the water. Network cards died. And, as usual, they want it fixed ASAP."

Trevor kept his eyes trained on the screen, analyzing the code, testing subsets of data, as well as looking for a way to insert a Trojan that, once triggered, would destroy the software as soon as it was used for the first time. If he could figure out a way to add that little time bomb to the program, he could get Cassandra out of harm's way before Mikhailov figured out what was going on. That was, if Trevor was allowed to leave.

Almost as if pulled in by his thoughts, the clack of the door being opened resonated from upstairs and Mikhailov, followed by his henchmen, descended to the room.

"Ivanov."

★ ★ ★ ★ ★

Cassandra stared out the open window at the river traffic flowing past the little apartment facing Fontanka River as the blaring car horns and bustle of people on the streets filled her ears. She took a sip from the cup she nursed in her hands. Even coffee tasted different without him. How pathetic was that? Watching a couple stop for a kiss before continuing on their way toward Sennaya Square, Cassandra's heart tightened into a wadded ball in her chest. She missed his firm lips. She even missed his smart-ass comments.

The early morning sun reflected off the water. For once, it wasn't raining, but the humidity was a heavy blanket in the air, and the chilly wind, a cutting knife. A typical late spring day in St. Petersburg. Cassandra brushed her hair from her face in frustration as she turned back to the room and eyed the computer screen, the dead graphic equalizer interface displayed prominently in its center.

Her stomach grumbled and Cassandra grimaced. She hadn't wanted to leave the apartment or the laptop for fear of missing his live broadcast. But the walls of the studio apartment were closing in and supplies were low. She needed food and fresh air. She set her cup aside, slipped on her boots, and grabbed her jacket and wallet. Her hand hesitated, hovering over the ticket bundles, remembering the day they had bought them and discussed the evasion plan. She snatched them and shoved them in her back pocket before she strode out the door.

The brisk wind cut across her cheeks and her ears burned slightly from its sting. She shoved her fists deeper in her coat pockets as she reached the corner of the block where the wind whipped around her like a Tasmanian devil. Cassandra's blustery thoughts matched the weather perfectly. Her mind drifted in a whirlwind to Trevor.

All she wanted was to be able to reach him somehow, grab him and run. But she knew it was impossible. Not with the few resources they had at their disposal. She hadn't made up her mind about contacting Boris regarding Trevor's confinement in the mansion. Not once had he contacted her in the days Trevor had been gone, and she still didn't know if she could really trust him.

George had sent over some transcripts to Jennifer and now it was a matter of sitting tight—again. Jessica hadn't been able to pinpoint any useful information or connections and had yet to say anything about what was going on with her. Cassandra's brows drew together as she walked the cold streets of St. Petersburg, fully engrossed in the chaos in her head. Among all the convolution of the days since Trevor had been stuck in the mansion, Cassandra had not rested, revving to get moving, to get things done. She hated sitting on her hands, waiting for the other shoe to drop.

The blare of a horn drew her out of her tempestuous musings. Her eyes took in her surroundings. Adrenaline spiked in her veins, chasing the cold that had become her constant companion of late. She shook her head and tucked her chin further into the collar of her coat as she gazed across the street.

Her eyes traveled the length of the stonewalls and the wrought iron gate holding the mansion she had only seen on video within its protective circle. Following the curve of the intricate design on the gate to the camera situated at the top of one of the pillars, the memory of the bruise on Trevor's back flashed before her eyes. *Damn him. It's even freaking higher than I imagined.*

A shiver held her in its grip as the light turned and she stepped into the crosswalk. Keeping her head down, she watched the gate from the corner of her eye until she reached the small garden where Trevor had hidden the transmitter. How the hell had she gotten there? Him. He drew her. She knew it was a ridiculous thought, but somehow she could feel him.

She ducked into the garden and found a bench far enough back that she wouldn't look suspicious, yet close enough that she could still see the gate and any activity. As she sat there, her mind was totally focused on Trevor. In the days he had been gone, mornings were the worst. She missed waking up to his spicy warm scent and his lean muscular body wrapped around hers. She missed fighting for the hot spray of the shower each time he joined her. Morning showers that usually ended up with more steam than...*Hell.*

A cold breeze crossed her knees and she tucked her arms tighter against her sides, her hands wadded the fabric inside her pockets. *Why am I torturing myself? What counts is that he's okay.* Each morning she would get some kind of message from him. "Picture in your head the Imperial March sounding each time someone rings at the door," "This morning I imagined taking a shower with you," or, "I love how you smell in the morning. Warm in all the right places. I miss that, *a ghrá.*" Stupid little messages, but they helped get her through the day. While she observed the house, her gut twisted in knots again. The same feeling that had followed her through the many days he'd been in there. So close, yet so far.

But even with that big bump in the road, she didn't allow herself to dwell in negativity. She used her pent-up energy and, yes, her worry to power her forward and through it. She tracked down as much as she could on Boris.

Jessica had thought at one point she had a lead on a family connection, but that didn't pan out. The data trail had simply dried up. Overall, he appeared squeaky clean—a little too clean, considering his association with Mikhailov. It should have marked him somehow, but it hadn't. His business did well, his accounts modest with no signs of large deposits. Jessica hadn't found any trace of additional off-shore accounts, so it didn't appear as if he was totally on Mikhailov's payroll. It was all in George's hands now.

Cassandra hadn't wanted to burden anyone with her worry. She knew that Jessica was getting concerned. She had even considered contacting Nathan as a precaution, but thought better of it. He would just add to her stress, insist she abandon Trevor and get the hell out of there.

Cassandra's body shuddered as icy cold fingers found their way up the back of her coat and into her boots, numbing her toes. It was getting late; Trevor would be out for a break soon. She exited the garden and, as she turned to the left, she saw a tall woman wearing tight black jeans, a leather biker jacket, and boots entering the mansion grounds after checking in with security. The same woman she had caught a glimpse of before on the feeds. An aura of confidence exuded from her long purposeful strides. As her dark ponytail swung out of sight, deep-seated curiosity took hold of Cassandra. *There's something about her.... Time to find out who you are, chica,* Cassandra mused as she hurried back to their apartment for her next fix of Trevor's voice.

Chapter Thirty-Four

Shredded

SOMETHING WAS GOING DOWN AND, whatever it was, it wasn't good. From their quick conversations over the last weeks, Jessica had picked up on the tension in Cassandra's voice. The words left unsaid spoke louder than the ones she voiced. Yet her friend had not revealed what was the cause of the tension, or what was really happening with them on their trip.

Although Jessica wanted to blast Cassandra for keeping secrets, she couldn't. Hadn't she been doing the same? Cassandra had sensed there was more then met the eye since their little midnight tête-à-tête. She had kept her relationship with Stephan under wraps, cherishing and nurturing it covertly as if it were a rare seedling, afraid it would wither the minute it was brought out into the open, under the glow of public acknowledgement and scrutiny.

Jessica thoroughly enjoyed having a part of him nobody else had. Whenever they were out for dinners, or pints at the pub, he behaved like the ultimate gentleman—calm, cool, and collected, gentle—even though Jessica could see the passionate, demanding, masterful Stephan in the gleam of his eyes, the one that came out in private, the one who touched her in ways that made her toes curl and her heart flip wildly in her chest, leaving her craving more, craving forever.

She didn't regret that she had held that information back, especially in light of Stephan's most recent behavior. At first, Jessica had been so caught up in assignments and worry for Cassandra that she had missed the first signs of change on his end—late nights at work, forgotten calls, broken promises. She had attributed it to the days of work he was trying to make up. Days he had fallen behind on as a result of their budding relationship.

Jessica missed lazy days in bed, exploring, challenging. The times Stephan had pressed her body tight against his lean muscular length, as if not wanting to let go, not wanting to be apart for a second. Her heart soared at the memory of the emotion that had surrounded her while cradled in his arms.

Uncertainty had been her constant companion of late. It had wrapped its tentacles around her, and they squeezed tighter with each clear avoidance. Tighter each time she caught a deep frown marring his handsome features whenever he was around her. Tighter still, each extra hour of the days spent without a word from him.

She hadn't seen or touched Stephan in days, their lack of contact again the result of late hours at the office with promises of seeing her soon. A soon that never happened. Her heart cracked a little more with each broken promise. So different from those first few weeks, when he had almost begged her to wait for him at his house.

Each day without seeing Stephan had been torturous. Jessica knew it was impulsive, but she needed to snuff the uncertainty that had been holding her hostage at his indifference. She could taste her excitement on her tongue and her hands shook like an addict needing her next fix as she stepped up to the Brennan Enterprises security desk. She had headed to his office for the second time, hoping for a repeat of the temptation and good dose of rough loving she'd received the first time around.

Just as before, the guard cleared her through. Standing before Stephan's door, her heart pounded out of control; need, a barely checked fire waiting to be fanned by his touch. Jessica steeled herself, took a deep breath, and knocked on the door.

"Come in."

She stuck her head in. "Surprise!" But the look in his eyes was nothing as it had been before. There was no glimmer of pleasure or a wickedness shining in them. They were flat, cold, dead. Her heart fractured a little more.

"Jessica. What are you doing here?" His voice was brisk and to the point.

"I came to rescue my prince again."

His expression shut down even more. A deep frown creased his brow as his gaze turned back to the papers in his hand. "You shouldn't be here. I told you I would see you tomorrow."

Dread pounded like a sledgehammer in her head and she blurted out, "What's going on, Stephan?"

He lifted his head and stared into her eyes. His hesitation spoke louder than words. Her heart plummeted to her stomach and her knees grew wobbly. After a few moments, he squeezed his eyes shut. Wanting to touch him, ease the frown from his brow, she took a step forward. But before she could reach him, his eyes snapped open. The sorrow that bled from them sent a blanket of ice spreading under her skin. The warning in his stare stopped her in her tracks.

"Jessica," his tone was dark, unforgiving. "We can't do this anymore."

"What are you saying, Stephan?"

"I am trying to ease us out of it, but it's not working."

The pain that flooded Jessica's eyes pierced Stephan's chest. It took all he had not to take back those harmful words. He had been avoiding her, avoiding a confrontation. He had justified the distance, kidding himself that he was simply looking for a way to let her down gently, mitigate her pain like a well-orchestrated business deal. But no amount of careful wording would lessen the pain he was inflicting on her. On them.

When her future was filled with all she was meant to have—deserved to have—a beautiful home filled with the carefree laughter of children and a loving husband. He prayed she would understand and forgive him.

Another sharp stabbing pain sliced into his heart with the smooth efficiency of a well-edged sword as he imagined another man giving her all he couldn't. Another man waking up beside her every morning, rolling over, and plunging into the warmth of her body, coaxing moans of pleasure from her sweet lips. He shook his head and scrubbed his face. Sweet Mary, his thoughts were going to kill him.

"Ease us out of what exactly?"

"I am terminating our agreement. It's time to part."

"What are you talking about?! Terminate our agreement? When did you decide that? Don't I have a say?"

"I've wanted to talk to you about it for a little while. I just couldn't find the right time…or way." He avoided her eyes, preventing her from seeing how close to the edge he was. How much he wanted her. Needed her.

"You gotta be kidding me."

"No, Jessica. I would never joke about something like this. We had a great run, but it's time to move on."

"What the hell! Where did this come from? Have you found someone else? Did I do something? What? Tell me?!"

"Don't." His command was set in stone. If she argued, he wouldn't be able to resist. "We talked about this, remember? When either one of us said it was over, the other would walk away without any argument." Nothing Stephan had ever said before in his life had been harder to verbalize. The only time he had felt that devastated was when he had delivered the news to Trevor about Conor and Maeve. Not even Layla's desertion had left him feeling so torn inside. He was doing Jessica a favor. He tried to keep that in mind, but it didn't help excise the feeling of being shredded from the inside out.

Jessica stood motionless in the middle of the room. She shivered as a deep freeze enveloped her when she took in his lack of expression. "Is that the agreement you had with Terese, too?" she spat out impulsively.

"I didn't have to remind her of it."

Jessica cringed. There was the inference to age again. When would he understand that she wasn't a young impressionable woman? That she was a woman who knew and understood what she wanted? That she wanted *him*? She searched his eyes and found none of the warmth, even love, she had seen in them before. Jessica felt her forever escaping through her fingers like fine sand. "You're really serious. You want me to leave."

"Yes." One sharp word that cut to the bone.

"You know I am staying in Dublin. That we will be crossing paths at functions…at Trevor and Cassie's."

"I am aware. Yes," Stephan answered through clenched teeth.

She thought she heard a small tremble to his voice, but the icy glint in his eyes confirmed she had to be mistaken. Jessica hugged herself in an attempt to ease the pain squeezing her chest, the emotions choking her. Her thoughts scattered as she processed everything that had been said.

She wanted to scream like a child, break something, slam doors. She wanted to make him see what he was doing to her. She wanted to expose the shattering pain consuming her each second he stared at her with those cold eyes. Instead, she did the mature thing—bottled her rage and screams of frustration deep inside. Later, when she was alone, she would let it loose; but she knew she would never be the same. "Okay, message heard loud and clear. When can I come home—I mean, go to your house to pick up my things?"

Her mention of his house as "home" dealt another deep blow to his heart. That was the way he wanted it to be. He wanted his house to be her home, their home. Instead, he had to resign himself to living in the big place all by himself. Could he even do it, now that she had filled every nook and cranny with her essence and memories? Smiles through bathroom mirrors while brushing their teeth. Her perfume lingering in the hall as she passed. Her warmth against him while watching a movie or the news. Meals shared over the kitchen table. Nights. Nights of heated groans and whispers echoing in his room. The fist that had gripped his chest shifted deeper and took a tight hold of his heart. Squeezing it so hard he felt it would be pulverized at any minute. He closed his eyes, afraid he couldn't hang on to the pretense much longer if he continued to gaze at her.

"I'm staying here for the night. You can do it at any time at your leisure." He would miss seeing her clothes hanging next to his. Her sexy undies in his drawers.

"Wow. Was I a fool? I never thought we would burn out this quickly. I thought we would fan the fire, keep it banked."

"I warned you."

"You led me to believe...I thought we were—" Jessica shook her head and her shoulders lowered slightly under the weight of her sorrow. "You never warned me you were a love 'em and leave 'em type of guy. Who knew?" She threw up her hands and paced the room. "Now I know how Terese must have felt. I can't tell you how that pisses me off to no end."

"I did not—I'm not..." —he had never tired of her. He could never tire of her. How could he when the woman had taken his heart and flipped his life inside out? Had become the woman he loved more than life itself? Once he had tasted a life with Jessica, he realized that with Layla he had been young, and in love with the idea of being in love. It was because of the depth and veracity of his love for Jessica that he was ending their relationship now. Hopefully, one day she would be grateful— "...excusing my behavior to you, Jessica."

Jessica breathed in deeply. "Alrighty then....Since you won't be home tonight, I'll collect my things now." Her chuckle held a sense of sadness. "I guess it's a good thing this ended so fast, or there would have been more to move out. No worries. I should be out of your hair within the hour."

She hesitated, and when he made no move toward her, turned around and walked to the door.

As she extended her hand to the handle, he spoke from his desk. "Thank you."

Her head dropped forward, his words robbed her of air; she couldn't breathe. A knot of rage, jealousy, hatred, and…love churned in the pit of her stomach. A sob bubbled from her chest, and, before she totally lost it, she jerked the door open and walked out without a backward glance.

She would remove herself from his home, his life; she only wished she could also cut him from her heart in that moment. That would take longer and require a full-blown exorcism. More than ever, she wished Cassandra was home. She needed her friend to console her, to take her side, and kick Stephan's ass for her. But more than ever, she needed Cassandra to tell her that she would be okay.

As Stephan watched Jessica leave, a deathly numbness pervaded his body. He could barely believe he had found the strength to send her away. When she had reached for the door, he had wanted to call her back, make her stay. *Fuck altruism!* He wanted her for the "to have and to hold," for the "until death do us part." He wanted to tell her about all the events that made him who he was, turn the reins of their relationship over, and let her decide where to take it. Then clarity came and he knew she would accomplish more in life without the restrictions imposed on her by his hang-ups, his limitations. He would do anything for her happiness, and letting her go was the least he could do to make that happen.

He dropped his head back against the chair, closed his eyes, and let the wave of loss he had been holding back wash over him. He raked his fingers through his hair and stared at the ceiling, lost in thought, lost in a movie of memories from the last weeks with her as they lit up the screen in his mind. It was only then that he allowed the tears he had suppressed so skillfully to roll freely from the corners of his eyes.

Chapter Thirty-Five

Snake Pit

THE SLIDE OF METAL AND turn of a doorknob jerked Trevor from his restless sleep, and he scrambled from the bed to face whomever was coming through the door. Dread flooded him when Deminov stepped into the room and shut the door behind him. Leaning lazily back against it, Deminov crossed his arms and his legs at the ankles. Trevor was wary of his calm demeanor and mimicked him by leaning against the opposite wall. His gut knotted. *What the fuck does he want?*

His big mouth got the better of him. "Sorry. I don't swing that way, Deminov."

Deminov's eyes narrowed and a nasty gleam shone from them. "Always such a smart ass. You should watch that little habit." The angry edge to his voice accentuated his accent.

Trevor's blood ran cold. Mikhailov wasn't a patient man. His little warning had sounded loud and clear: "Deliver or else." *Was this his "or else"?*

"Why is it taking so long, Ivanov? Mikhailov is not happy."

Trevor shrugged. "For one, people like you waking me up in the middle of the night. I need my geek sleep, helps keep my brain nimble."

In two strides, Deminov grabbed him by the throat, his face inches from his. Trevor gasped for breath and his ears rang from the impact against the wall. He held Deminov's glare and clutched the henchman's wrist, wiggling the fingers of his other hand under the henchmen's grip. "Dude, chill out," he gritted through clenched teeth.

Deminov leaned in even closer, his thumb pressed against Trevor's jaw, forcing his head to the side, and lowered his voice to almost a whisper. "Listen to me carefully. I will only say this once. You have three days to finish the work. Three. Days. Be sure you use your time wisely."

Trevor felt the warmth of Deminov's breath against his ear. *This* was the "or else."

Deminov tightened his grip on Trevor's neck and stars appeared before his eyes. *Fuck that!* Trevor grunted and spat out, "Keep...this...up—" Trevor swung his knee up into Deminov's gut and pulled back on three of his fingers wrapped around his neck. Deminov cursed and fell to his knees like a log. Trevor leapt away from him and rested his hands on his legs, sucking in deep gulping breaths. "—and you will have to finish it yourself," he gasped out as the sound of loud banging on the door filled the small room.

As Deminov pushed up from the floor, Trevor could have sworn he saw his death sentence written in his eyes. "What is it?" Deminov barked out in Russian at whoever interrupted their little parley, keeping his hateful gaze on Trevor the entire time.

"We are needed. Now," a woman's muffled voice responded from the other side of the door.

Deminov held his gaze a moment longer; Trevor could see the evil in the depths of his eyes. *Oh, yeah. He was definitely seeing red.* Once

Deminov turned on his heel and slammed the door shut again, Trevor's body sagged in relief. Sitting on the edge of the bed, he rubbed at his neck. Deminov was jonesing for him, and it was just a matter of time before he found a way to make his warped fantasy a reality.

"Shite!" Trevor exclaimed out loud as he eyed the shoe sitting on the nightstand. Cassandra had either already heard the live broadcast of the little altercation or would hear it later. She would not like the approaching deadline. They were in such a mess. If only he could look her in her eyes—eyes that always reminded him of warm whiskey—and tell her it would be okay. "It will be okay, Cassie. I have it under control."

Trying to lighten the mood, he joked, "So what character do you think Deminov is? Nate is already the Hulk, all green and shit. I got it! Abomination! You know, the KGB agent who became stronger than the Hulk after an overexposure to gamma ray radiation." Trevor tapped his lip with the tip of his finger. "Hmm...in his first story he kills the Hulk. I might have a use for him yet. Must investigate." In his mind, he could hear Cassandra's laughter. She would totally get where he was coming from. Flopping back on the small bed, Trevor tried to dislodge the rock that sat like a heavy weight in his gut.

The strain of being away from Cassandra was slowly eroding his confidence. Some nights he wondered in silence if that was it for them. If he would make it out alive. But then his usual stubborn self would take over and steel his determination to return to the comfort of her arms. After all, he had promised her he would. Every night.

The stakes had just risen a notch; he needed to move his ass and get it done. There was one thing in his favor: Dmitriy was becoming more comfortable with him, which could turn out to be extremely useful. The wheels in Trevor's head turned at an even pace as he began to plan his strategy, whatever the hell it was. He closed his eyes, but knew that sleep had flown right out the door with Deminov.

★ ★ ★ ★ ★

Trevor changed and waited for Dmitriy, just as he did each morning. Soon he heard the familiar clacking of keys and the door opened.

"Good morning," Dmitriy greeted.

"Is it?" Trevor's frustration was clear in the tone of his voice.

"You must be getting tired of being here," Dmitriy prompted after a few minutes as they walked toward the mainframe room.

"You have *no* idea."

"How are you doing with the programming?"

"Coming along. Clearly not as fast as Mikhailov expected. Deminov paid me a visit overnight. I have three days to get it done."

Dmitriy shot him a sympathetic look. "Are you going to be able to finish it? The other developer that failed—"

"I'm getting there." Trevor's response was abrupt. He didn't want voiced possibilities jinxing his drive. "It's a complex program. The algorithm seems to work on some subsets of data, but doesn't on others. I'm still looking for the break in the code."

"I know hardware and networking, but what you just said was Greek to me."

Trevor chuckled. "The program decrypts some things but not others, so technically it's still broken."

"Ah…you're fucked."

"Yep." He would be in even more trouble if he couldn't find a solution to his file extraction dilemma soon. The clock was ticking. "I'm going to start a new subset today and hopefully make some progress. I just need more time on the computer."

"I would strongly recommend you do. If not—"

"You don't have to remind me," Trevor grumbled as they arrived at the entrance of the subterranean room. "And here we go again, into the cone of silence…."

Dmitriy unwittingly laughed at what he thought was a joke. In reality, it was his way of passing a status update to Cassandra. Another day in the hole. Another day closer to getting back to her.

★ ★ ★ ★ ★

"Have I said I absolutely hate the cone of silence? Seriously!" Cassandra muttered and then sighed deeply. It would be a few hours before she heard from him again. Slipping some money in her pocket and grabbing her coat off the bed, she headed out. She had been living off coffee and had pretty much chugged it all. She planned to be back in time to hear him again. Just as Trevor went about his forced routine in the mansion, Cassandra had kept some semblance of normalcy in her life—if she didn't, she would go insane.

Based on the information that Trevor had passed to her, it appeared that his babysitter had taken a shine to him and was not a threat. Nothing had really popped when she did a quick check on his name. But then again, when push came to shove, you never knew.

Her thoughts flowed to the woman she had seen at the mansion. Something about her made her hair stand on end. As luck would have it, Trevor mentioned a woman by the name of Nikol Petrovna who was joined at the hip with Deminov. He had only seen her in passing. Had no interaction with her, even though he said she seemed to be watching him closely. There was something about her he also could not pin down. Cassandra hoped to ID her soon and then have Jessica and George on her case.

★ ★ ★ ★ ★

Trevor was so entranced in the debugging of the program he hadn't realized how quickly time had flown. Success was within his grasp. He had identified a flaw in the algorithm that could possibly be the source of the bug. Trevor had three more days to fix it and find a way to remove the files Boris wanted; somehow, that part was proving to be more challenging than finishing development on the high-level encryption software. Go figure. He had also written a Trojan virus he planned to embed in the decrypter at the last minute after he had demonstrated the software's functionality to Mikhailov.

"I'm heading for lunch." Trevor almost jumped when he heard Dmitriy speak right beside him. "You have to be hungry by now. Want me to get you a sandwich? Something light? A drink?" Trevor understood Dmitriy's concern. He knew that leaving the room for meals would reduce the time he had to get the job done.

"Sure, a sandwich and drink would be great."

"Anything specific?"

"Nope. Whatever Tatiana gives you is fine. I'll eat anything."

Trevor kept his eyes glued to the computer screen while his brain did cartwheels around the whole file transfer problem. There had to be a vulnerable point in the network and he was going to find it. As he retraced the steps he took to burrow his way into the network, something stood out in his mind. *Computer equipment.* Dmitriy had been looking at computer equipment online. Buying the replacement network cards. *Damn it. Why didn't I catch that earlier?* Dmitriy's computer was connected to the internet, while the one Trevor had been assigned to was not.

Trevor's pulse beat in a rapid thrum in his veins. He couldn't find a way in through to the mainframe before, but now that he was inside, he could find a way out. He could create a backdoor from Dmitriy's computer to his laptop back at the apartment since he could easily gain root access to it.

Calculating that Dmitriy would take at least half an hour to come back from lunch, he rushed to his computer. Taking Dmitriy's scat, he reached down and worked the micro thumb drive he had smuggled in on his first day on the job from the hem of his pant leg. He inserted the device in the front USB port and then opened the command prompt. Using the root kit files saved on the thumb drive, he quickly opened a connection to his laptop, all the while wishing he could also upload himself back there.

Once done, he checked the type of access privileges Dmitriy's computer had for the mainframe. Without blinking an eye, Trevor opened the advanced security tool and changed them from read-only to full access. It would grant him permissions to not only read and copy the files he needed, but also install the program he would use to erase the whole damn mainframe before anybody got wind of it.

Trevor began to copy the files he had flagged as must-have. Documents, lists, databases, and other files, together with a text file clearly named for Cassandra, were all bundled into a zipped file. The file size was daunting and he was afraid the connection would crap out before the transfer was completed. If that happened, it would mean starting all over again from scratch. He mentally crossed his fingers and initiated the upload. His anxious eyes followed the percentage on the progress bar.

His gaze jumped to the stairs with each scratch, each sound. Time dragged along painfully; a nervous energy possessed his foot—which tapped the floor in sync with each passing second—and his fingers, which drummed to the same tune beside the mouse.

"Come on! Damn slow connection! Freaking feels like dial-up," he grumbled to himself.

Sweat beaded on his brow as the progress bar inched higher—and just as it almost kissed the 100 percent mark, it stalled.

"*Fuck me!* Move!" Almost as if scared by his cursing, the bar jumped forward and, just as it reached full transfer, the click of the key turning in the lock bounced down the stairs.

A rush of adrenaline jacked his bloodstream, revving his heart. He dragged the mouse in quick jerks, closing all open windows. As he heard the door bang against the wall at the top of the stairs, he rushed for his chair. Glancing back at the computer he had just abandoned, the butt of the thumb drive still lodged in the port snared his gaze. Shite! With a push of his foot, Trevor rolled his chair to Dmitriy's station, snatched the drive, and rolled back to his own.

Dmitriy stepped off the last step into the room as Trevor palmed and furtively slipped the drive into his shoe. Trevor turned and smiled as Dmitriy approached his station carrying a tray, which he set next to Trevor's monitor. The tray held a decent looking sandwich and a beverage can.

"Enjoy," Dmitriy gestured toward the tray.

Suddenly starved, Trevor quickly inhaled the roast beef sandwich, washing it down with long gulps of the carbonated drink.

"Wow…I told Tanka to make something quick and light. Had I known you had the appetite of a wolf, I would have brought more." Dmitriy seemed impressed by the speed at which Trevor had scarfed down the sandwich.

"It was delicious. Please pass my compliments and thanks to Tatiana when you return the tray to her."

"You'll be able to do it yourself. She's coming to pick it up soon."

Trevor needed Dmitriy out of the room again. He settled back in his chair, inhaling and exhaling deeply to center himself as he studied his screen and filtered through his options. If he could get his hands on Dmitriy's computer once more, he could install the data eraser and solve all his problems.

His checklist was becoming shorter. Trevor had copied the files Boris had requested—more like demanded in exchange for their incursion into the snake pit—to his computer. He also had the ability to embed the Trojan virus in the decrypter like a time bomb set to explode in their faces later. The only item left to check off was the complete and irreversible deletion of the mainframe and backup files Dmitriy had on site, ensuring the completion of the job as agreed with Mark Devlin. Making sure his ass was out of there before Mikhailov discovered the damage to the servers would definitely be an added bonus.

★ ★ ★ ★ ★

It had been a long day wrapped around the computer searching for data on the mysterious woman. Armed with the name and every variation of its spelling, Cassandra had come up empty. Not even a picture on the internet. The lack of information returned on her queries only sparked her curiosity more. Whatever Nikol Petrovna's story was, she was a ghost.

Exiting the bathroom, Cassandra checked the graphic equalizer on her laptop's screen for any activity as she toweled dry her hair. The bars were still. An eerie feeling of being watched jerked her around and she stood silent as a statue, listening. The busy street outside her window was quieting, and life in the complex was settling for the night. Turning off the lamp next to the bed, Cassandra crossed to the window and, staying within the shadow of the curtains, checked the street below. Nothing seemed out of the ordinary. *Jumpy much?* she chided herself.

Cassandra flicked her wrist and checked the time. Soon they would fall into their evening routine. Dinner and listening to his monologue. Not quite the date she would've liked, but it was better than nothing. She slipped into one of Trevor's geeky tees and chuckled at the phrase across its chest—Geek Inside. "I wish," Cassandra muttered as she smoothed it over her hips and sat in front of her laptop.

Seconds later, the bars on her screen bounced. Doors opening and closing, voices deep in conversation, and the clank of silverware came across the feed. Underneath it all, she caught Trevor in conversation with Dmitriy. Dinner was surreal; the audio so clear, Cassandra could almost close her eyes and envision the scene in the room. Almost as if she was sitting there right next to her husband.

Silence settled over the connection and Cassandra knew he was back in his makeshift cell. Trevor's quiet voice came across the feed. "Great news. I got the files, Cassie." Cassandra's heart stalled for a split second in her chest before it revved into high gear. *Finally!* Her body hummed with excitement as she listened. "Everything we need for Boris. I was able to hack my way out. Check my laptop. Look for a zipped file named 'Full Backup.' I can't stay late, love. They're only giving me thirty minutes to catch a nap, then back in the hole. They have a hard-on for me to get this done."

While he was still talking, she quickly checked his hard drive and decompressed the file. Clicking through the contents, she saw that it appeared to contain everything Boris had hoped to get his hands on. She was about to close it when a text file named *"a_bhean.txt"* caught her eye.

Cassandra was almost afraid to see what it held. Did he know something more? With a deep shaky breath, she opened it. *I am a part of you and you are part of me. I'll hold you in my arms soon, a bhean.* Tears instantly rolled down her cheeks. It was a message that he knew she would understand. "Damn him."

Chapter Thirty-Six

Hidden Delights

J ESSICA ADMIRED CASSANDRA AND TREVOR'S office. They sure had a sweet set-up—top of the line computers, multiple monitors, full office paraphernalia. Their desks faced each other so that they could talk freely—and probably tease the hell out of each other during time spent managing their new business. She could picture Trevor orchestrating a full-on symphony of data crunching and code writing.

A smile curved her lips as she approached their desks. They clearly displayed their personalities. Cassandra's, neatly organized, not a file in sight, clean surfaces everywhere, just like her old office back home. Then there was Trevor's…papers scattered all over, printouts, notepads scrawled with chicken scratch. The man was a disaster in the making, albeit a bright one.

She noticed the basket holding mail on Cassandra's desk and a wide grin spread across her face. Cassandra had anxiously shared her birthday di-lemma on what to get Trevor earlier in the year. She remembered how nervous Cassandra had been about her gift. *"What do you get the geek who has freaking everything under the sun?"* she had asked over and over again. Jessica had told her to stop thinking so hard and then she would know. Oh, boy. Had she ever. Cassandra had mentioned that Jessica's gift basket of edible body oils had been her inspiration. That, and a pair of service handcuffs. Jessica grimaced. The mental image created by that comment had no place being in her head. It must have been a success, because the basket now held a prominent position on Cassandra's desk.

As it had been happening more and more lately, Jessica's eyes welled with unshed tears at the thought of her friends. Thinking of them and the steady, crazy relationship they had brought Stephan and what she had lost to mind. After leaving him the day he dumped her, she had walked into the Bauer's empty house and her body had begun to shake out of control. She never made it up that first flight of stairs. She had simply sat there, staring at the moonlight playing through the curtains and shifting along the floor as tears spilled in salty rivulets from her eyes. She had cried so much she had made herself sick. She hadn't felt the same ever since.

She couldn't remember how long she had sat there with misery as her companion. The room had eventually lightened, drawing her from her tribulation and forcing her to bed. As she lay there alone, tears had once again forced their way from her eyes. She missed the cradle of his arms, his harsh groans as they made love, the beating of his heart under her ear soothing her to sleep. She missed all of him deeply; it was as if a part of her had been ripped away, leaving an empty chasm, an open wound behind.

It had been a few days since and, desperate to escape her thoughts even for a little bit, Jessica fretted over what to do or where to go. The only people she had ever socialized with in Ireland were Cassandra, Trevor and…Stephan. She had not met anyone else yet, had no sphere of friends in her new world. Picking up the stack of papers from the basket on Cassandra's desk, she rifled through them until a postcard caught her eye. Lillie's Bordello—touted as being Dublin's most renowned and prestigious nightclub. *Possibilities. Just on Grafton Street. Not that far. Going.* Tossing the stack back in the basket, Jessica jogged up the short flight of stairs and zipped to the guest bathroom.

An hour later, she stood outside the front door waiting impatiently for the cab she'd called. She wanted to get going before she changed her mind. She had slicked and pinned her hair in a classic style, displaying the long gentle curve of her neck, and had slipped into an unadorned little black dress set off by hot red platform heels that showcased her shapely legs. Jessica's heart was pounding with nervousness and her body was buzzing with energy.

Jumping in the cab the minute it stopped out front, Jessica sat back and stared out the window during the short ride to the nightclub. This would be her first evening out on her own in Dublin. Her heart wasn't really into it, but her head was ruling this outing and she was damned if she was going to mope some more around the house. Evenings were the hardest. That's when images of moments spent with Stephan bombarded her at every toss and turn. She hoped to be rid of those images for at least one night. One night in which she would return home and fall into bed for a full night of uninterrupted sleep.

Lillie's swanky lounge with its burgundy walls and cream seating was just the kind of place Jessica would have hung out at back home. For the last many months, nightclubs had slowly lost their appeal. She hoped that night would get her back into the swing of things.

Squaring her shoulders, Jessica moved deeper into the club and found a table in a dark corner. The hostess stopped by and took her drink order, a dirty martini. Why the hell not? She wasn't interested in a pint, the usual drink she had with Stephan. Lost in thought, she missed the hostess setting her drink in front of her until the music called to her. Sipping her drink, she watched the action, couples dancing, their bodies moving in time with the music, the heat of the dance floor contagious and tantalizing.

Jessica ignored several men who passed by her table in hopes of catching her eye. She wasn't interested in what they had to offer. She had taken the first step in an attempt to heal her aching heart by going out, but her stomach churned in knots and her hand tightened around her glass each time her thoughts strayed.

It would take more than a night out to close that wound and she was sure a scar would be left behind when it did. Was he working? Was he out with another woman? Doing the same things *they* shared? Holding the woman tight against him the same way he had held her? Jealousy reared its ugly green head and a bitter taste filled her mouth.

Jessica's anguish choked her and she downed the martini in two quick swallows. Setting her glass on the table, Jessica realized she should have never come. The evening out on her own was making her feel worse, not better. She was scooting out of the booth when a familiar voice reached her ears amidst the commotion in the nightclub.

"Sweet Mary, thank you for bringing the woman of my dreams into my life."

Jessica whipped her head in the direction of the same Irish drawl she had heard at the airport on the day of her arrival. A smile spread across her face as she tipped her head back and looked straight into Sean's mossy green eyes.

"Damn. Does that line ever work?"

A grin quirked the corner of his mouth. "There's always a first."

"Yeah, Yeah." Her laugh bubbled up and spilled over. "Where have I heard that line before?"

His grin widened as he slid into the booth next to her and kissed her cheek. "Jessica. How are you?"

"You remember!"

"Of course I do, lass. My heart's been pining away for the American girl who never used my card. I bet you tossed it as soon as you reached your friend and the guy she was with."

"That guy happens to be her husband, and no, look—" Jessica reached into her purse and pulled the small slightly worn card from her wallet, "—here is it. Not tossed."

"Good to know I left an impression on you." Sean waved at the hostess, and shortly after another martini and a pint were left on the table.

"Wow, now that's what I call service."

Sean chuckled. "Nah. They know me. I work here."

"Ah…perks. So, where were you arriving from that day at the airport?"

"Australia. Had spent the winter there. Who wants to freeze in Ireland when they can burn in Australia?"

"True." She laughed at his enthusiasm.

They talked for hours. She learned about Sean's love for adventure. His time in Australia and other warm, tropical countries, which explained the golden tone of his skin. His wild streak had taken him to amazing places—Egypt, South Africa, Thailand, Brazil—all on a shoestring budget, living on temporary jobs and loving each second of it. He was a cool guy. If only she hadn't lost her heart long before she'd laid eyes on him. But his enthusiasm and youthful attitude would never be able to warm her blood the way Stephan's secure, strict, and even domineering one did. Stephan didn't just warm her blood, he set it aflame.

She released a deep breath and Sean cocked his head. "Am I boring you already?"

"No. Not at all. It's been a trying week. I just need a good night's sleep to restore my energy." Jessica had been so stressed over the sudden way Stephan kicked her out of his life that she could barely sleep at night. She tossed and turned, searching for a comfortable position that could never exist without his arms around her. As a consequence, she found herself dozing at the worst times during the day. Good thing she wasn't working for Cassandra's father anymore, or she would have found herself repeating Cassandra's snore-and-drool routine at team meetings.

She collected her purse and straightened on the seat, ready to take her leave, when Sean pushed to his feet. "I'll take you home. Are you far from here?"

"Not really. I was planning on walking home, taking in some fresh air. "

"Even better. I'm not sure I should be driving after a few pints anyway. It'll sober me up."

She didn't argue. She found that his company took her mind off her problems. Standing, she allowed Sean to guide her to the door.

"I need to settle my tab before we leave."

"Don't worry about it. I'll take care of it later."

"But—"

"No buts. My treat. If you are worried about paying me back, just give me the pleasure of your company another time." His jovial approach had no hidden intentions. Jessie was a master of decoding male innuendo.

Sean nodded at the hostess on their way to the door and received a wide understanding smile back. Once outside, in true gentleman fashion, Sean took off his jacket and guarded Jessica's shoulders against the brisk night air. After a short walk full of jokes and laughter, they arrived at the Bauer residence.

"You live here?" His surprised tone made her chuckle.

"I own the place. Cool isn't it? Nah, just joking. It belongs to my friend, Cassandra, and her husband, Trevor. I'm staying with them until I can move into my own place." She unlocked the door and hesitated. A near stranger. Harmless, nonetheless. She shouldn't let him in, but she didn't want to be all by herself in the big house again. Against her better judgment, she found herself asking, "Want to come in for a chat? Finish sobering up before heading back?"

Sean held her gaze and all humor bled from them as a gleam of heat flared. "I can hang for a bit. I'd love to spend some more time talking to you, Jessica."

"Come on in, then." She opened the door and crossed the threshold, with Sean following close behind.

★ ★ ★ ★ ★

Earlier that afternoon, Stephan had reached his limit. Nobody could ever blame him for not being a hardheaded Irishman. It had taken him a while to face the music, but once he had, he realized he wanted Jessica back. So bad, he would risk anything. Even telling her why he had ended their agreement. Give her a piece of him he had never shared with any other woman since Layla.

He had arrived at the Bauers' house and knocked on the door only to realize she wasn't in. He waited impatiently in his car for her return so he could apologize, spill his guts, and place the reins of his—their—future in her hands.

He would grovel if needed. Sometime within the last few days, he came to the realization that his treatment of her was high-handed. Patronizing, really. Assuming that hiding the truth behind his motives was protecting her from hurt. Jessica was young, but she was a very mature, opinionated, intelligent woman. She had made it clear she had wanted him long before she had ever set foot in Ireland. Stephan was certain that if he hadn't fled her house that first day, their relationship would have ignited then and there. She was clear as crystal, she had nothing to hide. He, on the other hand….

If the love he had seen in her eyes before was still alive, if she found it in her heart to listen to what he had to say, he would bare himself before her. And then, if she agreed to take him back, he could try to undo the damage he had done and they would find ways to handle the future as it unfolded.

His thoughts tumbled back to that first night without her. He had walked into a home empty of her things but still saturated with her essence— her scent permeating the air, the furniture rearranged to make things cozier—the images burned in his mind. Unable to face the large imposing bed where they had shared so many intimate moments, he sat in his library and drank himself into a stupor to dull the memories. Needless to say, he never made it to his bed that night.

Stephan hadn't fared any better the next day. He had taken a couple of personal days to pull himself together, but being trapped in the house with all of the memories of her—her smile, her voice, her mischievous eyes—crowded him at every turn. He didn't know what was more torturous, staying at home or going to the office, where the vision of Jessica bent over his desk, his palm print on her rosy ass, haunted him.

During the last few days, Stephan had time to reminisce about Layla and all the past heartache. Through it all, he could still remember the good times, the smiles, and the happiness they'd shared. He wanted much more from Jessica, much more than the couple of years he'd had with Layla. Forever wouldn't be enough. But even if they ended up as he feared, at least he would've—they would've—collected those happy moments, and he would be grateful for each and every one of them. He was ready to take what he wanted—and all he wanted was to take her home and hold her tight for as long as he could. No more fear of what ifs, no more fear of events that might never happen.

Movement on the street caught his eye. Anticipation flooded his veins, disappointment close on its heels. It wasn't Jessica. Just a couple on their way home after an evening out. As he glanced at his watch, out of the corner of his eye he noticed the couple had stopped in front of Cassandra and Trevor's home. Sitting in his car, parked across the street from the house, he gave them his full attention and realized that the woman with the glossy slicked-back hair and hot red shoes was indeed Jessica.

Stephan froze in his sedan's smooth leather seat and a blast of pain bloomed in his chest, almost knocking him forward over the steering wheel. His hands shook, a loud buzz rang in his ears as he watched the tall, lean young man walk her to the door. When he followed her inside and the door closed behind them, Stephan hung his head and squeezed his eyes shut. He never thought a broken heart could inflict such physical pain. He had thought the pain of sending her away had been intense. It was nothing compared to the burning fire churning inside him at that moment.

He was hurdled down an emotional rollercoaster, completely numb and speechless one second, angry and resentful the next. He left his car and started across the street. He wanted to storm the house, beat the crap out of the piece of shit that was at that moment possibly touching her, kissing her. She was his. Nobody else's.

Then reality came crashing down hard and he stopped in his tracks. He had driven her away with that exact purpose in mind. To let her choose someone else. Someone with whom she could have a longer, happier future. He had fucked up his own life. He had let her go, expecting her to move on even if he wasn't planning to do the same.

Stephan retraced his steps to his car and slipped back behind the wheel. Defeat was bitter on his tongue. She had been swift in finding a replacement for him. The truth of what he had witnessed delivered the mercy blow. If she had found it so easy to replace him, it meant she didn't really love him the way he thought she did. Stephan had reached the end of the road. He exhaled deeply, turned the engine, and drove toward a house where memories of her would torture him for a long time to come.

★ ★ ★ ★ ★

"So…who is he?"

"He who?"

"The guy who put that shadow in your eyes."

Jessica sat across from Sean in the media room. She had made them a pot of strong coffee and they had talked some more. Laughed some more. Still, her mind circled back to Stephan. She couldn't help comparing the two men. Whichever way she looked at it, Stephan always had the advantage. She loved his maturity, his calm demeanor, his take-control-leave-no-prisoner attitude. Sean sounded like a kid in a toy store. Cute kid, but still…not someone with whom she would choose to spend the rest of her life. She much preferred Stephan's hidden delights.

"Is it that transparent?"

"Yeah. It is. You had a different smile when I first met you. This new one has sadness in the background. As if you were thinking of good memories and mourning someone you've lost."

"Morbid connection much?"

Sean's expression took on a somber quality. "No. I mean…after you go through the death of a loved one and through all the phases of grief, you eventually find yourself remembering the good things you lived, experienced with that person. The smile in your face has that type of sadness."

He seemed to speak from experience.

"I get it. The thing is, I haven't gone through the phases of grief. I can barely accept everything that's happened."

"Want to talk about it? I'm a good listener."

"Do you want to talk about your own loss? Those types of deep thoughts don't just pop out of nowhere."

Sean's lips curved in a sad smile and he shook his head. "Not really."

"Me neither. I want to forget I was stupid enough to think he would be interested in me. At least, for the long run."

"He's a dumbass, whoever he is." Sean caressed her cheek with the back of his finger.

A smile spread on her lips. "I think I agree with you on that one. He'll miss out on being loved fully and completely. So yeah...it's his loss."

"Damn. Yeah. You're a goner."

"Guilty as charged."

"Again...*t-amadán*."

"I think I've heard Trevor refer to Nate with that word...it can't be anything good." Sean shot her a puzzled look. "Let's not go there. It's complicated," she explained.

Sean laughed. "The word means asshole. That's what your guy is."

"I wish he was mine." She laid her head against the padded back of the chair and sighed.

Sean stood. "I should be leaving. It has been a pleasure spending time with you, Jessica, but I have to get back to work. I have to help them close." He grabbed his jacket from the chair and they made their way to the door in a camaraderie born of the small shared secrets. "You still have my card. Call me. I have a broad shoulder. No strings attached."

"I appreciate it. We'll see. Can't promise anything."

"See you soon." Sean headed back in the direction of the nightclub, hands tucked in his pockets, collar pulled up. He looked as lonely as she felt.

If only…. Jessica brushed Stephan from her mind again and, closing the door, headed upstairs to her room, thanking the fates that she and Stephan had never shared her bed. If they had, she wouldn't have been able to handle lying among the memories. *He didn't seem to have the same issue,* she thought as she slipped out of her clothes and under the covers for another fitful night.

Chapter Thirty-Seven

Interesting Connections

H E SIGNED THE LAST OF the documents and handed them back to his secretary with a stiff, polite smile. He tapped his fingers on the desk and fidgeted in his seat as he watched her stride briskly toward the door. The minute she walked out, he grabbed his cell phone and punched in the long number in a quick and memorized succession.

The phone rang only a couple of times before Mikhailov answered with a curt, "Da."

"You have the program. Why is it taking so long for you to transfer my money? It's been over a month!" the caller spoke in a low, inflamed voice, in tune with the workplace environment. It wasn't as if his office had thin walls, but he didn't want their conversation to be overheard by his nosy secretary, who could walk back in at any time.

His nerves were getting the best of him. He itched to get his hands on the money and to be able to fill in the hole he'd dug before Devlin discovered it. He wasn't a forceful person by nature, but his bad decisions over the past year had pushed him into a spiral and now he found himself between a rock and hard place. There was no time or space for niceties.

The Russian man replied in heavily accented English, "You gave us a broken program. You do not get the money until I know it works as you say it will."

"What the hell are you talking about?" he all but snarled. "I handed you a piece of software you would never have been able to create from scratch!" He raked his hair with his fingers, his anxiety levels peaked to a new high. Raising his voice wouldn't help his cause, but he needed the money. Now. Not whenever Mikhailov could figure out how to get the software working. That was Mikhailov's problem. He had done his part.

"You need to be more careful of what you say on the phone." Mikhailov's tone was calm, despite the seething anger oozing from it.

Dealing with the Russian mafia boss, a dangerous shark, hadn't been the smartest decision—but then, there hadn't been a lot of options left from which to choose. He took a deep breath, lowered his voice, and apologized. "Sorry, but I can't wait until you have verified the program's utility. I need payment now."

"You will be paid when the program is finished and useful to me." Mikhailov was unmoved by his plea.

His response was followed by a moment of silence, and he thought the Russian was about to hang up on him. "Wait! Wait! Can you at least give me an advance? I guarantee you the program will do what you want!" Reduced to begging. God! *I'm so pathetic.*

Mikhailov chuckled. "Your peon has tried that already. Sergei told him the same. As I said, you will get the money when the program is fully functional."

A sheen of perspiration appeared on his brow as a nauseating despair sat like a boulder in the pit of his stomach. How would he cover his ass? All possible avenues had been exhausted. "And when do you think that will happen?" *Please be soon. Please say soon*, he chanted in his head as he waited for the answer.

"I do not know. Our last good developer who was working on it start-ed sniffing around like a wild boar and had to make a long trip to our version of GULAG. He will not be coming back." Mikhailov's words bled disgust, as if thoughts of the developer had left a rotten taste in his mouth. "We have a new one working on it right now, but so far I have not seen results. He seems to be good. A friend recommended him. I am expecting good news soon."

He pressed further. "How soon?"

Mikhailov's tone was heavy with sarcasm. "As soon as he finishes it, or the next developer does if this one cannot keep his nose out of my business."

The caller sighed. Realization that nothing would change Mikhailov's mind in regard to the payment hit him square in the face. "Okay, then. I guess I'll have to wait."

Mikhailov scoffed. "Of course you will. There is nothing else you can do. Keep in mind, you have a lot more to lose than I do if our little business deal is exposed."

He blanched at the mention of his precarious situation and his hand trembled slightly. "You don't have to remind me. I'm well aware of that."

Mikhailov's voice hardened. "Do not call again."

The call disconnected abruptly. He slammed his cell phone on the desk and leaned back in his comfortable office chair, releasing the deep breath he had been holding. If Mikhailov didn't get the decrypter finished soon, his chances of covering up his stupidity were gone. His family would lose everything.

The ping of his cell startled him and his eyes jerked to his phone. He picked it up and the image on its screen punched the air out of his lungs. It froze the blood in his veins. He grew lightheaded and was grateful he was sitting, otherwise it would have knocked his legs out from under him. With trembling fingers, he paged down to the text below it.

Such a beautiful family, no? Family is everything. Do not call again. My connections reach far.

Chapter Thirty-Eight

Qué Pasa

J ESSICA WANTED TO BEAT HER head against the desk. Each and every search query on the name Cassandra had provided had come up empty. She thought about the latest information request from Cassandra. It had been more cryptic than ever.

Jessie, check out this name. Petrovna. Nikol. Need anything you can find. Assume Russian descent. No pictures found. Only have description. 5"10–5"11. 140 pounds. Chestnut brown hair. Blue eyes. Need asap.

Drumming her fingers on the keyboard, she stared at it and racked her brain for any tricks to use in her search. She felt she was letting her good friend down. It was times like this that she missed Matt and his spunky wit. He always knew what to say to spur her synapse when it shorted. Disappointment welled in her chest. She had been counting on finding something to redeem herself for the failure she had encountered with

Kostas. It was curious that two of Cassandra's requests had come up with zero back to back.

A niggling tickled the back of her mind and she tried to grasp its meaning as it played hide-and-seek with her. She would call Matt in the morning and pick his brain. Even a brief conversation could be the ticket to getting her on track. Finished for the day, she pushed from the desk and pushed the puzzle to the back of her mind.

★ ★ ★ ★ ★

Wrapped in a blanket, Jessica wiped a tear from her cheek. She downed the last of the broth as she sat on the couch watching a movie on Trevor's sacred cow, a seventy-inch LED flat-screen television. The damn movie, about a woman who, on impulse, travels to Ireland with the intent of proposing to her boyfriend and instead finds the love of her life in an Irishman with dark hair and blue eyes, hit too close to home.

She couldn't hold it inside any longer, she needed Cassandra. She needed to bare her soul to someone who cared about her. Pulling her laptop onto her knees, she opened a chat window.

Cassie, still around? I know it's late and you might be on your way to bed, but can you talk?

Immediately a video call request popped up and Cassandra's familiar face filled the screen. "Here! Too keyed-up to sleep. Still need to handle a few things. What's the qué pasa, chica?"

Jessica studied her friend's image on the screen. "Damn, Cassie. Why the dark circles under your eyes? Sick or something? Why didn't you tell me?"

She heard Cassandra's quick intake of breath and frowned. "What's going on, Cassandra Cristina?"

Cassandra held her gaze. "Nothing I can't handle. No worries." Her gaze narrowed and she leaned closer. "What the hell is going on with you? You look like hell! Have you been sick? Has something happened?"

Jessica closed her eyes briefly, and then sent her friend a pleading look. "Promise me something first." A mix of curiosity and concern deepened Cassandra's creamy brown irises to almost chocolate. When she nodded,

Jessica exhaled a long breath. "Let me finish before you say anything. Okay?"

"Alright, but I can't promise anything."

Jessica rolled her eyes. "I know…Chatty Cathy Syndrome."

A soft smile curled the corner of Cassandra's mouth. "Whatever."

"Here's the deal. I was seeing Stephan."

"I knew it! Hold on. You said, 'was.' Past tense. You aren't seeing him anymore? You broke it off? Got tired of him already?"

Jessica held up her hands and chuckled. "Damn, Cassie. Two words: Slow. Down. Let me talk. You promised." Cassandra's eyes shifted to the left, almost as if checking something. "Everything okay, Cassie?"

"What? Yes. Yes." Cassandra returned her gaze to Jessica. "Okay. Shutting up now. Spill already."

Jessica sat back and crossed her arms as she watched emotions she couldn't define cross and then clear from her good friend's face. Something for later exploration. *Stop stalling, Jess.* "Remember when we talked just before you left and I told you what happened on the day of your wedding? Well, Stephan was one of the reasons I accepted your job offer."

"Okay. I get it. That's why you both were so weird at the bar and why you went to his office."

"Yes. I wanted to see if he was interested. Make sure I hadn't imagined what I had seen in his eyes. I wasn't wrong. He was definitely interested. The day you left he called and invited me out for a drink." Jessica paused, searching for the right words.

"Ah…that explains why your panties were in a bunch that day you met Terese."

Jessica's heart pinched at the mention of Terese. Was he back with her? Shaking her head, she pushed them from her mind. "Anyway. He offered a relationship with no strings attached. If either of us wanted out, we would walk away. I jumped at it, Cassie. I knew the first day I met him he was the one. I wanted him any way I could have him."

"Why didn't you tell me?" Cassandra's tone was slightly hurt.

"Selfishness, I guess. I've wanted this for so long, I just wanted to keep him to myself. We had been seeing each other up until a few days ago, when he told me it was over." Tears pooled in her eyes, blurring her vision, and she wiped them with the corner of the blanket.

Cassandra's eyes narrowed. "I'm going to kill him."

Jessica's heart filled with love for Cassandra. She had known her friend would stand up for her and it warmed her to no end that she didn't disappoint. Her matter-of-fact tone said it all.

"I don't know what happened, Cassie. One minute everything was wonderful. I even thought…I even thought he was changing his mind. That he wanted more. The next thing I know, he's pulling away. Shutting me out, and then telling me we're over." Jessica's voice caught.

"Oh, Jess…."

"I can't tell you how sick I've been over it, Cassie. My head hurts from trying to rationalize it and I am dead tired. It's hard to get up in the morning. Really hard to face the day without him. I can't even think of food without getting grossed out. And you know how much I love food. I miss him. I miss everything."

"Did he say why? I mean, Stephan is one of the most rational men I know. He is not a spur-of-the-moment kind of man. Hell, I have to schedule appointments with Máire just to be sure he shows up for dinner." Cassandra's tone was troubled.

A soft smile flowed across Jessica's lips. "So like him. Don't you love it?" The smile bled away just as quickly. "No. I think he is having an issue with the age difference. It kept cropping up. Stupid man. I'm old enough to know what I want."

"I don't know what to say. To channel Trev, Stephan is an *eejit*."

Jessica caught the look of worry that flared in Cassandra's eyes. "Cassie, don't worry about me." She didn't want her friend stressing over her personal life when the Russian business deal was becoming so convoluted.

Cassandra shook her head. "I can't help but worry about you. We brought you in and then bailed on you right after you got there. Left you all alone in a new city and country." Cassandra's voice was full of regret as she studied Jessica with a critical eye. "You really look like crap, by the way."

Jessica grinned. "Always the flatterer. Just so you know, I feel as bad as I look. I've felt like crap for a couple of days now."

"You should get checked, just in case. We don't want you at death's door by the time we get home. Tell you what, here's the number for my general practitioner. Anne O'Malley. You'll love her. The type of person you would want to hang out with at a bar. She's really good and I know she'll see you on short notice. Tell her you're my best friend and I recommended you. She should remember your name. I mentioned you to her before." Cassandra shrugged, "What can I say, the time we hosed Matt's computer is a funny story."

Jessica captured the name and number, saving it to her laptop. "Okay, I'll call first thing in the morning. To be honest, I just want to feel like myself again." Jessica heard a burst of noise coming from Cassandra's end of the call and watched her face lose all animation. "What's going on?"

Cassandra's eyes darted to the left and then back to her. "Nothing to worry about. I gotta go. Don't forget to call me after you see her. Oh, and we will talk more about Stephan later if you want. Damn, Trevor's going to flip—"

The video cut off abruptly and Jessica stared at the screen. Anxiety knotted her stomach. She didn't want to cause any problems between Stephan and Trevor. She should have asked Cassandra to keep it to herself, but she knew that wouldn't have been fair to her friend; she shared everything with Trevor. With a deep sigh, Jessica rubbed her eyes. *Ah, hell. That's not going to be pretty.*

Chapter Thirty-Nine

Brain vs. Brawn

D MITRIY'S HEART WAS IN HIS throat and he felt as if he was choking on it. He stuck his hands in his pockets to stop them from trembling as he walked down the hall to his uncle's office. Over time, since joining his household, he had learned that to be called to Uncle Mikhailov's lair was never a good thing. Standing before the carved oak door, Dmitriy tried to muster the courage to knock on it.

He could hear the angry discussion taking place in the room. Sergei was in there too. With a deep breath, he reached out a fist but cowered at the possibilities that meeting could lead to. *Better if I come back later, let him cool off.* He had never been the confrontational type, so avoiding a potential argument seemed to be the best course of action. Turning on his heel, he was about to take a step away when the door swung open and Sergei grabbed him by the collar, jerking him back through the door into the room.

"Where do you think you are going?" Sergei sneered. Holding Dmitriy in a tight grip by the scruff of his neck, Sergei dragged him further into the room and shoved him toward his uncle's desk.

Dmitriy caught his toe on the rug and stumbled, falling hard on one knee. Pain shot straight to his hip and he hissed out, *"Shit!"* He pushed back to his feet and scrambled to the middle of the room, away from the large walnut desk, putting some distance between him and Sergei.

"Uncle, I was told you wanted to see me." Dmitriy had no clue why he had been called like a school boy before his uncle.

Mikhailov studied him through narrowed eyes. Under his close scrutiny, Dmitriy's nervousness grew, his mouth dried, his stomach churned, and a thin sheen of perspiration covered his brow. He had seen the same deadly piercing gaze directed at others many times before—most never survived the encounter. The hair on the back of his neck stood on end.

"What have I done?!"

Mikhailov walked around the desk and stood in front of him. Before Dmitriy knew what hit him, Sergei's fist connected with his face. He staggered under the force of the blow, his cry of pain hung in the air as his head snapped back. Blood dripped between his fingers as he nursed his face in his hands, his eye throbbing, the flesh around it swelling in angry response to the direct hit, blinding him. He cringed away from Sergei and squinted up at his uncle in shock.

"Why?!" he cried out.

"What the fuck were you thinking by leaving Ivanov alone yesterday? The guard reported your visit to the kitchen." Mikhailov's voice raised an octave, his expression cold and uncaring.

"But…but Uncle, I thought you said you wanted him to finish the program. He needs time to figure it out. If…if he stays in the room it saves time and he can get more done," Dmitriy stuttered.

"Yes, idiot! And I told you to stay with him!" Mikhailov grated harshly, his patience frayed.

Dmitriy wiped the blood dripping down his chin with the back of his hand and rebutted, "You said to cater to him. And I did!"

Before Dmitriy could breathe another word, pain exploded in his gut and a scream ripped from his throat as his body collapsed around the fist that connected with his stomach. The soft Oriental rug caressed his burning face and cradled him as he lay curled in a fetal position, sobbing softly. *Please make this go away. I have done nothing wrong! Bastard!* He sucked in big gulps of air and fought through the pain.

In the distance, a phone rang followed by his uncle's muffled voice. "I asked not to be disturbed. This better be good." There was a brief pause and the click of the phone dropping in the cradle.

Dmitriy glanced up at Sergei, who wore a cruel gleam of excitement in his eyes.

"Sergei. Enough. Let him go." With a frown, Sergei stepped back.

"We have bigger fish to fry." Mikhailov looked down at Dmitriy in disgust and continued. "And you, stupid, go get Ivanov and get back to work. Stay with him. Do not let him out of your sight, or you will be erased from my bloodline next time."

Sergei reached down and unceremoniously grabbed Dmitriy by the arm. Jerking him to his feet, Sergei dragged him from the room and dumped him in the hall. "Move your ass!" he ordered, slamming the door closed.

The cold tile of the hallway floor soothed the heat radiating from the side of Dmitriy's face as he lay prone on the floor. He tried to assess the damage, but the pain was just one big ball of fire. When he could function again, he dragged himself to his feet in a slow, careful motion. He braced himself with an arm against the wall, willing the lightheadedness to pass.

When he could stand unaided, he stumbled down the hallway, away from pain and toward sanctuary—the computer room. Anger and hatred fueled his every step. He cursed his uncle and the time he had wasted kissing his feet for the last few years in hopes of being acknowledged for his efforts. He detoured to the kitchen—his other sanctuary. When he walked through the archway, Tatiana gasped and rushed to his side.

"What happened?!" she cried out, helping him to a stool before running to the sink for a towel. Wetting the towel in cold water, she rushed to his side and began wiping the blood from his face, shushing him each time he flinched from her touch.

"I won't be seeing you much today. I have to keep an eye on Ivanov. That means I will not be leaving the computer room for meals. Can you please bring us something to eat later?" He studied the curve of her cheek as she tended to him with gentle hands.

She nodded without making eye contact and replied softly. "It's okay. I understand. You must do as you are told. I'll fix you both something." Then, with some hesitation, she whispered shyly, "I...I will leave my door unlocked tonight. You can slip in after the others have gone to bed."

Dmitriy's hand covered and held hers. Softly lifting her chin with his other hand, he urged her to meet his eyes. "Are you sure?" Stunned, all Dmitriy can do was stare into her eyes. He had waited so long for that, for those words. Tatiana nodded, her answer a soft smile. His heart soared as he eased forward and kissed her gently on the lips.

"I have to go. He is waiting for me. I will come to you later." He gently squeezed her hand as he moved away.

Tatiana's tenderness had taken some of the pain and discomfort from the beating, but Dmitriy's mind still swirled with anger over the treatment he'd received from his uncle and that bastard, Sergei. More than ever, he was unsure whether he would ever earn his uncle's approval, or if all his effort and dedication could ever compete with Sergei's status within the Glazov.

Tatiana had been the reason he had accepted the job in Russia and the only motivation to further his cause and stay within his uncle's good graces. Dmitriy would do anything he could to remain at the mansion and continue his pursuit of Tatiana's love.

His hope was to wear her down and convince her to marry him. Once she agreed, they would move to Moscow and start afresh. Approaching the guest room to take on his babysitting duties, he was again filled with rage over Sergei's treatment of him. One day he would show Sergei that brains were better than brawn.

Chapter Forty

No Fucking Way!

CASSANDRA'S DOCTOR HAD BEEN AS nice as she had built her up to be. Dr. O'Malley was a five-foot, four-inch ball of fire with flaming red hair, startling green eyes, a dusting of freckles across her nose, and a feisty personality to match. Her wide friendly smile was engaging and made Jessica feel comfortable right away. The day before, Dr. O'Malley had put her through every imaginable exam under the sun, and some that Jessica hadn't even heard of. Holy Moses, the woman was an efficient tyrant. No wonder Cassandra loved her so much.

Jessica cursed. She needed to move her butt if she wanted to make her appointment to go over the results in time. She hated having to leave the warm, cozy cocoon of her bed so early, but it was the only time available on such short notice. She rolled out of her comfortable position, grumbling for having promised Cassandra she would take better care of herself. Once dressed, she grabbed her purse and jacket and headed out the door.

★ ★ ★ ★ ★

No fucking way! Jessica's mind screamed and swirled with information she couldn't quite seem to comprehend. Her ears were hot and her heart raced a mile a minute as she piled into her car. On the way home, her eyes kept straying to the paper bag and envelope on the passenger seat, and her heart did a somersault in her chest each time.

Pulling up to the curb, Jessica cut the engine and dropped her head on the steering wheel. *No fucking way!* She squeezed her eyes tightly and tried to breathe without hyperventilating. "Pull it together!" she murmured as she grabbed the things off the seat and walked on rubbery legs into the lonely house.

★ ★ ★ ★ ★

Jessica was tearing a path through the rug in Cassandra's living room as she paced back and forth, trying to wrap her head around what had just happened. She squeezed her eyes shut, blinking to clear the film of denial that coated them, and ran her fingers through her hair in agitation. She couldn't wait until later to talk to Cassandra. She needed to hear her friend's reassurances to keep her sanity in check.

Sitting at the dining room table, Jessica pulled the laptop closer and opened chat.

Cassie, let me know when you can talk.

Hold on! Give me a second. Cassandra's text was quick. Shortly after, a video chat request came through.

"Hey, Cassie."

"Jessie, we'll have to make it quick. I'm in the middle of something." Concern flooded Cassandra's eyes. "You look kind of pale. What happened? What did the doctor say?! Oh god, I poisoned you didn't I? How long does it take to get sick off bad food? Was it the paella? Geez! That was a month ago. Did I leave something else in the fridge?

Jessica couldn't help but laugh. "I wish."

Cassandra's eyes sharpened. "Wish what? Bad paella poisoning?"

Jessica sighed. "Yes."

"Jessica Marie Forrester. You better start making sense, woman, or I'm shipping your ass back to the States!"

"I'm pregnant."

"I mean, I should have cleaned out the refrigerator before I left," Cassandra continued as Jessica waited for her friend's brain to catch up with her ears. "Lord knows how long some of the veggies have been there. Leftovers, too—" Understanding flooded Cassandra's eyes and her mouth dropped open. She stared at Jessica as if she too were struggling with the news. "Holy shit!"

"I don't understand how this happened."

Cassandra shot a droll look at Jessica. "Part A inserts into part B—"

"Shut up, Cassandra. This isn't a joking matter," Jessica berated her.

"I know! I know! I'm just trying to understand. I mean these things happen. Not often…but they do."

"We were careful. Always used protect—" A shocked look snapped into place across Jessica's face. "Oh my god. The office—"

Cassandra's eyebrows rose. "Office? What office? My office? Eww, Jessica." Jessica narrowed her eyes at Cassandra and her mouth snapped shut. "Sorry, Jessie. Just a little overwhelmed at the moment. Mouth taking over and foot joining it."

"I don't know what to do." Jessica's voice trembled with each word.

Her friend eyed her. "Okay. So we are pretty sure you're pregnant. You told me you love Stephan. You still do, right?" Jessica nodded. "Okay. 'Nough said. You *have* to tell him." Jessica gave Cassandra a sour look. "Don't look at me like that. You have to. It's only fair to him. He deserves to know."

"You didn't see his face, Cassie." Jessica's voice hitched. "He was over me. If I tell him now, he'll think I was trying to trap him. I made it no secret that I wanted him for ever after. He'll hate me."

Cassandra's eyes turned from the video call and a frown creased her brow. "Shit. I have to go. Look at me, Missy." Cassandra snared her eyes. "You need to think about this very carefully. I'm like your older sister, and, as such, I would never guide you wrong. I say you *have* to tell him. *Tell* him. No matter what, he deserves to know. We should be out of here in a couple of days, I hope. When I get there, we'll figure out the fallout. Do not do anything crazy, okay? *Promise me."*

Cassandra held her gaze until Jessica nodded in agreement. "Okay then. Gotta go. It'll be okay. Hey! Does that mean I'm an auntie?" Jessica rolled her eyes at Cassandra's excited tone. "Damn…that foot just won't get out of the way. Bye."

When the connection cut off, Jessica chuckled and shook her head at the force of nature that was her friend. Leave it to Cassandra to spell it as it was. To make her laugh even when she felt like she could splinter into a thousand pieces with just the hint of a breeze. She was glad that she had been able to get the whole Stephan thing off her chest and share the news.

Jessica switched the lights off and, on her way to her room, panic set in again. Her heart hammered against her ribs and her legs grew wobbly. She stumbled through the door and plopped on the edge of the bed, dropping her head between her knees. She was pregnant with the man of her dream's child. And that scared her more than anything ever had before. She hadn't looked at another man since she had set eyes on Stephan all those months ago. That had not been his reality.

Joy and anguish warred in her chest and wreaked havoc in her head. A sob caught in her throat as she sat up and pulled the prenatal vitamins from the bag lying on her bed. Staring blindly at the little plastic bottle, her mind reeled. How could this have happened to her? To them? Should she even tell him, like Cassandra had advised? Would he believe her, or think it was a trick to get him back? Above all, would he be happy? She'd seen the look on his face that day in the restaurant. He didn't want a family. In that moment, she'd never felt more alone in her life.

Chapter Forty-One

Courtesy Visit

PAVEL ZAREV WAS STANDING BY the window looking out over St. Petersburg when he heard a knock on the door. Turning to face it, he called out in a curt demand, "Come in."

Vitaly Karyshev, his right-hand man and longtime friend, walked into the office, a serious expression on his face. "Edik has traced the withdrawal. The money was deposited into another account in the same bank."

Pavel had fumed over the hack discovered by one of his accountants during a routine money transfer he had requested be made to an associate's account. "Good. Then tell him to return it to mine—with interest. Did he find out who took it?" Fury leached into Pavel's voice. "I will show whoever did this they cannot steal from Pavel Zarev and live. It is like prison all over again." Vitaly nodded in agreement.

Pavel continued with his musings out loud. "Suppose someone in prison told you to fuck off and people around you heard it. You would have no choice but to pull a knife and cut into the bastard, otherwise you would lose respect. In prison, anyone with self-respect would respond to such words with retaliation, deeds. I want who did this dead. Planted in the woods," Pavel ordered coldly.

Vitaly dipped his head in understanding. "Edik was able to pull a name for the other account."

Pavel raised an eyebrow, waiting for his henchman to spit out the name.

Vitaly appeared to hesitate. He eyed Pavel warily and then finally blurted, "Mikhailov."

"Son of a bitch!" Zarev pounded on his desk with closed fists, his eyes darted with anger. "He is dead!"

"There is more. The money—it is no longer there. They moved it somewhere. We have no way to pull it back from the account."

Vitaly's words fueled Pavel's anger. Heat suffused his face. He slammed his fist on the desk again, sending the items dancing across the wooden surface. "If Mikhailov thinks he is getting out of this alive, he is wrong! Nobody messes with me and lives to brag about it!"

This was not a question of pride anymore. It was survival of the fittest. Pavel knew that if he accepted the theft without retaliation, it would be the end for him. Fights between gangs in Russia came down to more than money. It was all about defending their honor, reputation, power, and territory. Accepting such an offense showed weakness, an open invitation for other gangs to try the same: his organization would become the prey.

"Gather the others. Tell them to arm themselves with as much ammunition as they can carry. Load the cars." Pavel paused, mentally planning their course of action, and added, "Call in whoever you can. Instruct them to meet us at Mikhailov's mansion. He is about to be paid a courtesy visit."

Chapter Forty-Two

Clusterfuck

T REVOR'S THREE DAYS WERE UP. He had to deliver the damn decrypter by the end of that day or shit would hit the fan. He wasn't concerned about handing the finished product to Mikhailov. The program would literally implode and self-destruct like the message in a *Mission Impossible* movie once he added the Trojan virus to it. Sometime after he demonstrated the decrypter's capabilities and before he left the mansion, he would find a way to slip the code in and recompile it. For now, his concerns focused solely on the destruction of the data stored on the mainframe and backup.

Without that crucial step, his effort to inject the virus in the software would be for nothing. Mikhailov would still have the source files and could easily hire someone else to finish the job. If, and only if, he could find someone skilled enough to handle the code. The time he had spent in that hole away from Cassandra would be in vain if he didn't accomplish that one crucial task. The completion of the job and retrieval of his father's notes in Prague depended on its full success.

The clacking of keys against the door indicated his new friend had arrived to release him. Dmitriy was later than usual, and Trevor was chafing, eager to get away from the small room. When the door opened, a roughed-up Dmitriy stood just outside. The left side of his face was swollen and bruised, his left eye a mere slit, the damage clearly caused by a well-aimed fist. He avoided Trevor's gaze as he dabbed a handkerchief against his bloodied nose.

"What the fuck, man?!" Dmitriy, who appeared flustered and embarrassed, like a child who had been spanked in front of friends, ignored his startled comment. Trevor watched him closely as they walked to the mainframe room. He was puzzled, but, not wanting to embarrass Dmitriy further, held his tongue in check. Trevor would probe him later to find out who had used him as a punching bag and why.

Once the door clicked locked behind them and they reached the subterranean room, Trevor headed straight to his usual workstation and continued with his charade, initiating the sequence of commands to open the programming tool and subsequently the decrypter files. Dmitriy moved to his own computer and sat quietly, dabbing at his bloody nose.

Trevor glanced over at Dmitriy. Impatient to find out what exactly had happened to him, Trevor broke the silence. "If it's a new fashion statement you're going for, you missed the boat on that one." He had hoped his smart-ass remark would bait him, drag him out of his shell. When Dmitriy didn't bite, he shrugged. Unable to ignore the ticking of the clock, Trevor returned his attention to figuring out how to accomplish the last part of his job.

★ ★ ★ ★ ★

Time was teasing and slowly driving Cassandra mad. The knowledge that Trevor didn't have much time left was unnerving. Her confidence in his ability to complete the task and get out of the shark tank alive, once rock solid, was now cracked and chipped at the edges. It had been a while since Trevor's last broadcast. Once he'd disappeared into the hole, she'd double-checked everything. Cassandra caught sight of the corner of the airline tickets peeking out from under her notebook and remembered that she needed to change their flights, since they were leaving later than expected. The penalty fee would be a bitch, but more than worth it to leave Russia and the mafia behind.

Cassandra finished clearing out the last of their belongings and returned to her laptop just as the incoming chat window alert flashed on the screen. Clicking it, she saw a curt message from George.

Stand by.

"Shit. Come on, George! Don't leave me hanging!" Pushing her chair back, her stomach tied up in knots as she paced the room, waiting for him to come back online. Ten minutes later, the chat window flashed with activity a second time.

Cassie, are you there? Can you talk?

Yes.

A voice call request promptly popped up on the screen.

"What do you have, George?"

"Is Trevor with you? Hey, Trev. You're both going to want to hear this!" When Cassandra didn't respond right away, George's tone became inquisitive. "Cassie? Trev?"

"Trevor isn't here at the moment." She paused, trying to find a way to introduce the subject. "We have a small development."

"What kind of development?"

Cassandra released a deep breath. George wasn't going to be happy with her answer. *She* wasn't happy with the answer. "He's been in the mansion for over two weeks now, George. As you know, physical access was the only option in this case, but we ran into some minor complications."

"Shit, Cassandra! Minor complications? Ah, hell! Please say he isn't the developer I've heard being discussed on the feeds."

Cassandra could hear the anxiety creeping into his voice and in her mind's eye could see him raking his fingers through his hair again and again in frustration. She could almost see his hair standing on end.

"Well…we didn't think things would get this prickly. But we've got it handled." Cassandra opened a blank document to capture any valuable information for her file. "What do you have? Anything useful to us?"

"That friend of your father's? It took me a while, but I managed to track down new information on him. I am sending you a few files. Check it out."

Cassandra saved the incoming files to her desktop and opened them as soon as they transferred. Her breath hitched and her head spun as she absorbed the information they contained.

"Holy hell!" Cassandra sat dismayed by another confirmation that wolves amongst them were wearing sheep's clothing. "This is big. I need to let Trevor know. Damn it! I wish he had ears!"

"Wait, what? What do you mean 'had ears'?"

"He doesn't have a receiver, only a transmitter. And even that only works when he is out of the room he's been working in. Some sort of strong signal dampening."

"Damn, Cassie. This is bad…. We need to find a way to pass this info to him."

Stunned, Cassandra's eyes grew bigger as she read each new line. A fist squeezed her heart and her breath accelerated in tandem. Trevor was in the lion's den, oblivious to the fact that he was a pawn being used by both sides in a dangerous game.

★ ★ ★ ★ ★

Trevor eyed his keeper for the hundredth time. He had observed Dmitriy's bruise changing hues to a deeper purple as the day went by. He didn't seem to be going anywhere anytime soon and hadn't said much since they'd settled to work. All Trevor's attempts at small talk had only resulted in nods or grunts and the occasional chuckle, but nothing productive had been exchanged, which was very unusual for them. They usually enjoyed full geek-out conversations throughout the day.

Trevor decided on the direct approach. "What happened to you?"

Dmitriy was silent for a long time. Trevor watched as a frown creased his brow, his eyes narrowed, and his expression darkened. Anger seemed to get the better of him. "Sergei."

"What did you do? Block his porn?" he teased with a cocky smirk. Instead of a chuckle or laughter, Dmitriy shot him a resentful look.

"You really want to know? This,"—Dmitriy pointed at his own face—"is because of you."

Trevor immediately went on alert. His pulse beat wildly, a loud drum in his ears. *Does Mikhailov know why I'm here? Did Tomlin get wind I was hired and alerted Mikhailov about a foreigner heading to Russia?* The "what-ifs" swirled in his head until Dmitriy's next words pulled him back from the abyss.

"Indirectly. I left you unattended yesterday. Uncle Vladimir didn't quite like that."

Trevor let out a long breath of relief. His anxiety spike was a knee-jerk reaction. It was clear that he would be in much rougher shape than Dmitriy by now if Mikhailov knew of his connections and what he'd been commissioned to do. "And he let Sergei beat you? A member of his family? Just because of that?"

Although the treatment Dmitriy had received was appalling, in reality Dmitriy had been damn lucky he was family. Considering what Trevor knew about Sergei and Mikhailov, had it been anyone else, he or she would've received a treatment of the definitive kind.

Dmitriy scoffed and continued to give Trevor details on what had transpired earlier. "Fucker. I've been helping his cause for a long time. I have information he would pay a lot to keep under wraps. And this is how he treats me?! His sister's only son?!" Driven by anger, he didn't realize how telling the details were. Sergei would probably beat him to a pulp if that little talk ever reached his ears.

By having access to all the information the network carried, Dmitriy had become a valuable commodity, dead or alive. In that part of the world, with his connections, it didn't take much to sign your own death warrant. Poor guy was between a rock and a hard place and didn't even realize it.

Dmitriy continued on a roll, ranting about his uncle and Sergei, spilling Mikhailov's plans to dive heavy into the world of online fraud. He expounded on Mikhailov's dealings with smaller gangs specializing in phishing and hacking, similar to the group that had hacked into a major online gaming network and stolen thousands of user files not long ago. No wonder Mikhailov was so obsessed with the data stored in the server. That mainframe was the ultimate online fraud tool—a con artist's golden egg.

By taking such a forward approach toward online fraud, Mikhailov would be ahead of the game in the digital age and, if successful, he would become the top dog in all of Russia. The decrypter would play a huge part in jumpstarting his success, giving him access to decoding credit card information, PINs, and passwords stored in those files. *Holy shit!*

Trevor's face must have reflected his convoluted thoughts because, in that very moment, Dmitriy seemed to realize he'd been talking way too much, for far too long. His mouth snapped shut and he pushed from his desk. Standing, he stared at Trevor. He opened his mouth and snapped it shut again, raking his fingers through his hair as he began to pace the room.

A heavy bang hit the door and the sound of the locks turning reverberated down the stairs, startling them both. Dmitriy rushed up the stairs, leaving Trevor alone in the room. Sliding the chair closer to the foot of the stairs, Trevor overheard Dmitriy and the guard arguing in Russian.

"They are here."

"What do you mean? Who is here?"

"The Tambov. They had balls. They are outside the gates. And they are amassing numbers."

"Shit. Does my uncle know?"

"Of course he does! Sergei was the one who spotted them."

"I need to see this."

Suddenly, silence engulfed the room. There had been no slamming of doors, no clicking of bolts. Trevor pushed out of his chair and crept up the stairs. At the top, he tested the handle and confirmed the heavy metal door was unlocked. In their haste, they had forgotten protocol. Cracking the door, Trevor looked around, but they were nowhere in sight. Whatever was going down had to be huge to make them leave without any thought to possible punishment for their neglect.

Trevor didn't have to be slapped in the head to know that the perfect opportunity to wipe the mainframe clean and to find a way out of the mansion had just dropped in his lap. As he ducked back in the door, a loud boom sounded from the front of the mansion, followed by screams and running feet. A rapid succession of pops echoed from out front. *Gunshots!* He froze and, within seconds, filtered through the different scenarios in his mental Rolodex.

The words exchanged by Dmitriy and the guard, the knowledge that Mikhailov had been playing with fire, taunting his rivals by stealing their money from under their noses—all pieces combined helped him reach the most plausible explanation. They were at war.

Pavel Zarev must have caught wind of who had hacked his account. *Shite!* The whole situation had become a total clusterfuck. The one thing Trevor had never counted on was firepower.

Without any other options, knowing that there would be hard consequences to what he was about to do, Trevor spoke clearly so Cassandra could hear him, "*Mí-ádh!* I will love you always!" He prayed the message reached her loud and clear.

Confident she would follow their plans to the letter, Trevor rushed downstairs to finish what he had started. It was now or never.

★ ★ ★ ★ ★

"*Mí-ádh!*" The shock of hearing the Irish word for *bad luck* was like a death grip, freezing her and all thoughts, holding her hostage for a split second before she exploded into action. Cassandra raced around the room, shutting everything down, locking windows, pulling curtains closed. Blocking all emotion, she kicked into autopilot. She had a job to do: run.

Chapter Forty-Three

Bloody Hell!

T REVOR HIT THE BOTTOM OF the stairs and rushed to Dmitriy's computer. The ricochet of gunfire echoed from the open door. It sounded as if the confrontation was getting hairier by the minute.

Considering the computer room's location and its importance to the organization, chances were someone would soon come looking for the same data Trevor was trying to delete. Without much thought, he retrieved the micro thumb drive from the hem of his pants. "My lucky charm," he murmured. As he connected the device to Dmitriy's computer, he made a mental note to carry the same device with him on any future jobs.

Trevor saved the finished decrypter's source data he had worked on to the thumb drive and initiated the installation of the software used by all US government offices to erase confidential data from their computers. It guaranteed that no trace of the data could be restored once deleted.

More shots fired. Not just handguns. Rapid fire indicated heavy armory was at play. "Bloody hell! *Come on!* Come on!" he growled at the screen, watching the progress bar.

Trevor let out a huge sigh of relief when the process completed without a hitch. His eyes darted between the staircase and the screen while he scanned through the software's configuration and checked all necessary options to run the highest level of deletion possible. He then added a password to the program's preferences, ensuring that only he had authorization to terminate it. Once that was set, Trevor selected the mainframe as primary target and the backup storage as secondary.

He was about to run the program when the pounding of approaching feet reverberated at the top of the stairs and Dmitriy came running down, a crazed look on his face, wielding a gun in his hand. Adrenaline jacked into Trevor's system as he tapped a finger, one single key press, initiating the destruction process. The deal was sealed, there was no going back. "Ivanov! Zarev's gang is attacking! We need—" He stopped mid-sentence as Trevor turned in the chair to face him. "What the fuck are you doing?"

The flush of excitement coloring Dmitriy's face turned a brighter red and his eyes grew wide as his gaze shifted from Trevor to the screen. "What are you doing?!" His eyes grew tight around the corners and narrowed as he began to stalk toward Trevor.

Trevor eyed him warily; from the awkward way Dmitriy held the gun, he was positive the man had never handled one before. He probably preferred his fingers on a keyboard, not on a gun's trigger. Trevor had been like that once. That was, until Cassandra burst on the scene and forced him to develop his marksmanship skills. Now he was just as comfortable with the gun as he was his keyboard.

Going on instinct, Trevor shot for more time. "I assume you don't want the data taken by whoever is raiding the house? Right?"

Understanding seeped into Dmitriy's alarmed expression when he drew even closer and saw the data destruction software window displayed on the screen. File names scrolled at a rapid clip.

"You are so dead! Stop it, now!" Dmitriy pressed the gun to Trevor's temple, his face distorted with anger as he twisted the muzzle like a screw into Trevor's skin. "I said to stop the process!"

Trevor sat motionless, ignoring his request. Dmitriy expelled a shaky breath, pushed past him, and began to type commands, clicking buttons as he tried to abort the program. The progress bar on the screen continued to inch forward at a fast rate. "Stop the fucking process. *Now!*" His eyes bulged and spit flew out of his mouth with each furious word as he shoved Trevor's shoulder.

Trevor raised his hands from the keyboard and shook his head. "Sorry. No can do."

Dmitriy's expression fluttered between anger and helplessness. "Why? Why are you doing this? He'll kill you!"

Dmitriy was a brilliant network engineer but, when it came to his uncle, he was naïve. "Yep, and he'll kill you, too." Trevor paused for effect. "You know that, right? Remember the beating you took this morning? Just for leaving me alone?"

In the span of a second, a dozen different expressions skipped across Dmitriy's face, and Trevor knew he had gotten his drift. "Mikhailov won't even bother to do it himself. Without blinking an eye, he will turn you over to Sergei again. You know I'm telling the truth. Deep inside…you know."

Anger bled into Dmitriy's eyes and he burst out, waving the gun, "This is your fault! You caused all this! Your actions are the reason Zarev is retaliating against us and now you're deleting the files?!" Suddenly, the muzzle was pressed against Trevor's temple again and Dmitriy hissed through clenched teeth, "I should kill you myself!"

"Your uncle ordered me to steal the money from Zarev. It was your uncle who provoked his anger, not me." Trevor watched Dmitriy closely. "My goal is to retrieve something your uncle stole from my employer."

Dmitriy's eyes clouded with uncertainty and his hold on the gun relaxed, easing the pressure against Trevor's temple. "What do you mean?"

Trevor sighed deeply. "The decrypter he stole. I was hired to find and delete it." The commotion above ground grew louder; from the sound of it, it was creeping closer to them. Trevor looked at Dmitriy straight in the eyes. "Dmitriy, we don't have time for a pow-wow. Join me. I'm your only chance. If you stay, you are dead either way. I have connections. I can give you a chance at a new start away from your uncle. A normal life. No threats. No beatings. Just let me finish what I need to do. You have to decide now!"

Gunshots and screams could be heard topside, moving closer and closer. It sounded like Zarev had brought a whole arsenal to annihilate Mikhailov's gang for good. "Fuck it! You need to figure it out. *Now!* As soon as the data destruction is complete, I'm out of here, with or *without* you," Trevor pressed. "I'm not sure how I'll get out of here with a bloody war raging outside, but I'll sure as hell find a way! Do you really want to face Mikhailov after this?"

Dmitriy hesitated for a second before he blurted out, "Okay. I'll help you." Squaring his shoulders, his voice hardened. "But Tatiana comes, too."

A grin quirked the corner of Trevor's mouth and he shook his head. "About freaking time. Fine. She comes with us." Dmitriy exhaled a long deep breath of relief and his hold on the gun slacked.

Standing, Trevor drew close and clapped Dmitriy on the back. Distracted, Dmitriy didn't react when Trevor twisted the gun from his hand, disarming him before he knew what hit him. "I better hold on to this. I think we are both safer if I handle it."

Trevor slipped the gun into his waistband. "As soon as the process is finished, we're getting the hell out of here. You lead the way to Tatiana."

Buzzing with nervous energy, Dmitriy watched the progress bar on the screen with Trevor. "I know a way out. There's a big tree in the back. It grows close to the back wall of the property. We can use it to scale the wall. There's a ravine on the other side. It's part of a park. Once over, we can hide in the bushes."

Trevor shook his head. "No. We have to put as much distance as possible between us and the mansion. Where does the park exit? To a busy street?

Transit?"

Dmitriy nodded. "Yes."

At that moment, the bar displayed 100 percent completion—erasure success. The mainframe and backup unit had been fully annihilated. The data Mikhailov lusted over, blown to bits.

Another series of shots rang out. "That was too close for comfort. We need to go, now!" Grabbing the USB stick from the computer, Trevor rushed to the stairs, Dmitriy on his heels. He nudged the door and peered outside. "All clear," he whispered, and darted down the hall with Dmitriy close behind.

"This way! Shorter!" Dmitriy hissed, tugging at Trevor's arm and dragging him through a detour to the kitchen.

"We gotta be quick!" Trevor reminded him in a rough whisper. That detour needed to be a grab-and-run operation. Sporadic gunfire sounded from somewhere in the house. Soon, the police would come knocking or one of the gangs would cry uncle. Whatever the case, they needed to move their asses before that happened.

Dmitriy entered the kitchen at a run, skidding across the floor, his head turning left and right, searching. A cutting board with sliced vegetables and a discarded knife sat on the large wooden table. It appeared as if the women had been caught by surprise in the middle of fixing lunch. He glanced at Trevor, panic in his eyes. "Where is she?" He yelled in Russian, "*Tatiana! Tanka!* Where are you!"

"Dmitriy! Here!" a soft voice cried out in stuttered words filled with fear. Dmitriy immediately dropped to the floor and extended his arm under the table.

"Tatiana!" Dmitriy grabbed her outstretched hand and pulled her tight against him, shushing her as she broke down in uncontrollable sobs. "It's okay. Don't cry, Tanka. We're getting out of here."

"No! They'll kill us."

Losing patience, Trevor took Tatiana by the shoulders, looked her directly in the eyes, and spoke to her in perfect Russian. "Tatiana, you have to trust us. We need to get out of here now, or we will be trapped. If we do not find a way out of here right now, we are all going to die. Do you understand?" He felt the weight of Dmitriy's glare on him, surprise and accusation in his eyes. Trevor shrugged a shoulder.

Dmitriy's whispers of comfort and Trevor's words finally pierced Tatiana's fear and her expression hardened as she stood straighter, brushing at the tears on her cheeks. "I am good. I am good."

She was a determined little thing, and Trevor could see why Dmitriy was drawn to her. Trevor turned Tatiana around and urged her to follow Dmitriy, whispering, "You can't make any noises. We don't want to call attention to ourselves. Dmitriy will lead the way. I will be right behind you, covering your backs."

Loud voices came from the end of the hall. Trevor's pulse quickened. Pulling the gun from his waistband, he pushed them to the double French doors leading to the backyard. "Go, *go!*"

Dmitriy grabbed Tatiana's hand and tugged her behind him. Popping his head around the door jamb, Dmitriy scanned the perimeter then gave Trevor a curt nod. "Clear."

Once they slipped out the back door, they followed Dmitriy's lead, running through the property to the back garden wall. Just as they reached the half-moon bench at the base of the old English Oak, they heard two men yelling at each other from the distance and the sounds of doors being opened and slammed shut.

"Where are they? Did you check the rest of the mansion?"

"They were not seen at the front. Someone opened the door."

"Maybe Dmitriy took him to safety."

"Call Sergei."

"He won't like it."

"Doesn't matter, he will tell us what to do."

The two men rushed back toward the front of the mansion, their conversation fading as they moved deeper into the house. Trevor's stomach cramped with anxiety. They needed to get out of there quickly. Mikhailov would not leave one stone unturned while searching the property. And once he figured out that his files were gone, Dmitriy and Trevor would be at the top of his shit list, bumping even Zarev, who currently reigned supreme.

That thought triggered a memory. Boris's reaction to Zarev's name during the interview. Was Boris playing both sides? Were the files he wanted for Zarev? Was he the catalyst to Zarev's violent retaliation? All those questions spiraled in Trevor's head. If Boris wanted possession of the information in Mikhailov's documents so badly, why would he provoke an attack knowing Trevor was in the mansion trying to secure them for him? It didn't make any sense. But then again, clashes between gangs were a common occurrence. Could this be a simple coincidence? Filing those uncertainties for later, Trevor herded the couple forward.

"How do we get up there?" Trevor pointed to the top of the solid stone wall.

Dmitriy's eyes slanted to meet his look of concern and a smug smile curved his lips. "I spent part of my childhood here. I have used it many times to sneak to the ravine for boyish adventure."

Dmitriy brought Tatiana's hand to his lips for a kiss and jumped up on the stone bench. Using the knots on the rough tree bark and the faults in the old stone wall as makeshift steps, Dmitriy shimmied his way up, one foot at a time, until he reached the top. Swinging a leg over, he straddled the wall and gestured for Tatiana. "Come. You can do it."

Tatiana followed his example while Trevor kept guard of the perimeter, each movement, each new pop making him jumpy. The sounds of the bloody confrontation taking place in the house were eerie to his ears—surreal, even.

As Tatiana got closer, Dmitriy extended a hand and helped her up to the top of the wall. He then swung his leg to the other side and initiated his descent.

Trevor slipped the gun back in the waistband of his pants and followed suit. They had made it look so easy. Thank the Irish gods Cassandra had whipped his ass into shape, or he would have fallen on his face. He cursed his need for an adrenaline rush. That one had become a whitewater rapids ride without the raft.

Midway to the top, he heard the sound of sprinting feet heading in their direction. Glancing up, he saw Tatiana's skirt disappearing as she slipped out of sight, followed by a soft rustle of bushes and then silence.

Peeking from behind the tree, Trevor recognized Alexander, one of Mikhailov's guards. He watched as the heavily armed man, breathing hard from the run, poked the bushes at the back of the house with the muzzle of his AK-47. Trevor drew and held a deep breath, motionless while visualizing Cassandra's face, his promise to return to her in one piece a looping mantra in his head.

"Alexander! They went this way!" another voice shouted from somewhere out front. The guard's head snapped up and he took off running. Sneaking another look from behind the tree, Trevor watched as he disappeared in the direction of the house.

Anticipating the man would be back, Trevor rushed his ascent, pulling himself up just as Dmitriy had done. Straddling the wall, he squinted into the wooded area for any sign of the couple on the other side. A sense of dread invaded him when he considered the possibility that they had bailed on him. A quick "Psst!" reached his ears, then another. Searching in the direction from where the sound originated, Trevor spotted Dmitriy's head popping out from the bushes.

Dmitriy waved at Trevor, urging him down. "Come on!"

Scanning the backside of the wall, Trevor spotted the uneven stones he could use as foot holds. "Give me a second!" he called down in a low voice.

Supporting his weight on his hands, he swung his leg to the other side and, shoving his toe onto the first foothold, eased over the wall. Facing the house, he noticed movement in the yard and heard snarling dogs. The damn dogs were on the loose again. He hated those big dogs. They were too smart for their own good. It was just a matter of time before they picked up their scent. He glimpsed down for the next foothold.

"Halt!" a familiar voice yelled.

Startled, Trevor stared down into Sergei's dead cold eyes. The henchman sneered just before he pulled the trigger. A grunt whooshed from Trevor's chest when burning pain speared through his shoulder. He let go of the wall and crumbled to the ground, falling on a bed of soft springy moss. Blinding pain radiated from the left side of his body. "Fuck!" he cursed, rolling to his back. Perspiration beaded his brow as he cradled his drooping arm closer to him. Warm blood oozed from the wound and stained his shirt. A metallic tang coated his tongue, his ears felt like they had been stuffed with cotton as his vision faded to black.

Chapter Forty-Four

Running

Cassandra moved purposefully around the apartment, gathering the last items needed for her evasion. Returning to the makeshift desks, she shoved Trevor's laptop into her pack and reached for her own. Just then, the equalizer on the screen blipped and a commotion filtered through the connection. Her knuckles turned white as she squeezed the handle of the pack, listening intently for more signs of Trevor. Cassandra knew she should disconnect all the equipment, pack, and leave, but she couldn't bring herself to do it.

Trevor's urgent whisper came loud and clear through the speakers, *"We gotta be quick!"* Adrenaline coursed hot and fast in her blood as she overheard footsteps running and heavy gunfire in the background. What the hell was going on in there?

Soon after, she heard a second voice, which she recognized as Dmitriy's, cry out, *"Where is she?"* And then he switched to Russian. A woman's voice answered his call.

A frantic conversation took place between Dmitriy and the woman. Suddenly, Trevor's firm tone sounded again and the woman stopped crying. Minutes later, following another brief dialogue in Russian, Cassandra heard Trevor call out, *"Go, go!"*

She heard the thumping of running feet and heavy breathing. They were escaping, running. Cassandra knew she should do the same but her feet were fused to the floor. She had to know that he was safe. Once he was off the property, she would gather their things and leave as planned. Until then, she listened intently to their every move, waiting for another word from Trevor.

"How do we get up there?" Her heart sank to her knees. Trevor hadn't been lucky with heights of late. She braced herself for what would come next. Men's voices speaking excitedly in Russian came across the signal and she heard Trevor's sigh of relief when they faded in the distance.

"Come on!" Dmitriy urged, an undertone of panic in his voice.

"Move it, Trev! Get the hell down from wherever you are! No more climbing for you, mister!" she grumbled, even though she knew he had no way of hearing her.

"Give me a second!" She almost felt like he had responded directly to her. A small smile cracked on her lips. He would be out of there in a minute and she would be back in his arms in a few hours.

"Halt!" She recognized that voice. Her stomach sank to her feet. She had heard that voice the day Trevor received his unwanted visit in the middle of the night. Sergei. Mikhailov's henchman and resident psycho.

A loud pop rang out. "Trevor!" she cried when his grunt echoed in the room, followed by static. The connection had been severed. *That was a shot. I know it was. He is not dead. He is not dead. Get moving, Cassie.*

Sick to her stomach, hands shaking out of control, Cassandra put a wall around her heart and focused her thoughts. She forced a shutdown of her computer, shoved it in with Trevor's, and slung the backpack over her shoulder. Grabbing her Grach, she checked the safety before stuffing it into the band of her jeans at the small of her back as she bolted through the room to the front door, where two duffel bags waited on the floor.

Cassandra scanned the hallway before she slipped out, locking the door behind her. With both bags in hand, she double-timed it down the stairs, spilled out on to the sidewalk, and hurried off in the direction of the Sennaya Metro Station. By her calculations, the whole trip to the safe house would take a couple of hours, barring any delays. At the most, she expected to arrive there around early evening. *Trevor better be there.*

She weaved past businessmen and women, mothers and children, and the elderly going about their daily grind, oblivious to the turmoil churning inside her. Cassandra wanted to yell, scream, make them aware someone she cared deeply about, someone she loved, was in danger. But life went on untouched by the pandemonium buffeting them from all sides.

Cassandra's heart hammered against her ribs as she reached the entrance of the metro. She made her way through the throng of people toward the turnstile. As the metal slot sucked the ticket from her fingers, she pushed her way through and mingled with the many passengers waiting on the platform. She glanced at the digital board and sighed heavily. She would be on the next train out of there.

★ ★ ★ ★ ★

Trevor woke to an excruciating pain radiating from his shoulder. Hands tugged and pulled at his body and voices penetrated his consciousness. Voices he recognized—Dmitriy and Tatiana. He tried to move, but the pain was like a hot poker spearing through him. He sucked in air, fighting through the agony that would have dropped him to his knees had he not already been lying on the ground. Darkness threatened to overtake him once again, but he pushed through it.

"Lift him so I can wrap his arm," Tatiana told Dmitriy; when he did, another burst of burning pain seared through his upper body as she wrapped what looked like strips of cloth from her skirt tightly around his chest and arm. Dmitriy covered Trevor's mouth to muffle the cries that broke from his lips and were sure to give away their location.

Breathing harshly through his nose, Trevor's head fell back against the ground.

"What the hell happened?" Dmitriy whispered.

Even drowning in pain, Trevor couldn't prevent the amused chuckle that escaped his lips. "Damn. You sound like my wife...fucking Sergei happened."

"Wife?" Dmitriy shot another accusing look at Trevor and shook his head. "Never mind. We don't have time. We have to get out of here. What do we do now?"

"How bad is my arm? Did you check it while I was out?" Trevor asked in Russian, hoping one of them had had the presence of mind to take advantage of that natural anesthesia—unconsciousness.

"Yes. Tatiana checked."

"I think the bullet went straight through. I cleaned the wound the best I could. It's still bleeding, but not as bad as before. It will do for now. The arm doesn't seem to be broken. You will need an x-ray to be sure." Trevor raised an eyebrow at Tatiana's impressive thoroughness and expertise.

She shrugged and said offhandedly, "Three younger brothers and living on a farm in the middle of nowhere makes you learn that kind of thing. They hunted a lot." Trevor tried to smile at her, but could only manage a grimace.

"What do we do now?" Dmitriy asked again.

"We need to get out of here. I'll need your help. I won't get far on my own."

They helped Trevor into a sitting position and gave him a second to catch his breath before draping his good arm over Dmitriy's shoulders. Tatiana supported him by the waist as they eased him to his feet.

"Shite!" Trevor hissed. Pain blinded him, his hearing muffled, and he thought he would pass out again. "Give me a second." Trevor squeezed his eyes shut and gulped big gasps of air until his head cleared and he could breathe again. "Okay, I'm good. Let's go."

Dimity shouldered Trevor's weight and became his human crutch, leading them on an excruciating race against time. They all worried Sergei would catch up with them. It wouldn't be pretty if he did.

The minutes it took to reach the edge of the park were the longest of Trevor's life. When they reached the busy road, and before they continued on their way to the closest metro station, Dmitriy took off his sweater and covered Trevor's shoulders with it to conceal the blood staining his shirt.

"Not that this will help much, but thank you," Trevor grunted.

Dmitriy frowned. "What do you mean? At least it will cover the blood."

"Yeah, but have you seen your face?" Trevor smirked. "We are a curious pair, bloodied and bruised. All courtesy of Sergei."

When Dmitriy gripped Trevor's arm again and draped it around his neck, Trevor groaned and stumbled against him.

"Steady, my friend. I'm sorry I moved too quickly." Dmitriy's tone was apologetic.

Trevor flashed him a mischievous grin. "Don't be. You just gave me a brilliant idea. Follow my lead." He leaned heavily against Dmitriy and cried out in Russian, slurring his words. "Vodka! More vodka! Where is my bottle?" He shifted his head in Tatiana's direction and narrowed his eyes. "Are you hiding it?"

Tatiana caught on quickly and did what she could to further their ruse. "You, my brother, have had enough. We need to get you home so you can sleep it off."

"Come," Dmitriy urged, leading a stumbling Trevor in the direction of the metro.

At the counter, Dmitriy pulled out his wallet and was about to hand the cashier his credit card when Trevor gripped his hand. "No," Trevor whispered in English.

"What do you mean? We need to pay to get in."

"I know. No credit cards. They can trace that. I'm sure one of the hackers working for your uncle could. Use cash."

Understanding shone in Dmitriy's eyes for a second before dismay took over. "I have no cash on me." Panic flooded his expression. "How are we going to get out of here now?"

Trevor had the emergency train and bus passes in his back pocket, but they were useless. There was no way he could make it without Dmitriy and Tatiana's help, and he wouldn't leave them behind, even if he could.

Trevor's shoulder throbbed, numbness setting in, and perspiration soaked the back of his shirt. The wound needed attention soon or he could develop an infection. While the pain wasn't as bad as before, it still made him grit his teeth each time he was jostled.

Trevor hissed low through his teeth in Russian, "We need to get out of St. Petersburg. I—we—need to head North."

Tatiana considered his words for a second and a gleam of excitement bled into her eyes. "The Udelnaya flea market! I know several of the vendors there. The majority of them live outside of St. Petersburg. I bet we can find a ride out of here with one of them."

The idea of being tossed around in the back of a truck was not appealing, but it was the best idea they had at that moment. Nobody would think to look for them in a flea market truck heading out of town.

Dmitriy had come to the same conclusion because he turned on his heels. "The market is this way." Tatiana looked at Dmitriy in surprise. He shrugged and added, "I followed you a few times to make sure you were safe. I was worried." She grinned and squeezed his hand.

Witnessing their small intimate moment pinched at Trevor's heart, reminding him of Cassandra and his need to see her, touch her again. Leaning heavily on the two, Trevor sucked in a deep breath and nodded to Tatiana. "Lead the way."

★ ★ ★ ★ ★

Nikol's emotions were in turmoil. One moment she was cozily embedded in Mikhailov's organization, earning a position to take him and her true target down. The next, she was in the middle of a full-fledged gun battle having to protect her back against friend—if that was what she could call Mikhailov's trusted guards—and foe alike.

She had lost sight of Sergei when the first shots sounded and chaos ensued. Nikol wasn't impressed by the firepower the two gangs had built over the years. She had lived long enough amongst them to understand their capabilities and the reach of their influence in society, not to mention how fiercely they defended their territory.

As much as the unexpected tumult was detrimental to her goal, it could possibly move her closer to success in her venture. The target of her operation was the server room—the only room to which she still didn't have access. Crouched in the library, armed to the teeth, Nikol regrouped and headed off in its direction, hoping that in the middle of the melee the guards had been sloppy in their supervision of the door.

Loud bangs and pops reverberated from several points in the property, and the air reeked of gunpowder as she scurried down the hallway to the server room. She carefully checked her perimeter and slowly climbed down the stairs, holding her stance in the event someone was still down there. Her heart soared at seeing the mainframe. She was so close to the treasure it contained she could taste success, taste the pleasure of having all those idiots who thought she wasn't good enough choke on their tongues.

Finding the computer that had direct access to the mainframe, she tried to pull up the files stored in it. Nothing. Everything had been erased.

"Damn it!" Someone had deleted the evidence she needed to bring him down. Nikol stood and kicked the chair in a burst of anger, sending it scattering across the room. She would have to find another way. She had collected some already, but the files would be icing on the cake and seal the deal without argument.

Sergei. He had just become the key to getting more evidence. Back in the hall, Nikol made her way to the great room, the last place she had seen him, and, as she passed a window, caught sight of him running toward the back of the property as if the bats of hell were on his heels. Cutting through the kitchen, she sprinted through the disarray and out the back door, scrambling through the bushes in the direction he had taken.

Nikol hunched over and cut across the colorful flowerbeds, crushing the beautiful blooms under her heavy boots. A shot rang out. As she rounded the path, she found Sergei with his gun aimed at the top of the stone wall. A masochistic spark lit his eyes—the one that always gave her the creeps. "Who are you shooting at? Shouldn't you be helping us inside? Zarev's men are breaking through," she yelled, running to join him. Her heart was in her throat, choking her as she bent over trying to catch her breath.

Sergei stared at the top of the wall a second more before dropping his arm at his side. A wicked, nasty grin curved the corners of his mouth. "The new guy," he spat.

"What new guy?" Nikol surveyed the area. "Where's the body?"

"He was on the wall. The swine was trying to escape. He toppled to the other side like a dead pig." Satisfaction dripped from his every word.

Nikol took a step toward the wall. "Where do you think you are going?" Sergei demanded.

"To check the body."

Sergei laughed. "He's not going anywhere. We will go around through the park. Easier than breaking a neck going over the wall." He cocked his head. "Follow me, little Nikol, and you will see. I have been waiting for this hunt a long time. A pity he was such poor prey. "

Nikol's mind was troubled. Sergei preyed upon those who threatened his position. Dmitriy, Mikhailov's nephew, had a place of honor on his shit list for being Mikhailov's legitimate successor within the gang. There was only one other person Sergei seemed to hate more than he hated Dmitriy, and for some reason that was Ivanov. Kostas's programmer. Another innocent lamb brought into the lion's den to be slaughtered. Nikol crossed her arms and held her ground. "I'm not going anywhere until you tell me what you are talking about and who you took down."

In two large steps, Sergei reached her side, jerked her to him, and dug his gun in the flesh of her cheek. "Why do you always have to question me?" he ground out in a low, rough voice. "Just do what you are told, for once."

He shoved her toward the house. Stumbling, Nikol caught herself. Biting back her rage as she straightened, she glanced up straight into the muzzle of the gun he pointed at her. Schooling her features, she nodded. She wasn't sure she could hold back the disgust she held for him from coloring her voice if she spoke. Her finger itched to pull the trigger, but she couldn't. Not yet.

Sergei smiled knowingly as he gestured with the gun toward the house. "You first; cannot have you sticking a bullet inside me, can we?"

Sergei's words hit home, calling up memories of two nights before.

The banging at her door pulled her from a restless sleep and seemed never-ending.

"Open this door, little Nikol!" Sergei demanded, his voice slurring over the words.

"Go away! You are drunk, Deminov!" Nikol had yelled back. *"You are drunk and,"*—she had whispered under her breath—*"an ass."*

The door had crashed open, splinters of wood shooting everywhere. Nikol had scrambled to get out of bed and from the vulnerable position she was caught in, but Sergei had tackled her back against it, pinning her beneath him.

Nikol had fought him furiously. She had scissored her legs around his neck, squeezing tight as she leveraged herself on her shoulders in a firm plank position, holding him back. He had tried to break the hold, but she had punched his face, gripped the crown of his hair, and reached under her pillow for her gun. With Sergei in his intoxicated state, she had the advantage of strength and speed. Before he had been able to break the hold, she had swung the gun around and nested the muzzle smack in the middle of his forehead.

Sergei had eyed her warily then, her actions penetrating his semi-drunk haze. She had stared him in the eyes, hers hard and unforgiving. *"Move and I put a bullet through your head."*

His eyes had narrowed, a sneer marred his mouth. *"You owe me, bitch. No one denies me."*

His arrogant words had pissed her off and had spurred her anger. She had tightened her thighs around his neck and a smirk had crept over her mouth as his face turned a deeper hue of red. Her frustrations at the time it was taking to complete her assignment in the mansion had finally exploded with his breaching of her door minutes earlier.

Nikol had pinned his gaze. A loud clicking sound had filled the room as she had cocked the hammer of the gun. *"I never agreed to such payment. I have told you no repeatedly. I do not enjoy alpha males. Or jackasses. You should respect that. Try it again,"*—she had tightened her thighs and twisted to the side, flipping over him and pinning him on his back. His hands had once again clawed at her hips and tried to push her off him. She had held tight, pressing her weight down on him, squeezing his head between her knees, and swinging the gun behind her, pressing the muzzle tight against the tender flesh of his semi-hard cock—*"and I will make it so no woman can ever give you a blowjob again. Be happy I do not put a bullet in you right now."*

The memory faded quickly into the present situation. "If I wanted to, I would have done so by now," Nikol shrugged, ignoring the heated look he tossed her way. "How do we get there?" She needed to find out if Sergei had truly killed the developer. If he was still alive, he could be of use to her.

The two of them snuck through the side garden to the front of the mansion where the confrontation had started, Sergei in the lead. Their progress was delayed by some of Zarev's men still lurking out front. Sergei took them down with rapid discharge of his Strike One pistol. By the time they burst through the gates on foot, the police vans and cars were turning the corner.

Sirens blasted and lights flashed as the Special Rapid Response Unit—the Russian police's tactical team—pulled up to the front of the mansion. The original confrontation that had died down as the gangs aided their fallen brothers and regrouped was newly amplified by concussion blasts and tear gas being dispatched by the police to contain the upheaval.

Sergei holstered his pistol inside his jacket and mingled with the crowd of curious bystanders and gawkers that had gathered around the front of the property. Nikol followed as he weaved through them. After the police flooded the mansion like a tidal wave, Sergei took off at a run down the sidewalk bordering the mansion walls. Without a second thought, Nikol followed him, shoving the lingering pedestrians aside in her rush.

She caught up with Sergei and they ran the few blocks it took to reach the park. When he veered into the wooded area withdrawing his pistol, Nikol cursed under her breath and chased after him. Drawing even, she registered the cold calculating look in his eyes, his goal to make sure his prey was dead. Nikol followed Sergei's curt directions until they reached the area behind the mansion and the spot he was certain the body had landed when it had dropped from the wall.

Lush green moss and lichen covered the soft ground in the secluded and shaded area. Tall fern-like vegetation hid the less-travelled manmade paths through the woods. A cool breeze blew the branches of the many oak trees scattered around the lot, their long branches giving them the appearance of tentacled creatures. She shivered as the cool air brushed over the perspiration coating her skin.

She slowed to a stop when a flash of color appeared in the distance at the opposite end from which they had come. She took a step to investigate it, but was distracted by Sergei's loud curses. She smirked and followed the source of the foul language. Satisfaction flowed through her. It seemed his prey was not so dead—and a little smarter than Sergei had given him credit.

She wiped the enjoyment from her face when the angry rampage reached her ears. Sergei's face was a most unflattering shade of red and his fist wound tight around his gun. He looked like a kid having a temper tantrum after losing his favorite toy. "Where is the body?"

Sergei shoved past her. "It is gone. The bastard survived." His attention was caught by something on the ground and he crouched to study it. As he brushed the ferns and foliage out of the way, a growl of anger rolled from his lips.

"What is it?" Nikol peeked over his shoulder at the ground in front of him.

"The bastard was not alone. He had help. See?" He pointed to the different sole imprints on the dirt. "There are more than one set of footprints here." An evil deadly smile bloomed across his face as he looked up at her, and a peppering of goose bumps spread across her arms. "Now we hunt."

Chapter Forty-Five

Insane Bastard

WIND SWOOSHED DOWN THE TUNNEL as the train to Parnas barreled into the station. Once the doors opened, Cassandra merged with the flow of passengers boarding the train. Dropping the duffels at her feet, she gripped the overhead bar and a wave of relief washed over her. With the first leg of her journey underway, she had time to think again.

It was the first time since the shot rang through the speakers that she was not in a flurry of activity. Her numb mind jumpstarted and body began to shake as all thoughts converged on Trevor. Shock held her in its tight embrace. What could have gone wrong? Everything was moving like clockwork, albeit warped from their original plan. Cassandra could clearly hear his cocky words from that first day echoing in her mind as he had walked up to the mansion: *"So far, so good, a ghrá. Hopefully, this will be a walk in the park."*

It hadn't been a walk in the park. At the time, neither of them had a clue as to what awaited him inside those walls, nor the restrictions forced on him that first day. The same way neither of them had anticipated they'd have to deploy their contingency plan.

She never really expected to hear the word *"Mí-ádh"* uttered in a rushed whisper, or the words *"I will love you always"* spoken in a tone crowded with finality before silence had enveloped the signal. Cassandra squeezed her eyes shut. *He is not dead. He's too damn stubborn. He promised.*

She swallowed the scream that clawed at her throat and leaned her head against her outstretched arm. She listened to the droning sound of train wheels clacking along the tracks, and counted the stops in her head as it sped through the tunnel—a simple task to distract her from further dark thoughts.

Tears welled as concern continued to rip at her heart. *I should've done something. Stayed. Gone to him,* she badgered herself and, at the same time, reprimanded herself for the weakness. *Focus, Cassie. You have a job to do.* The plan was simple. If he was a no-show after twenty-four hours, she would hightail it back to Ireland.

The jolt of the train changing tracks snapped Cassandra back to awareness. She opened her eyes only to glance straight into the sympathetic faded ones of a petite, white-haired elderly woman sitting on the seat in front of her. Brushing the wetness from her cheek and unable to bear the pity she saw in the depth of the woman's eyes, Cassandra shifted her gaze to the transit map above the door.

A while later, at the announcement of the approaching Parnas station, Cassandra adjusted the strap of the backpack into a more comfortable position and reached for the bags. She shuffled around a few other passengers to position herself in front of the sliding doors, and burst out of them as soon as they opened. She shoved her way through the crowd of passengers, mumbling "Excuse me" as she maneuvered around them, heading for the stairs and the bus—the next leg of her journey.

Reaching the top of the stairs, Cassandra squinted in the bright sunlight and spotted the bus parked across the street. Adrenaline spiked her veins as she sprinted for it. Cars skidded to a stop bare inches from her, but she hardly gave them a glance. She focused on her one goal—catching that bus before it left the station.

Once boarded, Cassandra scanned the area around the station for any sign that she had been followed as she shuffled behind the other passengers to her seat. She took the aisle seat in the emergency exit row and, still running on autopilot, set the duffel bags between her feet and the backpack on her lap. Under the shield of the backpack, she slowly shifted the Grach from her back to the front of her waistband, tucking it within easy reach.

Settling down for the ride, she rubbed the sweat trailing from her brow with her sleeve and plucked at her t-shirt. As her body cooled, a flurry of goose bumps raced along her arms and her sweaty shirt, now icy cold, stuck to her skin. Rubbing her arms, she reached into one of the duffel bags for a jacket. She pulled out the first one she grabbed. It was blue. Trevor's. Her breath caught in her throat, almost choking her, and her heartbeat pounded in her ears.

Anxiety bubbled up again and she dropped her head forward, resting her chin on her chest. "Breathe, just breathe!" she whispered.

"Pardon me?" the woman seated across the aisle, wearing blue jeans, a green jacket, and holding a tourist guide, asked with an Australian accent.

Shaking her head and displaying a friendly smile, Cassandra responded, "I'm sorry. I must have been talking to myself."

"I do that all the time." The woman's blue eyes wrinkled at the corners and she flashed an understanding smile before returning her attention to the book in her hands.

Cassandra sucked in a deep breath and released it in a heavy sigh as she stuffed Trevor's jacket back in the bag and pulled out her own. Exhausted, she slipped it on and dropped her head back against the headrest. She tried to block all worry for Trevor by visualizing the contingency checklist in her mind—scout the area around the safe house; connect to the satellite feed; contact Nathan and George; and, finally, wait for Trevor to show up, if he hadn't already.

The bus ride went on forever, the multiple stops along the way, heavy traffic, and noise of the diesel engine grating on her nerves, causing her head to pound. Eventually, the monotony of the ride lulled her into a semi-doze.

As the bus slowed, Cassandra's head snapped up. Instantly alert, she shouldered her backpack and zipped her jacket to conceal the gun. She grabbed her bags and exited the bus as soon as the doors opened. Anxious, she took a minute to get her bearings. The road that led to the safe house was off to the right. Shrugging the backpack into a more comfortable position on her shoulder and taking a better grip on the bags, she headed in that direction.

★ ★ ★ ★ ★

Trevor was slowing them down. Dmitriy and Tatiana helped him, but the last few steps had just about killed him. With each step, it became harder to hide his discomfort from Tatiana's concerned eyes.

"This is ridiculous," she gestured to Trevor and glanced between the two of them. "You men are so stubborn. Look at him," she pointed at Trevor. "He cannot walk any further. I beg you. Flag down a cab. It is only a short distance."

Trevor knew she was right. His shoulder burned, perspiration trailed down the sides of his face soaking his shirt, making it stick to him like a second skin. He couldn't take another step. He nodded at Dmitriy. "Do it. It's risky but—"

"Let them trace the transaction. They still won't be able to find our destination." Dmitriy withdrew his entire daily limit at the closest ATM and they jumped into the first cab they flagged down. "At least now we have cab fare and enough to tide us over."

Once in the cab, silence descended upon them, each lost in their own thoughts. Dmitriy held Tatiana's hand in his, his thumb caressing the underside of her wrist. The gentle caress didn't go unnoticed. Trevor sagged in the seat, wishing it was his hand caressing Cassandra's. He hoped the market would provide them with their ticket out of St. Petersburg; if not, they would become easy targets in a city where Mikhailov's reach ran deep.

"Do you know the market emerged during the reign of the Soviet Union and existed illegally for about fifty years?" Tatiana broke the quiet. "During the hard times of Perestroika, many dwellers from St. Petersburg and the surrounding suburbs survived and supported their families by selling goods at this flea market. Many of them still sell their wares there today. To them, Udelnaya is more than a market; it is their way of life."

Tatiana's description had not done the market justice. Trevor was taken aback as they hopped out of the cab. The immensity of the Udelnaya flea market was a surprise. The deep, earthy odor of the damp, packed dirt mixed with that of tarnished antique wares and used clothing saturated the air. The wide area was littered with small tables, stands, and blankets spread helter-skelter on the ground—all covered in used and new items alike; clothes hung from lines strung between trees, vans and trucks parked in the area with doors open to display wares lined inside and to pick up purchases.

Visitors crowded the place, foreigners and locals alike, looking for the best deal they could find. The sunny day gave the market a festive atmosphere, even though to the majority of the sellers and traders the place was a job, a necessity.

Tatiana turned to them. "Wait here. Let me see if I can find my friends."

"I will come with you." Dmitriy insisted.

"No, Dmitriy. They could be anywhere. We cannot drag Ivanov around, and he cannot stay by himself. Let me find them and talk to them first." She left before they could protest further.

★ ★ ★ ★ ★

Nikol followed Deminov as he tracked the footprint trail left behind on the soft ground to the road bordering the north side of the park. She observed as he pulled out his cell phone. "How are you going to find him?"

"The Glazov has eyes and ears everywhere. I will find him." Sergei placed a call and it was answered right away. "Ilya, call your cousin and tell him to keep an eye out for a foreigner. New face. Dark hair. Blue eyes. One hundred eighty-five centimeters. Around eighty kilos. One of our own might be helping him." After a pause, he added, "I don't know who, idiot. If I did, I wouldn't be calling you. Send a car for me." He gave Ilya their location and then made another call. "Vladimir."

Mikhailov's voice boomed over the speaker and Nikol could overhear the conversation. "Where are you? You disappeared at the worst time." Mikhailov's voice was cold, unforgiving.

"I am on pursuit of the developer. He has escaped."

"Fucking swine. The computer room was compromised. The files erased. He must be working for Pavel. Dmitriy is also missing. They must have collaborated to steal from me." Mikhailov's voice was cold as steel. "Kill the developer. Bring my nephew"—he spat the word—"to me. Maybe he can fix this mess before I wipe him from my bloodline forever."

Nikol tensed as Sergei's eyes became flat and as unreadable as stone. He glanced at the Bvlgari watch banded to his wrist as he disconnected the call. "Dmitriy is missing. As soon as the car is here, we will find them both."

★ ★ ★ ★ ★

Trevor leaned heavily on Dmitriy as they moved to the side and found a spot where they could sit and wait for Tatiana's return. He grunted as Dmitriy helped him to the ground and inspected the wound. "Not what I envisioned when I told you to join me, that I could help you. It seems the roles have been reversed, mate."

Dmitriy looked him in the eyes. "You will still be able to help us, right? I'm depending on it. You're my ticket away from my uncle. If Sergei finds me…" He didn't need to finish. The meaning was clear. He shook his head. "It would be even worse for Tatiana."

Trevor knew exactly the scenario Dmitriy was painting in his head. He would never wish that to happen to Cassandra.

The shuffle of soft steps approaching drew their attention and they both looked up to see Tatiana hurrying toward them with a smug smile on her face. "I got us a ride. Come with me."

Tatiana moved to Trevor's side and help Dmitriy support him as they walked to the center of the market. As they approached a stand, little more than a tarp stretched out on the ground, Trevor observed an older couple sitting on foldable chairs by the tarp. From the looks of things, they sold an eclectic mix of goods—all sorts of personal items, clothes, antique glass containers—anything they didn't need for themselves. It was obvious that they were looking for ways to supplement their meager state income.

Tatiana smiled at the older woman. "These are the friends I told you about, Babushka." Trevor assumed that Tatiana had to be very good friends with her, since the endearing term was only used when addressing one's own grandmother or close elderly friends. "This is Dmitriy and Ivanov."

Tatiana turned back them. "This is Zoya and her husband Yakov. They are friends of my family who lived near my grandparents when I was a child. Now they live in a little village called Vyun, far north of St. Petersburg. They come regularly to the market. I am only able to visit with them when they are here."

Zoya and Yakov eyed Dmitriy and Trevor warily. The woman asked Tatiana, "Who is your man?"

A flood of rosy color swept across Tatiana's cheeks. "Not my man, Babushka. Boyfriend," she sputtered as she pointed out Dmitriy, who inhaled deeply and grinned, happiness shining through his eyes.

"What is wrong with your friends?" Yakov nodded at both men.

"We were attacked. Ivanov is in worse shape. We are trying to get him home," Dmitriy answered promptly with a half-truth.

Trevor addressed the older man directly. "Can you help us? I was hoping you could give us a ride."

Yakov hesitated a moment and then directed his gaze to Tatiana. "We will. But we do this for you, Tanka."

Relief washed over Trevor. One step closer to reaching Cassandra.

"The market closes in an hour. We'll pack and leave soon."

Dmitriy looked Trevor's way. "I should help them pack so we can get out of here faster." He said, easing Trevor to the ground.

Trevor cradled his throbbing arm tightly against his side while Dmitriy and Tatiana helped Zoya and Yakov box their goods.

★ ★ ★ ★ ★

Sergei pounded his hand against the steering wheel and swerved to avoid hitting another car parked on the side. Nikol eyed him warily and wanted to kick herself in the ass for not taking the wheel in the first place. Sergei was better wielding an AK-47 then he was maneuvering through traffic. His anger mounted with each phone call, each lead that didn't pan out.

"Sergei, pull over. Let me drive." Nikol kept the tone of her voice low and even.

Sergei grabbed his pistol from the center console and aimed it at her. "Shut your mouth." His voice shook, the veins popped on his temple as he rasped out the words.

He was a man on the edge. *Insane bastard.* Nikol threw up her hands. "Easy. No need to splat us like flies on a windshield before we can find them."

Relief fluttered in her chest when he dropped the gun on his lap with a huff and turned his attention back to the road. Nikol's shoulder slammed against the door when Sergei pulled hard on the wheel and swung the car around to make a second pass along the avenue where one of the informants had spotted Ivanov. Nikol hit the answer on the car's bluetooth system when Sergei's phone buzzed.

"Sergei?" An unfamiliar voice burst across the speakers.

"Da. What is it, Yury? I do not have time for your whining."

Yury stammered. "I thought I was supposed to handle the collections today at the market. Did you pull me?"

"What the hell are you talking about?" Sergei spat.

"I just saw Dmitriy walking into the market. Why would you send a nerd to do my job? You told me this was mine."

Sergei eased back in his seat and a curtain of calm settled across his expression. "You saw Dmitriy? At Udelnaya?"

"Yes. I just said that. Should I leave?"

"No. Follow him. I am on my way." Sergei's hand shot out and gripped Nikol by the back of the neck. He yanked her by the hair toward him and planted a bruising kiss on her lips. Nikol jerked back, wincing in pain and pulling at the seatbelt that had cut into her shoulder. Sergei laughed at the disgust he must have seen in her eyes and narrowed his own. "You will learn to like my kisses."

Fury almost choked her, but Nikol held her tongue. Sergei's temper was uncontrollable. To provoke him further in the speeding car could quite possibly leave her brain splattered on the window. Sergei punched the gas and the car surged forward in the direction of the Udelnaya flea market and his prey. The time had come. Nikol began to strategize her next move in the deadly game she had been playing most of her career.

Nikol's hands were slightly cramped from the death grip she had on the dashboard and the "oh shit" handle above the passenger window. The streets were filled with heavy midafternoon traffic, and Sergei, in his fury to reach the flea market, almost rear-ended every double-parked car and ran every red light they encountered.

Mother of God! Nikol squeezed her eyes shut as Sergei planted his foot on the pedal and accelerated through another red light, swerving around the white semi pulling into the intersection. When the truck's horn sounded, Nikol could have sworn that her life passed before her eyes. She was not impressed. When she could pry her eyelids apart, she glanced at Sergei from the corner of her eye. The grim set of his mouth and grip on the steering wheel said it all. He was pissed—rip-roaring pissed—and out for blood.

Skidding to a stop in front of the market, Sergei killed the engine and barreled out of the car. Curses rolled from her lips as she struggled with the seatbelt and bolted after him. Nikol tracked him as he ran into the market, talking urgently on the phone.

She picked up her pace, following Sergei through the obstacle course of merchandise, clotheslines, and tourists. Adrenaline was her fuel. She couldn't let him find Dmitriy and Ivanov on his own. If so, they were dead men, and valuable information would slip through her fingers. With a burst of determination, Nikol caught up to Sergei. "Do you know where he is?"

Sergei slowed to a walk and she followed suit. He scanned the place, searching for his targets. "This way." A wicked gleam shone in his eyes, a sick sneer pulled at the corner of his mouth.

He inched his hand into his jacket and she heard the cocking of his gun. Nikol's heart raced, her breathing accelerated. She was aware of each movement, each patron around them. The hustle and bustle of the market sounded loud to her ears. Unsure of Sergei's plans, she followed his example and palmed the grip of her HK concealed under her jacket as she waited for the right time to act.

★ ★ ★ ★ ★

Dmitriy took the last box from Tatiana and set it in the trunk of the dilapidated older model Lada Riva.

"That's the last of it." Tatiana brushed her hands off on her torn skirt. "We can leave now." Her voice was tight and strained.

He turned and gave her an encouraging smile. "Stay here. I will get Ivanov."

"No. I am coming with you. With my help we can move him faster."

Dmitriy smiled broadly and grasped her hand. "Come then." Turning to Yakov, he called out, "We will be right back with Ivanov."

"His wound will need a thorough cleaning as soon as we get to the farm," Tatiana worried.

Suddenly, she jerked his arm and Dmitriy looked over his shoulder at her.

Tatiana's hand covered her mouth and her eyes were wide open. "What's wrong?" He turned his head in the direction she was staring and his heart bottomed out—Sergei. And he had company. His eyes darted to Ivanov and, on contact, he could see that Ivanov also realized something was up by their expressions. Dmitriy waved his hand behind him and hissed, "Run Tatiana. *Run!*

The sound of her pounding feet disappeared in the distance about the same time a loud group of Japanese tourists following their guide hurdled down the path toward Sergei and became the perfect cover. Dmitriy stooped low and, mingling with the crowd, hurried to Ivanov's side.

"What is it?" Ivanov rasped, pain coating his every word as Dmitriy looped his arm over his shoulder in a rush to get out of there before Sergei saw them.

"Sergei," Dmitriy responded under his breath.

"Fuck! We must have been spotted." Ivanov flashed the sweater showing the gun tucked in his waistband. "Tell me when." Ivanov hissed through his teeth.

Dmitriy gave a slight shake of his head. "No, Ivanov. He is not alone. We need to go, now!" Dmitriy helped him to his feet. As they straightened, the tourists who had been their shield moved down another aisle and Dmitriy's eyes collided with Sergei's.

Snared by Sergei's gaze, Dmitriy whispered under his breath, "He saw us."

Ivanov's head slumped down. "Damn it. So close."

Dmitriy swallowed hard. Concern for their lives warred in his heart. He took a deep breath and called out, "What are you doing here Sergei? Shouldn't you be with my uncle?"

Nikol's pulse fluttered and revved as adrenaline flooded her system a second time. Shooting a wary glance at Sergei, she knew from the serene look on his face, the glazed gleam in his eyes, and the twisted smirk on his lips that he had transcended to his happy place—the world in which he was master and all were there for his pleasure, which ran from pain to torture and defilement.

"Your uncle is the one who sent me. He wants you home. You have work to do." Sergei's tone was condescending and full of contempt.

Sergei closed the distance in a cocky gait. Dmitriy shifted to the side, leaving Ivanov to stand on his own two feet. "Ivanov! Look up," Sergei's voice rose and spit shot from his mouth. "I want to look in your eyes when I plug a bullet in your head."

Ivanov lifted his head, eyes full of rage, and glared at Sergei. Nikol's brows rose in surprise when he spoke in perfect Russian. "What kept you so long? Glad to see you still have a big hard-on for me. But as I told you before, I do not swing that way."

As the words died from Ivanov's lips, Sergei yelled, his face contorting in a snarl. Nikol watched as, in a fluid movement, Ivanov pulled a gun from under his sweater and shoved it under Sergei's chin.

"Gun!" someone yelled. Tourists and vendors alike screamed and scattered in all directions.

"Cocky son of a bitch!" Sergei yelled, reaching for his own gun.

Shit! Shit! Nikol's mind screamed and she made her move. Suddenly everyone froze. Sergei cursed, his finger flexing on the trigger. "Don't," Nikol bit out, digging the muzzle of her gun into his temple.

Sergei dropped his arm. "Think about what you are doing, little Nikol," he sneered, pressing his head harder against the cold metal barrel of her HK.

She spat at his feet. "You should have done what you were told for a change. I cannot let you kill them both." Sergei shifted and Nikol pulled back the hammer. "Do it and you drop." Out of the corner of her eye, she saw Ivanov withdraw his gun and Dmitriy drape Ivanov's good arm across his shoulders. She yelled at them, "Get out of here. Go!" Ivanov hesitated, eyes puzzled and assessing. *"Run!"* Dmitriy tugged on his arm and they both blended into the crowd.

"No!" Sergei swung his arm back.

Nikol dropped to a squat and kicked his legs out from under him. Sergei's yell of rage mingled with the echoes of the shot that blasted from his pistol when he hit the ground. Pandemonium ensued as people—tourists and vendors—scrambled for cover. She blocked the sounds of running feet and screams from her mind, narrowing her focus on the lowlife in front of her.

Sergei flipped back to his feet and, in a fluid move, kicked the pistol from her grasp. Nikol shook her hand, hissing at the pain that burned up her arm. Sergei laughed low in his throat as he swung a right hook aimed at her temple.

Anticipating the hit, she blocked it, grabbing his wrist and countering with a right hook to his face. Sergei caught the punch before it reached his jaw. He grinned tauntingly. His grip, a vice squeezing the bones of her fist, brought tears to her eyes as she fought through the pain.

"Give up now, little Nikol. I know you. Know your moves." Her heart shifted into overdrive, a thin film of perspiration covered her skin, and frustration fanned her anger as she struggled to release his hold.

Hatred colored her voice and her mouth curled in contempt. "You know nothing about me. And I am not your little Nikol!" As the last words spilled from her lips, she tightened her grip on his wrist, jerked him closer, and kicked him in the middle of his chest.

Sergei grunted as air rushed from his lungs. His body hunched over, curling in on itself. Without missing a beat, Nikol took a step forward and jabbed her right arm upward. The uppercut connected with the underside of his jaw. Another grunt filled the air as his head snapped back and the force of the punch twisted his body, dropping him to his knees.

Sergei breathed heavily, a mix of blood and spit dribbled from his mouth as he scrambled back to his feet. Wiping his mouth with the back of his hand, he eyed her with contempt. "Your ass is mine. I will take great pleasure in keeping one of your fingers as a trophy," he growled before rushing her and throwing a strike at her jaw.

Nikol wasn't fast enough and took a solid hit to the shoulder. The force of the punch was staggering, almost knocking her to her knees. As his momentum turned him sideways, she caught her balance and bounced back, grunting out loud, as she delivered a powerful left hook to his kidney.

Sergei expelled a loud ragged breath and slumped over. Before he could recover, Nikol swung her fist back, catching him on the cheek, and followed with a roundhouse kick to the side of his head. His head popped to the side and he lost his balance, catching himself before he fell. "Bitch!" he yelled, backhanding her.

Throbbing pain radiated from Nikol's cheekbone and a soft cry escaped as she went down on her knees. Sucking in deep gulps of air, she scrambled to her feet and spun to face him. Sergei stalked toward her, but before he could reach her, she delivered a reverse back kick to his jaw, dropping him to the ground.

She lifted his head, digging her fingers into the sides of it, and swung back her knee. Before it connected, Sergei grabbed her leg and twisted it to the side. Nikol cried out as she slammed back against the ground. The impact drove the air from her lungs, leaving her gasping like a guppy on dry land.

Rolling to all fours, she almost retched when the toe of Sergei's shoe slammed into her gut. The force of the kick lifted her body from the ground and dropped her on her side, agony a painful lover squeezing her chest.

Sergei thrived on her pain, taunting her. "Did I hurt you? Are you having fun yet?" Sergei's voice held a rasp of excitement, savoring the anticipation of his victory and having her at his mercy.

She knew she wouldn't be able to hold out much longer, and there was no way in hell she would fall to him. A flash of light hit her eye and glancing left, she spotted her gun lying on the ground, just out of reach. Hope gave her a new burst of energy. As Sergei circled behind her, she leveraged off her hands and kicked back at him with both feet, knocking his legs from under him. He landed on his stomach with a heavy thud.

Nikol rolled sideways out of his grasp, sliding the back of her hand along the dirt and under the grip of her pistol. Wrapping her fingers firmly around it, she lifted it from the ground as she continued to roll to her knees. Sergei's battle cry, "Bitch! You die!" filled the air as he ran at her.

Her pulse was loud in her ears and her vision narrowed to Sergei's chest. She held him in her sights and popped off two consecutive shots. Blood bloomed from the holes burrowed into his chest. Her breath hitched when he dropped to his knees and looked up at her. Her death hovered in his eyes as he began walking on his knees toward her with an outstretched hand. "Fuck you, bastard!" she yelled, squeezing the trigger again, riddling him with bullets until he lay flat on his face, a pool of blood encircling him.

Swallowing hard, Nikol fell back on her elbows and let out a small gasp of relief. Wiping the sweat from her eyes with the back of her hand, she painfully rose to her feet and rested her hands on her knees, trying to catch her breath.

Silence filled the air, followed by the shuffle of tourists and vendors emerging from their hiding places. When the murmurs started and sirens sounded in the distance, Nikol knew she needed to move. Pushing from her knees, she stood, studying Sergei's lifeless body as she returned her gun to her waistband.

The bastard was really dead. She now had a target on her back. His death was not without witnesses—one of them Mikhailov's man, to whom Sergei had spoken earlier. Dusting off her hands and pushing her hair from her face, she winced when her fingers brushed her cheek. Turning on her heel, without a backward glance, Nikol headed off in the direction Dmitriy had dragged Ivanov.

★ ★ ★ ★ ★

As they weaved through the busy market, a shot rang out. Screams filled the air, people scurried and scattered around them, herding them down the trail toward the parking lot. Trevor felt like a pinball bouncing between Dmitriy and the panicked crowd. He gritted his teeth when his arm collided with a woman's purse. Red colored his vision and his knees buckled.

"Hang on. We're almost there," Dmitriy urged. "There they are. *Tatiana!*"

"Dmitriy!"

Tatiana's voice was music to Trevor's ears. As Yakov jumped into the driver's seat and turned the engine, Tatiana met them halfway. She wrapped an arm around Trevor's waist and helped Dmitriy half drag him the rest of the way to the car. She entered from one side and helped slide him across the seat until he was wedged between them both.

"What happened? How did you get away?!" she asked anxiously.

"Petrovna let us go!" Trevor rasped out.

Dmitriy slammed his door shut and stuck his hand out the window, banging on the outside on the side of the car, *"Go! Go!"* The old man punched the gas and gunned it out of the lot, onto the busy street, heading north.

★ ★ ★ ★ ★

As soon as Yakov had turned onto the highway, Trevor had fallen into an exhausted restorative sleep. It was amazing what a nap could do. No wonder babies spent the majority of their time in that oblivious state. Trevor fidgeted, trying to find a more comfortable position without knocking his arm into Tatiana, who was glued to the door, trying to give him as much room as possible on the seat.

"Are we there yet?" The Russian words flowed off Trevor's tongue.

Dmitriy shifted to glance at him. "We are almost there."

"The good news is your wound stopped bleeding," Tatiana smiled encouragingly. "The small farm is located just on the outskirts of town. I will clean and redress it when we get there."

Trevor breathed a sigh of relief and rested his head back. Looking through the windshield, he watched the car eat up the road as they passed through the small village. The veil of dusk was slowly descending upon the serene countryside. So different from the chaos they'd left behind.

Petrovna's actions at the market still puzzled Trevor. The first time he had met her he had known there was something about her that was different from the goons Mikhailov had under his roof. Maybe Cassandra had uncovered more details regarding who she was before all hell had broken loose. He filed that curiosity for later perusal.

A short while later, Yakov turned on to a dirt road, which opened to a small, faded-white farmhouse with a half-broken porch running along the front. Zoya looked back at them. "Welcome to our humble home."

Exhausted, they all piled out of the car. Trevor's shoulder hurt like a bitch; all he wanted was to be on his way. "How do we get to Vyborg from here?"

Zoya turned to their motley crew, "Do not be stupid, boy. Come in. Eat. It is late."

"Ivanov. Be reasonable. We have not eaten since this morning." Dmitriy's tone was pleading. "It would be rude to refuse. We will leave as soon as we can."

Had Trevor been alone he would have been on his way, but now the responsibility for Dmitriy and Tatiana's lives weighed heavily on his shoulders. "Okay, we eat, but then we are gone."

"Thank you."

Once Zoya and Tatiana finished tending to Trevor's wound, Zoya went about getting their meal ready, and a little while later called them to the table. The thick stew let out a delicious aroma of spices and hearty meat. Its mouth-watering scent wafted to his nose and filled the room, mixing with the rich scent of the warm crusty bread their hostess had set on the table. His stomach rumbled and he realized how hungry he truly was. He wasn't alone. They all dug in and scarfed the delicious homey meal.

During dinner, while watching the affinity the couple had for Tatiana, a new idea popped into Trevor's head. It would be like killing two birds with one stone. Once finished, he took Dmitriy and Tatiana aside. "I have no idea where we are right now, but I need to reach Vyborg as quickly as possible."

Tatiana patted his hand soothingly. "I can ask them how we can make it there."

Trevor reached out and caught her hand in his. "Not us. Me. Do you think your friends will let you two stay here for a couple of days?"

Tatiana frowned and narrowed her gaze at him. "Are you dumping us?"

"No. You are both safer here. Nobody will know to look for you on a remote farm. Whoever is looking for us will be looking for three people, not just one."

"But your wound—"

"I think I can handle it. I am not in as bad a shape as I was before. Besides, you and Zoya have already cleaned and packed it nicely." He cupped his shoulder. "The way you stabilized my arm, I think it is fused against my side. For the record, all that probing and poking hurt like a bitch. I do not think I will ever be able to look at another shot of vodka again. Please thank Yakov for the shirt." Trevor read the concern in Tatiana's steady gaze and squeezed her hand. "Really. I am good to go. Besides, I cannot wait any longer. I have resources in Vyborg that will help us all, but I am under a deadline."

Reluctantly, Dmitriy nodded and Tatiana hurried off to find out how to get to Vyborg from their location. She returned in no time at all. "Yakov and Zoya agreed to let Dmitriy and me stay a bit longer. He has offered to give you a ride to Vaskelovo. It is a fifteen-minute drive from here. From there you can hitch a ride to Vyborg."

"No," Dmitriy said, reaching to his pocket. "Take the money. Not much, but it should be enough to get you there."

"It is perfect. I will send for you." Once at the safe house, he would contact Stephan to make arrangements to hire Dmitriy. They would find a position for him at Brennan Enterprises until things settled. Trevor's gaze shifted to Tatiana. "Can Yakov leave now?"

Tatiana reached for Dmitriy's hand and smiled at Trevor. "Just say when."

"When," Trevor answered promptly.

Chapter Forty-Six

Where's Waldo?

CASSANDRA APPROACHED THE PROPERTY, STAYING to the tree line and the cover of the woods. Locating an old, decaying fallen tree, she stashed the backpack and duffel bags inside it and covered everything with fallen needles and brush. Light filtered through the leaves of the branches overhead, and the smell of warm sod, flowers, and old foliage flowed on the breeze. Crouching next to the tree, Cassandra pulled the Grach from her waistband, released the safety, and pulled the slide, cocking the gun.

She studied the landscape—the neglected flowerbeds around the back porch, the patchwork fence lining the property. A true testament to the lack of care given to its upkeep. An eerie quiet broken every so often by the songs of birds and buzzing of bees embraced the house and surrounding yard.

Inching forward, Cassandra made her way around the house, eyeing the area to be sure she was really alone. Only silence greeted her as she scouted the perimeter, hoping to find some sign that Trevor had beaten her there. Disappointment weighed heavily in her heart when she found no external indication that the house had received any visitors recently.

She tested the handle to the back door. Finding it locked, she ran her fingers along the wooden siding, searching for the hidden panel Nathan had mentioned, locating it at shoulder height next to the doorframe. She disabled the alarms and, holding her gun in one hand, quietly pushed the door open. Cassandra checked as far as she could see, then eased inside, closing and locking the door behind her.

It was bright enough inside that she could see the small serviceable kitchen was clear. Inching her way into the hallway, Cassandra's mouth dried and her heart raced. She raised her gun and gripped it with both hands, moving incrementally around the next doorway. Slicing the area with her sight and gun barrel, she took a deep breath and surged into the room, sweeping it for any unauthorized personnel. The room was clear.

She ventured back into the hallway and prowled the rest of the house, checking each room the same way. A very thin layer of dust covered the furniture, and nothing appeared to have been disturbed recently. It was as Nathan said it would be—empty. Once she closed all the blackout curtains and switched on a lamp in the living room, she slipped back out to the woods to retrieve her bags.

Back inside, Cassandra took inventory. Nonperishable goods lined the kitchen cabinets; the fridge was empty. Walking into the main bedroom and directly to the imposing armoire, which took up a good chunk of the room, she opened its doors. An assortment of men's and women's clothing hung in the stand-alone closet. Parting them, she studied the base of the cabinet with a critical eye. Near the bottom left corner, she spied a depression in the wood. Squatting, Cassandra pushed the dent until she heard a soft click and the fake bottom popped open. Lifting the piece of wood higher revealed a small digital keypad embedded in a metal safe.

She sifted through her memory, keyed the required code, and listened for the soft beeps. The door of the safe cracked and Cassandra completed a quick sweep of the cache of weapons cocooned inside—several M16s and SIGs as well as ammo for each. "Armed and in charge," she murmured. Hoping to avoid having to dip into the cache, she secured the armoire and returned to the main living area.

Retracing her steps through the kitchen, she spotted a half-empty bottle of vodka sitting in a corner on the counter. *Thank you, Mr. Whoever!* Cassandra grabbed the bottle and returned to the living room. She sat on the couch, staring at the clear liquid swishing in the bottle calling her name, and wanted nothing better than to drown herself in the bottom of it. Shaking her head, she set it aside and instead reached for the bags, dragging them toward her, and rummaged through them, pulling out their contents. Opening one of the bottles she had stashed, her sandpaper-dry mouth welcomed the fresh water that flowed over her tongue.

Her hand began to shake and she tightened her grip on the bottle, squishing it. She was crashing and burning. Cassandra dropped the empty bottle on the coffee table and reached for the vodka. Twisting off the cap, she brought the smooth, cool lip of the bottle to her mouth and sucked back a good swig. The clear liquid burned a fiery trail down her throat, but even the liquid heat wasn't enough to melt the ice that had fortified her heart. *Hang tight; you're not finished yet. No rest for the wicked, as Trevor would say...Shit...Trevor.*

Shaking her head, Cassandra pulled out Kostas's other housewarming gifts, lining Trevor's gun and ammunition on the table. Taking a deep breath, she cocked and engaged the safety on his.

She then retrieved her backpack, pulled out the laptops, and set them up on the table, connecting the small peripherals with precise and quick movements. With that task completed, the first strands of frustration slinked their way in her chest. *Is he injured? A prisoner? Or safe and on his way to meet me?* The possibility that he could be dead was just too much to process or accept.

The graphic equalizer was a flat line. She didn't expect any fluctuation. Without the help of the amplifier, Trevor would have to be within a short radius for any signal to be picked up, but in the hopes she would hear his approach, she left the equipment running.

A deep grumble reverberated in her stomach. Startled, she realized how hungry she was, and tore into the bag of nuts she had brought with her. Up until that moment, her numb mind and body had been running on adrenaline, blocking all feelings, focusing on the necessary tasks at hand. Her training and her father's teachings, the glue holding her together, prevented her from splintering into a million pieces.

Darkness crept into the room. She rechecked all the doors and, grabbing Trevor's laptop from the table, sat on the floor with her back against the front door to wait out the night. Her position gave her a clear view of the room and the hallway beyond. Pulling the handgun from her waistband, Cassandra sat it next to her and opened the laptop. With a few quick strokes, she checked for any messages, any sign of life. Nothing.

Ah, hell! George! He was going to blame himself for not passing the critical information to them sooner. Using the satellite link, Cassandra sent a message to George. Next, she sent a similar one to Nathan. The one-liner's meaning was clear. *Oh yeah, this situation could definitely be classified as fucked up beyond all recognition.*

★ ★ ★ ★ ★

George paced his office, his hair standing on end, the chaotic result of passing his fingers numerous times through it. It had been over sixteen hours since his last communication with Cassandra. He knew his good friend and his wife were knee-deep in shit. His only hope was that he had gotten the information to them in time. His pocket vibrated and he reached for his cell, finding a message from Cassandra. *Thank freaking geek gods.* His elation died the instant he read her cryptic email. *We've been compromised. Keep ears on for Trevor.*

"Fuck!" Through the glass window, he saw nobody on the floor paid any attention to him. He was known to let loose foul words every once in a while, and they had become desensitized to his outbursts.

George sighed deeply as a sense of dread clawed its way up his back, his worry thick in the air. Slumping in his chair, he rested his elbows on his desk and his head on his hands. *Think, George, Think!*

Without anything to go on, he turned his attention back to his keyboard.

His fingers spit out commands, searching and finding all calls made and received by Mikhailov's cell phones within the last few days. It seemed that whatever had happened earlier that day had disturbed the hive. He hoped to find something useful in the transcripts that could lead him to Trevor's whereabouts.

The query results returned several calls exchanged amongst them and other numbers not previously captured. Pulling the transcripts, George forwarded them to Jennifer, requesting help in translating the conversations.

Reaching for his phone, he replied to Cassandra's earlier email. *Ears on. Will keep you posted.* Pushing back from his desk, George rocked in his chair as he waited for the requested translations. His priority had now become tracking Trevor's whereabouts and easing Cassandra's and his own fears.

★ ★ ★ ★ ★

Boris contemplated his next move while lounging comfortably in his small study. He was close to having everything for which he had worked so hard in his hands. The side of his mouth curved and eyes gleamed at the thought of their expressions when he delivered what he'd promised. A part of him felt sorry for having pressured Robert's family into service and capitalizing on Trevor's skills. But the other, the one that had given up so much over the years to get to that point, wasn't. He needed to get that behind him.

A soft creak sounded on the porch and Boris cocked his head, listening for any more disturbances. Another creak sounded. *What the hell?* Boris switched into action. In a fluid move, he turned off the table lamp next to him, drowning the room in darkness, while palming his gun and cell phone from the table. He dropped to the floor and, keeping to the shadows, slid to the window. He pushed the curtain aside slowly, just enough to peek out, and spotted two shadows moving toward the front door. His heart hammered in his chest; his mind became void of all thoughts until self-preservation took over. On his stomach, he elbowed his way to the hall and the kitchen beyond.

Reaching the pantry, he eased inside and, just as the door closed, gunfire peppered the house. Boris flattened to the floor and shifted the potato bin, revealing the hidden trapdoor. He dove into the dark, damp crawl space, pausing only to close the trapdoor above him before he wormed at a fast pace toward the end of the passage. As he scurried, his thoughts returned to the two men he had glimpsed on his porch.

Considering he had been playing both major gangs in St. Petersburg, he couldn't tell for sure to which the men belonged. But one of them looked like Lev, a foot soldier in Mikhailov's organization. At the end of the tunnel, he burst out into the field beyond his house, grateful he'd had the foresight to plan an escape route all those years ago. The game he played was a dangerous one, and he had to be prepared in the event that one day his game was up.

Under the cover of night, he looked back at his house in the distance. A savage curse burst from his lips. About ten men surrounded the house and were still riddling it with bullets. Boris watched the brutal action for a few minutes and confirmed the identity of at least two of Mikhailov's men among the trigger-happy thugs. Mikhailov was out to get him. *Has Trevor been caught? Did he disclose our deal?*

His rancor overcame him, hardening his resolve. All those years he had sacrificed—his dignity, the love of his life—all for nothing. To come this far, this close to the final result, only to watch it all go down the toilet. With the strong possibility that Trevor was either in Deminov's hands or on the run, Boris had an obligation to fulfill: his promise to Trevor. But first, he had to reach Cassandra.

Keeping low to the ground, Boris backed further and further from the house. He hit the tree line and wound his way deeper into the woods. Staying out of clear sight from the road, he ran south in the direction of town.

If he was lucky, Trevor had made it out alive and had been able to smuggle the data out before all hell broke loose. If that was the case, Boris wanted to get his hands on it as soon as possible. Find Cassandra, and he might quite possibly find Trevor.

Once he had placed enough distance between him and the house, he pulled out his cell phone and, after a moment's hesitation, he made the dreaded call.

"Da?" The voice on the other end sounded furious at the late intrusion.

Hating that he had to ask the favor, he cleared his throat. "I need help."

★ ★ ★ ★ ★

Nathan had been in St. Petersburg under official orders for well over twenty-four hours. Three days before, Director Franklin had debriefed the team on a rookie babysitting assignment. Everybody, including him, had groaned at the thought of being deployed on that mission until Franklin had mentioned the location—St. Petersburg, Russia. He couldn't resist the tempting opportunity to be closer to Cassandra.

Ever since she had hooked up with the Blarney Stone, contact between them had been minimal. When she had made contact, it was always with work-related questions: "Hey, can you check this out for me? Can you get me access to…?" The odd request of a couple of weeks back had pissed him off and gotten under his skin. Something was up.

With that thought in mind, Nathan had raised his hand. "I'll do it."

Franklin had lifted his eyebrow. "You? Are you serious? This isn't the type of assignment I'd have expected you to jump at."

Sensing all eyes on him, he had shrugged. "What can I say? Maybe the newbies will benefit from all this." He tapped his head. "Who better than me to whip them into shape? Besides, I have more field experience than anyone here."

Franklin had frowned, but accepted his offer, probably relieved at having the decision to assign someone taken out of his hands.

The babysitting mission was to oversee the security detail for a low-profile diplomat in Russia being handled by fresh-off-the-farm and newly deployed agents. But Nathan had his own agenda. He planned on checking up on Cassandra and the asshole to see what they were up to, and to make sure she was safe.

Nathan had arrived in St. Petersburg around dinnertime the day before, the address he'd received from Robert safely stored in his phone. He'd checked into his agency-assigned hotel room and hit the sack. He wanted to be in top form in the morning when he confronted Cassandra and Bauer regarding their activities in Russia. However, his plans were waylaid. Instead, he found himself tied up with work for the whole day.

Nathan was beat, still under jetlag's influence, and feeling miserable. To top it off, he was performing a task that always put his boxers in a bunch—typing. Not a pretty combination. Rubbing the back of his neck, he glanced at the clock. One in the morning and he was still stuck at the embassy. *At some point, I'll get to the fucking hotel room tonight.* Closing his eyes and leaning his head back against the chair, he let his mind wander.

He knew he should have warned Cassandra of his arrival. *She is definitely going to blow a gasket,* he admitted to himself. He put the finishing touches on the report, adding his thoughts regarding the new recruits assigned to the diplomatic security detail, and hit send. With a fist pump, he stood and arched his back in a big stretch.

Nathan's neglected stomach rumbled. As he grabbed his trench coat off the rack, his focus once again turned to Cassandra. *Shit, I'll definitely have to face the music tomorrow morning, when I show up at their doorstep unannounced and, most likely, unwanted.* Yet he would attain deep satisfaction in watching Bauer burn when he pointed out his shortcomings. Maybe Cassandra would finally realize her husband was a nuisance, worthy only of a temporary fling. *She had already been shot because of him, for fuck's sake. What else is he getting her into? If she ever....*

Nathan's mood veered sharply to anger. Shrugging on his coat, he headed out the door. At the elevator, he repeatedly pushed the button, impatient to get out of there. He would straighten things with Cassandra the next day and remove her from the Irishman's influence before it was too damn late.

Exiting the embassy into the cool night air, his plan was to get a burger at the hotel and some much-needed shuteye. The vibration of his cell against his thigh startled him and he fumbled around inside his pocket for it. His chest tightened when he checked his inbox. An email from Cassandra.

Curious, he opened it. It had arrived a few hours earlier while he been knee-deep into the report. The sight of her new last name in the sender's field fanned his anger. A sour taste filled his mouth at the thought of the Irishman's arms around her. He would need a lot of bleach to scrub that image from his head.

Scrolling to the body of the email, his chest tightened even more and his blood ran cold at the sight of the single word, *FUBAR*. Stunned to see the acronym used by Cassandra, he could only stare at the cell in his hand. "Holy Fuck, Cass!" he exclaimed as the meaning behind her message sliced through his mind like a sharp knife. All thoughts of food vanished in a blink of an eye.

Pulling up the logs from the safe house on his phone, he found evidence that the code had been used within the last eight hours. Nathan replied. *Are you safe? Are you hurt?* He cursed and paced the sidewalk, waiting on her response.

After a few minutes, Nathan ignored all precaution and jumped into the car. He loaded the coordinates to the safe house into his phone's GPS and buckled in. He revved the engine and gunned it. The back end of the car fishtailed and rubber burned into the asphalt as he shot out of the embassy parking lot, heading north. His first thought was to reach Cassandra to make sure she was safe and unharmed. His next centered on how much pain he would inflict to that fucking bastard she'd married for putting her life at risk again.

★ ★ ★ ★ ★

Cassandra brushed her hair back from her face. Her tailbone was numb and her legs cramped from siting too long in one position on the cold, hard wooden floor. Setting the laptop aside, she slowly rolled to her feet and worked the kinks and blood flow back into her stiff muscles.

A flash of loneliness stabbed at her, and heaviness sat in her chest. Evenings had lost their appeal since Trevor's sequester in the mansion. That night would be the worst of them all, without his voice to soothe her. Edgy and restless, Cassandra occupied herself with rearranging the bags. She wanted to leave at a moment's notice once Trevor arrived. A sob escaped her and her father's voice sounded in her head. *"Man up, Cassandra Cristina."*

"Yes, Sir." Her words echoed through the room. She repacked the duffel bags— passports, wallets, three-hundred dollars in rubles, and plane tickets to Prague—and set them by the entrance. She wandered to the window and moved the curtain aside. Scanning the property and seeing no movement, she returned to her spot on the floor to wait. "Damn it, Trevor! You better get your ass here or I will track you down and kill you myself!"

She glanced at the computer clock; it had been over twelve hours since their last contact. Cassandra's shoulders drooped under the weight of exhaustion beating at her. Shifting into a more comfortable position, she let her head rest back against the door. From under hooded eyes, she stared blindly down the hall as images began to flash in her mind—the first day Trevor charmed his way into her heart with a single word. The first night in each other's arms. His proposal. Their wedding.

Cassandra squeezed her eyes shut and tears seeped from them, little trails of salty fingers dripping down her cheeks. *I'd know if he were gone... wouldn't I?* "You're a part of me; I am a part of you." Words whispered against her ear. Her eyes snapped wide open and darted around the room. His gentle whispered words, just a memory in her head. Dejected and anxious, the stress of the day finally crashed down on her, leeching the last of her reserves, and her eyelids grew even heavier. Cassandra instinctively reached for the gun and pressed it tightly against her thigh. Her knuckles gleamed white under the tension of her grip as a fitful sleep overcame her.

Darkness pulled her into its tight embrace. Cassandra's eyes tracked frantically back and forth across the dark room and her body twitched, searching for escape. *"Mí-ádh!"* rang out in the room, soon followed by, *"I will love you always."*

"Trevor!" she screamed as she fell through nothingness, hand outstretched, reaching for his. Cassandra's body jerked and her eyes snapped open, blinded by the darkness. Scrambling to sit upright, she drew in deep gulping breaths and concentrated on slowing her racing heart.

She tightened her grip on the gun and raised it, aiming it down the hallway until the cobweb of her dream faded away. "A dream. A freaking dream," she muttered, scrubbing her face with a hand, unable to shake its hold on her. Her eyes grew used to the darkness, and the empty room slowly revealed itself to her. Lowering the gun, reality kicked her square in the chest. He was just a dream. Not real. Not there.

Cassandra pulled her knees tight against her chest and rested her forehead on them. Her thoughts continued to spiral out of control. Trevor is quick and resourceful. *He knows what he's doing. Fuck! Those people are brutal.* A flashing bar on the screen caught her eye. Straightening, Cassandra pulled the laptop closer and opened the window. Two email messages from George appeared. The first, received hours earlier, was a reply to her initial communication, advising her that he had his "ears on" and would keep her posted.

She opened the more recent message. *Nothing solid so far. Bad news. I still don't know where he is. The good news. No one appears to have any clue where he is either. I'm searching. It's like looking for fucking Waldo. Hang tight. Hang on, Cassie. I'll find him."*

Cassandra's heart infused with hope and a half smile quirked her lips. *Waldo.* She wished she had more resources in Russia that could help with locating Trevor. Powerful resources.

Boris! Why didn't I think of him sooner? Cassandra's thought slapped her up the head. Armed with the information George had passed on, she was more confident of his help. Pulling her cell from her pocket, she made the call. Each unanswered ring was like a death knell. On the fifth ring, the line connected with a click and then silence. She asked tentatively, "Boris? Is that you?"

"Where are you?" Boris's voice boomed over the connection. "I have been looking for you. I went by your apartment. It was empty. Are you okay? Is Trevor with you?" His familiar voice was strained and filled with worry.

"I'm safe for now. I'm not sure about Trevor; we lost contact after he escaped the mansion. I thought you would know!" Anger coated her voice. Anger at Boris for dragging them into a bigger mess then it should have been. "You and I need to talk. You have some explaining to do."

"Where are you? I will come to you."

Chapter Forty-Seven

Curve Ball

JESSICA KNEW CASSANDRA WAS RIGHT. She needed to tell Stephan. The rules of engagement had been broken and warped to no end by that little twist of fate. Whatever his reason for drawing a line between them, it had been overridden by the shared responsibility over the indelible connection growing inside her.

Stephan's baby. She had warred over the responsibilities a child brought to the surface. Would she be a good mother? Was she ready to take on such a huge task, a career all on its own? Her initial fear and concern had morphed into exhilaration and joy. Once she was able to see the bright side of the curve ball thrown at her, she wanted that baby more than anything in the world.

Her only concern was Stephan's reaction to it. Jessica knew he would be shocked. Her pregnancy dismantled his so carefully outlined plans. The "when I say it's over, it's over" rule had been crossed off the slate when they both had forgotten to use precautions that one night in his office. Yet, Jessica consoled herself that the impact of her pregnancy would be a positive one. She had observed him when they had been in public places. His eyes had lingered on babies and rounded pregnant bellies. Eyes filled with craving and longing—a longing he seemed to deny himself for some reason.

The emotional attachment they'd developed through the many weeks they had been intimate encouraged her to believe he would give them a new chance, remove all their boundaries and limits, and let their relationship run free, even bloom. Jessica wasn't going to give him an ultimatum or impose fatherhood on him. She would give him a choice. Whether or not he wanted to be a part of their child's life would be his decision to make. Her emotions fluttered from hope to downright fear at the prospect that he could reject them both.

Cassandra was thrilled with the prospect of being an honorary auntie. Their child would be, without a doubt, spoiled rotten. And if Stephan decided not to be a part of their lives, Jessica would console herself at knowing she would have a little part of him for herself forever.

It was late when Jessica parked in front of Stephan's house. The lights shone through the windows on the main floor and, through the sheer curtains, she observed as a shadow moved in the sitting room by the front window. Once the decision to tell him solidified in her mind, she couldn't wait a minute longer to follow up on it. The sooner she got it off of her chest, the sooner she would be able to focus on the things that mattered.

Taking a deep, ragged breath, Jessica made her way to the door with uncertain steps. She rang the bell and waited for what seemed like an eternity, switching her weight from one foot to the other. Her heart grew heavier with each second and her palms began to sweat. He was home. She knew it. *Is he avoiding me? Does he have company?* She grew light-headed and disappointment formed a hard lump in her throat. *This is a bad idea.* She was about to turn away when the door opened.

For an instant, Stephan's eyes glimmered with delight at seeing her standing at his door. The moment was short-lived, quickly replaced by the business mask he presented to clients and acquaintances. "Jessica. What brings you here?"

"Can I come in?" The fact that she had to ask caused a pang in her chest.

Stephan hesitated and then opened the door wider, gesturing for her to come inside. Instead of leading her into the living room where they had spent happier moments together, Stephan led her down the hall to his study. His actions spoke louder than words. She wasn't welcome. He waited for her to sit before taking his chair on the other side of his imposing desk. Stephan looked at her over his clasped hands. "So…?"

Jessica tilted her chin up and held his gaze. "It's my turn to say we need to talk."

He raised an eyebrow. "How so?"

Her eyes wandered around the study and returned to his. "Would you prefer to go somewhere more public? Maybe the Brazen Head?"

"It depends on why you are here. Should I be concerned for my virtue?" The spark of humor in his voice gave her hope that not all had been lost.

"I can't guarantee your virtue will be left intact. If I recall correctly, your office had a wild effect on my senses. Your study might just do the same." She followed the direction of his gaze to the edge of the desk. Desire instantly flooded his eyes and she could tell he was recalling the event just as she was.

"Have you come here to tempt me into repeating it?"

Stephan's teasing and the humorous glint in his eyes gave her hope that maybe he would be receptive to her news after all. "Possibly. It will depend on you."

His expression changed abruptly, as if he was reminded of his own decision to avoid her. "You know it can't happen, Jessica. It's over."

"Just hear me out. I have something important to tell you."

He nodded. "I'm listening."

She took a deep breath to compose herself. Her heart raced in her chest and her palms grew clammy. She was a hormonal mess. She couldn't hold off any longer. It was now or never.

"I'm pregnant."

His eyes narrowed to thin slashes and his face turned to stone the second the words left her lips. Her heart sank to her feet and she closed her eyes in pain. She had expected him to be shocked, but she'd never anticipated the disgusted expression that covered his face.

She grew lightheaded again and her hands began to tremble. Clasping them tightly in her lap, she waited anxiously for something, anything, a word from him. After several moments of thick, heavy silence she blurted out, "Talk to me. Say something."

Stephan's stare was unwavering as he studied her. "To be honest, I'm at a loss for words. Stunned, really. I knew you had a tenacious streak, but I never thought you'd go this far."

"What are you talking about? Don't talk as if you don't have as much responsibility in it as I do. We were both careless that night in your office." Her tone was strong. Confident.

Stephan paused and a glint of something she couldn't recognize crossed his eyes. "Why are you doing this? Are you looking to get even because I ended it before you were ready to?"

"Are you trying to say I planned for this to happen? To get pregnant with your child to get you back?"

Stephan scoffed sarcastically. "Un-fucking-believable. Who the hell are you? I have to say, you are a very good actress. You do sound so very sincere."

"Stephan. I *am* pregnant. Only a couple of weeks along, but pregnant nonetheless. It didn't happen by itself. It takes two to tango."

She didn't think his eyes could harden any more than they did. This time they glowed with rage. A rage she hadn't expected or foreseen from him.

"Of all the things I imagined happening between us." He paused, clenching his teeth as if to contain the anger burning in his eyes. His voice pitched low and was full of unadulterated pain. "Of all the things I thought you capable of to drive me mad. This was not one of them."

"This?"

"I saw you. Jessica. I saw you the other night with *him*."

"What are you talking about?" She became frantic, trying to comprehend what he was implying.

"I saw you walking into Trevor and Cassandra's house with that young guy."

"What young guy? Sean?" A deep frown creased her forehead. "He's just a friend. What does he have to do with anything?"

"Does he know you are trying to pass his child off as mine?"

"His child? Sean's?" Blood rose to her head, her cheeks heated and her pulse pounded in her ears. Anger reddened her vision. "Are you fucking insane? This is your baby!"

"That's where you're wrong, Jessica."

"I never slept with Sean."

"You certainly didn't. I am sure you were wide awake making that child." His tone was inflammatory.

"Why are you doing this? Hurting me this way?"

"How do you think I feel, knowing you were with someone else when you said you wanted me?"

Tears flowed down her cheeks and fell to her lap as she stared at him, trying to make sense of his words. "I don't just want you. I love you."

Stephan pinned her with tortuous eyes. "And this is how you show it? Passing off your boyfriend's child as mine?"

"Whether you believe me or not, this is your son or daughter growing inside me. No one else's."

A glimmer of hope flashed in his eyes but vanished instantly. Stephan pulled a sharp intake of breath before his cold eyes settled on Jessica again, cutting her to the bone. "You see? I knew things would get complicated. I knew the day would come when you would want a child. You're young. Your clock would start ticking and when I couldn't give you what you wanted, needed, you'd leave."

For weeks, she had wanted to know more about him and now he was giving her a glimpse into his core, into what made him who he was. She wanted to see it all now. The good and the bad. She held her breath, waiting for him to continue.

"I knew your youth would make things worse, but I just couldn't help myself. I had to have you. Thought that maybe we could forget everything else but the feelings we draw from each other. What I feel for you is raw, all-consuming. Stupidly, I thought I could draw a line and obey it myself. We both ignored that line when it came down to it and I accept my part of the blame; but I never, in a million years, expected you to stoop so low. The idea that you were with someone else right after you left my bed is sickening. I never took you for a liar or a manipulative woman. But you are one."

Anguish blasted her from every angle. She couldn't understand what he meant. "Why can't you just accept you're going to be a father?"

"Because I *know* there's no way this child can be mine." His absolute belief in his pain-infused words gave her pause.

"But it *is*!"

"It *can't* be." He collapsed in his chair and his mouth formed a grim line. "I'm sterile."

The air expunged from Jessica's lungs and her heart missed a beat. Wide-eyed, she shook her head. "No way! Listen to me! You are *wrong*. If that's the case, why did you use protection when you made love to me?"

"Force of habit. I'm a responsible adult. Birth control is not the only reason people wear condoms, Jessica." Stephan rubbed his eyes with a thumb and forefinger, then lowered his hand to the desk, clenching his fist.

Thoughts swirled in her head and she felt detached from reality for a second. Then it all came crashing down on her. Every time she saw his longing eyes trailing an infant, every time he covertly observed little ones at play, he wasn't denying himself one; he thought he couldn't have one for himself. *But he was wrong!*

"Stephan, *listen* to me! I don't care what you say. This *is* your child."

"Stop the pretenses, Jessica. It can't be true. There was a test done a long time ago." The calmness with which he said the words brought chills to her spine. Stephan exhaled a deep breath and shook his head. "This is pointless."

Jessica understood that nothing she could possibly say would get through to him at that time. She had to find a different way to reach him or simply give up. "Fine. You don't seem to be open to the possibility that your test, whenever it was done, could be wrong. For the record, I'm keeping *our* child. If you'd like to be sure, you are welcome to request a paternity test once he or she is born. If not, it's your loss. This would be your chance to have what you've craved for so long."

"I never—"

"Oh, yeah you did." Jessica rubbed her brow to hold back the headache that was creeping up on her. "Don't lie to yourself. If and when you're ready to accept the fact that maybe those tests were wrong, accept that I'm all you need in your life, you know where to find us. But don't take too long, or I might be the one passing on the offer."

Jessica stood, her back straight; she couldn't hold back the love from shining in her eyes as she gazed on him for what might be the last time. Her voice trembled when she spoke. "Goodbye, Stephan."

The minute the door slammed closed, Stephan leaned back in his chair and raked his hair with both hands. He stared blindly into space as he wrapped his head around what had just happened. Jessica's announcement brought back the painful memories of eighteen years back. Layla.

He had met her through a friend and they'd clicked right away. They'd dated for a short time before she had officially moved in with him. She'd had long-term plans, and he had been right there with her.

They both had held good jobs and had shared wide circle of friends. The only things that had been missing from the perfect picture were the wedding rings, the house with a white picket fence, and the racket of children. Their only contention had been over marriage; Layla had been adamant that they didn't need the wedding rings or the papers, and she wasn't alone. Ireland's lack of a divorce law pushed many young couples to cohabitate without the long-lasting commitment of marriage.

Her words still rang loudly in his ears. *"What if things go sour and we can't get divorced?"*

"We love each other. Why focus on the what-ifs? Why not take it seriously, make it forever?" had been his usual reply.

Over time, Layla had begun to yearn for a child. Stephan had seen it as the perfect opportunity to weaken her defenses and gently guide her to the altar. But while Stephan preferred to have a tight knot before bringing children into the world, Layla wanted them without the need for a definitive tie. It was during one of their arguments about it that she had confessed she had stopped taking her pills months before without success. They had argued about her tactics, but in the end, they had reached an agreement: they would actively try to conceive, and when it happened, she would marry him. Months had passed without a hint of a baby. He had soothed her, saying those things could take a long time, that maybe they just had to relax a little, go on vacation somewhere warm.

Layla hadn't seen it that way. She had become anxious and proposed they go through fertility testing. The day she had received the results he had been at work. Layla had called from home, crying inconsolably; he had been barely able to understand a word she had said. By the time he had gotten home, she had already packed and left. All that was left of her was a note on the table.

Stephan,

We can't continue this way. You can't give me what I want and I can't be who you want me to be. I wish you all the happiness in the world and that you find someone who can fulfill your every wish. I hope to find the same for myself one day.

Love,

Layla

Each word had burned his mind irrevocably. He had sunk into a world of hurt and disappointment. His infertility became a source of shame that he hid deep inside, shying away from evolving relationships, avoiding the disclosure of what he viewed as a handicap.

Layla had wanted a baby more than she had loved or wanted a life with him. He believed others would eventually come to feel the same way. For many years, avoidance of deeper connections had worked beautifully.

All things went to hell in a hand basket when he met Jessica. He had known he was in trouble the minute he had laid eyes on her. Her youth screamed joy and laughter and of babies who would look like angelic imps, blonde and blue-eyed, just like their mother. A pang of wistfulness hit him square in the chest. He had known it was coming, had seen the signs when he'd caught Jessica enthralled by the baby that day—one of the reasons that had pushed him to put an end to things, to them.

He still couldn't believe she had gone to such great lengths. The extreme of getting pregnant by another man and to claim it was his. She was impulsive and determined, but the Jessica he knew was not manipulative and evil. The deep pain he had witnessed in her eyes came back to haunt him.

Suddenly, he needed to get out of the house. The walls closed down on him, he needed to find a place where he could clear his head and think, drown himself in a pint or two. He jumped to his feet, grabbed his jacket and keys, and rushed out of the house as if the dogs of hell were nipping at his heels.

Chapter Forty-Eight

Dumbass

THE DRIVE TO THE SAFE house hadn't done much to improve Nathan's mood. Too many questions simmered in his head, heating his temper to a boiling point. What were they really doing in Russia that required having a safe house as backup? What had made Cassandra run there? He slammed his hand against the wheel. This time he planned on having the answers straight up.

Dawn was still hours away and it had been several miles since Nathan had passed any other cars on the highway. Anxious to reach Cassandra, he pressed his foot on the pedal harder and harder, his stomach twisting in knots as his car ate up the miles. *Is she hurt? Is the asshole with her? Is he hurt?* The idea of Bauer in pain appealed to him. After savoring the image, Nathan shook his head. It would be too good to be true. He glanced at his phone's screen. Thirty more miles to go. It couldn't go by fast enough.

Just before reaching the coordinates, and taking into account he had no intelligence on what had caused Cassandra to flee to the safe house, Nathan pulled off onto a side access road and parked the car behind a grove of large trees, out of clear sight from the road.

According to the GPS, the safe house was located on the other side of those woods. He checked his email. Still no reply from Cassandra. Out of the car, Nathan shrugged off his trench and tossed it back on the seat. After a swift scan of the area, he palmed his SIG and took off jogging along the edge of the road until he reached a hidden driveway off to the right.

There was a crisp bite to the early morning air, and the woods were teeming with life. Nathan veered through the trees, cutting into the tree line surrounding the house. The sounds of crickets serenaded his ears and small animals rustled in the underbrush as he made his way across.

He stumbled right into the safe house's backyard and, crouching in the cover of the shrubs, cased the house. After a few minutes of observation, his concern grew when he couldn't detect any indoor activity. Under the dim moonlight, he crept to the back door. After hearing the soft beep from the hidden keypad, Nathan turned the handle and eased the door open. Concern was like a heavy fist gripping his chest as he peered and inched forward into the small dark kitchen just far enough to clear the door.

Squinting down the hall at the kitchen door, Cassandra's heart dropped to her stomach when a creak sounded on the planks of the back porch. Her eyes were tight and gritty and her ears had been playing tricks on her for the past hour. She could no longer count on one hand the number of times she had thought she had heard the door creak.

She almost let it pass until the ping of the security pad spurred her into action. Rolling to her feet in a smooth flowing motion, she grabbed Trevor's gun from the coffee table, turned the lamp off, bathing the room in darkness, and quietly sprinted down the hall to the kitchen. Gripping her gun in one hand and Trevor's in the other, she stayed low and listened. Her pulse raced out of control. *Please be Trevor! Keep it cool, Cassie.* She took a position behind the door and released the safeties on both pistols.

Cassandra held her breath as the door eased open. With eyes already adapted to the darkness, she watched the shadowy figure step through the door. Disappointment punched her in the chest and she winced inwardly. She was intimately familiar with Trevor's gait and knew right away that it couldn't be him.

She gauged that the intruder outweighed her by a good hundred pounds and was taller by some eight inches. On soft feet, she slipped behind him and kicked the door shut as she dug one Grach against his lower back and the other kissed the base of the intruder's skull.

"Don't move!" she hissed harshly. "Do and you'll get one in the kidney. Or one straight in the pea brain. Maybe both."

She pressed the muzzles of the guns tighter into his body when he shifted his weight. "Don't give me an excuse. Put your hands behind your head!" The intruder complied, an indication he understood exactly what she'd said.

Cassandra followed procedure; keeping one gun pressed tightly against his neck, she slipped the other in her waistband and disarmed the intruder.

"Cass...." The masculine tone was raw and husky, and she struggled to place it.

Jabbing his lower back with the barrel of his own gun, she nudged him forward. "Move. Slowly. Who are you? How do you know my name?"

"Jeezus. Cass. It's me, Nathan."

"Liar! Hit the switch." Once the kitchen was flooded with light, her jaw almost hit the floor. "Shit! It is you! What the hell are you doing here?"

Nathan turned and looked at her, his angry eyes narrowed to slits. "What? No welcome hug?"

"What the hell, Nate!" She shot him a disgusted look, handing him back his gun and lowering hers. Resetting the security system, she walked past him without a backward glance.

He followed her, switching the lights off and leaving the kitchen back in darkness. Nathan closed the distance between them, rapidly catching up when Cassandra turned the table lamp on again. Grabbing her arm, Nathan spun her around to face him. "What the hell are you doing here?" His voice was full of rage and there was a possessive desperation in it. "Where the fuck is your husband?" He spat the word at her.

She watched his jaw clench when his eyes found the two contingency bags at the entrance. He turned his turbulent gaze to her. "What has that damn Irishman gotten you into?"

Cassandra strained against his grip and jerked her arm back. She pressed her lips together in anger. She could no longer stand his cynical expression without retort. "Shut the fuck up, Nate! Before you say something we'll both regret." Her patience had worn thin and she felt like clocking him good.

"Is there money involved? The greedy bastard is using you to help pad his account, isn't he? I never thought you—"

Her eyes flashed furiously. Her hand curled into a fist and, moving of its own volition, caught him across the jaw. Nathan's head snapped back.

"Fuck!" he hissed out.

"You don't know him! And apparently, you really don't know me either! He doesn't need that…he doesn't need the money."

A vein pulsed in his forehead and his lips pressed into a thin line as he rubbed his jaw. "What the hell was that for?" His eyes filled with a mix of fury and disbelief.

Cassandra stood toe to toe with him and, tilting her head back, held his gaze. "You know nothing about him or us. So back the fuck off!"

"I'll back off Cass, if, and only if, I find that I gave you to someone who really deserves you."

Her face became a marble effigy of contempt, her low voice simmered with barely checked anger. "You. Did. Not. Give. Me. Away," each word punctuated by a jab of her finger against the middle of his chest. Nathan flinched, but Cassandra was past the point of no return. "As much as you seem to think you had me at some point, I was never yours. Never!"

"You can't ignore the fact that we are perfect for each other. Made for each other. Come back with me. Back to the CIA. I can protect you there. I can keep you safe! We can leave now."

"See? That's where you get it all wrong, Nate. I don't need you to protect me. I don't want you to protect me." His eyes narrowed, but Cassandra pushed on. "All the years I struggled to be the perfect daughter, perfect employee, perfect partner, perfect...whatever. It was exhausting and demanding. Trevor, he gets it right. He *understands* me. He *trusts* me. He lets me be me."

"Cass, you should have said something. I would've—"

"What? Understood? Changed? Either way, it wouldn't have been as natural as it is between Trevor and me. He loves me as I am, always has from day one. He admires my strengths and, for some weird reason, loves my faults more. I don't have to second-guess what he's thinking or how to please him, the same way he doesn't have to work hard at pleasing me. What we have is real love. Not the idea of love you seem to have created in your own mind."

Nathan scoffed. "He loves you, and yet he put you in danger. Dragged you to Russia. Made you run for the hills. Left you alone to fend for yourself!"

All Cassandra could do was shake her head in response to his comments. She backed away from him, rubbing her arm and met his icy gaze straight on. "Wrong again. He didn't drag me into anything. Where he goes, I go willingly. I came here as his wife and partner to help him. He didn't put me in danger; in fact, he kept me out of it while putting his own life on the line." She cocked her head and placed her hands on her hips. "And, as for my running for the hills? It was part of our contingency plan to remove me from harm's way, you dumbass! So here I am. Safe and sound while my husband, the man I love more than life itself, could quite possibly be lying somewhere injured, or worse, dead. So, don't you dare sit here on your high horse condemning someone who has done everything he can to protect my ass."

A sob took a strangle hold on her throat. *Oh God! Don't let him be dead.* Cassandra struggled to control herself before she did something rash. Swallowing hard, she wrapped her arms around her waist and turned her back to him.

Nathan was like a dog with a bone. "Why Cass? You still haven't told me why you're really here. Is he involved in something dirty? Something you can't even tell your own father about? I talked to Robert. He only knows the same bullshit you've been dishing me."

Sighing deeply, a part of her wanted to tell Nathan to go to hell. But her other half had an overwhelming need to have him understand what Trevor meant to her once and for all. It pained her that her friend's view of Trevor was distorted by misplaced jealousy. All she wanted was for Nathan to see Trevor for who he really was.

Cassandra sat on the edge of the couch studying the hard planes of Nathan's face for a moment. "Okay, fine. You deserve to hear why I've been asking for so many favors and sounding edgy. We're in Russia because Trevor was promised information in exchange for the retrieval of some stolen data."

A calculating look blanketed his expression. "What do you mean, 'information'?"

"The information revolves around Trevor's parents. They vanished into thin air almost six years ago. Nobody knows how or why. They were never found. We need to know what happened to them."

Nathan's eyes hardened. "And what did the job entail, Cass?" His tone was angry and unforgiving.

Cassandra knew from experience that he wouldn't let it go. "A mafia organization from St. Petersburg stole a powerful decrypter in development phase. If they managed to finish the development of the software, our client would be blamed for all the financial chaos that would ensue."

Nathan cursed under his breath and threw his arms up. "What the fuck was he thinking?! He could have come to me! Passed on the information to the CIA!" His tone rose as he paced in front of her. "Hell, he used to work for the NSA, for fuck's sake!"

Cassandra watched Nathan circle like a caged tiger in front of her and kept her own temper in check. "Yes, we could have; but we were honoring our client's wishes to avoid government agency involvement unless absolutely necessary." He stopped midstride and stared at her in disbelief. "Don't give me that look. This is a job. It is what we do—"

Before she could explain further, a noise reverberated down the hall. Cassandra cocked her head to listen as she signaled Nathan to remain quiet. The noise sounded again—the creak of wood on the back porch followed by the beep of the keypad. She shot a questioning look straight at Nathan.

Seeing the look, Nathan mouthed, "No tail."

Both sprang into action like old times. Exchanging a series of hand signals, they quietly jogged toward the kitchen. Nathan took point covering the door and Cassandra fell back, taking a position in the hallway, covering both Nathan and the door.

Her heart pounded and swelled with hope that Trevor had finally made it. It took all her strength to not rush the door and yank it open. For all she knew, it could be one of Mikhailov's goons. Nodding to Nathan, she took a firmer grip on her gun, waiting for whoever it was to enter the kitchen, while he pressed back against the wall in the shadow of the cabinets, waiting for the opportunity to catch the trespasser off guard.

Cassandra wanted to yell at him to be careful in case it was Trevor, but had to content herself with shooting him a telling glance, hoping he would catch her drift. Her attention remained riveted on the door and her breath came in raspy gasps of anticipation. For the second time that night, a shadow eased into the house.

★ ★ ★ ★ ★

Trevor managed to reach Zelenogorsk and catch last train to Vyborg with the luck of the Irish. After Yakov had dropped him off at the closest village, he had used Dmitriy's money to procure a ride to the train station. With his left arm immobilized against his chest, courtesy of Tatiana's proficient hands, he was able to sleep for the length of the two trips. Whatever she had cleaned the wound with, possibly some farm ointment or such, was working wonders. Although still in pain, it was bearable and his shoulder didn't throb like it did earlier.

He arrived in Vyborg shortly before three in the morning and quickly located the street that would take him to the safe house. The ache of his shoulder faded to the background and the ache in his heart—the one as a result of knowing Cassandra was within reach—was front and center. *Did she make it this far? Walk this same path? Is she as anxious to see me as I am to see her?*

The house was dark, an eerie shadow squatting in the dim moonlight. No glow of light peeked through the windows. That worried him the most. A sick feeling overwhelmed him. *What could have possibly delayed her arrival? Is she in any danger?* A new resolve solidified in his mind. If push came to shove, he would throw the damn plan and itinerary out the window. If she hadn't arrived by noon, he wouldn't leave Russia. He would move heaven and hell to find her and take her home. Trevor rolled his sore shoulder and skulked to the back of the house. Following Cassandra's instructions, he entered the memorized code. A soft beep sounded and a green light flashed, indicating the door was unlocked.

★ ★ ★ ★ ★

As soon as the shadow crossed the threshold, Nathan rammed the barrel of his gun against the back of intruder's head. The intruder froze in his tracks. The steady motion of his arm moving out from his body and his stance sent a surge of adrenaline like a drug into Cassandra's blood, her heart thrummed out of control in her chest and, without any hesitation, she took off at a run toward them.

"Cass! No!" Nathan yelled, cocking the hammer of his gun.

Chapter Forty-Nine

Freakin' Rabbits

"NATE, NO! DROP IT! IT'S Trevor!" Cassandra yelled, leaving her position and rushing toward the two men.

Trevor ignored the muzzle pressed to his temple and met her halfway, sweeping his arm around her waist and gathering her tight against him.

"*A ghrá!*" His voice was thick and unsteady as he buried his face in the crook of her neck.

"Trevor!" she sobbed, cupping the back of his head and wrapping her arms around his shoulders, her gun still tightly clenched held in her hand.

"Fucking bullshit!" Nathan grumbled flipping the lights on. Taking the gun from her, he snarled, "Let me have that before you kill one of us."

Cassandra felt the rapid beat of Trevor's heart synching with hers as they thrummed out of control in their chests. She cupped his face and pressed her lips tight against his. The relief of ending the many days of separation burning the ties that had held her heart in a tight grip since the last day she kissed him goodbye flowed over her. His familiar musky scent invaded her, comforting, soothing her frayed nerves.

Within seconds, Trevor took control of the kiss, thrusting his tongue past her lips, exploring her mouth, drowning her in wave after wave of need and desire. She had dreamed of being crushed in his embrace again, and there he was, holding her, crushing her, the images of her dreams now a reality.

"Hell! Just get a room!" Nathan's growl penetrated her consciousness.

They broke the kiss with a big sigh, resting forehead to forehead, eyes locked, both working at catching their breaths.

After a moment, Cassandra pulled back and took in his appearance—stained pants, his left arm bound to his chest under a shirt she didn't recognize, the tightness around his mouth, the pain in his eyes.

She narrowed her gaze. "I heard dogs and gunshots. I heard you cry out. What happened? Were you hit? How'd you get here? Are you in pain? Is all that blood—" Cassandra snapped her mouth shut.

Trevor grinned. "Wow, I've missed even that." He pushed the loose wisps of her hair behind her ear.

Her hand covered his and pressed it against her cheek. He weaved his fingers with hers, squeezing her hand as if knowing the effort it took her to hold it together. The gesture brought a smile to her face, the first in hours, days. "What the hell took you so long? Take the scenic route?"

Chuckling, Trevor kissed her knuckles. "Something like that."

The smile faded from Cassandra's eyes. "Shit, Trevor." She gently placed her hand on his chest. "How bad is this?"

Trevor shrugged dismissively. "Meh."

His scrunched face and the flare of pain in his eyes told a different story. An overwhelming need to check his injury for herself and take his pain away swept over her. "Nate, I spotted a first aid kit under the bathroom sink. Get it, will you?"

Nathan grumbled, "He's survived this long."

"Nate. Please."

"Wuss!" he muttered as he stepped from the room.

Trevor muttered under his, "Someone had some recent exposure to gamma rays...."

"Trevor!" Cassandra shushed him, but couldn't hold back a little smile from touching her lips. She led Trevor into the living room and gently eased him onto the couch. He sagged against it with a deep sigh before tipping his head back and closing his eyes. Cassandra took a seat on the coffee table across from him and placed her hand on his knee, the physical contact a way to reassure herself that he was really there, that it wasn't one of her crazy dreams.

Trevor covered her hand with his, rubbing his thumb along the inside of her wrist, a simple gesture that swelled her heart and sent a rush of moisture into her eyes. Silence filled the room, but the unspoken words that flowed between them never quieted.

Nathan's brisk step echoed from the hall. Cassandra brushed the corners of her eyes, fighting hard against the tears she refused to let fall. She took a deep, long pull of air and exhaled it slowly.

A deep frown furrowed Nathan's brow as he barged in and tossed the kit at her. Cassandra caught it with both hands, ignoring his childish behavior as she set the kit on her lap. "Trevor?"

Trevor grunted in response. Unwilling to cause him more pain, she let him have his space. After a few more minutes of silence, she couldn't stand it anymore. "Okay mister. Stop stalling. Tell me what happened."

He flinched and opened his eyes to gaze into hers. "It's a long story. Got any popcorn? Beer?" Trevor tried to make light of the situation, but his wife wouldn't have any of it.

Her whiskey-brown eyes fixed on him and her mouth formed a grim line.

"Quit being a smart ass. I want to know what the hell happened. I lost years of my life yesterday."

His smile faded as he searched her face, trying to reach into her thoughts, and his stomach tightened at the distress he had caused her. He knew Cassandra and, by the gleam that was flashing from her eyes, he would be on the receiving end of a good badgering once she had pulled the entire story, down to the smallest detail, out of him. *God, I love her.*

"This ought to be good," Nelson sneered, leaning against the doorframe, his arms tightly crossed over his chest, a look of disdain coloring his eyes.

"Fuck off, Nelson." When Nelson's hands curled into fists, Trevor smirked. He returned his attention to Cassandra and began his recollection of the whole story, from the time they lost contact to the time he reached the safe house. As he unveiled each grueling chapter in his journey to reach her, Cassandra's grip on his hand grew tighter and tighter. When he reached the chapter involving Deminov and Petrovna, Cassandra's eyes grew wider and Nelson cursed under his breath. "And here I am," he finished with a cocky grin, relieved the ordeal was behind him.

Aware of Nelson's disapproving presence in the room, Trevor ignored him, focusing solely on Cassandra's lovely face. The burn of Nelson's gaze bore through him. Trevor turned to him and their eyes connected briefly. At that moment, Trevor realized that something had changed. Nelson's body language and the old hatred in his eyes born on the day they met no longer carried the heat they once did. It wasn't completely gone, but it wasn't as prevalent either. In its place seemed to sit a painful acceptance. The marginally friendly look was quickly gone once he realized Trevor was well aware of it. The familiar pure, wholesome dislike was back in full force.

Cassandra rolled her eyes at them both. "Now what?"

Trevor returned his gaze to his wife's. "I need a shower and a few hours of sleep before we can even think of leaving." He leaned forward, kissed the tip of her nose, and touched the soft silky skin of her cheek with his good hand. His thoughts were clear now that she was close to him. He was almost feeling like himself, his usual wickedness and good humor surfacing once in Cassandra's proximity. "While storytelling and gift of gab is in this Irishman's blood, I would rather be horizontal."

Nelson groaned from where he stood at the door. Trevor ignored his outburst and studied Cassandra closely. His heart tumbled in his chest. Dark shadows circled her eyes and her shoulders curved under the weight of exhaustion. "You look like you could use some sleep too, Cassie girl."

Cassandra held the hand he had placed on her cheek and nuzzled it before dropping a soft kiss on the center of his palm. The touch of her soft lips sent a flash of heat tearing through him and a pang resonated in his heart. During their exchange, Nate continued to study them. From the corner of his eye, Trevor saw him listening intently to their conversation and watching their interaction—the way they looked at each other, touched, and caressed as they talked. That was fine with Trevor.

Pushing from the doorframe, Nelson took a step further into the room and interrupted them. "Do you still need me to stay?"

Cassandra replied, keeping her eyes on Trevor, "Since you're here, I was hoping you'd help us." She paused before adding, "We can't go back to St. Petersburg. It isn't safe. The safest route would be across the border into Finland. From there we can find our own way to Prague."

Nelson nodded; his face was closed and clear of all emotion. "Fine. We can talk in the morning before I head out."

Trevor frowned, looking from one to the other. A strange vibe hung in the air. Something tense, unlike the usual friendliness and familiarity they displayed in the past. Trevor's curiosity was piqued and he made a mental note to ask Cassandra about it later. The only things he wanted and needed were a hot shower and Cassandra in his arms. "Where is the shower?"

"I'll show you." Cassandra helped him to his feet and grabbed the first aid kit. As they walked past Nelson, she called over her shoulder, "Nate, you can take the bedroom at the end of the hall. I'm sure you can find pillows and blankets there somewhere."

"No, thanks. I will make myself comfortable here."

"It's your call." Cassandra could feel Nathan's gaze drilling into her back as she led Trevor down the hall into the bedroom with the large armoire. Entering the room, she flipped on the light and set the first aid kit on the dresser while Trevor headed into the bathroom. Moments later, the shower kicked on.

She walked into the bathroom to find him fumbling one-handed with the buttons of his shirt and cursing under his breath. She brushed his hands aside. "Here, you stubborn Irishman. Let me do that." His hiss of pain as she pushed the shirt off his shoulders gripped her stomach and squeezed it so tight she thought she'd be sick. She dropped a kiss on his lips. "Sorry."

"Do that again," he grinned.

She smiled softly at his attempt at humor and pressed her lips against his again. As the shirt dropped from her fingers to the floor, the full extent of his injury hit her. Her breath hitched and she cringed inside, her attention riveted on the stained dressing wrapped around his shoulder from front to back. Her hand hovered over the dressing. "You really were shot." Her voice was filled with fear and accusation. "I heard the shot go off. But it didn't feel real until just now."

"I'm okay, Cassie. Friends helped me."

Cassandra's heart sputtered and her knees grew weak. "You've been shot," she repeated, shaking her head, slightly dazed.

"It's just a little sore." Pain colored his tone and he grimaced again. "But hey, now we're even. Later, you can show me your scar and I'll show you mine." He flashed a crooked grin and wiggled his eyebrows.

"Shit, Trevor! That's not funny." She pointed a finger at him. "That's it, buster. No more wall climbing for you. First you fall on your back, and now you've been shot like a target at an amusement part. You're bloody lucky you didn't freaking break your neck!" Her eyes grew wide as she gently removed the dressing and stared at the injury just below his clavicle. "Holy shit! If it had hit you four inches down—" All of a sudden everything came crashing in. A sob crept up her throat and she swallowed hard, capturing it, preventing it from escaping her lips.

Trevor brushed his knuckle gently along the side of her face. The tenderness in his touch was more than she could bear at that moment. "It looks worse than it is. It hardly hurts now." There was a softness in his tone as his eyes melted lovingly into hers.

Cassandra sniffed loudly and wiped her nose with the back of her hand. "Yeah, yeah! So says you," she whispered as she reached for the button and zipper of his pants.

Making quick work of them, she slid her hands inside, grazing over his hips and pushing the pants off to the floor. His warm skin tempted her, but she clamped down on her need. His came first. She turned and held back the curtain so he could step into the shower.

As he stepped in, her eyes swept over him and pain pierced her. The entire left side—front and back—was one massive bruise, and there was a slightly larger hole where the bullet had come out. Steam billowed above the shower, fogging the mirror in the small bathroom. Trevor raised his face to the spray, letting the water flow over him. His shoulders hunched over, as if weighed down by fatigue.

Disrobing, Cassandra stepped in behind him and slid her hands gently, possessively, up his back. His muscles twitched and rippled under her touch. She wanted to feel every inch of him, to reassure herself that he was whole, safe. How many times did she replay that scene in her mind while waiting for him?

"Hell, Trevor," Cassandra whispered, kissing his shoulder as she eased her arms around him and pressed her length against his back. "Pure hell is where I have lived these past hours. When I heard your words and then silence, my heart…shattered."

Trevor turned and wrapped his good arm around her waist, pulling her tight against his chest. "It was the hardest thing I have ever had to do *a ghrá*, but I needed to know you would be safe." He brought his lips down to hers and kissed her.

His kiss was gentle and sweet. When they parted lips, she pressed a kiss on his chest and stepped back. "Shush. I don't want to think about that now."

She worked the soap in her hands and began washing every inch of him, concentrating on easing his pain and, at the same time, hers. She massaged shampoo in his hair and studied him closely as he rested his head against the tile, letting the water rinse the lather from it.

Cassandra's heart beat wildly in her chest as her eyes traced the lines of his lean, battered body. Trevor's shoulders no longer drooped so prominently, and the tension that had marred his face minutes earlier had eased. More than two weeks had gone by since she had last touched him like that. Cassandra reached up and brushed his hair back, rinsing the rest of the soap from it. Lulled by the heat of the water and her touch, his eyes grew heavy and dimmed with exhaustion. When the water's temperature cooled, she shut it off. "Come on, Trev. It's getting cold."

Trevor didn't want to move from the soothing heat and comfort he found in there, but he was struggling to remain upright. When he stepped out, Cassandra patted him dry, taking extra care of the area around the entry and exit wounds, before wrapping the towel around herself and herding him to the bedroom.

She sat him down on the edge of the bed and retrieved the first aid kit from the dresser. "We need to dress the wound and bind your arm again, mister." She cleaned the damaged flesh with antiseptics and bound his arm while he watched her steady hands work on him. Trevor saw the strain in her features, the furrowed brow, and knew that she was hurting for him. The whole process stung him all over again, but he held it in as well as he could. He didn't want to distress her even further.

Once done, he pushed the pillow against the headboard and leaned back against it gingerly, avoiding stress to the patch-up Job Cassandra had given him. The effects of a clean shower and bandages left him relaxed and sedated all at once.

The room darkened when Cassandra turned off the switch, leaving them in the soft glow of the bathroom light. From under half-mast eyes, Trevor watched his wife as she released the corner of the towel tucked between her breasts. His cocked jerked in response when she tugged the towel from around her body and use it to briskly dry her hair before tossing it to the bathroom floor. His heart lurched, his pulse quickened, as his stark-naked wife joined him on the bed.

The weight of her head and the tickle of silky wet hair on his chest soothed him as she curved her body into his, her heat radiating through him like a furnace. He tucked her tighter against his side and Cassandra shifted into a more comfortable position, sliding her leg between his and gently resting her arm on his chest, fingertips caressing his bandaged arm.

Contentment for having her so close, skin to skin, invaded him in a rush, and Trevor released a deep sigh. Her scent permeated the room, filling his nostrils, and making him more aware of the time spent apart from each other, as well as the danger they both had faced.

He tightened his grip around her and rested his chin on her head. With Nelson standing guard in the living room, they both could comfortably surrender to a deep and restoring sleep.

★ ★ ★ ★ ★

Lying on his back, Nathan tucked his arm behind his head and tried to make himself comfortable on the couch. His mind ran through all the information gleaned within the last hour over and over again. He had been wrong about many things. As hard as it was for Nathan to admit it, he now understood that what Cassandra felt for Bauer was not infatuation, but true love.

During their conversation before the Irishman had arrived, she'd had that crazed look in her eyes. The same look he'd seen on the faces of people who had lost loved ones in tragic circumstances. A look that he had hoped would register on Cassandra's face should something ever happened to him. It had been there all right, only it had been for Bauer instead.

Nathan flinched as images of Cassandra and Bauer whirled in his mind. But for the first time, he admitted to himself that his fight for her was over. Fidgeting on the couch, Nathan tossed and turned as he listened for any disturbances. All was quiet, including the back of the house where the bedrooms were located.

Exhaling deeply, he set his gun at hand's reach and folded his arms across his chest, hoping to grab some shuteye before they had to be up and on the road. The long hours at work, the panicked drive, and the jetlag finally beat him into oblivion.

★ ★ ★ ★ ★

Sliding into awareness, Cassandra held her breath, hoping the wonderful dream she'd had was real. Shaking the last threads of sleep, she let her senses roam free. The warmth at her side enveloped her in a soothing cocoon. Breathing in deeply, a mixture of scents—clean and spicy—filled her nostrils and pierced her heart with images of Trevor's arrival.

In the low illumination provided by the bathroom light, she could see Trevor was still in the same position he had been in when they had drifted off earlier. Resting her head on her hand, Cassandra gently traced the outline of the bandage with her fingers. He would be stuck with a sling for several more weeks.

She watched the steady rise and fall of her hand on his chest. A need to feel more of him, all of him, slammed into her, sucking the air from her lungs, sending a flow of dampness between her thighs. She rose to her elbow and her pulse beat a tad faster as she took in the length of his lean, muscular body. The line of his neck tempted her lips and the ridges of his abs called to her fingers. Of their own accord, they glided across the muscles of his flat stomach. A smile curved her lips as his cock twitched and hardened under her touch, as if cognizant of her deepest desires.

Cassandra rose and eased her leg across his body, straddling him and bracing herself on her knees. She looked down on a still deeply asleep Trevor, his eyelashes fluttering against his cheeks, his mouth slightly parted, little puffs of air escaping past his lips. The events of the past hours, the injury, had taken a heavy toll on him. He remained undisturbed by her movements as she positioned his erection. She held her breath and in a single motion, slowly lowered her body onto his.

Trevor jerked awake and was instantly alert as Cassandra's warmth engulfed him, her muscles tightening around him. His breath hissed when she withdrew and impaled herself on his throbbing cock again, his moan mingled with hers as she ground her clit against his groin.

The feel of her skin against his, her juices coating the juncture of their bodies, was better than the erotic dream he had been immersed in moments before. In his dream, her fingers were wrapped around his cock, the movement of her hand sliding up and down along his length, driving him mad. A dream so vivid, it had caused his cock to grow hard and a heavy ache in his balls. Reality was so much richer.

Trevor's heart seized in his chest when his eyes locked with hers and he saw the swirl of emotion in them. "Cassie—" his voice broke with huskiness as he brushed his hand in a soft caress from her thigh to her curvy hip.

She arched her body against his and moaned softly, "I needed you, Trevor."

The emotions reflected in her eyes matched those constricting around his chest. He needed her more. "*A bhean,*" he whispered. A soft smile curved Cassandra's lips at his words as she pressed against him. Her movements were slow, controlled, seeking both his and her pleasure without causing him more pain. His cock, clutched deep inside her, twitched and pulsed in response. Undulating her body, Cassandra kept a slow, sensual pace, lifting with her knees and slowly easing down again and again on him.

His good hand gripped at her hip and his heels dug into the mattress each time she withdrew and lowered her body. Trevor thought he had died and gone to heaven when her taut nipples grazed his chest as she leaned over him until her lips hovered above his.

"Shite, Cassie! I've missed you. This!" he whispered harshly, raising his head, closing the gap between them, and sealing his mouth to hers. Supporting her weight on her hands, she teased, scraped his lips with her teeth. Her beautiful thick hair fell around him in a rippling curtain as she nipped at his lips and licked along their seam before plunging her tongue deep inside.

Trevor fisted her hair as he angled his head, taking control and intensifying the kiss, mimicking the action of their bodies with his tongue, sliding and dancing with hers. She continued to move her hips, alternating between shallow and deep penetrations. A groan rumbled deep in his chest with each skin-to-skin, groin-to-groin contact, with each circling of her hips and grinding motion. He mimicked her movement and pushed his hips off the bed, thrusting deeper into her. A moan escaped her mouth and rolled into his. Breaking from the kiss, her hair cascaded down her back as she arched her graceful body and rested her hands on his thighs, exposing her round breasts to him.

The raw love etched on her face was too much to withstand. He swallowed the pain and, supporting himself on his good arm, covered her breast with his mouth, laving, sucking, licking her engorged nipple, then repeated the same on the other as she cupped them in offering to him.

"Jeezus, Trevor! I've missed you, too! This...us!" Her breath hitched and her walls squeezed him tightly.

He knew the signs. She was close—so very close to the edge. Easing back to the bed, he clenched his teeth when his balls tightened and he prayed he could hold on. "God, Cassie girl!" he whispered.

Trevor brushed her clit with his thumb, triggering a flood of moisture from her. A shiver of anticipation shook her when his thumb caressed her a second time, and then again and again, playing her like a tightly strung guitar. Quicker and quicker, in a circular motion, he rubbed her throbbing clit and she rocked hard against him, her thighs tightening as the first wave of an orgasm swept over her.

Cassandra's nails dug deep into Trevor's thighs with the first release. Her entire body shuddered and stiffened. *"Trevor!"* she cried out as wave after wave continued to tumble over her. Trevor was relentless, each flick of his thumb sending little jolts of electricity through her. With a sob she took hold of his thumb and squeezed it as she rode him to the edge, pulsing around him, gripping him deep within.

Trevor's body began to tremble and he groaned in a ragged breath, *"A ghrá!"*

"Trevor, now!" she cried out again, feeling a second wave reaching for her. "With me!" she rasped, reaching back to roll his balls between her fingers.

Pleasure burned through him like hot lava, firing his senses, licking the edges of his perception, and making him numb to anything but the woman above him. He buried the worries about what was to happen in the near future and let go, giving himself to her. *"I'm coming!"* he yelled, exploding in a powerful release, pumping in spurts deep inside her as the strong contractions of her own release rippled and clamped around his shaft. Their moans mingled in the silence of the room, creating a sensual song to their lovemaking.

With one last sweet, slow exhale of breath, Cassandra collapsed on top of him. Chests heaving, they lay spent, until, slowly, the frantic breathing eased and their galloping hearts synched into a normal rhythm.

All of Trevor's thoughts centered on Cassandra's limp body and the loving care she had taken, how she made him feel. Brushing her hair from her face, he placed a soft kiss on her forehead. He knew words weren't needed, but he still wanted her to hear them. His fingers tenderly traced the line of her cheekbone and curved under her chin, lifting her face to him. Snaring her gaze, he whispered, "I love you, Cassandra Cristina Brennan. I have since the day you crowded my desk." She smiled sweetly and covered his hand with hers, pressing his palm to her cheek.

Suddenly, her eyes grew wide. "Oh, my god. Am I hurting you? Damn, you must feel like a beached whale landed on you!" She tried to move, but Trevor quickly wrapped his arm around her, pinning her against him, and burst out laughing.

"Shite, Cassie! Don't make me laugh! That hurts like hell!"

"I told you!" Her voice held a degree of concern and she tried to move away again.

He tightened his hold. "Nope. I meant laughing hurt. Not having you ravish me. That was all good love...better than good."

"Note to self: making love after being shot in the shoulder doesn't hurt, but laughing does." She opened in a wide smile and relaxed against him. "It's a good thing that only laughing hurts, because you won't be doing much of that where you're going."

"And where might that be?" Trevor raised an eyebrow.

Cassandra grinned. "While you were out sightseeing we received the confirmation from boot camp."

"Ah, no. No way in hell. I just earned a get-out-of-jail-free card on that one after what I've been through. Think dogs, walls, and Sergei. Oh, my."

A soft chuckle rumbled against his chest. "I'll have to think about it," she muttered sleepily.

"You better," he sighed contently.

★ ★ ★ ★ ★

Nathan's eyes popped open at the same time his hand snapped for his gun. He rolled to his back, gripping it in both hands. Jerked awake by a noise he couldn't quite pinpoint, his senses were on high alert as he sat up. Rising from the couch, he moved carefully around the house, trying to identify what had disturbed his sleep, checking for anything out of the ordinary.

On his way down the hall, he paused at Cassandra's room. It only took him a matter of seconds to register what had woken him—her soft voice and the Irishman's heavier one moaning and murmuring to each other.

Nathan's heart stuttered to a stop and the blood rushed from his head. Fuck! Shifting his weight to the balls of his feet, he backed away from the door, seeking escape. His eyes locked on the kitchen back door and, without hesitation, he walked swiftly down the hall. Reaching the door, Nathan quickly disabled the security system and stormed out into the night.

Pacing within the shadows of the tree line, Nathan rubbed his face with his hands and ran his fingers through his hair in agitation. The reality of what he witnessed between the two earlier should have prepared him for what he had just overheard. But it hadn't. *No fucking way I'm going back in there.* "Freakin' rabbits," he grumbled.

Chapter Fifty

Valkyrie

IT HADN'T TAKEN NIKOL LONG to find out who had helped Dmitriy and Ivanov. The market had been packed with vendors who had witnessed their escape and who knew the couple with whom they had left. A little persuasion—Nikol-style—worked wonders, especially when they had been exposed to what she could do in the form of the body sprawled on the ground. Armed with the location of the farm where the couple lived, she had planned to jump into Sergei's car and head out in pursuit, but the police, already on high alert due to the earlier conflict, had responded faster than expected and had pounced on her.

She had been dragged to the closest police station and, once they had verified her credentials, Nikol had been turned over to her own department. Back in the hands of Colonel General Olegovich and the usual inquisition squad, she had sat unconcerned through the same bullshit bureaucracy she experienced each time she entered the building. Long hours spent defending her position and covering her ass. Long hours spent justifying her actions against a long list of transgressions, including the killing of Sergei in the market—a clear-cut case of self-defense.

Nikol's reports had been flawless but for one thing: she had omitted the real reason they had been at the market—the very personal reason why she had accepted the mission in the first place. Nikol had also omitted that once she left the station, she would be chasing after information that could help her and her family find closure. She would eliminate the cause of so much pain, a pain that had haunted them, had burned in her chest and mind for many years. As soon as they had given her the green light to leave, she had jumped in her car and headed toward her goal.

By the time Nikol cut the lights and rolled to a stop outside the old di-lapidated farmhouse, it was close to three in the morning. She drew her HK, keeping it at her side as she approached and knocked on the door.

The front light sputtered, flooding the porch in a muted glow. A sur-prised and sleepy old man opened the door. "Can I help you?"

"I am looking for two men and a woman. I think you can help me."

The man inched the door closed and looked out over her shoulder. "There is only me and my wife."

Nikol glanced at the outside of the house. It had seen better days. Rag-ged floral curtains covered the front windows and time had inflicted clear damage on the property. She gazed into the eyes of the old man and stuck out her hand. "My name is Nikol Petrovna." She caught the flash of rec-ognition that briefly lit his eyes. "I see you have heard of me."

The old man crossed his arms defensively. "I do not know of these people you ask for."

Nikol nodded in the direction of the old Lada. "That is your car, no? Your name is Yakov. Your wife, Zoya. Yes?" The man hesitated, but nodded affirmatively. "You were seen leaving the market with the people I am looking for stowed in your car."

Fear crept into his eyes. "They are not here—and even if they were, why would I tell you?" He glanced at the gun in her hand, swallowed deeply, and took a step away from her. "You will kill them, kill us all."

Nikol holstered her gun and dropped her hands to her side, palms open. "Yakov, if I had wanted them dead, they would have died earlier today at the market. I just want to talk to them. They have information that could help me."

Yakov stared hard at her as if trying to get in her head. Finally, he gave a curt nod and pulled the door open. "Come in."

Nikol breathed a sigh of relief and followed him. The inside of the house showed almost as much wear as the outside. The faded, chipped paint of the walls, the un-matched chairs arranged by the fire, the hand-stitched pillows sitting on their seats were a statement of the couple's impoverished state. The room was homey and clean. No dust collected on the little statues of farm animals or traditional Russian dolls peppering the surfaces.

An older woman approached them, wringing her hands nervously. Yakov draped his arm around her shoulder and kissed her temple. "Zoya. This is Nikol. Nikol Petrovna." Zoya's eyes widened and she glanced sharply at her husband. "She is here to talk with our guests."

"But Yakov—" Panic screamed in her words.

Dmitry came into view with the woman she recognized from the mansion, her hand tightly clasped in his. "It is fine, Zoya."

"Dmitriy." Nikol nodded in greeting.

"Petrovna." He nodded back, a questioning look in his eyes. "Sergei?" The woman with Dmitriy gasped and edged closer to him.

"Dead." Nikol's voice was firm, without inflection. She looked over his shoulder. "Where is Ivanov?"

"He's not here." Dmitry stood with his legs apart, as if bracing for her to make a move.

"I know you were your uncle's IT guy. The servers were wiped clean during the chaos. Do you have a copy of the data?"

Dmitriy frowned. A confused expression shadowed his face as if he was struggling to understand the reason for her questions. His voice wavered. "There are no copies. Ivanov destroyed everything."

"Ivanov? Did he make a copy of anything?"

"I do not know. When I got back to the room he had already initiated the process."

"Got back? You left him alone?" Ivanov had proved he was more than just a developer, not to be underestimated. Nikol couldn't help but wonder if he was in league with Kostas. If he was, why hadn't Kostas come to his aid when everything went to hell?

A red flush spread across Dmitriy's cheeks. "Yes." Understanding suddenly crept into his eyes.

"I need to find him. Do you know where he is?"

"Why should I tell you?" Defiance colored his voice.

"The data is a critical piece of evidence. It will help seal the fate of some very bad people."

His eyes widened. "Evidence? So you are...."

"Gang Squad. St. Petersburg Central Internal Affairs Directorate." She watched his eyes grow even wider. "So as you can see, I do not wish to hurt him. I proved that, have I not? I helped you both before. Saved you from Sergei."

Indecision warred in Dmitriy's eyes as he turned to look down into the woman's at his side. She shook her head and he flashed her a brief smile. Turning back to Nikol, he sighed. "He mentioned Vyborg. That is all we know."

Yakov spoke up. "I dropped him off in town. He planned to catch the train."

An overwhelming rush of excitement filled Nikol. "Thank you." She turned on her heel and headed out the door. Success was a sweet taste on her tongue. Soon she would have everything for which she had worked so hard.

★ ★ ★ ★ ★

Nathan watched dawn's fingers creep across the black-blue starry night and cursed under his breath. He hadn't been able to find a comfortable position or catch any shuteye outside. Sitting under the thick cover of the trees on the north side of the property, the echo of Cassandra's voice mingled with that of the Blarney Stone resounded repeatedly in his head. What bothered him most was that the damn Irishman was growing on him. Observing Bauer's tender eyes and the respect he held for Cassandra shamed Nathan. How he had ever mistaken her calm demeanor for help-lessness was beyond him.

Who am I kidding? Nathan had created an image of her in his mind, one molded to his expectations—a woman to be protected, and dependent on him for that protection. Nathan shook his head. Definitely not the Cassandra he had found in the house that night.

Giving up on finding a soft spot on the hard ground, he stood and stretched the cramped muscles of his shoulders. He leaned back against the rough bark of a tree trunk, debating on whether to bite the bullet and head back inside in search of a more comfortable accommodation, hope-fully a padded one. The sound of crunching tires along the road reached his ears and Nathan tilted his head. *What the hell?*

Adrenaline pumped into his blood. His mind shifted gears. Nathan drew his gun and ducked to the ground. Squatting behind the bushes, he eyed the entrance to the property. The safe house had been specifically chosen for its remoteness and access route, one way in and out. The car creeping up the drive was not there by accident.

Nathan watched as the vehicle turned into the unpaved driveway. He tracked the progress of the dark sedan from the shadows as it purred its way around the side, toward the back. The driver pulled to a stop and cut the engine just short of the house. Nathan stealthily shifted his position so he had a full view of the car. The driver sat motionless, head turned toward the house.

After a few minutes, the driver stepped out, shutting the door quietly. He walked casually toward the house, empty handed. Nathan moved along the tree line and kept the driver in his crosshairs, covering his approach to the back of the house. *Turn away, man. You don't want to go there.* Nathan watched closely as the man stepped up onto the porch and scrutinized the door.

Suddenly, the porch lit up and the door opened. Bauer stood on the threshold dressed only in jeans, the gauze and sling around his arm stark white in the glare of the harsh light. The two men studied each other and exchanged words, their voices too low to be overheard. Nathan stifled a curse when Bauer stepped aside and gestured for the man to enter. *Shit!* Nathan was pissed. Neither Cassandra nor Bauer had mentioned expecting visitors.

Nathan paced behind the trees, running a hand through his hair. He breathed in and looked up into the early morning sky, shaking his head. Those two lived dangerously. He watched the leaves on the trees flutter in the breeze and heard a rooster crow. Morning was fast approaching and exhaustion was pulling at him. With his temper under control, he turned back and stared at the house. There had to be a good reason for their unannounced guest to be there. Determined to find out what was going on, Nathan took a step toward the edge of the tree line.

The crunch of fallen twigs and the rustle of leaves jerked his attention to the opposite side of the property. Fading back into the bushes, Nathan crouched and watched the area. The sounds were spaced, soft snaps and scrapes at intervals. In the dim morning light, Nathan caught sight of a hunched-over figure darting across the yard to the parked sedan. The new visitor tested the handle and opened the passenger side. He gripped his SIG firmly as the figure slipped into the tree line, moving toward Nathan's position as he edged around to the back of the house following the same path the earlier visitor had taken. Assuming it might be another unannounced guest, Nathan eased closer to the edge of the property and waited. If the intruder wasn't a friendly, it would suit him just fine. He was itching for an outlet to relieve his pent-up frustration.

His jaw clenched and his shoulder muscles tightened when the figure moved only a few yards in front of him and the snap of the cocking of a gun pierced the air. That sound changed everything. While the first guest had been unarmed and looked like he was there for a casual visit, this one was geared for a first-person shooter game. Nathan had found his outlet.

Fate must have been on Nikol's side. She had been scouring the streets, stalking known informant hidey-holes and questioning people about newly arrived faces in Vyborg. Summer was a busy season in the well-visited town. Tourists came and went and nobody really cared about one new face. She had been about to give up for the night when, by chance, she had caught sight of the familiar sedan driving past her on the street. She had pulled out behind it and followed it covertly out of town to the remote house.

Parking her car in the woods, she prowled in the cover of the trees and through the property to the sedan parked on the side of the house. A quick check confirmed that he was indeed in there.

Nikol sat on her haunches watching the back door. A slash of light lit up the window when someone peeked outside. She could almost hear the loud thumps of her heart in her chest. She could taste triumph. Excitement was a drug running free in her veins. Everything she needed to exact revenge once and for all was inside that house.

A chill curved its way along her spine and she snapped her head around, searching the dark woods behind her. She could have sworn she was being watched. *Focus, Nikol. The bastard is dead. Not waiting around to jump you.* She turned her attention back to the door. *Now or never.* She stood and cocked her HK. She sucked in and exhaled a deep breath as she left the shelter of the trees, running for the back of the house.

With a muttered curse, Nathan bolted from his cover, his gait stealthy and his gun clenched tightly in his hand as he ran all-out after the shadowy figure. He hit the porch at a leap and body-slammed the target into the house, pressing his forearm across the intruder's neck. A loud breathless grunt burst from the intruder and the heavy gun slipped from his hand, falling with a loud thunk to the porch.

The man of slight build and some five inches shorter than him kicked back, slamming the heel of his boot into Nathan's knee. Simultaneously, he twisted his body, throwing his elbow with a sharp jab, snapping Nathan's head back and dropping him to his knees. Nathan hissed as pain radiated from his knee and merged with the throbbing pain at his temple.

Before he could catch his breath, a sharp blow hit the center of his chest and a yell spilled out as he sailed through the air off the porch, landing on his back with a loud thud, the impact popping his gun from his hand.

Stars spun in front of his eyes and nausea overtook him as he rolled to his side and rested on his elbow, sucking long drags of air into his constricted lungs. *Fuck!* Before he could take a second breath, the intruder, with catlike grace, jumped from the porch and kicked him a second time. Pain amplified in the middle of his chest as he fell to the ground. The imprint of his boot throbbed like a newly inked tattoo on his chest. Nathan growled in fury as he rolled to his knees and glanced up.

He had expected to see the face of a hardened criminal, but found instead the bruised face of an angel filled with the fury of the hounds of hell. His heart lurched and the shock of the vision in front of him left him dumbstruck. Before he could come to his senses, she backhanded him, knocking him sideways to the ground. Nathan groaned and wiped the blood from his mouth with the back of his hand, the coppery tang burning his tongue. While attempting to stand again, he ducked and missed the right hook aimed at his head, but he was too slow to avoid the toe of her boot. It snapped in a swift kick, catching him under the jaw and sending him flying backwards. His last thought as his eyes rolled into the back of his head and his body dropped like a log to the ground was, *Fucking Valkyrie.*

Chapter Fifty-One

Revelations

NIKOL STOOD OVER THE SPRAWLED body of her attacker, heaving with the exertion of the fight. In the soft light of dawn, she studied the man's angular face, his aquiline nose, the well-defined lips, the cleft chin, and short haircut. She hadn't been able to register the color of his eyes but, by his coloring, she assumed they were light. It was an attractive but unfamiliar face. Nobody she had seen in the mansion or among the many mug shots she had memorized. She committed his face to memory. The bastard was now another on her watch list.

The door flung open. "What the hell!" A woman's curse filled the air and Nikol spun to find the dark muzzle of a pistol aimed at her forehead. The woman was barefoot and dressed in a button-down shirt, her dark hair a rumpled halo spilling around her shoulders. As the woman stepped closer to the edge of the porch, Nikol's eyes darted to her Heckler & Koch lying by the door.

"Nuh uh...I wouldn't if I were you," the woman warned in English, a language Nikol understood well, as she stepped back and eased to a squat to retrieve the gun. Standing, she aimed both at Nikol.

"Cassandra!" Ivanov stormed up behind the woman and Kostas spilled out behind them. Ivanov pulled up short when he saw her. "You! How did you get here? Dmitriy! You better not have touched him." The Russian words rolled smoothly off his tongue.

"Ivano—" She barely registered the growl which sounded behind her before a heavy crushing weight crashed into her back, dropping her face first to the wet grass. Her lungs labored in her chest and burned from the effort to breathe under the pressure of the tank sitting on top of her, pinning her. A low, deep voice snarled against her ear, "You're going to pay for that."

"Fuck, Nathan! What the hell are you doing?!" the woman Ivanov called Cassandra yelled at the monkey on her back. Her voice brimmed with concern and smoldering anger. Nikol felt a large strong hand tighten on her shoulder. "Back off, Nate! I have her covered!" Cassandra's voice was low and hard.

Nikol gritted her teeth and bit back a groan when a hand fisted her ponytail and the back of her jacket, jerking her to her feet. A cry spilled from her lips when the man pushed her from behind and her knees collapsed against the hard edges of the porch steps.

Fury was a tight ball sitting in her chest. She hissed as she turned her head and spat at him, "You are going to pay for that." The man's light grassy-green eyes turned to stone and his hand balled into a fist at his side. Nikol raised her chin defiantly.

"Let her stand, Nelson," Ivanov's voice ordered. She glanced up to see both him and Cassandra with their guns trained on her.

With a backward glance, she pushed to her feet and eyed them warily. She watched as Ivanov tucked his gun at his waistband and rested his hand possessively at the woman's lower back. Cassandra gestured at her with the flick of Nikol's own HK muzzle. "Let's take the party inside."

As Nathan followed the group to the living room, his eyes touched on the ponytail swinging back and forth ahead of him and anger simmered hot—anger directed at the woman who had just handed him his ass on a platter. Nathan cracked his jaw. It still ached and his head still spun from the beating she so effortlessly delivered.

His eyes followed the lines of her long, lean athletic figure; he found himself admiring how she had handled herself. Her legs encased in dark jeans went for miles, ending with a tight curvy ass. Nathan shook his head and tried to gather his scattered wits. He wanted answers now. *Who is the man? Who the hell is the Valkyrie? And why is it that everybody seems to know each other?* "What the fuck is going on here?" Nathan's voice, clipped and flippant, reflected his frustration. "Who the hell are these people?"

The older man stood to the side, his stance relaxed, eyes studying everything, mostly glued to the harpy.

"That's Boris," Cassandra answered with a narrowed look at the man.

"Boris who?"

"Well, now that is the question of the day. Who exactly are you Mr. Boris Kostas? Care to explain to us why I shouldn't just shoot you where you stand for putting our lives in danger?"

"Cassandra...I do need to apologize for not telling you what you were getting into, but it was for the greater good," Boris said sheepishly.

"Can someone explain in plain English what the fuck is going on?" Nathan growled.

Bauer joined him. "Ditto."

The woman's lips pressed into a thin line and her eyes narrowed on the man they were all scrutinizing. Nathan had seen the hatred in her eyes when she had directed it at him, but the look she was throwing at Boris defined the phrase "if looks could kill."

He was pulled from his musings by Cassandra's icy-cold voice. "I'd love

to know what the fuck is going on, too. As for who Boris is, let me introduce you. Meet Special Agent Boris Kostas of the Federal Security Service
of the Russian Federation."

All heads snapped back to Boris and they all wore similar curious, confused expressions.

Nathan burst out, "Jeezus, Cass. How did you two get involved with an
FSB agent, and why is he here?"

Trevor frowned and fought to grasp the implications of what was unfold-
ing in front of him, specifically the look of shock that had briefly fluttered across Petrovna's face on finding out that little detail. "Hold on a
second! Cassie, when and how the hell did you find that out?"

Cassandra shot him a quick glance. "George dropped that little bomb
right before all hell broke loose. When Jessie and I both came up empty,
I asked for his help. I don't have all the pieces yet. I know he's FSB, but
that's about it." She paused and studied Boris's frowning face. "It took
George a few days of digging. And you know George. If the info was
easily available, he would have found it in no time flat. This was buried
deeper than Jimmy Hoffa."

Trevor snorted at her reference. "And why would that be?" Trevor continued to scrutinize Boris. His face displayed surprise. *Interesting.* Almost as
if he hadn't expected anyone would be able to uncover any information
on him at all. But then, he probably had never encountered anyone like
George before either. The man was one of a kind, his tenacity even made
Trevor break out in a sweat.

Trevor's attention slid to Petrovna and Nelson. Animosity pulsed in a
thick wave between them. Petrovna sat in the corner of the couch with an
arm resting casually on the armrest, the clenching and unclenching of her
fist signaling her agitation as she glared sourly at Nelson. His expression
was a mirror image of hers as he kept his gun trained on her. The two
looked worse for wear, as if they had been put through a meat grinder.
Petrovna's gaze darted to Boris and hatred flared brighter. Boris himself
stood near the hall entry, out of harm's way, observing the two with a
puzzled look in his face.

Trevor almost laughed at the entire comical scene. Five people stuck in a house in the middle of nowhere, ready to do one or more of each other harm. He eased himself next to Cassandra on the couch and got the party started. "Let's start at the beginning, why don't we? Boris, why didn't you tell us about your associations? You would have gotten our full cooperation from day one if you had been up front."

Trevor's question dusted off memories of the days and emotions Boris had dealt with over the years. The many good things that he had forfeited for the sake of a job. A job that he believed was helping to improve his fellow countryman's lives. "To be honest, I never expected I would need to tell you anything. I have been living undercover for a very long time." Out of the corner of his eye he saw the woman's head snap up, a deep crease furrowed her brow and disbelief clouded her narrowed eyes.

"Maybe far too long." To give himself time to gather his thoughts, Boris took the chair across from them and addressed Cassandra. "It was shortly after I met your father. A KGB officer offered me a position after my performance during the 1980 Summer Olympics in Moscow and the US-Soviet peace talks in the mid-80's. At the time, I saw no wrong in doing so. I was young, had no family, not many friends, and was dedicated to the service. My introduction to the organized crime unit was under total secrecy. No one was to know I worked for the KGB; otherwise, I would be of no use to the agency."

Boris paused just long enough to catch his breath. "With the change of times, the collapse of the Soviet Estate, and dissolution of the KGB, my role was carried over to its successor organization, the FSK, and subsequently to the FSB. That is why even though Robert was a very dear friend of mine, I was unable to tell him about my new position or activities. I left the army under the guise of joining the police force to assume the façade of a corrupt officer. An easy assignment really, since corruption within the police is commonplace."

Nikol sat as if turned to stone. Her eyes never left Boris's face. She listened intently to his words and tried to make sense of the facts as he laid them out. Questions droned in her head. Everything that she had grown up believing, everything she had focused on her entire life, had been unraveled in just a single minute. She struggled to hold on to the cold mask covering her emotions—the surprise and shock stemming from Boris's revelations.

Boris sighed deeply, drawing Nikol back from her internal struggle. "It is a sad reality when the population trusts more the mob than they do the police. During the time I was in the police force, I ran guns, passed on information, and cultivated a reputation—all legwork in preparation for the new role ahead of me: taking down the largest gang in St. Petersburg."

"Zarev's?" Trevor interrupted, and Boris nodded. "How did you become involved with Mikhailov's instead?"

"By chance." Boris found himself reliving that memory. Tumbling once again in the turbulence that had bled from Mikhailov's eyes that fateful day. "Mikhailov's wife was murdered by a minor gang in retaliation for some wrongdoing committed by his men. He sought me out. He had heard about my access to the investigation reports and wanted information." He closed his eyes and squeezed them tight to push that memory away.

"You flipped her killers. You gave him their names," the woman said.

The intonations of that voice sent him spinning into another memory, the memory of someone who haunted his dreams each night. His eyes snapped open and his brow wrinkled with his contemptuous thoughts. He studied the woman and tried to understand the niggling that had pierced him each time he had seen her. Hearing her voice for the first time played with the edges of his perception, evading his efforts to pinpoint what it was about her that was so familiar to him.

"Yes. It haunts me to this day, but it was something that, at the time, I just viewed as poetic justice. They had killed an innocent woman. It was only fair that they were punished for that. With the information in hand, Vladimir delivered his justice swiftly. The men were never found, but we all knew they were no longer among the living. The gang in question disappeared from the mafia scene shortly after."

Cassandra leaned forward. "Why us? Why did you use us to get the files? If what you say is true, you were in, friends at that point. Why not try to secure them yourself?"

"Vladimir is a very cautious man, even more so after his wife was killed. He doesn't engage in lasting personal involvements, so we couldn't bribe a lover to get the files for us. Although I have had a close association with him for years, he never allowed me into his inner circle until recently, and I never had access to his data storage. Your arrival was heaven-sent. I couldn't ignore the fact that you were my ticket to those files."

"How do you plan to use them?" Trevor quirked his eyebrow questioningly.

Boris's eyes widened. "So you did manage to get the files out." A profound relief invaded him. That information released all the tension he'd been bottling inside and he slumped in his chair. "I was not sure. I have to admit, I was surprised to see you here. Mikhailov's men ambushed my house last night. I was certain you had been caught and squeezed for details. I did not quite expect you to have managed to retrieve the files, especially after I received the call from Cassandra telling me—" he scoffed, "—ordering me, to come here."

"Oh…make no mistake, if Trevor hadn't made it out you would not be sitting so comfortably," Cassandra snipped. "We have the data. But you're not getting it until you answer Trevor's question."

Boris measured her with a cool, appraising look as he considered how much to divulge of his activities. Trevor's stay in the mansion had given him quite a lot of the insight already. Whatever Boris said would only fill in the gaps. "It's the last piece of information I need to bring down both gangs. I have acquired a significant volume of sensitive information through our Signals Analysis Department during the many years I have been undercover, but we discovered that Vladimir was apparently involved in seeding some of the incriminating information regarding Zarev's operation to the police, trying to flip him, possibly hoping we would take Zarev down for him, paving the way for his own organization to move in and take over. We cannot allow that. Vladimir is a smart man. His organization has grown in strength and reputation. If we only take out Zarev's gang we will have a bigger problem on our hands. We want both. But we need to have all our ducks in a row, as you say, before we can sweep in and close down their operations."

"Okay, I get that we were an opportunity you couldn't pass up. But now what? If Mikhailov is as smart as you say, he must have connected the dots and will be gunning for all of you," Cassandra reasoned.

"You better add Dmitriy into the mix," Trevor quipped. "He can't go back to St. Petersburg either."

"My superior is just waiting for me to give the green light to proceed with the arrests. I need to have the files to justify them, otherwise they will just find their way out again."

"Fine, as long as that guarantees our exit from the country unharmed," Trevor demanded.

"But of course! Once they are all behind bars, we will make sure he and his associates stay there for a long time. A great number of gang members from both organizations are already under arrest thanks to the little war that took place yesterday."

"Do not trust him." All eyes swung in the woman's direction.

Cocking his head, Boris studied her a moment. "What about you? I do not think you are who you pretend to be. Federal Service? Undercover?"

"Yes. St. Petersburg Central Internal Affairs Directorate," she responded matter-of-factly with a hostile glare.

"What is your directive?"

She raised an eyebrow and her condescending smile was slow and deliberate. "Apparently my directive was to facilitate your directive. I was recruited to infiltrate Mikhailov's gang to retrieve the data you could not get your hands on." Her voice held a heavy dose of sarcasm.

"Bastards!" Boris burst in rage. "They never trusted my methods."

"Nobody trusted your methods. They are filthy," she spat at him.

The rest of the people in the room faded to the background as Boris's full attention focused on the officer lurking in the corner of the couch, her contempt beating at him. "Why would you say such a thing? We have never crossed paths before now."

The hatred in her eyes was back in full force at his words. "I have to say, you covered your tracks well. You are almost one of them. How you could turn your back on your family for a job is beyond imaginable. Family should be number one in anybody's life. Blood ties matter."

"What are you talking about?"

"You. Your loyalty to the service when you had no loyalty to your own wife."

Boris's breath hitched as his wife's image flashed in his mind. "Alina." The name spilled from his lips in a reverent whisper.

"Yes. Alina."

Boris was confused. That part of his life had been buried long ago. Very few people were even left that remembered he was married. "How do you know this?"

Nikol's eyes narrowed to slits. "I know this is true because Alina Petrovna…is my mother."

"No! It cannot be." Boris jumped to his feet and began to pace. His pulse raged in his ears and he couldn't rationalize the news. When Alina had left, as far as he knew, she had not been carrying his child. He stopped abruptly in front of the young woman claiming to be Alina's daughter and studied her. The tilt of her head as she glared back at him, almost daring him to deny her words; the dark brown hair, the curve of her defiant chin. *Alina.* The last telling sign—even as he recognized he still couldn't accept—her eyes. The spitting image of his own mother's. He shook his head.

"It *is* the truth."

"She hid you from me. Why?"

"What did you expect? She thought you were a gang member. She thought you a thief and a criminal. You should have told her."

"And what? Involve her in the chaos? Have her end up like Mikhailov's wife? When she left, my heart was broken, but I knew she was better off. Would be safe. I never expected her to hide our child from me."

"Do not call me yours." Nikol's voice simmered low. "I am *not* your daughter. You are not my father. I hated you for what you did to my mother. For being nothing more than a criminal." Boris paled. "You have been my personal target for many years. You are the reason I ended up in undercover operations with the gang squad. I was hoping for evidence to bring you down. Searching for the same files I was ironically assigned to steal for you. I wanted you to pay." She continued with a staid calmness, "I would just as happily put a bullet in your head, but that would break my mother's heart. For some reason I cannot understand, she still cares about you."

Boris's heart shattered. All those years. Those wasted years. To hear that she still cared. "Alina. Where is she?"

"You will have to earn that information, *Papa*," Nikol sneered. Disgust dripped from her lips.

Silence descended on the room. He glanced toward the blond man referred to as Nathan Nelson and was relieved to see he had holstered his gun. A glint of camaraderie flashed in his eyes as Nelson held his gaze. Boris saw sympathy radiating from Cassandra's eyes and cool assessment in Trevor's. Boris scrubbed his face with his hands and rubbed his tired eyes as he took his seat again.

Nikol, his daughter, couldn't stand the sight of him, and from the hatred and repugnance that sparkled in her eyes, he would have no luck convincing her to give him a chance to prove himself to her. He needed time to think, time to regroup. Time to locate his wife. Alina, after all these years, still cared. That changed everything. With a deep, weary sigh, Boris looked Trevor in the eye. "I've answered your question. The files?"

Nikol kept her eyes trained on Cassandra while the woman walked to one of the duffel bags near the door and returned with an external hard drive, which she placed on the table. Back at the couch, she nodded to it. "It's all here."

Boris turned the drive over in his hands almost as if he couldn't quite believe he had it. A satisfied smile curved his lips. "Thank you, Trevor."

Trevor, which she now knew to be his true name, shrugged. "I wish I could say it was my pleasure."

"I thank you just the same." Boris stood. "I need to get back to St. Petersburg so we can shut them down. Cassie," he nodded to her and then turned to look directly at Nikol. Her heart stuttered in her chest. Here was the man that had haunted her dreams. Dreams of a family. Dreams of a father's guiding hand. Dream of a mother's smiling face. Nikol witnessed the play of emotions across his features—indecision, hope, sadness—and hardened her heart. The unexpected turn of events had derailed all of her. She had a goal, she had a purpose before. Her dreams of vengeance deflated like a popped balloon. Once she was alone, she would pull everything out and explore her options.

Boris must have seen the finality of the decision in her eyes because he immediately turned on his heel and, as he headed for the kitchen, called over his shoulder to Trevor, "I will contact you as soon as everything is clear."

The sound of the door slamming behind him brought with it a new uncomfortable silence. Nikol knew that she should leave too, but could not find the energy to move. It didn't help that the man, Nelson, continued to stare in her direction.

Trevor broke the silence. "Well that was fun."

"About as much fun as a root canal," Cassandra grimaced.

"Nikol?"

"Yes?" Nikol responded to Trevor's questioning tone.

"I have to ask. Dmitriy and Tatiana?"

"They are still where you left them at the farm. They are safe for the moment. But I would recommend moving them out of there as soon as possible. I was able to track them. Others might, too."

Trevor stood and held out his hand to Cassandra. "We'll do that in a few hours. We need to catch some shuteye. It's been a long couple of weeks. I am tired and sore." He turned his head to Nelson. "I would appreciate it if you could stay a little longer. I'd like to discuss something with you before you go."

When Nelson nodded his head affirmatively, Trevor led Cassandra to the hall. At the entry, Cassandra pulled up short and turned back to face Nikol. A small smile quirked the side of her mouth. "I just have to say this. Girl, you've got some mad moves. You knocked him out—" Cassandra stopped and chuckled when a growl sounded deep in Nelson's chest. "Anyway. Stay and regroup before you go."

Nikol couldn't hold back a little smirk at the memory of Nelson flying back through the air. "Thank you for the offer, but I cannot stay. I have to check in."

Cassandra nodded in understanding and joined Trevor, who wrapped his arm around her neck and led her away, laughing at something she whispered to him.

The minute the sound of the door closing at the end of the hall reached them, Nelson's brow pulled into an affronted frown. Nikol raised an eyebrow at the clear dislike displayed on his features.

He then stared directly into her eyes, his green gaze burning like the fires of hell, a tormented pissed-off look she knew all too well. She stared back and, as the minutes passed, each narrowed their eyes to slits, both determined to win the staring contest they'd started. She wasn't leaving until she was named the victor, even if that meant killing the son of a bitch in front of her.

Chapter Fifty-Two

Mistaken

T HE SATURDAY CROWD PACKED THE Brazen Head. The mouthwatering aroma of traditional Irish food coiled in the air, drawing passersby and regular patrons alike. Stephan's mood matched the sorrowful songs in the background. His favorite dish tasted like ash on his tongue.

He could still hear Jessica's parting words, "*...you know where to find us. But don't take too long, or I might be the one passing on the offer.*" He had reflected on the words every waking moment since. They had forced him to take a long hard look at himself and his desires. After some soul-searching, he had found his answer. Stephan had made peace with his past and knew what he had to do to fix the future.

Jessica's news gave him a second chance at life. He would accept that

child as his own. Marry Jessica and leave everything, including her association with Sean, behind them. If he didn't grab hold of the opportunity
Jessica had presented to him, he would lose not only her but a chance at
a life he had always wanted—a woman who loved him, a child to spoil,
the house with a white picket fence. He would deal with his trust issues
as they formed their life together, while he lived, breathed, and enjoyed
Jessica's company and a child he planned to call his own. It didn't matter
who the child's real father was, only that he sure as hell would be that
baby's dad. He would do everything in his power to make that happen.

Stephan stood and dropped a few notes on the table to cover his tab. A
smile formed on his lips and his step had a new spring to it as he walked
out into the fresh air. The walk home would clear his head and help him
focus. He would need all the courage he could muster to knock on her
door.

He shoved his hands in his pockets and, as he rounded the first corner,
almost ran into a family exiting a restaurant. The man had his arms full
carrying a younger child, and the woman coaxed another little girl tugging on her hand as they headed toward a parked car. The angle of the
woman's head and hand gestures as she spoke to the little tike stroked
his memory. His steps faltered and his brow furrowed as he chased the
elusive memory. Distracted, he stopped and cocked his head, observing
their progress.

At that moment, the woman looked up and their eyes collided. A broad
smile filled the woman's face and knocked the air from his lungs. She
detoured toward him with the little girl skipping at her heels. "Oh my
god! Stephan!"

"Layla." A strange cold sense of aloofness numbed his senses, a deep
shock at seeing her after so many years. Crossing paths with her so unexpectedly gave him pause.

She caught up with him, wrapped her arms around him, and dropped a
kiss on his cheek. "It's so good to see you. It's been years."

His arms automatically wrapped around her, then dropped to his sides as
she stepped back. "Ages." His voice shook more than he would have liked

as he looked down into the curious eyes of the little Asian girl attached to her hand.

"Layla?" Stephan's eyes flew to the man approaching them with the toddler cuddled in his arms.

Layla flashed the man a sunny smile. "John, this is an old friend of mine, Stephan. Stephan, this is my husband."

"Nice to meet you." John's warm tone spoke of his friendly nature.

Stephan accepted John's extended hand. "Likewise."

Layla must have seen the questioning look on his face as he gazed on the children because she responded immediately, "We were celebrating. John and I have just arrived from China. These are our new little daughters. We fell in love with them on our first visit to the orphanage there. We are blessed to have found the two sisters. The international adoption process was a grueling road, but now that they are here, we can finally be a family."

Stephan brushed the bangs from the little girl's forehead. "They're beautiful. Congratulations to you both."

"Layla, we'll wait for you at the car. It was nice meeting you, Stephan." John nodded his head and took the other little girl by the hand.

Layla smiled happily after them. A sad chuckle escaped Stephan and she turned back to him with a questioning gaze. "What a pair we are." He shook his head. "I seem to be attracted to women who want children, and you are attracted to men who can't give them to you."

Layla's expression turned to puzzlement. "What do you mean?"

"I mean, you had to adopt after all, even though all you have ever wanted was to grow big with your own. I bet you must have been disappointed to find out you had the same problem with John. Is there an epidemic in Ireland?" He chuckled again sarcastically. "Sorry, I guess I had a few too many pints."

Horror flooded Layla's eyes. A flush flashed across her cheeks as she shook her head and reached for his hand. "Oh my god, Stephan. You thought it was your fault? Oh, Stephan." The sympathy in her eyes and sadness coloring her voice sent his heart careening in his chest. "Stephan, I think you might have gotten things confused. It's always been me. I'm the one who can't conceive."

Stephan's world turned upside down at that moment. His ears rang and his legs turned to jelly. He stumbled and would have fallen on his face if Layla hadn't reached for his other arm, steadying him. "What do you mean?"

"I told you. Over the phone. I left you the note."

"No, the note said I couldn't give you what you wanted. I thought you meant…that I…that it was my fault you couldn't get—"

"No! Dear lord. No! I said you couldn't give me what I wanted because I believed you were only interested in a child of your own blood."

He squeezed his eyes shut and shook his head in denial. "No. You were what mattered most to me. I would have done anything to make you happy. Including taking the step you just now took with John."

"Stephan. Look at me." Stephan opened his eyes and she held his gaze. "I'm sorry my message wasn't clear. I never meant to hurt you. I just couldn't face the fact that you would see me differently. Expect things from me I couldn't give you. Want me to be someone I couldn't be. A mother to your biological children."

"I couldn't have cared less about blood ties. I wanted you to marry me, grow old with me. You were the one pushing for a child. I just wanted the commitment. With you. Then." His voice sounded stifled and unnatural even to his own ears.

She shook her head. "I. Am. So. Sorry. I was so hurt, so out of my head by the news I gave little thought to the rest. I buried myself in a hole of self-pity for a long time. Then, I met John. He made me feel alive again. He's the one who prompted me to consider adoption."

Stephan rubbed his eyes and sighed. "I am happy you finally got what you wanted, Layla. I truly am."

"How about you? Did you find your happily ever after you always talked about?"

A soft smile twitched the corner of his mouth. "You remember that, do you?" His smile faded as Jessica's image filled his mind. "Come to think of it, I actually have. But I might have just blown it with her. How do you ask someone for forgiveness after being an utter jackass?"

Layla laughed and smiled up at him. "By using those exact words."

A car's horn sounded in the distance and Layla briefly glanced over her shoulder. "The girls are probably antsy. I have to go." She pulled him into her arms and squeezed him tight. "It was really good seeing you again. Please keep in touch." She pulled a card from her purse and handed it to him. "Give me a call after you have managed to gain that forgiveness. I am sure that whoever she is, she's a special woman. I'd like to meet her someday."

"She is very special. And yes…I'd like that."

Stephan leaned down and kissed her cheek. "Goodbye, Layla."

"Goodbye, Stephan." She piled into the passenger seat of the car and waved as they drove away.

A cold tingling spread under his skin, his palms began to sweat, and his thoughts were a jumbled mess. All those years. His emotions were on a turbulent rollercoaster beginning with confusion, spiraling into anger, and flipping into jubilation. Jessica carried *his* child.

Exhilaration coursed through him. His soft chuckle grew into a quiet laugh and then into booming laughter. It grew even louder as passersby gave him strange looks. If only they knew. Once the frenzy of the emotions bubbling inside him died down, he could breathe again. It dawned on him that he wasn't bitter. He wasn't angry with Layla. Those mistaken words forged who he had become. A good friend to Conor and Maeve. A top executive. A guardian to Trevor. The man that Jessica loved. And yes, a father to be.

A big smile spread across his face as he changed directions and headed to

St. Stephen's Green in search of atonement and forgiveness. In search of the future he always dreamed of.

★ ★ ★ ★ ★

Jessica was tired of embracing the porcelain altar. It was one thing to pray to the god of food and drink after an evening of too many Cosmopolitans; another to spend the entire morning paying tribute at even the thought of the tiniest crumb. Having survived another bout of nausea, Jessica made one last attempt at a light lunch.

She shook her head and snorted when the Imperial March reverberated through the house. "Only Trevor." Leaving the kettle on, Jessica sauntered in her bare feet down to the foyer and across the cool smooth wooden floor to the door. There were already several packages upstairs waiting for Trevor. At that rate, she would be on a first-name basis with the couriers.

"Yes, I can sign…" she began as she opened the door. Her jaw dropped open when her eyes crashed into Stephan's. Lightheadedness overwhelmed her and she blinked several times. *Oh hell. You will not be sick. Don't you dare get sick.* "Stephan! What…" The memory of the day before swiftly crushed the hope fluttering in her stomach. His words had fractured a wide chasm in her ability to trust him. "Trevor isn't here. He and Cassie aren't back yet."

Her heart did a big cartwheel as his eyes roamed over her figure and darkened with emotion. His lips twitched. "That's why I couldn't find it." Blushing, she self-consciously adjusted the hem of the button-down shirt and shrugged.

"Can I come in?" His quiet effervescent tone gave her pause. At a loss for words, Jessica didn't want to hear any more of his absurd accusations. A piercing pain found its way through her heart again, the same pain she'd experienced the day before when he had cut her to pieces with his harsh words. It hurt that he had so easily believed her a manipulative liar. Stephan should have known better.

"Jessica?" The rich timbre of his voice cut through her jumbled reflections.

She raised her chin with a cool stare. "I'm not sure this is a good idea."

She pushed the door closed but he blocked it with his foot.

"Jessica…please. Hear me out. I have a lot to say."

"I don't want to hear what you have to say right now."

He moved closer to the door and held her gaze. "I reckon I'm an idiot. You have every right to tell me to piss off. But you have to hear me out." His eyes darted to her tummy. "Please? For the sake of our child?"

"There is no *our* child. You said it yourself. You said I…that I…." Jessica shook her head and pushed the door again.

"No!" Stephan held the door open. "Please, Jessica. Give me a chance to explain."

His eyes clung to hers and she found herself drowning in the longing and tenderness spilling from their depth.

"Jessica…." Without a word, she shook her head.

Stephan's shoulders slumped and the light fled from his eyes. He turned his back and, with unsteady fingers, scrubbed through his hair before he turned again to face her. A new determination filled his eyes.

"I'm not running away from us anymore, Jessica. The few times I did only brought on more hurt. I'm staying put until you hear me out. I'll camp on this doorstep if I have to. As you said, you may be the one declining the offer. But at least let me put it on the table." He cast one last imploring look at her.

Jessica closed the door and sagged back against it. Her heart raced and her head spun. She couldn't let him go without knowing what he wanted. With a huff, she jerked the door open and almost ran into him.

He stood at the door waiting for her, his arms folded across his chest and a muscle quivering at his jaw. *Stubborn man.* She opened the door wider and he stepped through.

"Upstairs?" His eyes carried a strong resolve as he waited for her answer.

When she nodded, Stephan gestured her to precede him. As she walked up the stairs, she had a sensation of floating, as if all the heartache she had been carrying had fallen from her shoulders. Her stomach rolled and she pressed a hand against it.

At the top, she hesitated and then led the way to the living room. The curtains framing the front windows fluttered as a soft breeze flowed across the sill and into the room, tickling her skin. The smell of cut grass, fabric warmed by sunshine, and the laughter of Dubliners walking the street eased her nerves. The hiss of steam followed by the whistle of the teakettle pierced the air. She took a deep breath and turned to face him. "Would you like some tea?"

Without waiting for his answer, she walked ahead of him in the direction of the well-equipped kitchen and, with trembling hands, opened the cabinet, pulling down two cups. A prickling sensation invaded her when his soles scuffed the floor as he approached her from behind. Her heart beat faster, her breath accelerated; her hands trembled even more when his breath caressed her shoulder. She squeezed her eyes shut.

"Stephan, don't."

"Don't?"

"Don't use the power you have over my heart to burrow your way back in it."

"I wouldn't do that. I want to earn your trust and your love again."

"You will need to work much harder."

"I know." He set his hands on her shoulders and turned her around to face him. His heart stuttered when his eyes met the hurt in hers. In a defensive gesture, she brushed his hands off and folded her arms across her chest.

"I was wrong."

"About?"

"Everything." He put his fingers under her chin and tilted her face up so he could clearly see her eyes. "I thought of my infertility"—he pressed his finger against her lips, blocking her protest—"as an irreparable defect. Mostly because of how I found out about it all those years ago. For most of my adulthood, in my mind, I didn't measure up." He paused. "Then you swept into it and blew all my preconceptions to smithereens. I wanted to be perfect for you."

She bled for the man in front of her—a man who, despite his external confidence and harshness, was soft inside. Jessica began to place the pieces of the puzzle that hadn't quite fit before. They now made a clearer picture, an understanding as to why he'd reacted so badly on seeing her walking beside another man. Someone he had considered to be better than himself. "You were perfect for me."

"But above all, I wanted you to have everything you wanted in life, even if it meant letting you go. I didn't want to. My conscience battled my heart over that decision. But in the end, my conscience won." He squeezed his eyes.

"And you sent me away." Understanding hit her full force. His reactions, his distance, a self-flagellation of sorts. She wanted to kick him for being so stubborn.

"I thought I was doing you a favor. Setting you free so you could find the perfect man. A younger man that would give you everything I couldn't—or thought I couldn't."

"You had no right to take that decision out of my hands. I'm not a little kid. I'm a rational woman who makes her own decisions and knows what she wants. I wanted you."

"I know that now. My patronizing behavior was inexcusable. I'm sorry for that. Last night, I had a long hard look at my life and discovered something I had deliberately ignored. I had spent it in fear. Fear of rejection. Fear of being denied something I craved so much. In my misguided attempts to retain some semblance of control and avoid pain, I denied you. I rejected you. I hurt us both in the end. This morning, I knew I had to come to you, beg your forgiveness. Beg you to let me be a part of your lives. I didn't care who the real father was, only that it was your child. A part of you. You have my heart, and any child of yours will too."

His words rang true in her ears. The unwavering love in his eyes warmed her heart, melted the ice that had caged it since the day he had told her to leave. Jessica's eyes clung to his. "What are you trying to say?"

"A good friend gave me a piece of sage advice. I'm here to say I'm a total and utter jackass. I'm here to grovel with the knowledge that you carry a small piece of me inside you."

Her pulse careened and heart pounded at the weight of his admission. "What made you change your mind?"

Stephan shook his head. "Doesn't matter. You were, are, and will always be the most important thing that has ever happened in my life. You tore down the walls I had built around my bruised heart and healed it. You made me whole even when I viewed myself as a lesser man. I want a life with you, Jessica. I need you." Her eyes glittered with unshed tears and his hand slid down her arm, taking her hand to his lips. "I *love* you, Jessica Forrester. Please tell me I'm not too late." Stephan could barely recognize his own strangled voice.

"I don't think I have ever heard you say please." Jessica's expression grew serious and pensive.

"Please tell me you can still have some love left for me in your heart."

"Wow. Twice." A glint of humor crossed her eyes.

Her amused words drove him out of his mind. He all but growled, "This isn't a joking matter, Jessica. Tell me what I need to hear."

"Now, there's the Stephan I know," she nodded, and smoothed her hands on his chest, resting one above his heart. It beat erratically under her warm touch.

"You still haven't answered," he prompted again, barely able to say the words but hoping her touch signaled good things to come.

"I'm not sure what to say."

"Say you love me."

"Why should I?" She lifted her chin and a defiant spark shone in her eyes.

"Because I'm not leaving until you do. Even if I have to spend all day, all night reminding you of what we shared and rekindling love you once had for me."

"And how do you plan on doing that?"

"The only way I know." He threaded his fingers through her hair and pulled her to him, covering her lips with his, taking her mouth in a ravenous kiss.

She melted, wrapping her arms around his neck, and cradling his head with her hands. A burning heat flared out of control and all the longing she'd held inside for the past week poured into that kiss. Her tongue flicked inside his hot, moist mouth as his hand moved to the back of her head and fisted her hair, holding her to him.

Stephan's other hand edged down along her body, skimming her lower back and the curve of her ass, pressing her snug against the hard ridge of his erection trapped between them.

She broke the kiss and whispered against his lips, "I've missed you, Stephan—" Before she could finish, his mouth devoured hers again. Her heart raced out of control with each lick, each suck, each delicious nip.

Hungrier for her touch and her taste with every passing moment, Stephan lifted her off the floor and she wrapped her legs around his hips. His mind splintered when she plundered his mouth with her tongue, thrusting it deep. Undiluted desire speared through him. His legs bumped into the dining room table and he dropped her ass on it.

His hands flew to the buttons of the shirt she had stolen, shakily unfastening them and shoving it off her shoulders to reveal the skimpiest of lacey bras covering her now fuller breasts. Her silky skin glowed with a rosy blush in the soft sunlight filtering through the windows. The poignant picture shot straight through his heart.

Her breath came in harsh gasps as if her lungs were fighting for air. Blood surged again into his tight aching cock. He slipped his fingers under the straps and gently eased them from her shoulders, unwrapping the beautiful mounds to his appreciative eyes. His gaze was riveted to the rounder curves, darker nipples, and translucent skin. A deep groan echoed in the room.

He lowered his mouth to them and paid homage, suckling, nibbling, flicking them with his tongue. Teasing them into puckered tips, blowing his hot breath over the moist skin. Jessica's moan was a sweet serenade to his ears. His cock jumped in synch with each hitched breath she took for each little bite at the pebbled nipples.

"Beautiful," a reverent whisper escaped him.

Stephan's heart hammered out of control as his hands skimmed along the curve of her calves to her hips and his fingers traced the sides of the tiny swatch of cloth still covering the juncture of her legs. His breath grew ragged and his pulse raced as his finger trailed from her belly button across the silk and down between her thighs. "So wet."

The moisture on the fabric was a telltale sign, one he rejoiced to find. After hitching her ass to slip her panties off, he spread her thighs apart, baring her to him. "Mine." A wicked smile spread on her face as her eyes met his.

"Has always been. Only yours." She sat up and reached for his face, caressing his cheek. "I've missed you, Prince Charming."

Stephan took a deep breath, pulled her hand to his lips, and placed a soft kiss in her palm. "I missed you too, Jessica. Let me show you how much."

The bright sun shining through the windows was like a spotlight on the beautiful image in front of him, her mussed light hair a deep contrast with the dark wood of the table, her creamy skin rosy and flushed in the right places. He closed his eyes and breathed her in. His senses picked up on the sound of her accelerated breathing and the sweet honey essence of the desire coating her folds.

Jessica rose to her elbows and glanced down the length of her body. Anticipation twisted a knot in her stomach as he lowered his face and placed a chaste kiss on the tender skin below her belly button. Goose bumps bloomed across her skin at the first feather-light touch of his lips. Dragging deep gasps of air, Jessica spilled back to the table, her fingers flexing and tightening around the edge. "Stephan…" His name escaped her lips in a low, drawn-out, needy moan.

His hands were everywhere, palming, squeezing, gripping her flesh. Skimming along her still flat stomach to her swollen, sensitive breast. His fingertips circled her achy nipple before taking it between them, tugging and pinching. Her breath hissed through her teeth as the combination of the sensitivity from the first weeks of pregnancy and the pleasure of his fingers playing her like a piano sent shooting electric pulses straight to her throbbing clit.

Stephan's cock twitched and pulsed in a sensual echo of Jessica's soft cry as he rolled the beaded nipple, playing with it, twisting it between his fingers while laving the other with his tongue.

"Stephan!" she cried out as he deepened his explorations, slipping his fingers between her thighs and into her heat. Jessica pushed from the table and reached for him. Tangling her hands in his hair, she jerked his mouth to hers in a deep searing kiss. Her hand dropped to his side, caressing the length of his body, stroking and brushing along his skin. The scent of her juices flooded him with need. He withdrew from the contact to shed his clothes hurriedly, stripping his shirt, undoing his pants, and releasing his throbbing cock while tracing the curvy lines of her body with his eyes.

She pushed back and followed his blazing gaze as it burned a path on her already fevered skin. "It's been a hell of a week. I've wished for this way too long." Her heart flipped in her chest. She spread her thighs wider in invitation, cradling his heavy erection against her when he took his position between them. She circled his waist with her legs and hooked her ankles at his back.

Another low moan rumbled deep in his chest and his breath hissed between his teeth. "You're killing me," he ground out harshly as his hips surged, driving his cock deep inside her. Jessica's body arched into his and their groans mingled as she ground her clit against his groin.

Her engulfing heat almost brought him to his knees. "Oh, God!" The words burst from his mouth as he drove inside her, alternating between quick short thrusts and long hard ones. The feel of her hands roaming his body, pinching his nipples, coupled with the rippling of her impending orgasm around his cock were enough to drive him crazy.

He closed his eyes and absorbed the whole of the moment. The moans and soft gasps of breaths mingled with the wet sounds of flesh against flesh, the scent of arousal permeating the air around them, the fire in his blood burning hotter with each deep thrust. Reaching for the juncture of their bodies, he rubbed her clit in circular motions in synch with his driving thrusts.

"Stephan!" Her little screams escalated his pleasure. His balls pulled tight inside him and a pulsing tingle radiated from his spine, signaling the approaching edge of oblivion. "Stephan! I love you!" she cried out. Her inner muscles flexed and clamped down on his engorged cock, squeezing him tight.

"Sweet Mary, Jessica!" She wrapped her arms around his back and held him tight, meeting him thrust for thrust as he bucked out of control. "Jessica!" he yelled out as his hot sperm spurted inside her.

Her body squeezed his, milking each pulse of his cock to the last drop, holding on to him as if she would never let go. He leaned over her, holding her eyes with his, caging her as he supported his weight on his splayed hands.

"Well, this is definitely the best makeup sex I could ever have imagined. We should break up more often," she joked.

His smile died and his expression turned solemn. "Don't ever say that. I never want to experience that again. Marry me, Jessica. Be mine. Give me forever."

"I've been yours forever."

He kissed her plump ravished lips and broke their intimate contact. "Let me take you to bed and show you how much I missed you all over again."

A glow of motherhood and love radiated from the smile that spread across her face, flooding him in warmth. A warmth that would fill his life for many years to come. "Yes...."

Chapter Fifty-Three

T.M.I.

THE WEEKS SPENT APART HAD nearly been the death of him. Not only because Trevor had missed the warmth and comfort of Cassandra's body, but also the reassurance of her presence, the emotional anchor she provided just by being there, with him. The early morning hours had provided them with joyous reacquainting. It also brought back the personal focus of their mission. The business side of it had been handled and they could now head out for Prague to receive their hard-won payment: his father's notes.

Questions jostled in his head and he couldn't remain in bed any longer. Without disturbing Cassandra, Trevor slipped from the bed and padded out of the room. A good cup of tea should do him wonders.

As he took the first step toward the main living area, the creak of Nelson's bedroom door reached him from the opposite end of the hall. *Great. Just what I didn't need. Morning breakfast with Captain America.*

He rolled his eyes at the prospect and prepared himself to the face the music. *Might as well deal with it before Cassandra gets up.* Expecting to see Nelson's sourpuss, Trevor's eyebrows raised in amusement at the sight of Nikol backing quietly out of his room with her jacket, holster, and boots bundled in her arms. His brows furrowed as she juggled her belongings and gently closed the door.

When she turned and saw him, she froze. Her eyes narrowed and her lips pursed, as if trying to decide whether or not to acknowledge him. After a brief second, she shrugged, nodded in his direction, and headed to the kitchen. An amused smile quirked the corner of his lips and he chuckled. Nikol's mussed hair and partially buttoned man's shirt made for an interesting piece of conversation. The telltale abrasions of a man's five o'clock shadow branded the skin of her face and neck, and her swollen lips reminded him of the current state of Cassandra's—well loved. He followed her, still smiling at the thought of Nelson and Nikol together. That could definitely work in his favor. He headed straight for the cabinets to search for teabags and a kettle while Nikol walked straight to the back door.

"So…you…Nelson?" he prompted in Russian as he searched the cabinets.

"There's no me…Nelson," she replied in kind. "I must go now. Disable the security so I can leave without waking everyone."

"Afraid he will try to stop you?"

"He couldn't stop me even if he tried."

Trevor hesitated. The hope that Nelson would have found a reason to leave Cassandra alone vanished quickly. "Are you sure? I mean…look at you."

"Good sex is good sex," she shrugged.

"Whoa! Too much information."

His attempts at humor were a total failure. Not once did her stony façade crack. "Are you going to disable the code or do I walk out and leave the house blaring?"

Trevor shook his head. "Fine." He punched in the code. "Anything you want me to pass on to him?"

When the soft beep sounded, Nikol opened the door to leave and hesitated. Her head turned toward the hallway and a flicker of an undefinable emotion flared hot. "No," she answered tersely, closing the door behind her.

* * * * *

Not finding a single teabag, Trevor made do with a pot of coffee. The aroma would surely raise Cassandra from her deep slumber easier than a bullhorn blast. Sitting at the kitchen table, Trevor worked on composing an email to Mark Devlin on his laptop when he heard the stirring of life in the hallway. Seconds later, Cassandra strolled in with a sleepy smile on her face and her hair in disarray, both results of their night of loving.

Her rumpled, relaxed appearance sent a lick of pure lust straight to his cock. The image of himself raising her to the counter and taking her then and there, his face buried between her thighs, her taste on his tongue, gave him an instant hard-on. If Nelson hadn't been in the house, he would have made that image a reality. Instead, he greeted her with a smile. "Good morning, *a bhean*."

She smiled back and grabbed a cup, filling it with the dark brew. "Hmm… you do know how to please a woman, Mr. Bauer."

"I sure hope it's not just with my talent at making the perfect pot of coffee."

Her eyes gleamed as she took a sip from her cup and chuckled. "No worries there. My list of your more pleasurable talents is a long one." Her eyes took on an innocent quality. "Maybe I should upload it as a list to the web. Let everyone know how talented my geek really is."

At that moment, they heard footsteps from the hallway and Nelson walked in as disheveled as Nikol had been, minus his shirt. His heavy-lidded eyes hid his thoughts as he squinted, peering around the room.

Trevor's smile widened. "There's coffee in the pot. Help yourself."

Nelson grumbled and walked to the pot sitting on the counter. He poured himself a big cup, eyes still searching around, looking for evidence of something Trevor could only imagine was Nikol's presence. He took a big gulp of coffee and when his eyes met Trevor's amused ones, understanding filled them. Nathan froze.

Trevor turned his eyes back to the email on his screen and attached the files containing the details Cassandra, Jessica, and George had compiled during his stint in the mansion. Devlin was in for a surprise. The damning information was enough to seal the fate of the mastermind behind the hack.

Cassandra glanced at Trevor as she searched the cabinets for something to eat, her message clear: behave.

"So, what are your plans?" Nelson asked him.

Trevor eyed him, puzzled at the absence of the angry tone that usually simmered below Nelson's voice. "We fly to Prague as soon as Boris gives us the green light. Then back to Dublin. You?"

"St. Petersburg to get my luggage and straight to Langley." Trevor could clearly see the unasked questions in Nelson's eyes. An uneasy silence descended upon them while Cassandra busied herself with making them all some porridge.

Once ready, she left the bowls on the counter to cool down. "You guys are driving me nuts. The testosterone in here is getting thick. I'm going to take a shower." Her eyes narrowed. "No knives, guns, or fists allowed, children. Be good, or else." She headed for the bedroom, leaving the two men alone in the small kitchen.

The atmosphere became heavy with tension. Nelson's agitation beat at Trevor. Impressed by his control, Trevor tossed him a bone. "She left earlier."

Nelson's head jerked and he held Trevor's gaze. "Did she say anything?"

"Nope."

Nelson's face paled and his glance shot to the kitchen door. "I need to get moving. Did you need anything else from me before I go?" His voice was distant.

"As a matter of fact. Dmitriy and Tatiana. I need you to help me get them out of the country. I'm sure you can find a way to remove them from Russia under wraps."

Nelson looked at Trevor as if he had grown a second head. "Are you asking me to help you get two possible fugitives across the border?"

"Yep. Do you have a problem with that?"

"You know, you're ballsier than I thought you were." Nelson shook his head and chuckled. "I'm beginning to see what she sees in you."

Trevor knew Nelson was spoiling for a fight but couldn't hold back his smart mouth. "You mean what she couldn't see in you?"

Nelson inhaled deeply and temper flared in his eyes. Surprisingly, he didn't retaliate. "Yes. So…what's your idea for making your brilliant escape scheme a reality?"

"I need to get them to Ireland. If you can get them on a plane to Dublin, I'll have someone meet them at the airport."

"I'll see what I can do. I assume you want them out of Russia as soon as possible."

"Yes. I don't want to leave them behind."

"I'll be in touch." Nelson stood and began gathering his things. "Tell Cass…never mind," he caught himself, his eyes lost in thought.

Trevor had never seen the man so insecure of himself. For the first time since dancing a few rounds in the NSA conference room a year or so ago, he felt sorry for him. He put himself in Nelson's shoes and cringed at the sting Nikol's disappearing act must have left. "I'll be waiting to hear from you."

Nelson nodded, disabled the security system, and left without a backward glance.

Chapter Fifty-Four

More Time

*O*N THE INTERNATIONAL FRONT, DETAILS *of a massive anti-gang operation in Russia have now been released to the public. The St. Petersburg police have disclosed a record number of arrests in a case that spans through two major mafia gangs and a number of smaller associates. The operation also included the takedown of one of the gang's strongholds after a gun battle ensued.*

Pavel Zarev and Vladimir Mikhailov, heads of the two largest mafia organizations in St. Petersburg, have been arrested and are being held for arraignment. The case is said to be one of the most solid-built in the history of anti-gang operations in Russia. Unconfirmed sources have also revealed that digital evidence recovered from one of the strongholds was key to the arrests.

Roy Denner sat paralyzed in his cozy family room. The tightly gripped remote slipped from his clammy hand to the floor. His eyes darted to

Martha. It was Sunday morning and his wife puttered around the kitchen, unaware of the rapid beat of his heart or the pain that banded around his chest like some torture device tightening with each word of the newscast. His older son played with one of his many handheld game consoles at the dining room table while the twins played on the carpet by his feet. A picture-perfect evening with a family he had indulged to no end.

Each day had been an emotional rollercoaster as he had waited for news from Russia, news that could have put an end to his misery. His nerves had slowly been getting the best of him, burning a hole in his stomach. He grabbed the half-empty bottle of antacid from the side table and popped a couple of tablets in his mouth, chomping them to bits as the news continued to roll.

He lost himself in his thoughts and the reason for the knots twisting in his stomach. They had been fairly well off. He had a good job, cash in his pocket, and the latest gadgets money could buy. But he hadn't been satisfied. The lure of luxury RVs, boats, and vacations in Europe teased his mind. Greed had swept in and dug its talons deep. It wasn't called a deadly sin for nothing. It had blinded him to the already comfortable life he and his family enjoyed. But still he wanted more, needed more.

It had all started with a simple, innocent, stock tip. Prior to the collapse of the markets a few years back, a friend had pointed him to a sure-fire win and Roy had jumped in with both feet. The returns had been modest, but enough to purchase a vacation home on the East coast.

Soon, modest returns weren't enough. He began borrowing money from his children's education accounts, equity in the house, and loans against his retirement fund to invest in volatile stock market options. The returns had not been as great as he had anticipated, so he'd tried his hand again, hoping the third time would be a charm. Then, disaster hit.

Roy could still remember watching the stock markets plummet and the desperation of not knowing how to face Martha with the news that he had jeopardized everything they had worked so hard for, including the roof over their heads and their children's education. In a panic, he'd committed an even more shameful act. He had tapped into his own parents' nest egg.

His parents had saved for many years, nurturing a fund they called the dream house account. Because of his background in finance, they had entrusted him as manager of the account, hoping Roy would help them grow their funds so they could one day fulfill their dream of living abroad. They had yet to agree on a location where they both wanted to enjoy their golden years and, knowing his parents, he hadn't expected them to ever come to a decision. That it would remain a pipe dream.

Roy had been confident he would have plenty of time to replace the funds and that they would never find out about his withdrawals, since they didn't need to tap it for day-to-day expenses. Their pensions had been enough to cover those. But things didn't quite happen the way he'd expected. Over the past few years, he'd continued to bleed the fund in order to maintain the style of living his family had grown accustomed to. His plan was to wait for his luck to change. To repay every single penny once the market stabilized.

Five months back his luck had turned all right, but for the worse. His parents had popped in for a visit and had dropped a bomb. They'd found their dream home. Their eyes had shone with excitement as they had explained they were putting an offer on a cute little bungalow in the Caribbean and, if everything went according to plan, they would be moving in a few months.

On seeing the surprised expression etched on his face, his mother had commented, *"Don't worry, Roy. We'll come to visit, and you can always fly the whole family to spend time with us. Think of it as a vacation destination."* His heart had sunk to his feet.

As soon as they'd left, he had accessed their fund and grown lightheaded. He'd taken a substantial amount from their account, more than he'd even realized. Once they attempted to draw from it, his syphoning of the funds would be out in the open. He couldn't let his parents find out he'd failed them, failed his own family. He couldn't let that happen.

Desperate, he made another choice and robbed Peter to pay Paul. He doctored records, shaved off money from MDS's books, and used it to fill the hole he'd dug in his parents' dream just in the nick of time. Their offer went through and they were at that moment enjoying their golden

TO RUSSIA WITH LOVE

years in their little bungalow by the sea, with its two pink flamingos stuck in the sand like sentinels at their door. He shook his head and didn't know what disgusted him more: those damn flamingos, or how messed up things had gotten since.

The cycle had continued to get worse when a couple of weeks later, Mark Devlin had called a managers' meeting. He had announced that MDS had developed a groundbreaking piece of software that could change the landscape of the financial market. The program had the potential to generate a tidy sum of revenue and Devlin, expecting amazing returns, had decided to go public with MDS. Roy had panicked. He knew that a financial audit of the company had to happen first. All financial statements and transactions, management structure, and company holdings had to be in order and demonstrate a sound footing. When that took place, he would be in a world of hurt.

For nights, he'd agonized over how to cover up his stupidity, when, by chance, he had come across an article about online fraud in Russia and how widespread it was. That's when he'd realized the answer was in hand. The decrypter that Mark Devlin had mentioned. Its potential was his ticket out of hell. His mind had run circles around that piece of information and, in the end, he had mapped out a scheme that would save his ass. If he could find a buyer for the software without having the source of the infiltration traced back to him, he would secure the funds needed to replace the money and move on with his life.

The Russian connection in the article reminded him of an MDS employee from Russia he had disciplined in the past for fraudulent use of the company's credit card. He was the perfect mole. Easy to manipulate. Isolated. No friends. And a gambling habit that couldn't be sated. His money-flow issues rivaled Roy's own addiction to the stock market.

He had pulled Tomlin into his office under the pretense of reviewing the disciplinary action and had hooked him in with the offer of helping to pay his outstanding gambling debts. Tomlin had jumped at the opportunity. Roy had directed him to avoid all electronic means of communication. Instead, they had used handwritten notes delivered covertly between them to seal the deal. His instructions to Tomlin were straightforward. Use his Russian connections to find a buyer, set up a back door on the server, and coordinate the sweep of the decrypter file, leaving no trace of an infiltration behind.

Tomlin had come through with a buyer. A prominent businessman by the name of Vladimir Mikhailov. Anger flared high in his chest when he recalled the events that had foiled his best-laid plans. The hacker Mikhailov had put in charge of the server infiltration had misunderstood Tomlin's instruction and had not only copied the files, but deleted the original from the server as well. To compound matters, the software was not complete. It was still in development, a piece of information Devlin hadn't mentioned, and Mikhailov had refused to pay him until the software was fully operational. He scrubbed his face with his hands and didn't know whether to laugh or cry. His family was now safe from Mikhailov's reach, but his arrest in Russia also extinguished Roy's hopes of covering up his indiscretions.

As the rest of the newscast blared on the TV, Roy jumped from the couch and hurried to his office. Since the day Devlin had called his meeting and disclosed the upcoming IPO, Roy had put into place a backup plan in the event Mikhailov did not come through with payment—a family vacation to Cuba. A country without an extradition agreement with the US. It would be a long two-leg trip through Canada, but once there, they could remain out of the long arm of the American justice system.

His hands were clammy and sweat beaded on his forehead as he pulled up the airline website and exchanged their tickets for that evening. A big fee later and with confirmation of their new flight itinerary, he pushed away from his desk.

"Martha!" He walked into the kitchen and took her by the shoulders. "I just got word that the IPO audit has been scheduled for the same week we are supposed to be on vacation. I had to move our trip to Cuba up a couple of weeks. We need to fly out today instead."

"What? Are you going nuts?" Martha's expression was puzzled.

He kissed her lips. "Sure. We can do it. It's summer. No school."

"You expect us to be packed and ready to go now?" Concern colored her voice.

"The flights are booked and hotel all handled. We just need to be at the airport by three pm. If we pack now, we should be able to make it with no problem."

"What's going on, Roy?" Her eyes grew wide.

"Nothing bad. I don't want to lose the money we've already forked out. The tickets are non-refundable."

Martha was a practical woman. He knew that argument would win her agreement. "Fine."

"We need to hurry."

Roy could clearly see that Martha was not happy with the abruptness of his announcement, nor with his flimsy excuses to take off at a moment's notice, but, as usual, she caved to his request. Within record time, the family was packed and headed to the airport for a very long vacation.

★ ★ ★ ★ ★

Clearing security had been a breeze: not a lot of luggage to inspect, only a few electronics and cameras. Yet Roy's eyes were riveted on the security personnel, covertly watching them, looking for signs they were on to him. His stomach had cramped when it was his turn to remove his shoes and walk through the metal detector, but they had all been cleared for boarding and directed to their gate.

Waiting for their turn to board, Roy drummed his fingers on the hand rest and looked at the crystal face of the watch wrapped around his wrist. Since the attendant had stepped behind the counter to handle passengers' last-minute seat adjustments, Roy had kept his eyes trained on her every move, expectant of the boarding call.

His heart revved when the attendant finally moved to the gate and picked up the PA microphone. "Let's go. Get your things—they are about to call our flight." Martha scrambled to grab their carry-on bags and herded the boys in front of them toward the boarding lane.

The procession to the seats was painfully slow. Standing behind Martha, his eyes kept darting to the corridor, almost expecting to see sirens, police rushing the gate. His stomach cramped again and he bumped into

Martha, making her almost stumble over the twins. She turned around to look at him, a deep frown marring her face.

"Sorry," he mumbled, and continued their slow progression to the attendant who checked their boarding passes and directed them toward the ramp.

Once boarded, Roy sat on one side of the aisle with his eldest son and Martha on the other with the twins. He shifted uncomfortably in his seat, his sweat-drenched shirt stuck to his back and beads trailing from his brow. He wiped the back of his hand across his forehead and gulped in small draughts of air to ease his anxiety.

"Come on, come on. Finish boarding already." He could tell Martha was worried about his behavior from the looks she kept casting his way. Unable to give her the reassurances she needed, he stared straight ahead. When one attendant picked up the phone and another locked down the door, Roy almost wept with joy. He fell back against his seat and offered Martha a smile.

"Ladies and gentlemen, the Captain has turned on the Fasten Seat Belt sign. If you haven't already done so, please stow your carry-on luggage underneath the seat in front of you or in an overhead bin. Please take your seat and fasten your seat belt. And also make sure your seat back and folding trays are in their full upright position."

With each word the attendant spoke, his smile grew wider and he reached across the aisle to take Martha's hand in his. She glanced into his eyes. "Are you going to tell me what this is all really about? I have never seen such a frantic look on your face before."

A twinge pinched at his heart that yet again he was lying to her. It seemed the lies had gotten easier over the years. "There is nothing wrong. I'm just looking forward to spending sunsets on the beach with you and was worried we wouldn't make the flight. Everything is going to be okay."

"At this time, we request that all mobile phones, pagers, radios, and remote controlled toys be turned off for the full duration of the flight—"

When his wife turned her attention to the twins and helped them turn off their portable games, Roy breathed another sigh of relief. Each announcement, one step closer to take off. His entire body sagged and almost melted into his seat as the plane began to pull away from the gate.

As the safety instructions rolled on the television monitors, Roy racked his brain for anything that would help mask what he had done. Without the payoff from Mikhailov, his options were almost slim to none. The best he could hope for was to hide in Cuba until a solution presented itself. His biggest worry was how to break the news to Martha that they could not return to their home.

His son gripped his hand as the engines revved and the plane prepared for liftoff. Roy lowered his head and, in a low voice, consoled him. "It will be great. Like an amusement ride." His head snapped up when the engines wound down and the captain's voice came over the speaker.

"This is the Captain speaking. We're experiencing mechanical difficulties, and as a precaution will be returning to the gate. We apologize for this delay and appreciate your patience. Our number one goal is your safety. Thank you."

Roy's hands grew clammy and his breath burst in and out of him in shallow puffs. His mouth grew parched and he licked his lips several times. As the plane made the slow, agonizing turn back to the terminal, dizziness hit him and his vision grew dark. He could hear Martha's voice calling him. He lifted a hand and waved her off, hoping she would leave him alone. His mind raced and his gut clenched.

As the plane powered down, the attendant's voice boomed over the speaker. *"Ladies and gentlemen, please remain in your seats. We will depart as soon as the ground crew has checked the plane. ATC has given us an estimated delay of twenty minutes. Until then, sit tight and we'll keep you advised of any changes."*

Roy observed one of the attendants cross the aisle to the door and, moments later, bright daylight broke into the cabin. His eyebrows creased in a deep frown and his eyes locked on the attendant area. His heart dropped when two men in dark suits boarded the plane and walked down the narrow aisle, checking seat numbers. As they neared the row his family was sitting in, the man in the lead snared and held his gaze, passing him and stopping immediately behind his seat. The second man halted his progress at the row in front of him. "Mr. Roy Denner?"

Numbness consumed him, his ears rang, and he could feel every single set of eyes now trained on him like laser beams burning his skin. "Yes."

"You need to come with us, sir," the man who had been in the lead advised him in a low controlled voice. He didn't need any words to understand why they were there for him.

"Roy? Roy! What's happening?" Martha's panicked shrill echoed in the cabin.

Roy shot an apologetic look at his wife as he stood. "It will be okay, Martha," he murmured. His shoulders slumped and he stared at his feet as he shuffled down the aisle, escorted by the two men. *I can fix this. I just need more time.* An overwhelming sense of loss hit him and it became impossible to steady the erratic beat of his pulse. Who was he kidding? It would never be okay again.

Chapter Fifty-Five

Cloak and Dagger

CASSANDRA'S SOFT VOICE PENETRATED TREVOR'S thoughts. "We should be landing shortly. Do you want to stay for a few days instead of heading back to Dublin this afternoon?"

"No, *a ghrá*. I want to get back home."

"Okay. But if you change your mind later, we can stay." Love and understanding filled her eyes. She must have caught the nuances in his tone indicating his "I want" was clearly "I need."

Ireland was home to both of them, like an old comfortable recliner that lulled you into a relaxing sleep the moment you sat on it. Although Cassandra had become his safety blanket, his home away from home, he couldn't wait to get into his own bed where his feet didn't hang off the end, take a nice long shower without someone waiting outside, and use his own computer without restrictions. Two weeks with no internet access had almost been the death of him. Just the thought of it still had the power to give him a case of withdrawal jitters.

A lot had happened in the seventy-two hours since Trevor had been reunited with Cassandra. Nelson had arranged Dmitriy and Tatiana's extraction from Russia, and Trevor had contacted Stephan who, in turn, was to meet them at the airport in Dublin that same morning. Trevor and Cassandra had offered Dmitriy a position with Bauer Enterprises, which he had enthusiastically accepted. His skill set would be a huge asset to their budding business.

Mark Devlin had received the email containing enough documentation to take action against Roy Denner, MDS's CFO. The loss the company had incurred from his theft and from the delay in the final development of the program was in the millions.

Boris had accomplished his mission's objective, providing his superiors with the necessary evidence to keep Mikhailov and Zarev behind bars for a long time. Twenty-four hours later, a massive sting operation had been executed to perfection under the cover of the dark in the early hours of the morning. News coverage had been nonstop ever since, the event touted as the biggest mafia-related mass arrest in Russian history.

The disruption to their operations had left both mafia organizations headless and without direction. Once Trevor and Cassandra had received the green light from Boris, they had jumped on the earliest flight out of St. Petersburg.

Landing in Prague mid-morning, they swiftly made their way through airport security. Traveling light, with only their backpacks containing laptops and a change of clothing, they exited the airport and caught a taxi to downtown Prague.

The day was bright and warm, the summer sky blue and clear, a perfect day for sightseeing and enjoying popular tourist spots. Trevor watched the scenery as the cabbie maneuvered his way from the airport to their destination, the Grand Hotel Europa, where Mucha waited for them.

Cassandra cast a sideways glance at Trevor and could see tense lines around the grim set of his mouth. His stiff posture indicated his shoulder still bothered him. The good news was that, according to the medic Nathan had unexpectedly sent to the safe house, Trevor's wound was healing nicely and he had received a clean bill of health. She shook her head. *With his Irish luck, he'll have a prettier scar than mine.*

A thick silence filled the cab. The quiet rub of his thumb along the back of her hand was a sure indication that something else troubled him. Deep in her gut, she could tell he expected the meeting to end in another wild goose chase.

She truly hoped this time they would find a solid lead, not just another crumb. Sometimes it felt as if they had become Hansel and Gretel searching for the breadcrumbs that would lead them out of the forest and to Trevor's parents.

Anxious to have the meeting over and done with, she squeezed Trevor's hand to let him know she was there for him and left him to his musings. Her heart ached for him. It had to be harder to lose a loved one as an adult when the memories were clearer and stayed with you longer.

Arriving at Wenceslas Square, which was actually a very long avenue with a wonderfully designed garden in the center and traffic lanes running on both sides, the cabbie merged into the flow of traffic. "If you look out your window, you will see the National Museum," the cabbie commented as he maneuvered through the roundabout and headed south. After a few more minutes, he stopped in front of an amazingly bright yellow building and turned to look back at them. "Welcome to the Grand Hotel Europa."

A gem of the Art Nouveau architecture in Prague with its beautiful decorative frontage full of intricate details and sculptures, the hotel was a feast for the eyes.

Cassandra's eyes twinkled with marvel. "It's beautiful. I could spend hours standing right here admiring the artwork alone."

Trevor paid the cabbie and, slinging his backpack over his good shoulder, turned to face it with her. "It *is* nice." He lifted Cassandra's wrist and glanced at her watch. "But we don't have time. Come. We can't be late."

Tugging her wrist, he led the way to the entrance and, with a deep calming breath, held the door for her. The interior of the historic hotel was like a time warp to the elegant Edwardian era, with all the architectural fittings and furniture similar to how they would have appeared back in the early 1900s. The pleasant surprise on Cassandra's face as she looked around the elegant lobby gave him a hint that she felt the same way.

"Wow...." she whispered as the made their way to the dining room where Mucha should be waiting for them.

The dining room, with its strikingly elegant dark wood paneling and high ceilings, only had a few empty tables. An eclectic mix of languages flowed from the groups of tourists having breakfast before embarking on their exploration of Prague.

Antonín Mucha, described by Devlin as a tall, dark-haired man wearing glasses, was easy to spot. He sat alone, at a corner table by the window. A laptop messenger-style bag sat on the floor at his feet as he read the local newspaper. Trevor veered in his direction.

As they approached the table, Mucha's eyes met Trevor's. "Am I that obvious?"

"No. We're that good." A small smile curved the corner of Trevor's mouth. "Besides, Devlin gave us your description."

Mucha appeared to relax and, folding and setting his newspaper aside, he nodded to the chairs, indicating they should sit. Once settled and after the waiter left with their drink orders, Mucha cut to the chase.

He reached into his bag and pulled out a letter-sized manila envelope, laying it on the table in front of Trevor. "Devlin sent this with his regards."

Trevor took the envelope in his hand, weighing it. Noticing the light volume, he frowned and shot Mucha a questioning look.

"It's not much. Just a few sheets of paper I found tucked among my notes when I moved a little while ago," he explained as Trevor ran a finger under the seal, opened it, and pulled the sheets out.

His father's familiar scrawl covered the pages. Trevor swallowed hard. His father's handwriting was so similar to his own chicken-scratch. On closer inspection, it appeared to be some kind of shorthand, but nothing Trevor had ever seen or remembered his father using before. He passed the pages to Cassandra and watched the frown furrow her brow. "Is this all?"

"What you have is all I found," Mucha responded.

Trevor glanced at the sheets Cassandra returned to him. "How did you come in contact with Brennan?" His matter-of-fact tone disguised the anguish churning in his heart.

"Mr. Brennan was working on a breakthrough algorithm. He contacted me because he was curious about my research on voice recognition."

Trevor's curiosity piqued immediately. "What algorithm?"

"He didn't share any details, only that he was on the verge of a revolutionary breakthrough. The couple of times we met we mostly discussed my own work. He was excited; I could tell the wheels were turning in his head. The questions he asked me led me to believe that he was working on a classified project."

Trevor's frown deepened as he listened to Mucha. Cassandra reached under the table and took his hand in hers, squeezing it tightly. "What do you mean by classified?"

"I can't explain. All I can tell you is that, shortly after our conversation, he disappeared. It was all over the news. Since that day, all I can think about has been the conversation and his mention of the algorithm." Mucha shook his head and looked down at his tightly clasped hands on the table. "I'm sorry there isn't more. Until recently, I had no idea I had them or that they could be important. It was just by chance I discovered them while unpacking my office and recognized his handwriting."

Trevor shook his head. "Why did you sell them to Devlin?"

Mucha frowned. "Devlin hired me some six months ago. My resume outlined my experience and the many people I'd worked with. I listed Mr. Brennan as one of them. In a casual conversation after my interview, I mentioned how I had come across some of Mr. Brennan's notes mixed with mine. I don't recall him being very interested in that information at the time."

He paused; a thoughtful expression crossed his face before he continued. "A few months ago, he called me and asked me if I had disposed of the notes. When I told him I still had them, he sounded excited. Said he was interested in the sheets. I thought he was just curious to see them, so I sent them to him, thinking he would return them to me once he was done. A week later, a check arrived in the post. It was unexpected. He told me to consider it a bonus. I wasn't sure what to do, but didn't want to rock the boat with my new boss so I let it drop."

Trevor slumped back in his chair, questions careened in his mind as he tried to get his head around what to do next. *Will this quest ever end?*

Mucha slipped his bag over his shoulder and stood. "I am sorry I couldn't have been of more assistance. Mr. Brennan was a brilliant man. I enjoyed working with him and had been looking forward to more discussions with him regarding his algorithm."

Out of the corner of her eye, Cassandra saw Trevor's frown deepen and could tell by his pained expression that he, himself, wished the same— more time with his dad.

Pulling a card from his pocket, Mucha extended it to Cassandra. "My contact information, in case you have more questions." He returned his gaze to Trevor. "You look a lot like him, you know?" Trevor's eyes snapped to Mucha's. "I don't know how I can help, but please contact me if you think of anything."

Once Mucha disappeared from sight, Cassandra turned back to Trevor and watched quietly as he stuffed the sheets back into the envelope, his disappointment almost palpable.

Cassandra captured his hand and squeezed it. "Trevor, talk to me. What are you thinking about?"

"Nothing… Fuck! Everything," he huffed out a sigh. "What the hell was he into? Why would he never mention this algorithm? Why the cloak and dagger? He never filled Stephan in on it either."

"Maybe it wasn't his decision to make. Maybe he thought he had more time. Whatever the reason, we'll figure it out." She cupped his neck and rubbed her thumb along his jaw, the prickling of his unshaven skin rough against hers. "As you always say, no stone left unturned, right?"

A slight grin quirked the side of his mouth. "My own words back to haunt me! What would I do without you?"

Cassandra grinned. "Walk around aimlessly? Lost?"

Chuckling, Trevor leaned over and pressed his lips against hers. "Exactly!" He kissed her again. "We'll tackle it once we get home."

"We have a few hours to kill." Hoping to take his mind off his father and the notes in the envelope, she prompted, "Want to go for a walk? It would be a shame to waste this beautiful weather. Besides, this is my first time in Prague, remember?"

He stuffed the envelope in his backpack. "You're right. We should be out in the sun like lizards enjoying the day, not stuck in a terminal."

As they turned for the exit, Cassandra took his hand and smiled up at him. "Plus, I need to enjoy every single free second now. I'll be pretty busy helping Jessica with the wedding once we get home."

Trevor had been shocked to learn of the developments in Dublin. When he had called to make sure Dmitriy and Tatiana had arrived safe and sound, Stephan had broken the news of his upcoming wedding to Jessica, who was expecting their first child.

Trevor's eyes narrowed and his eyebrows slanted in a frown. "How the hell did that happen?" His tone was exalted. "And here I was thinking the old man's swimmers used walkers."

The humorous glint in his eyes gave him away. "Trevor!" Cassandra admonished him, unable to contain the smile that spread on her lips. "That's so wrong."

"What? He's the one playing the decrepit-old-man role. 'No hips were damaged in the making of this baby.'" A thoughtful look crossed his face. "We should get Jessica a t-shirt with that."

Cassandra burst out laughing, enjoying the return of her husband's humor. They walked down Wenceslas Square, enjoying the warmth of the sun, the colorful gardens, the carefree time together.

All of a sudden, Cassandra felt a tug on her arm. Swinging her head to look behind her, she found Trevor stopped in his tracks with a look of horror on his face.

"Trevor? What is it? What happened?"

Trevor's wide eyes met hers. His mouth opened and closed a few times as if at a loss for words. "Wait a minute. That means they're going to want us to babysit."

Cassandra rolled her eyes and shook her head.

"Don't shake your head at me, missy. You know they will. Hell. Does that mean we'll have to change diapers?" His nose wrinkled.

Cassandra could only stare at him dumbfounded. "You don't really—" Her eyes narrowed at the humor she caught shining in his eyes. She punched him in his good shoulder and grinned. She looked up at the sky. "Heaven help Jessica. You are going to drive her ape shit."

"So looking forward to," he smirked as he brought her hand to his lips and pulled her around to mingle with the tourists enjoying the afternoon heat.

Epilogue

Masks

TREVOR LAY ON HIS BACK watching the glittering layer of pinholes in the dark curtain of night. The soft moss grass tickled his neck and arms, the earthy scent tantalizing his nose. He inhaled deeply as he gazed up into the sky enjoying the quiet evening and the serenade of crickets flowing on the gentle breeze.

His eyes tracked across the night sky and a frown pulled at his brow as the stars vanished one by one from it, creating a bland, eerie void. In their place, images from the past showed like an old, grainy movie. One image in particular absorbed his attention—his father's laughter as they sat at the old dining table in their house in Sligo.

"This is the basics of encryption, Trevor."

Trevor's eyes shot to his father's, a mirror image of his own startling blue ones. A smile quirked Conor Brennan's handsome face, still unlined by age, his black hair neat and trim—a contrast to Trevor's unruly brown mop, which tended to stick out in all directions. "So, all I need to do is replace a letter with another?"

"Yes. As long as we have the key and others don't, our conversations are private. This is our secret, yours and mine. You can't share it with anyone."

"I won't, Dad." His gut churned and dread's tight fist squeezed his heart as his father's face gradually morphed into that of a stranger before his eyes. A face he had never seen before and whose dark, cold, emotionless eyes pierced his soul.

As he turned from the stranger, wide-eyed and befuddled in search of his father's familiar figure, a huge wave of water engulfed him. Its sheer force knocked him over and dragged him under its cold bone-biting depths, rolling and tumbling him head over heels.

Nausea gripped Trevor's stomach as he frantically fought against the current's pull, scissor-kicking to break free of its grasp, to reach the surface. Each kick, each stroke was torturous, and each time he breached the surface, a new wave dragged him back down. His arms and legs burned and grew heavier with each push.

A tight band gripped his throat and squeezed his lungs until he thought his head would pop. Unable to withstand the pressure, he broke the seal of his lips, expelling the last of his precious breath. Water invaded his mouth, choking him. He coughed and sputtered, gasping frantically for air. The vice around his chest grew tighter and his eyes grew dim.

"Trevor!" Cassandra's voice came through the veil.

"Cassie!" he screamed in his head.

"Trevor! Trevor, damn it! Wake up!" Straddling him, Cassandra cupped his face and kissed him. "Come on, baby. It's just a dream. Wake up, *a ghrá!*

His eyes popped open, drawn to her desperate call. Trevor froze in place until reality leaked into his awareness. He locked eyes with her, his anchor in the storm. As his muscles relaxed under her gentle hands, he exhaled a deep breath and squeezed his eyes shut.

Cassandra exhaled a breath of relief and sat back on his hips, pushing the hair from her face with a shaky hand. "Jeezus, Trevor. I couldn't wake you. You were choking and screaming." Her throaty voice hitched. "I had to actually sit on you to get you to wake up. Are you okay?"

"Yes…I'll be fine…I'm fine." He buried his face in the crook of his arm as the images and voices of his dream continued to bombard him. *What the fuck did they mean?*

Cassandra rubbed her hand in circles across his chest. "Trevor, your dreams have come back with a hell of a punch. They seem worse the more frustrated you get with your parents' case. Do you want to talk about it? It seemed to help the last time."

"I don't know, Cassie. This time, the dreams are haunting in their clarity." Trevor sat up and Cassandra shifted her weight so he could scoot back against the headboard. "I'm missing something. I know I am, I'm so fucking close to figuring it out, yet I can't see it clearly." Trevor rubbed his hand across his face in frustration.

"I wish there was something I could do."

"I know, *a ghrá*. There's nothing any of us can do at this moment. If only—" He leaned his head against the headboard and stared at the ceiling.

The heavy mask of disappointment etched on Trevor's face tore at Cassandra's heart. She knew that wasn't the end of their search; it was a new beginning, with a brand new direction already taking shape before them. A direction that he would lead her in when the road was clear. A direction they were both determined to take for the sake of their future.…

Craving more?

Don't miss the next novel in the

hot and thrilling

Countermeasure series

ALTERNATE

CONNECTION

More books in the

Countermeasure series

and

Countermeasure: Bytes of Life series:

COUNTERMEASURE

ECSTASY BY THE SEA

CUFFED AT MIDNIGHT

PASSION AT DAWN

ABOUT THE AUTHORS

CHRIS ALMEIDA (C. ALMEIDA)

Chris Almeida (also known as C. Almeida) began writing children's stories at a very young age. Born in Brazil but currently living in Toronto, Ontario, Canada, Chris's life took a totally different course when technology came into play, and the following 17 years were spent delving deep into the world of programming and web design.

It was in 2010, when Chris began role-playing online as a hobby, that writing wormed its way back into the picture—this time, writing storylines for the role-playing group.

The ideas and plots created for the game awoke the inner writer, and, a few months later, together with partner-in-crime Cecilia Aubrey, he began writing romantic erotica.

Now, still together, they have written a number of short stories and novels and are currently working on book two and three of their series, as well as several short stories as part of the spin-off series. Through it all they have continued to enjoy role-playing through their favorite characters.

CECILIA AUBREY (C. AUBREY)

Cecilia Aubrey (also known as C. Aubrey) has dabbled in writing on and off over the years. But it was in 2010, when she was offered a life-changing opportunity within a role-playing group, that writing placed itself front and center.

The development of story ideas, research, writing, and participation in bringing those stories to life spurred a desire to take writing to a higher level. A few months later, Cecilia and her partner in crime, Chris Almeida, began writing romantic erotica.

Together, they write suspense-driven erotic romance with sexy, technologically inclined men and woman, filled with intrigue and enough twists and turns to make a rollercoaster seem tame.

They have several published short stories to their credit and their first novel, COUNTERMEASURE, was published in January 2011. They are currently working on the second and third books in the COUNTER-MEASURE series.

Always gluttons for punishment, they have several projects in queue, screaming and waiting for their turn, including a spin-off series of shorts tied to their novels. Through all the chaos and laughter, they still hold true to their roots, bringing their favorite role-play characters and stories to life.

You can find us at:

http://caduobooks.com
http://countermeasureseries.com/
http://www.facebook.com/Counter.Measure.Series
http://www.facebook.com/CAlmeida.CAubrey.Authors
http://twitter.com/CAlmeidaCAubrey

www.ingramcontent.com/pod-product-compliance
Lightning Source LLC
Chambersburg PA
CBHW030538020726
47494CB00005B/1427